Reader's Digest
CONDENSED
BOOKS

KRISTIN HANNAH

COLLECTION

The Reader's Digest Association, Inc.
New York, NY / Montreal

We are committed to both the quality of our products and
the service we provide to our customers.
We value your comments, so please feel free to contact us.

The Reader's Digest Association, Inc.
Select Editions
44 South Broadway
White Plains, NY 10601

Reader's Digest Select Editions, also known as Condensed Books, is an ongoing series published every two to three months. The typical volume contains four outstanding books by different authors in condensed form. Anyone may receive this service by writing The Reader's Digest Association, Inc., 44 South Broadway, White Plains, NY 10601, visiting the web at www.rd.com/freebook, or calling our toll-free number: 800-463-8820.

For more Reader's Digest products and information, visit our website:
www.rd.com (in the United States)
www.readersdigest.ca (in Canada)

ISBN 978-1-60652-549-4

Printed in the United States of America

CONTENTS

DISTANT SHORES

ONE

Seattle, Washington

IT ALL started with a second martini.

"Come on," Meghann said, "have another drink."

"No way." Elizabeth didn't handle alcohol well. That had been proved conclusively back in 1976, when she'd been at the University of Washington.

"You can't refuse to drink at my forty-second birthday party. Remember how drunk I got last spring when you turned forty-five?"

What a debacle *that* had been.

Meghann raised her hand and flagged down the waitress, who hurried over. "We'll take two more martinis. And bring us a plate of nachos—heavy on the refried beans."

Elizabeth couldn't help smiling. "This is going to be ugly."

The waitress returned, set two elegant glasses down on the table, and picked up the empties.

"Here's to me," Meghann said, clinking glasses with Elizabeth.

For the next hour their conversation drifted down old roads and around old times. They'd been friends for more than twenty years. In the two decades since college, their lives had gone in opposite directions—Elizabeth had put all her energies into wife and motherhood; Meghann had become a first-rate divorce attorney—but their friendship had never wavered. For years, as Elizabeth and her family had moved from town to town, they'd kept in touch via e-mail and phone calls. Now, finally, they lived close enough to see each other on special occasions. It was one of the things Elizabeth loved most about living in Oregon.

By the time the third round of martinis was delivered, Meghann was laughing uproariously. She dug through the nachos, found one with a lot of cheese on it, and looked up at Elizabeth.

"Birdie? What's the matter?" she asked.

Elizabeth pushed the martini away and crossed her arms. It had become her favorite stance lately. Sometimes she found herself standing in a room alone, with her arms bound so tightly around her own chest that she couldn't draw an even breath. It was as if she were trying to trap something inside of her that wanted out.

"Birdie?" Meghann said again.

"It's nothing, really."

Meghann lowered her voice. "Look. I know something's wrong, Birdie. I'm your friend. I love you. Talk to me."

This was why Elizabeth didn't drink. When she was in such a weakened state, her unhappiness sometimes swelled to unmanageable proportions. She looked across the table at her best friend and knew she had to say something. She simply couldn't hold it all inside anymore.

Her marriage was failing. Thinking it was hard; saying it was almost unthinkable.

They loved each other, she and Jack, but it was a feeling wrought mostly of habit. The passion had been gone for a long time. More and more often it felt as if they were out of step, dancing to different music.

But Elizabeth couldn't possibly say that. Words had too much power. "I'm not very happy lately. That's all."

"What is it you want?" Meghann asked.

"It'll sound stupid."

"I'm half drunk. Nothing will sound stupid."

"I want . . . who I used to be."

"Oh, honey." Meghann sighed heavily. "I don't suppose you've talked to Jack about this."

"Every time we get close to talking about something that matters, I panic and say nothing's wrong."

"I had no idea you were this unhappy."

"That's the worst part of it. I'm not *un*happy, either." Elizabeth slumped forward. Her elbows made the table rattle. "I'm just empty."

"You're forty-five years old, and your kids are gone, and your marriage has gone stale, and you want to start over. My law practice is full of women like you."

"Oh, good. I'm not only unhappy, I'm a cliché, too."

"A cliché is just something that's commonly true. Do you want to leave Jack?"

Elizabeth looked down at the diamond ring she'd worn for twenty-four years. "I dream about leaving him. Living alone."

Meghann leaned toward her. "Look, Birdie, women come into my office every day saying they're not happy. Most end up trading everything for a nine-to-five job and a stack of bills, while hubby dearest waits ten seconds, then marries the salad-bar girl at Hooters. So here's a million dollars' worth of advice: If you're empty, it's not Jack's fault. It's your job to make Elizabeth Shore happy."

"I don't know how to do that anymore."

"Birdie, let's be martini-honest here. You used to be talented, independent, artistic, intellectual. In college we all thought you'd be the next Georgia O'Keefe. Now you decorate your house."

"That's not fai—"

"I'm a lawyer. Fair doesn't interest me." Meghann's voice softened. "I also know that Jack's job has been hard on you. I know how much you wanted a place where you could put down roots."

"You *don't* know," Elizabeth said. "We've lived in more than a dozen houses since we got married, in half that many cities. You've lived in Seattle forever. You don't know what it's like to always be the stranger in town. I know I've let my house become an obsession, but it's because I *belong* in Echo Beach, Meg. Finally. For the first time since I was a child, I have a home."

"Okay," Meghann said, "forget the house. How about this: I can't remember the last time I saw you paint."

Elizabeth drew back. This was something she definitely didn't want to talk about. "There wasn't time after the kids were born."

Meghann's expression was loving but steady. "There is now."

A subtle reminder that the girls were in college now, that Elizabeth's reason for being had moved on. Only a woman with no children would think it was so easy to begin again. Meg didn't know what it was like to devote twenty years of your life to children and then watch them walk away. On shows like *Oprah*, the experts said it left a hole in your life. They underestimated. It was a crater.

Still, Elizabeth had to admit that the same thought had occurred to her. She'd even tried to sketch a few times, but it was a terrible thing to reach for a talent too late and come up empty-handed. No wonder she'd poured all her creativity into her beloved house. "It takes passion to paint," she said now. "Or maybe just youth."

"Tell that to Grandma Moses." Meghann reached into her handbag and pulled out a small notepad with a pen stuck in the spiral column. She flipped the pad open and wrote something down, then ripped off the piece of paper and handed it to Elizabeth. "I've been waiting almost a year for the right time to recommend this to you."

The note said, "Women's Passion Support Group. Thursday, 7:00/Astoria Community College. Room 106."

"Meg, I—"

"Listen to me, Birdie. I have a lot of clients in Grays County, and I send them to this meeting. It's a group of women—mostly newly divorced—who get together to talk. They've all given up too much of themselves, and they're trying to find a way back."

Elizabeth stared at the note. It was one thing to get drunk and complain about her unhappiness to her best friend; it was quite another to walk into a room full of strange women and declare that she had no passion in her life.

She hoped her smile didn't look as brittle as it felt. "Thanks, Meg." Still smiling, she flagged down the waitress and ordered another martini.

Echo Beach, Oregon

THE bedside clock dropped one blocky red number after another into the darkness. At six thirty—a full thirty minutes early—Jack reached over and disabled the alarm.

He lay there staring at the light sneaking through the blinds. He could make out the barest hint of rain falling outside. Another gray, overcast day. Normal early December weather on the Oregon coast.

Elizabeth was asleep beside him, her silvery blond hair fanned across the white pillowcase.

In the earlier days of their marriage they had always slept

nestled together, but somewhere along the way they'd started needing space between them. Lately she'd begun sleeping along the mattress's very edge.

But today things were going to get better. Finally, at age forty-six, he was going to get another chance. A Seattle production company was starting a weekly sports program that would cover the highlights of Northwest sports. If he got the anchor job, he'd have to commute to Seattle three days a week, but that wouldn't be a hardship. It was a step up from the pissant local coverage he was doing.

He'd be *somebody* again.

For the last fifteen years he'd worked his ass off. In a series of crappy little towns he'd paid for his mistakes. Today, finally, he had a chance to get back into the game.

He got out of bed and winced in pain. This damp Oregon climate played hell with his knees. Grimacing, he limped toward the bathroom. As usual, he had to walk over fabric samples and paint chips. Birdie had been "redoing" their bedroom for months now. It was the same in the dining room. Stuff heaped in every corner, waiting for that rarest of moments: his wife actually making a decision.

He had already showered and shaved when she stumbled into the bathroom. "Morning," she said with a yawn. "You're up early."

He felt a flash of disappointment that she'd forgotten. "Today's the day, Birdie. I'm driving up to Seattle for that interview."

A tiny frown tugged at her brow. Then she obviously remembered. "Oh, yeah. I'm sure you'll get the job."

In the old days Birdie would have pumped up his ego, assured him that it would all work out in the end, that he was destined for greatness. But she'd grown tired. He'd failed to land so many jobs over the years, no wonder she'd stopped believing in him.

He'd tried to pretend he was happy here in Oregon, that all he wanted out of life was to be the noon sports anchor covering mostly high school sports in a midsize market. But Birdie knew he merely tolerated living in this nothing town.

She looked up at him. "Will the job make everything better, Jack?"

Her question sucked the air from his lungs. God, he was tired of this discussion. Her endless quest for the answer to *what's wrong with our lives?* was exhausting. Years ago he'd tried to tell her that all her happiness shouldn't depend on him. He'd watched as she'd given up more and more of herself. He couldn't stop it, or didn't stop it, and somehow it had become all his fault. He was sick to death of it. "Not today, Elizabeth."

She gave him the sudden hurt look he'd come to expect. "Of course. I know it's a big day for you."

"For *us*," he said, getting angry now.

Her smile was too bright to be real. "I picked a place for us to celebrate your new job."

The sudden change in subject was their way of smoothing over the rough spots in their marriage. "Where?"

"There's a bear camp in Alaska. You fly in and stay in tents and watch the grizzly bears in their natural environment." She moved hesitantly toward him. "I thought maybe if we could get away, have an adventure . . ."

He knew what she was thinking, and it wouldn't work. A new location was no more than a different stage upon which to act out the same old scenes. Still, he touched her face gently, hoping his cynicism didn't show. There was nothing he hated more than hurting her. "Sounds great. Do we get to share a sleeping bag?"

She smiled. "That can be arranged."

He pulled her against him, holding her close. "Maybe we could celebrate right here in our own bed when I get home."

"I could wear that Victoria's Secret thing you got me."

"I won't be able to concentrate all day."

As he pulled back from her, he looked down into her beautiful face. Once, not all that long ago, they'd loved each other unconditionally. He missed those days, those emotions.

Maybe. Maybe everything really could change for them today.

JACK loved the hustle and bustle of Seattle. The energy. It was the first time he'd been in a city on the go in a while.

He parked in front of a sleek concrete-and-glass building at the corner of Main Street and 106th. He sat in the car for a minute, gathering his confidence, then headed inside. On the seventeenth floor, he adjusted his silk tie and stepped into the reception area.

He thought, You're Jumpin' Jack Flash. They'd be lucky to get you. Then he walked up to the desk.

The receptionist smiled brightly. "May I help you?"

"Jackson Shore to see Mark Wilkerson."

"One moment, please."

A few moments later a woman walked toward him and offered her hand. "It's a pleasure to meet you, Mr. Shore. I'm Lori Hansen. My dad always said that you were the best quarterback the NFL ever had. Well, you and Joe, of course."

"Thank you."

"This way, please."

Jack followed her down a wide marble-floored corridor to a closed door. She knocked softly and opened it.

The man behind the desk was older than Jack had expected—maybe seventy. "Jackson," he said, rising. "Have a seat."

They shook hands; then Jack sat down.

Mark Wilkerson did not. He stood on the other side of the desk, an industry prototype for authority and power, in a black Armani suit. His was the largest independent production company in the Northwest.

Finally he sat down. "I've seen your tapes, Jack. You're good. I was surprised at how good, actually."

"Thank you."

"It's been, what, fifteen years since you played for the Jets?"

"Yeah. I blew out my knee. As I'm sure you know, I led my team to back-to-back Super Bowl wins."

"And you're a Heisman winner. Yes," Mark said, "your past triumphs are quite impressive."

Was there the slightest emphasis on *past*, or had Jack imagined that? "Thank you. I've paid my dues in local broadcasting, as you can see from my résumé. Ratings in Portland have gone up in the two years I've been at the station."

"What about the drugs?"

Just like that, Jack knew it was over. "That was a long time ago. When I was in the hospital, I got hooked on painkillers. The networks gave me a big chance—*Monday Night Football*—and I blew it. But it won't happen again. I've been clean for years."

"We're not a huge company, Jack. We can't afford the kind of scandals that are standard operating procedure at the networks. The truth is, I don't see how I can risk my success on you."

Jack used to think that losing football was rock bottom, the damp basement of his existence. It had been what sent him reaching for a bottle of pills in the first place.

But he'd been wrong. Nothing was worse than the slow, continual erosion of his self-esteem. Times like this wore a man down.

He stood up. It took all his strength to smile and say, "Well, thank you for seeing me." *Although you didn't, you officious ass. You didn't see me at all.*

Then he left the office.

For years Elizabeth had watched daytime television talk shows. The shrinks agreed that passion could be rekindled, that a love lost along the busy highway of raising a family could be regenerated.

She hoped it was true, because she and Jack were in trouble. After twenty-four years of marriage, they'd forgotten how to love each other. Now only the barest strand of their bond remained.

She couldn't keep pretending that things would get better on their own. She had to make it happen. That was another thing the shrinks agreed on. You had to act to get results.

Tonight she'd give them a new beginning.

She kept that goal in mind all day as she went about her chores. Finally she came home and made Jack's favorite dinner—coq au vin.

With the tantalizing aroma of chicken and wine filling the house, she got a fire going in the living-room hearth. She lit the cinnamon-scented candles that were her favorite, then dimmed the lights. By candlelight the yellow walls seemed to be as soft as melted butter. On either side of the blue-and-yellow toile sofa, two mahogany end tables glimmered with streaks of red and gold.

When everything was perfect, she showered. Then she burrowed through her lingerie drawer until she found the lacy white silk camisole and tap pants Jack had bought her for Valentine's Day a few years ago. She'd never worn them.

She frowned. They looked awfully small.

And her ass was awfully big.

The lingerie was size ten. A size too small. Not so much, really. . . . If only she could delete the memory of once being a size six.

She slipped the camisole over her head. Then she stepped gingerly into the tap pants and breathed a sigh of relief.

Tight but wearable.

She went to her closet, found the blue silk robe that had been another long-ago gift, and slipped into it. The fabric caressed her smooth, perfumed skin, and suddenly she felt sexy.

It was now six thirty, and she realized that Jack was late.

She poured herself a glass of wine and went into the living room to wait. By the time she'd drunk a second glass, she was worried.

By eight, dinner was ruined.

Then she heard his key in the front door.

Her first reaction was anger. "You're late" were the words that filled her mouth, but she took a calming breath and released the air slowly. For this one night she wanted to be Jack's mistress, not his wife. She poured him a glass of wine and headed toward the door.

He stood in the doorway, staring at her. And she knew.

"Hey, honey," he said without smiling. "Sorry I'm late." He didn't comment on anything—not the fire, the candles, her outfit.

She moved toward him, feeling suddenly self-conscious in her silk robe.

"I didn't get the job."

"What happened?" she asked softly.

"Wilkerson didn't want to gamble on a guy who used to do drugs." Jack gave her a smile so sad it broke her heart. "Some things don't ever go away, I guess."

She could see how badly he was hurting, but when she reached for him, he pulled away. She stared at him, feeling lost. She didn't know what to say. In the end, she took the safe route, yet as she spoke, it felt as if her bones were cracking. "Here. Have some wine."

He took the glass she offered, walked into the living room, and sat down. Then he opened his briefcase and pulled out a stack of papers. Without looking up, he said, "Can you turn on the lights? I can't see a damned thing here."

"Sure." She turned away from him quickly, before he could see how much he'd hurt her. "I'll get you something to eat."

"I love you, Birdie," he said to her back.

"Yeah," she answered softly. "I love you, too."

TWO

THE next morning, Elizabeth sat on a stool at the kitchen counter, her hands curled tightly around a mug of chamomile tea.

"Coffee?" Jack asked, pouring himself a cup.

"No, thanks. I'm trying to cut down on caffeine."

"Again?"

"Yes, again." She set her cup down on the granite countertop.

Jack looked tired, and no wonder. He'd tossed and turned all night long.

"Why don't you stay home today?" she said. "We could go Christmas shopping in town. The stores are all decorated."

"It's too cold."

She was silent. Once, it wouldn't have mattered if it were raining or snowing. Being together was the point. Now even the weather came between them.

He touched her shoulder and said softly, "I'm sorry."

The shame in his eyes almost undid her. "You'll get another chance, Jack."

"I love you, Birdie."

This time she knew he meant it. "I love you, too."

"So why isn't it enough?"

Elizabeth wanted to look away. "What do you mean?"

"Come on, Birdie, this is the discussion you always want to have, isn't it? The perpetual burning question: What's wrong with us? Well, now *I'm* asking it. Why isn't what we have enough?"

What she said next mattered; she knew that. They so rarely dared to approach the truth of their unhappiness. But she couldn't imagine being honest, saying, "I'm afraid we don't love each other anymore."

"I don't know" was all she could manage.

Jack's shoulders sagged. "You exhaust me, Elizabeth." He drew back from her. "You moan and whine about how unhappy you are, but when I finally try to discuss it, you won't say anything."

"Why should I? You never listen anyway."

They stared at each other, neither certain where to go from there.

"Okay, then," Jack said finally. "I'm off to work. Maybe today I'll score that big story."

With that, they merged back onto the comfortable highway of their lives. Jack might have briefly hit his turn signal, but in the end, no lane-changing was allowed.

JACK stood in front of the stadium, freezing in the chill breeze.

"There you have it," he said, giving the camera one of his patented PR smiles. "The two teams competing for this year's State Boys B-eight football championships. They might be small in size and number, but they more than make up for it in spirit and determination. From downtown Portland, this is Jackson Shore with your midday sports update."

The minute the camera light blinked off, he tossed the microphone to his cameraman. "Damn, it's cold out here," he said, buttoning up his coat. With a quick wave good-bye he walked back to the station. He could have waited for a ride, but the techies were taking forever breaking down their equipment.

Once inside the station's warmth, he got a mocha latte and headed into his office; then he sat down at his cheap metal desk.

There was a knock at his door. "Come in," he said.

It was Sally, one of the station's new production assistants. She was young and beautiful and ambitious. "I wanted to thank you for Tuesday night," she said.

Jack thought for a minute. "Oh, yeah. The Bridgeport Pub." A bunch of the producers and videographers had gone out after work. At the last minute Jack had invited Sally.

She smiled at him. "It was really nice of you to invite me along."

"I thought it'd be good for you to hang out with the producers a little. It's a tough business to break into."

She took a step closer. "I'd like to return the favor."

"Okay."

"Drew Grayland."

"The Panther center?"

"Yes. My little sister was at a party with him on Saturday night.

She said he was drinking and doing drugs, and he took a girl into his room. When the girl came out, she was crying, and her clothes were all ripped. Later that night a drunk driver hit a dog up on Cascade Street. The rumor is that Drew was driving and the campus police are covering it up. Thursday is the big U.C.L.A. game, you know."

Jack hadn't had a tip like this in . . . ever. "This could be big." He allowed himself to imagine it for a second—a national story, his face on every television in America.

"Can I be your assistant on it?" Sally asked.

"Of course. We'll need to see if that woman filed any charges against Grayland. We can't run with campus gossip."

Sally flipped open a small notepad and started taking notes.

"I'll talk to the news director," Jack said. "You get to work on questions and leads. We'll start with the campus police. Let's meet in the lobby in . . ." He looked at his watch. It was twelve forty-five. "Thirty minutes, okay?"

"Perfect."

When Sally grinned at him, he felt a flash of the old confidence.

By the time Elizabeth got home that evening, she was dog-tired. The library meeting had run overtime, and her book group had taken almost an hour to get started.

Exhausted, she tossed her purse on the kitchen table, went back outside, and settled into the rocking chair on the porch. The even, creaking motion of the chair soothed her ragged nerves.

The bronze ocean stretched out before her. The thick green lawn, still damp from an afternoon downpour, glittered in the fading sunlight. A pair of ancient Douglas firs bracketed the view perfectly.

A fleeting *if only* passed through her mind. She immediately discarded it. Her painting days were long behind her. But if she hadn't let that once hot passion grow cold, this was what she would paint.

She watched the sun sink slowly into the darkening sea, then got to her feet and went back inside. It was time to start dinner.

She had just walked through the front door when the phone rang. She answered it. "Hello?"

"Hey, kiddo, are you done saving the Oregon coast for the day?"

Elizabeth smiled. "Hey, Meg." She collapsed into a blue-and-yellow-striped chair. "What's going on?"

"Today's Thursday. I wanted to remind you about that meeting."

The passionless women. Elizabeth's smile faded. "Yeah," she said, "I remembered," although of course she hadn't.

"You're going?"

Yeah, right. "If I went, what would it be like?"

"A bunch of girlfriends getting together. They'll probably talk about how it feels to be lost in the middle of life."

That didn't sound so bad. "You really think it would help me?"

"Let's put it this way: If you don't go this week, I'll make next week such hell that by next Thursday you'll be begging to go."

Elizabeth couldn't help smiling. Years ago, when Meghann had suffered through a terrible, heartbreaking divorce, Elizabeth had treated her in exactly the same way. Tough love. Sometimes a friend had to strong-arm you; that was all there was to it. "Okay, I'll go."

After they hung up, Elizabeth checked the answering machine. There was a message from Jack. He was tracking down a big story and wouldn't be home until late.

"There you have it, sports fans," she said aloud. "I'm going to the meeting."

She took a shower, then went into her walk-in closet. She stared at her neatly organized clothes. So much of what she bought was bright and colorful—hand-painted scarves, batik prints. But the last thing she wanted to do now was stand out in the crowd.

Look, there. A woman with no passion.

She chose chocolate-brown wool pants and a cream-colored cashmere turtleneck. Then she pulled her straight blond hair back into a French braid, removed the dangly silver-and-turquoise earrings she usually wore, and put in a pair of pearl studs.

She studied herself in the mirror. "Perfect." She looked as bland as a wren.

She left Jack a note on the kitchen counter just in case he got home before she did. A wasted gesture, of course.

Twenty-five minutes later she pulled into the parking lot of the community college. Clutching her handbag tightly under her arm, she entered the building and moved down the hallway until she came to room 106. Without allowing herself a pause, she walked inside.

It was a small classroom. In the middle sat a semicircle of metal chairs, some of which held nervous-looking women. Off to the left a table held a coffeemaker and a tray of baked goods.

"Don't be shy. Come on in."

Startled, Elizabeth spun around and found herself nose to nose with a stunningly beautiful woman wearing a scarlet suit.

"I'm Sarah," the woman said, smiling brightly. "Welcome."

Elizabeth couldn't manage a smile. "I'm Elizabeth."

Sarah gave her shoulder a reassuring squeeze. "Everyone's nervous at first." She guided Elizabeth toward the circle of chairs.

Elizabeth sat down. Beside her was a tiny, bright-eyed young woman dressed in a denim jumpsuit and scuffed cowboy boots.

"I'm Joey," she said. "My husband left me to join a rock band. He plays the harmonica. Can you believe it?" She laughed.

Elizabeth nodded stiffly. Meanwhile, all around her, women chatted with one another. More women drifted into the room, took seats. Some joined in the conversation. Others, like Elizabeth, sat quietly.

Finally Sarah closed the door and took a seat in the middle of the group. "Welcome, ladies. It's nice to see so many new faces tonight. This is the Women's Passion Support Group." She smiled. "Don't worry, we're not as erotic as that sounds."

Laughter followed that remark, some of it nervous.

"Our objective is to help each other. We have something in common, and that something is a sense of loss. We've discovered that we've misplaced a vital part of ourselves. For lack of a better word, I call the missing element passion. To begin, let's go around the circle and share one dream each." Sarah turned to the woman next to her. "You've been here before, Mina. Why don't you begin?"

Mina, a plump, red-haired older woman, seemed entirely at ease. "I started coming to these meetings about six months ago, when my husband was diagnosed with Alzheimer's." She shook her head. "I couldn't imagine finding passion, but now I'm taking driving lessons. It's given me a new freedom. Next week I'll be going in for my final test. Hopefully, I'll drive here on my own next time."

The group applauded, and Mina giggled.

When the room quieted, the next woman began to speak. "My name is Fran. My husband ran off with his secretary. His male secretary. The only passion I have lately seems to center around buying a handgun. Unfortunately, I can't decide which one of us to shoot." She smiled nervously. "That was a joke."

Sarah leaned forward. "What do you love doing, Fran?"

"I loved being a wife." She paused, shrugged.

"Think about it, Fran," Sarah said. "What would you do if you knew you couldn't fail? Answer fast."

"Sing." Fran looked surprised by her answer. "I used to sing."

"I belong to a women's choir," Mina said. "We sing at nursing homes and hospitals. We're always looking for new members. Why don't you join us? We have a lot of fun."

Fran looked uncertain. "I'll think about it."

Several women started talking at once. Many of them had reached for unexpected things. Flying, skydiving, marathon running. The consensus was that anything could be a start.

"*That's* what we're about," Sarah said. "Finding your passion is finding your authentic self. The one you've buried beneath other people's needs." She nodded to the woman next to Fran, who immediately started talking. After her, another spoke, then another.

Elizabeth realized suddenly that it was her turn. She took a deep breath. "I'm Elizabeth. I'm a housewife with two daughters. Stephanie is almost twenty-one; Jamie is nineteen. I haven't been divorced or widowed. Everything that's wrong with my life is my own fault."

"Blame isn't what we're looking for," Sarah said. "We're interested in what you want from life—your dreams."

"I used to paint," she said. Surprisingly, it hurt to say the words out loud.

"I work at an art-supply store. Picture Perfect, on Chadwick," one of the women said. "Come down this Saturday, and I'll help you find everything you need."

Elizabeth had plenty of supplies. Paints and brushes were the least of what an artist needed. "There's no point, really."

"Don't be afraid," Sarah said. "Buy the paints, and see what happens."

"You're lucky," Joey said. "You actually have a passion. I've been coming to the meetings for months, and I still have no clue."

"I wish *I* could paint," added another woman.

Elizabeth looked at the faces around her. They believed this was helping her. In fact, it was making her feel worse. "Sure. I could do that," she said just to end her turn. "It might be fun to paint again."

She thought the women were going to start break-dancing.

FOR the next week Jack and Sally spent eighteen-hour days following the Drew Grayland story. They interviewed dozens of people, tracked down countless leads.

Innuendo, anecdote, gossip—these they found in abundance. By all accounts, Drew was a sleazy, not-too-bright young man who had an exceedingly high opinion of himself, an almost total disregard for other people's feelings, and an unshakable belief that society's rules didn't apply to him. In other words, he was a real pain in the ass.

He was also Oregon's brightest collegiate athlete, the best state basketball player in two decades. Speculation was high that he could lead the down-on-their-luck Panthers to their first ever NCAA championship season.

It was hardly surprising that no one in Panther athletics would talk to Jack or Sally. And nobody seemed to have seen the incident with the girl except Sally's sister. In short, they had no proof. No one liked Drew Grayland, it was clear, but no one would say anything on the record.

After another fruitless day, Jack and Sally went to a local steak house for dinner. They sat in a dimly lit booth.

"What now?" Sally asked.

Jack didn't know where to go from here. All he knew for sure was that he'd failed. Again. "Maybe you should take the story to someone else," he told Sally.

"We'll nail this story, Jack. You and me."

Sally's confidence never seemed to waver. Jack couldn't remember the last time someone had had such faith in him.

He looked at her. Even now her black eyes shone with optimism. And why not? She was twenty-six years old; it would be years before she learned the tarry taste of disappointment.

At her age he'd been the same way. After three stellar years at U.W. and that amazing Heisman win, he'd been a first-round draft pick—to a loser team who needed him desperately. He'd worked hard, played his heart out. Three years later the Jets picked him up.

That had been the first of his golden years.

In the fourth game of his first New York season, the starting quarterback had gotten hurt, and Jack's moment had come. He threw three touchdown passes in that game. By the end of that season, no one remembered the name of the quarterback he'd replaced. Jumpin' Jack Flash had been born. Crowds chanted his name; cameras flashed wherever he went. He led his team to back-to-back Super Bowl wins. It was the stuff of which legends were made. For years he'd been a superstar. A hero.

Then he'd been hit. Game over. Career ended.

"Jack?" Sally's voice pulled him back into the smoky bar. For a second there, he'd been gone. "What happened to you?"

He sighed. Here it comes, he thought.

She gazed at him earnestly. "When I was a little girl, my dad and I used to watch football together. You were his favorite player. He always said you were the best quarterback to play the game, and now you're in Portland, on the lowest-rated newscast in town. What happened?"

It felt dangerous suddenly, this moment—a slow, conscious skate toward the edge of intimacy. He knew better, of course. Every man his age did, but he'd been lonely for a long, long time, and just now that burden seemed heavier than before. "It started in the hospital."

Amazingly, he told her all of it—how he'd gotten addicted to his pain medications and blown his shot on *Monday Night Football*. It came back to him like a handful of broken glass, all sharp edges and reflected light. He knew that if he held it too tightly, his hand would bleed, but he couldn't stop himself.

He told her how he'd tried so hard to pretend that losing football didn't matter. But the game had been his life. Without it he'd anesthetized himself with pills and booze. His excesses had become legendary. He went from golden boy to party animal.

"After a stint in rehab," he said, "the only job I could get was for a local station in Albuquerque. It's been a long, slow climb back."

He looked at Sally and knew that something had changed between them. He tried to look away. Couldn't.

She touched his arm, and the touch was like an electric spark. "This story is going to make both of our careers."

He had to do something, he decided. Anything was better than sitting here, suddenly aching for a woman he couldn't have. "The campus is closing today for winter break," he said. "What do you say we go back, drive around? The administrators and staff will be gone. Maybe someone will talk when the wardens aren't around."

"It's worth a shot."

Jack paid the bill; then they left.

Back on campus, they looked for all their previous sources. They made themselves impossible to ignore, easy to find. Nothing.

Finally they pulled into the parking lot and sat in the car beneath a bright streetlamp. A silvery rain beaded the windshield.

"I guess that's that," Jack said at last. A glance at the dash clock revealed that it was one in the morning.

A knock at the window shocked both of them.

Jack rolled down the window. There, sidled close to the door, was a campus police officer, a man they'd tried to interview earlier.

"You're lookin' for dirt on Drew Grayland?" the officer whispered. "I can't stand by and do nothin' anymore. Here." He slipped a manila envelope through the open window.

Jack glanced down at the envelope. There were no markings on it of any kind. When he looked back outside, the officer was gone.

Jack opened the envelope and withdrew the papers, scanning them. "Oh, my God."

"What is it?" Sally asked.

"Incident reports. Four women have accused Drew of date rape."

"And he's never been arrested?"

Jack turned to look at her. "Never."

ELIZABETH checked her to-do list for the final time. Everything was done. By this time tomorrow she'd be at her dad's house, with her daughters and family, celebrating an old-fashioned Christmas.

After one last obsessive-compulsive pass through the house, she grabbed her purse and headed for the car.

She made it to Portland in good time. At the television station, she parked and went inside. Upstairs, she found Jack's office empty. Glancing worriedly at her watch, she hurried down to the studio, checked in, and slipped into the darkened room.

Jack was behind the big desk on set. In full makeup, with the lights bright on his face, he looked movie-star handsome. As usual. It was unfair, she thought suddenly, that he'd held on to his youth while hers seemed to be sliding south.

"In the past two years," he was saying, "four different women have made rape or sexual misconduct reports against Panther center Drew Grayland. Campus officials did not turn these reports over to the Portland police. Olympic University athletic director Bill Seagel had no comment today when apprised of the allegations, except to say that to his knowledge no criminal charges had been filed against Grayland. Coach Rivers confirmed that his star center will start against U.C.L.A. next week. We'll be bringing you live updates on this exclusive story as information becomes available."

Jack took off his microphone and stood up. As he crossed the room, he noticed Elizabeth and grinned broadly. He led her back to his office, laughing as he kicked the door shut behind them.

"Can you believe it, Birdie? I did it." He swept her into his arms and lifted her off her feet.

She laughed along with him. No one did success like her husband. It had always been that way. In the good times Jack was a rushing torrent of water that swept you away.

He loosened his hold, and she slid back down to the floor.

They stared at each other; their smiles slowly faded. After a long, awkward moment, she said, "Are you ready to go?" She glanced down at her watch. "Our plane leaves in two hours."

Jack frowned. "We leave tomorrow."

He'd done it again. She was proud of her control when she said simply, "No. We leave today. December twenty-second."

The door to his office smacked open. A young woman ran into the room. "You're not going to believe this," she said, rushing forward. She got halfway across the room before she realized that Jack wasn't alone. She stopped, smiled pleasantly at Elizabeth. "I'm sorry to interrupt. But this is big news. I'm Sally."

Elizabeth's smile was cinched tight. She was too angry with her husband to be sociable. "Hello, Sally."

"Jack, three more women filed complaints against Grayland.

And here's the really great news. I just took a call from one of them. She'll talk to you. On-camera."

"Meet me in the lobby in thirty minutes," he said. "We'll come up with a game plan."

"You got it." With a hurried nod to Elizabeth, Sally left the room.

Elizabeth looked at Jack. "Let me guess. You're not coming with me."

He took her in his arms. "Come on, baby," he murmured against her ear, "you know how much I need this. Like air."

And your needs are always important, aren't they, Jack?

"I'll make it up to you," he promised. "And I'll be at your dad's before Christmas Eve."

They were close enough to kiss, but Elizabeth couldn't imagine any more distance between them. "Mean it, Jackson," she said.

"I do."

"Okay, honey. I'll go on ahead."

He kissed her hard and let her go. "I love you, Birdie."

She wanted to answer but couldn't. He didn't seem to notice anyway. His mind had already followed young Sally out the door.

Later, as she walked through the TV station's empty parking lot, she wondered how often a woman could bend before she broke.

ELIZABETH hated to fly alone. She didn't say a single word except "thank you" on either of the flights, just kept her nose buried in a romance novel all the way to Tennessee.

At the rental-car agency in Nashville, she chose a white Ford Taurus and filled out the paperwork. When everything was finished, she got into the car and drove south. Each mile calmed her nerves.

She was back in her beloved Tennessee, the only place in the world beside Echo Beach that felt like home.

At the Springdale exit, she eased the car off the freeway, then drove through town. A mile out, the road thinned to two lanes, and on either side of it, empty tobacco fields stretched to the horizon.

She turned onto the gravel road that bordered her father's land. To the right, everything belonged to Edward Rhodes. Acres and acres of tilled red earth. Soon the crops would be planted. By July the corn would be as tall as a man and go on forever.

At last she came to the driveway. A huge scrollwork metal arch curved above the road. Swinging gently in the breeze was the copper sign that read SWEETWATER.

Elizabeth drove slowly down the driveway. The Federal-style brick house stood proudly in a manicured yard. Clipped evergreen hedges outlined the perimeter, the perfectly shaped line broken here and there by ancient walnut trees.

She parked in front of the carriage house turned garage and shut down the engine. Then she pulled her garment bag out of the car and headed up to the front door, where she rang the bell.

There were a few moments of silence. Finally Daddy opened the door. He wore a blue shirt and twill pants. His white hair was Albert Einstein wild, his smile big enough to break a girl's heart.

"Sugar beet," he said. His molasses-thick drawl stretched the words into taffy—*sugah beeat.* "We didn't expect y'all for another hour or so. Come on now, give your old man a hug."

She launched forward. His big arms curled around her, made her feel small again, young. When she drew back, he touched her face. "We missed you something awful." He glanced back down the hallway, calling, "Hurry up, Mother. Our little girl is home."

There was an immediate response. Elizabeth heard the Gatling gun sound of high heels on marble flooring. Then she smelled flowers—gardenias. Her stepmother's "signature" scent.

Anita came running around the corner, wearing cherry-red silk evening pants, black stiletto heels, and an absurdly low-cut gold spandex top. Her long, platinum-blond hair had been teased until it sat on top of her head like a dunce cap. When she saw Elizabeth, she let out a little screech. "Why, Birdie, we didn't expect y'all so soon." She started forward, as if she were going to hug Elizabeth, but at the last minute she came to a bumpy stop and sidled up to Daddy. "It's good to have you home, Birdie. It's been too long."

"Yes, it has."

"Well . . ." One of those awkward pauses fell, the kind that always punctuated Anita and Elizabeth's conversations. "I better check my cider. Daddy, you show our Birdie up to her room."

Elizabeth tried to keep her smile in place. Of all her stepmother's irritating habits (and they were legion), calling her husband Daddy was top of the heap.

He grabbed Elizabeth's garment bag and led her upstairs to her old bedroom. It was exactly as it had always been. Pale lemony walls, honey oak floors, white French provincial four-poster bed.

"So where's golden boy?" Daddy asked as he hung up her garment bag.

"He broke a big story and needed another day to wrap it up. He'll be here tomorrow."

"Too bad he couldn't fly down with you," he said slowly.

She couldn't look at him. "Yes."

Her father knew something was wrong between her and Jack. Of course he knew; he'd always seen through her. But he wouldn't push. "Your mother made us some hot cider," he said at last. "Let's go sit on the porch a spell."

"She's not my mother." The response was automatic. The moment Elizabeth said it, she wished she hadn't. "I'm sorry," she said.

There were other things she could say, excuses and explanations, but in the end, they amounted to empty words, and she and her father knew it. Elizabeth and Anita had never gotten along. It was years too late to change it . . . or to pretend otherwise.

Daddy heaved a big-chested sigh of disappointment, then said, "Walk your old man outside. Tell me about your excitin' life in that heathen Yankee rain forest."

As they'd done a thousand times before, they walked arm in arm down the curving mahogany staircase, crossed the black-and-white marble-floored entry, and headed for the kitchen.

Elizabeth steeled herself for another round of stiff conversation with her stepmother, but to her relief the kitchen was empty. Two mugs of cider sat on the butcher-block counter.

"She always remembers your sweet tooth," Daddy said.

Elizabeth nodded. "Go on out. I'll bring the cider."

Carrying the two mugs, she followed her father outside. The back porch wasn't really a porch; it was a portico-covered square of stone-tiled space. Beyond, huddled in darkness, was the yard with her mother's garden.

Several black wrought-iron chairs hugged the back of the house. Each one faced the sprawling garden. Elizabeth handed her father his cider, then sat down next to him.

"I'm glad you could make it home this year," he said.

Something about the way he said it bothered her. She looked at him sharply. "Is everything all right? Are you healthy?"

He laughed heartily. "Now, sugar beet, don't try to make me old before my time. I'm fine. I'm just glad you could make it down here, is all. I miss seein' you and my granddaughters."

"I believe you forgot to mention Jack," she observed dryly.

"Like you keep forgettin' to mention Anita. Hell's bells, honey, I reckon we're too old to be fabricatin' feelings. But as long as you're happy with golden boy, I'm happy with him." He paused, glanced sideways at her. "You are happy, aren't you?"

Elizabeth laughed, but even to her own ears it was a brittle sound, like glass hitting a tile floor. "Things are great. The house is finally coming together. You'll have to come see us this year."

Daddy turned to her suddenly. "I'm only gonna say this once, Birdie; then we can pretend I kept quiet." He lowered his voice. "You're missin' out on your own life. It's passin' you by."

The words were like a sucker punch. "How do you know that?"

"Just 'cause my glasses are thick as Coke bottles doesn't mean I can't still see my little girl's heart. I know an unhappy marriage when I see one."

"Come on, Daddy. You've been married two times, and wildly in love with both of your wives. You can't know about . . . whatever it is I'm going through."

"You think I never had my heart broken? Think again, missy. Your mama about killed me."

"Mama's death broke all our hearts. That's not the same thing."

He started to say something, then stopped.

She sensed that he'd been about to reveal something. "Daddy?"

He smiled, and she knew it had flown past them, whatever opportunity had almost existed. As usual, he wouldn't talk about Mama.

Elizabeth leaned back in her chair, stared out at the yard that had once seemed so big. She remembered another time in this yard, back when she'd been a little girl of six. It was after her mother's funeral. The moment she'd realized that Mama was really gone. Forever.

She'd been sitting in the grass listening to the distant buzz of adult conversation. When everyone had gone home, her father had finally come to her and squatted down. "You want to sleep in my room tonight, sugar beet?"

That was what he'd said to her. Nothing about Mama or grief or the endless sadness that was to come. Just one simple sentence that was the end of one life and the beginning of another.

Now, as she stared ahead, she said, "The moon looked just like this that night."

"What night?"

"Mama's funeral," she said softly, hearing her father's sharply indrawn breath when she mentioned the taboo subject.

He pushed to a stand. "I think I'll call it a night, Birdie." He leaned down and kissed her forehead.

She shouldn't have mentioned Mama. It had always been the surest way to get rid of her father. He was at the screen door by the time she found the courage to say softly, "You never talk about her."

He stopped. The door screeched open. She thought she heard him sigh. "No, I don't. Some wounds run deep, Birdie." His voice was as soft as she'd ever heard it. "You'd best remember that."

Then the door banged shut, and she was alone.

THREE

ANDREA Kinnear, the girl who had come forward to talk about Drew Grayland, lived in a small brick house near the university.

Jack stood in front of the house. His cameraman, Kirk, and Sally were next to him. He'd never done anything like this before, an on-camera interview with the victim of a violent crime, and he was nervous. He knocked on the door. It opened, and a small, pale young woman with carrot-red hair stood there. She wore a cotton skirt and a white blouse. "Hello, Mr. Shore. I'm Andrea."

Jack introduced Sally and Kirk. Then the three of them followed Andrea into a small living room that was crowded with furniture. She sat down, though her body remained stiffly upright, her hands clasped tightly together.

Jack took a seat opposite her. "I'm just going to ask you some very straightforward questions, Andrea." He frowned. She looked so fragile. "Are you sure you're okay with this?"

"It's just . . . humiliating."

Sally touched Jack's shoulder, then drew back. It was the signal; they were rolling film now. Jack leaned forward and said, "You have nothing to be ashamed of, Andrea."

She tried to smile. "How about stupidity? I didn't even get to know him. I saw him across the room and knew who he was—everyone knew him. I knew I wasn't pretty enough or cool enough, but I'd had a few drinks, and I was brave. So I went up to him and started a conversation. At first he was so nice. He looked at me like I was someone who mattered. When other girls came up to him, he blew them off." Andrea fingered a gold cross at her throat. "After a while the party started breaking up, and there were only a few people in the room. Drew leaned over and kissed me. It was so . . . gentlemanly. When he asked me up to his room, I said yes." Her lower lip trembled. "I shouldn't have done that."

Jack said, "You're nineteen, Andrea. Don't judge yourself too harshly. Trusting someone isn't a crime."

Her gaze found his. "What he did to me was a crime, though."

"What . . . did he do?" Jack winced at his own hesitation, hoping they could edit it out.

"At first we were just lying on the bed kissing, but he started getting aggressive. He held me down so I couldn't move, and his kisses . . . I couldn't breathe. I started pushing him away, but he grabbed me, hard. I started screaming for him to get off me."

Jack could see how hard she was trying not to cry.

"He hit me once in the face. It hurt so much I couldn't even cry. And then he was ripping my clothes off, yanking my underwear down. I heard them rip. Then . . . then . . ." Her eyes were suddenly glazed with tears. "He raped me."

Jack pulled out a handkerchief and handed it to her.

"Thank you," she whispered, wiping her eyes. It was a moment before she went on. "I don't even remember leaving the house. My roommate took me to the emergency room, but we had to wait forever. I finally gave up and went home."

Jack realized that his hands had balled into fists. "Did you tell anyone beside your roommate? Your parents, maybe?"

She made a little sound, maybe a sob. "I couldn't. I guess I'll have to tell them tonight. But I went to the campus police the next day. I wanted to make sure they knew what Drew had done to me."

"What happened?"

"An officer listened to my story, then left the room. About fifteen minutes later Bill Seagel came in. He's the Panther athletic director. He laid it all out for me. How I had no proof, no doctor's report, no witnesses. How I'd been drinking. He told me nothing would happen to Drew if I came forward, but my college years would be ruined. So I shut up about it."

"Why did you come forward now?"

"I saw your report on the news." She looked up again. "I didn't want him to be able to hurt anyone else."

"So you went to the Portland police."

"It probably won't do any good, you know. I waited too long and did everything wrong. But I feel better. At least I'm not afraid anymore. Do you think I did the right thing?"

Jack knew he shouldn't answer. This interview wouldn't be much good if he ruined his credibility by showing that he cared.

But she was sitting there staring at him through eyes that were heartbreakingly sad. And she was so darned young.

"I have a daughter just your age. Jamie. I pray that she is safe at college. But if anything bad ever happened to her, I'd hope she could be as brave as you've been today. You did the right thing."

Jack didn't realize until they'd said their good-byes and he and Sally were driving back to the station how shaken he was. "Damn," he said, thumping the steering wheel for emphasis. "I was about as detached as that girl's own father. My career is going to do a swan dive when this airs."

"Anyone who could sit with Andrea and not be moved has no right to ask her those questions. She deserved your emotion."

Jack and Sally spent the next four hours in the editing room. The poor holiday-crew editor finally threw his hands in the air. "That's it, Jacko. It's done, and I'm going home."

Jack glanced at the clock. It was ten p.m. Too late to stop by the news director's house. He'd have to do it in the morning. Unfortunately, he was scheduled to fly out at seven a.m.

There was no way he could make that flight.

Elizabeth would kill him.

THE Nashville airport was quieter than normal for the holidays. Elizabeth had arrived almost an hour early, and she had to bide her time. She could hardly wait to see her daughters.

Finally Stephanie emerged from the crowd of passengers. As usual, she was the picture of decorum—pressed khaki pants, white turtleneck, black blazer. Her chestnut-brown hair was held in place by a black velvet headband. Even as a child, Stephanie had had an invisible, unshakable grace. Everything she did, she did well.

Elizabeth ran forward and hugged her elder daughter fiercely. "Where's your sister?"

"There was a seating mix-up. We got separated."

Jamie was the last person out of the baggage claim area. She stood out from the crowd like some gothic scarecrow. First there was her height, almost six feet, and her hair color—corn-silk blond that fell in a wavy line to her waist. And then there was her outfit. Skintight black leather pants, black shirt, and black combat boots. The mascara around her blue eyes was as thick as soot.

She pushed through the crowd like a linebacker. "That was the worst flight of my life," she said instead of hello. "The child next to me should be institutionalized." She kissed Elizabeth's cheek. "Hi, Mom. You look tired. Where's Dad?"

Elizabeth laughed. "Thanks, honey. Your dad had to stay behind for a day. Some big story."

"Gee, what a shock." Jamie barely paused for a breath and started talking again. "Could they put *more* seats in that plane? I mean, you have to be Calista Flockhart to get out of your seat."

Jamie was still talking when they pulled up to the house.

Daddy and Anita were already on the porch; they'd probably been standing at the window, watching and waiting impatiently.

Jamie bounded out of the car, hair flying, arms outstretched, and launched herself into her grandfather's open arms.

Elizabeth and Stephanie gathered the bags and followed her.

Inside, the house smelled like Christmas. Fresh-cut evergreen boughs draped the mantel and corkscrewed up the banisters; the cinnamony scent of newly baked pumpkin pies lingered in the air.

They spent the rest of the day talking, playing cards, and wrapping presents. By midafternoon Stephanie and Anita had disappeared into the kitchen to make dressing and a vegetable casserole.

Elizabeth stayed in the living room playing poker for toothpicks with Jamie and Daddy.

"So, missy," Daddy said, puffing on his pipe as he studied his cards. "How're things at Georgetown?"

Jamie shrugged. "Hard."

That surprised Elizabeth. Jamie *never* admitted that anything was difficult. "Honey," she said, frowning, "what's wrong at school?"

"Don't lapse into melodrama, Mom. It's just a tough quarter."

"How's the swimming?" Daddy asked. "Are we gonna see you at the next Olympics?"

When she was eleven years old, the day she won her first race, Jamie had vowed to win an Olympic Gold.

"Of course," she answered, smiling brightly.

But there was something wrong with that smile, something off. Before Elizabeth could say anything, Anita walked into the room. She was holding the cordless phone. "Birdie, honey, it's Jack."

Elizabeth knew instantly. Bad news.

ELIZABETH hadn't slept well. All night she'd tossed and turned. Finally, at five a.m. the morning of Christmas Eve, she gave up, got dressed, and went downstairs.

Jack hadn't been able to get away yesterday. Of course he hadn't. Something important had come up. *The video, honey, it's first rate, but blah, blah, blah. I'll be there tomorrow night. I promise.*

Elizabeth made herself a cup of tea. Then she wandered into the living room. There, sitting on the coffee table, was a red cardboard ornament box. Her father must have left it out for her last night.

She put down her tea and reached for the ornament that was on top. It was a lovely white angel made of porcelain. Her mother had given it to her on her fourth birthday, the last present Elizabeth could recall. Each year she'd unwrapped it with special care and taken great pains to choose the perfect place for it on the tree.

"Hey, Mama," she said quietly, smiling down at the angel in her palm. She had so few memories of Mama; each one was valuable.

She hung the angel from the second-highest branch, then plugged in the lights and stood back. The tree looked beautiful, festooned with lights and decades' worth of decoration.

Anita walked into the room. She wore a frothy pink negligee and Barbie-doll mules. "I had a heck of a hard time finding that box."

Elizabeth turned around. "You left this box out for me?"

"You picture your daddy rootin' around in the attic for a certain box of Christmas ornaments, do you?"

Elizabeth smiled in spite of herself. "I guess not."

Anita sat down on the sofa, curled her feet up underneath her. The puffy pink pom-poms on her slippers disappeared. "I'm sorry Jack couldn't get here yesterday."

Elizabeth turned back to the tree. She didn't want to talk about this. "He's busy with some big story."

"That's what you said."

"Yes, it is," Elizabeth answered curtly.

Anita sighed dramatically. It was how they'd communicated—in fits and starts—ever since Daddy had brought his new wife home.

Elizabeth had been thirteen, a bad age. And Anita Bockner, the beautician from Lick Skillet, Alabama, was the last person she would have chosen to be her stepmother.

"This is your new mama, Birdie," Daddy had announced, and that was that. Mama had never been mentioned again. No pictures of her graced the mantels or the tables; no stories of her life had ever been spun into a wrap that would warm her lonely daughter.

Anita had tried to mother Elizabeth, but she'd gone about it all wrong. They had been oil and water from the beginning. For Edward's sake they'd learned to be polite. When things got too personal, one of them always changed the subject.

It was Elizabeth's turn now, but the doorbell rang before she could speak. She glanced at Anita. "Are you expecting anyone?"

Anita shrugged.

Elizabeth went to the front door, opened it.

Jack stood there looking rumpled and tired. "Hey, baby," he said, giving her a lopsided grin. "I woke up the news director at midnight and gave him the tape. Then I flew all night. Forgive me?"

Elizabeth smiled up at him. "Just when I think I'm going to trade you in for a newer model, you do something like this."

She let him pull her into his arms, and when he leaned down to kiss her, she kissed him back.

IN AN ordinary year, the week after Christmas was quiet. A time for taking down decorations and watching old movies on television.

Elizabeth hadn't been back in Echo Beach more than twenty-four hours when she realized that this was not going to be an ordinary year. They'd been in the Nashville airport on December 27 when Jack received the first phone call. She hadn't thought much about it at the time, hadn't yet understood that their life had altered in the past week. While she'd been relaxing with her family in Tennessee, things in Oregon had undergone a subtle shift.

Jack was a hero again.

The Drew Grayland story had broken on the day after Christmas. The next day, he'd been arrested and charged with rape. The story immediately went national.

From the second Jack and Elizabeth got home, the phone never stopped ringing. Everyone, it seemed, wanted to interview Jack. He'd become a story himself. After all these years in partial obscurity he was famous again—not a household name, but a somebody.

It wasn't as if just anybody had broken the Drew Grayland story.

Oh, no. The story had been brought to America by Jackson Shore, a man who'd once been a god, then stumbled and lost his way.

Jack had become the poster boy for redemption. And this new life of his was evident in everything he did. He walked taller, smiled brighter, slept better.

Unfortunately, as Jack grew, Elizabeth seemed to diminish. She couldn't quite make herself be happy for him, and that shamed her. But how could she admit to being jealous of her husband's happiness and success? So instead of telling him that she felt abandoned by his sudden happiness, she ripped the hell out of the dining room, a perfectly functional if boring room tucked between the kitchen and living room.

Like many of the original cottages along this part of the coast, the house had begun life as a summer getaway for a rich Portland family. Over the years, under a variety of owners, it had been remodeled and reshaped. By the time Jack and Elizabeth stumbled across it, in 1999, the place had become a jumbled mess.

All Jack had been able to see was the cost—a run-down house with peeling paint and outdated plumbing fixtures. Not to mention the commute. Echo Beach was quite a drive from Portland.

But Elizabeth had seen past all that to a beautiful little cottage with a wraparound porch and view to die for. For the only time in their marriage, she put her foot down, and Jack yielded.

She'd started work on the house immediately. In the last two years she'd made a remarkable number of changes. She'd ripped up yards of avocado green shag carpeting and found a beautiful oak floor beneath, which she'd refinished. She'd scraped fifty years' worth of paint off the kitchen cabinets and replaced the counter-tops with exquisite granite tiles.

Because she worked alone, her progress was slow. Although she'd finished the kitchen and living room, she was still a long way from done. Only last week the dining room had seemed to be a low priority, much less important than fixing up the master suite. But last night had changed her outlook. She wasn't even sure why.

She and Jack had been sitting in the living room watching television. The phone had rung every fifteen minutes, and he answered every time, talking endlessly about himself and the story.

Elizabeth had heard the resurrection in his voice, and it sparked a lot of memories. Few of them were good.

In the early years of their relationship, she'd loved football. Watching Jack play in college had been thrilling. Every time he won, he brought a dusting of victory home with him. They'd loved each other then—wildly, madly, deeply.

But time had changed that. Somewhere along the way he'd become a star, and stars acted differently from ordinary men. They stayed out all night and slept all day, ignoring their wives and children. They slept with other women.

She and Jack had barely made it through those dark and terrible times. What saved them, ironically, was the end of his fame. When he blew his knee out and got hooked on drugs, he'd needed Elizabeth again.

Last night, as she'd listened to him talk ad nauseam about himself, she'd glimpsed their future. It was a mirror image of the past.

And suddenly she'd looked into the dining room and thought, That wall needs French doors.

This morning, after Jack left for work, she'd gone to the hardware store, bought a dust mask and a sledgehammer, and set to work.

Now, almost eight hours later, a gaping hole in the dining-room wall showcased the winter-dead garden beyond. The hole was, she calculated, exactly the right size for a standard set of French doors.

Whistling happily, she stapled thick blue plastic sheeting across the opening. She'd have to order the doors tomorrow.

She made herself a cup of tea and went out onto the porch.

A full moon hung overhead, huge and blue-white against a silvery sky. She walked down the porch stairs and stepped out onto the mushy grass of her front yard. Suddenly a sound caught her attention. At first she thought it was the wind moaning through the trees. But there was no wind. Turning, she faced the ocean.

She heard it again. A plaintive, elegiac sound that lingered long after the final note had run out. She knew what it was.

She crossed the yard and stopped at the edge of the cliff steps. The rickety stairway snaked thirty feet straight down to a crescent of sand. Caution held her. It was dark, and the stairs could be slippery, dangerous.

Then she saw them. Killer whales, at least a dozen of them.

Their fins rose tall and straight out of the water.

She held on to the splintery railing and hurried down.

It sounded again, haunting and mournful, a music borne of water, carried by the waves themselves. Out there, a whale breached up from the water and slammed down again; a second later there was a great whooshing sound, and air and water sprayed up from one of the animal's blowholes.

Elizabeth was mesmerized. After the whales were gone, the sea erased all evidence of them. Moonlight shone down on the water as it had before.

She wished Jack were here. She would have turned to him, let him take her in his arms. But he wasn't home yet.

FOUR

JACK sat at his desk staring down at the notes spread out in front of him. Suddenly his phone rang. He picked it up. "Jackson Shore."

A voice he hadn't heard in years said, "Jumpin' Jack Flash, how the hell are you?"

"Warren." Jack leaned back in his chair. "Hey, Warlord, I

haven't heard from you since the last time you got married and wanted me for your best man. Is that it—are you marrying another one?"

"No, no. But listen. You know I'm a studio analyst at Fox. Well, the guys here came up with this idea for a new show. It's called *Good Sports*. They're picturing a combination of *Real Sports* and *Oprah*, if you can believe that. I'll be hosting it, and we'll be looking at athletes in a whole new way, trying to understand the pressures and heartbreaks. And highlighting the role models out there."

"That sounds great. Maybe I could be a guest sometime."

"Actually, we want you as more than a guest, and I begged for the chance to be the one to call you. The bigwigs—and me, of course—think you'd be a natural to co-anchor with me. Think of it, Jacko. It'd be like the old days. We'd be a team again."

"You're serious?"

"Of course I'm serious. Just be in New York tomorrow for an interview. Have your secretary call Bill Campbell at Fox. He'll arrange for your ticket. Then give my secretary your itinerary. I'll pick you up at Kennedy."

"I'll get the first flight out. And thanks, Warren. I mean it."

"It's not a sure thing, Jacko. But I know we'll knock 'em dead. See ya tomorrow."

Jack hung up the phone and immediately called Elizabeth.

"Hey, honey, you won't believe—" He stopped. What if he didn't get the job? He'd disappointed Birdie too often in the past. There was no point in building up her hopes for nothing. "I have to go to New York tomorrow. Can you pack me a suitcase?"

"New York? How come?"

He thought fast. "Some hotshot high school quarterback just signed a letter of intent with the Ducks. I gotta interview him."

"Oh, that's odd. How long will you be gone?"

"Two nights."

There was a pause on the other end. "What's going on, Jack?"

"Nothing. Everything's great." And it was. For once, it was. Everything was going to be different now. He'd get this job; he'd return home in triumph. Oh, she'd grumble about moving east, but in the end, she'd do the right thing. This would offer them a second chance. Finally.

ELIZABETH STOOD BACK, her arms crossed tightly.

Jack was by the front door, garment bag in hand. Even at this predawn hour he looked bright and eager, almost boyish.

For a moment, he was so handsome he took her breath away. Strangely, she remembered the first time he'd kissed her. A lifetime ago. She'd known with that one kiss that her life had been up-ended . . . that she'd love Jackson Shore until the day she died.

But was it enough?

"Maybe I could go with you," she said.

His smile faded as he dropped the garment bag and moved toward her. "Not this time, Birdie. I'll be running full speed. I wouldn't be able to spend any time with you."

She nodded. "Next time, then. I hate New York anyway."

He kissed her good-bye and stepped back. "I'll call you. I've got a room at the Carlyle. The phone number is on the fridge."

"Okay. Have a good trip. Good luck."

"Winners don't need luck."

She stood there, arms crossed, until long after he was gone. Then she made herself some breakfast and planned her day.

AMAZINGLY, the local hardware store had a lovely set of French doors on sale. Someone had ordered them and declined acceptance, so Elizabeth got them at a discounted price.

The only downside was that she had to increase the size of the opening by six inches, then frame the damn thing and mount the doors. The whole backbreaking process took hours.

Now her shoulders ached and her fingers were cramped up, but the doors were in place. She was standing there admiring them when she realized it was Thursday. Passionless women night.

Maybe she'd go. It wasn't as if she had anything better to do.

JACK liked everything about flying first class—the roomy, comfortable seats, the clean white trays that held edible food, the drinks that never stopped coming. He was almost sorry when they touched down in New York and it was time to leave the plane.

As promised, Warren was waiting for him in the terminal. He stood out from the crowd like a two-hundred-year-old Douglas fir in a new-growth forest. He was tall and expensively dressed, but that wasn't what separated him from the others.

The crown of celebrity sat comfortably on Warren's head. He moved forward, grinning. The crowd parted to let him pass.

Jack didn't think Warren even noticed. "Warlord, how the hell are you?" Jack said.

"Jumpin' Jack Flash," Warren answered loudly. He pulled Jack into a bear hug, then clapped an arm around his shoulder and guided him toward the exit. "God, it's good to see you."

Warren kept up a steady stream of conversation as they left the terminal, got into his red Viper, and roared onto the expressway.

It was a gray winter's day. Clouds sent a sputtering, drizzling sleet onto the windshield.

"Remember playing in this lousy weather?" Warren said.

Jack grinned. He and Warren had been teammates at the University of Washington in Seattle. He was sure they'd played in the sun—they must have—but he couldn't remember it. "Elizabeth and Mary used to wear Hefty garbage bags to the games, remember?"

Warren laughed. "What I remember about Mary is that I never shoulda married her."

They'd been a foursome back then: Jack and Elizabeth, Warren and Mary. They'd been inseparable at U.W. Then the draft had sent Warren to Denver and Jack to Pittsburgh. After several years they were reunited in New York. By that time Warren was married to Phyllis, and both he and Jack were superstars in the hectic, crazy world of the NFL. Jack had thought fame would last forever.

"How is Birdie?"

"Great. So are the girls. They're both at Georgetown now. Stephanie is still quiet and serious. She's graduating this June—with a degree in micro something or other."

"Just like her mom, huh? Birdie was the only straight-A student I ever knew."

Jack had forgotten how much his wife loved school. For years after graduation she'd talked about getting a master's in fine arts, but she'd never done it.

"Remember Callaghan's Pub? Throwing back brewskis."

And picking up girls. At least Warren hadn't said it out loud. Still, silence didn't change the past. Jack had spent a chunk of his youth in that bar, flirting with the endless stream of girls that followed football. Taking them to bed.

And all the while, Elizabeth had been in a ridiculously big

house on Long Island, raising their children alone. When he came home smelling of booze and smoke and other women's perfume, she always pretended not to notice.

Warren pulled up in front of the Carlyle Hotel, then turned to Jack. "We meet the head honchos tomorrow. Your audition is scheduled for ten thirty. I'll read with you."

Before Jack had a chance to reply, the car door opened. A uniformed man smiled at him. "Welcome to the Carlyle, sir."

Jack got out of the car and handed his garment bag to the bellman. "Thanks."

Warren leaned across the empty passenger seat. "I'll swing by around eight. We'll have breakfast at the hotel."

"Great. And Warren—thanks for all of this."

"Don't thank me until they offer you the job. Then I'll take cash." The electric window rolled soundlessly upward.

Jack watched the red Viper drive away. Then he checked into the hotel and went up to his room. The first thing he did was pour himself a drink. He glanced at the phone and knew he should call Birdie, but the thought exhausted him. He'd have to pretend he was in town to see some college athlete, and she'd blather on about fabrics. Still, he picked up the phone and dialed his home number.

On the fourth ring the answering machine picked up. "Hey, honey," he said. "I'm at the Carlyle, room five oh one. I love you."

Those words came automatically, but in the silence that followed, he found himself thinking about what they meant . . . and how long it had been since they were completely true.

He went to his window and stared out at the glittering Manhattan night. A watery reflection of his own face stared back at him. He closed his eyes and saw a younger, brighter version of himself. That man walked through another time and place, far from here.

Seattle. Dusk, on a cold winter's day . . .

He'd gone to the Delta Delta Gamma sorority house and been told that Elizabeth Rhodes always spent Sunday evenings in the Arboretum. He'd had no choice but to go looking for her there. Desperation had spurred him; there was nothing more desperate than a college football star with a failing grade.

He'd found her in the marshy trails along the edge of Lake Washington. She'd been painting. At first all he'd seen was her hair, gilded by the setting sun. She'd had on a blue Shetland sweater and denim overalls. A trio of paintbrushes stuck out of her back pocket.

He cleared his throat and said, "Elizabeth Rhodes?"

She spun around, and her beauty stunned him. "Who are you?"

"Jackson Shore. I got your name from Dr. Lindbloom. He said you might have room in your tutoring schedule for a new student." He grinned sheepishly. "I'm flunking out of lit one oh one."

Her ocean-green eyes narrowed. "Let me guess: athlete."

"Football."

The smile she gave him was thin. "Look, I'd love to help, but—"

"That's great. When can we get together?"

She sighed. After a long moment she said, "I suppose I could meet with you tonight."

"Tonight? Homework on a Sunday night? I don't think so."

"Then I'm sorry. You'll have to find someone else. I only take students who really care about their classes."

He closed the distance between them. "I need you."

She gazed up at him. As the look went on, she started to blush. "Fine. I'll meet you tomorrow morning at the library. Ten forty. If you want help, be on time."

That had been the beginning.

Jack had fallen in love with Elizabeth fast, and it hadn't taken him long to charm her. He'd promised her the moon and the stars, vowed to love her forever. He'd meant it, too. Believed in it.

They hadn't done anything wrong, either one of them.

They simply hadn't understood how long forever was.

ELIZABETH paused outside the closed classroom door, then went inside to the Women's Passion Support Group meeting.

The faces were familiar this time, and welcoming. Mina stood talking to Fran, who seemed to be listening intently.

At the front of the room, Sarah clapped her hands together. "Good evening, ladies. It's great to see so many familiar faces."

The women all sat down.

Sarah was in the middle of her opening remarks when Mina popped to her feet. She was smiling. "I drove here! I can go any-where now."

The applause was thunderous.

Elizabeth was surprised by how deeply those few words affected her. *I can go anywhere now.*

When the applause died down, Sarah led the group in a discussion that delved into previously expressed dreams.

Cute little Joey, who worked as a waitress at Pig-in-a-Blanket, was the first to speak. "I did think about *someone's* dreams this week. One of my customers left this on the table." She pulled out a paintbrush and handed it to Elizabeth. "Is that, like, karma, or what?"

It was a Big K quality paintbrush, probably from a child's paint-by-number set. A cheap little brush no self-respecting artist would ever use. So why did Elizabeth feel like crying?

"Thank you, Joey," she said, taking the brush. When she touched it, her heart did a funny little flop.

"Tell us about your painting," Sarah said.

Elizabeth took a deep breath. "In college, my professors said I had talent. I was accepted into several fine arts graduate programs."

"Did you go?" Joey asked, her voice hushed with awe.

"No. After the girls were born, there wasn't time. Later I tried to go back to my painting, but when I picked up a brush, nothing happened." She looked around at the women's faces. Every one of them understood. Sometimes you missed your chance.

And yet . . . when she looked down at the paintbrush in her hand, something happened. Nothing major, but something.

Suddenly Elizabeth couldn't think about anything else.

After the meeting she drove straight home and rushed up to her bedroom. She opened her closet, shoved the clothes aside, and dropped to her knees.

There it was: a cardboard box filled with old supplies. She pulled it toward her, inhaling the long-forgotten scent of dried paint.

Smiling, she got to her feet and walked to the French doors that opened out onto the second-floor balcony. She pressed a finger to the cool glass, staring out at the night-darkened sea.

If there was anywhere she could paint again, it would be here. She closed her eyes, daring to imagine a shiny new future.

JACK drove slowly down the twisting road that led to his house. Although Stormwatch Lane ran for almost a half a mile, there were no other dwellings along the way. For most of its distance the road was bordered on the west by a sheer cliff. Below it lay the wind-blown Pacific Ocean.

He pulled into the carport and parked, then grabbed his garment bag and walked to the front door.

Inside, the house smelled of cinnamony candles. "Elizabeth?"

There was no answer. He headed up to their bedroom.

She was standing at the window, with her back to him.

"A penny for your thoughts," he said.

She spun around. "You scared me."

"I caught an earlier flight."

She glanced out to sea again. "That was lucky."

Already he'd lost her attention. But his news would get it back. He started to say something, but her voice stopped him.

"It's such a beautiful night. There are so many colors in the darkness. It makes me want to paint again." She turned to look at him, finally. "I went to this meeting tonight, and—"

"I have a surprise. Remember Warren Mitchell?"

"Of course I do. He's what . . . a studio analyst for Fox now?"

"He was. The guys at Fox just offered him a cushy one-hour once-a-week gig. Sort of a sports talk show."

"God knows we need more men talking about sports."

Jack was taken aback by that. "This will be a whole new kind of show. They've contracted for twenty-six episodes. They'll be filming in the Fox studio in New York."

"That's great for Warren."

"And for us." Jack grinned. "I'm going to co-host the show."

"What?"

"That's why I really went to New York. To audition."

"You *lied* to me?"

She made it sound worse than it was. "I didn't want to disappoint you again. But this time I got the job. Think of it, honey. We'll start over. And we'll only be a few hours from D.C. You'll be able to take the train down to see the girls at school."

"A few hours from D.C.? What are you talking about?"

This was the tricky part. "We have to move to New York."

"*What?*"

He winced as guilt reared its ugly head. "I know I promised this would be the last move, but they offered me so much money you wouldn't believe it. Everything can be ours now."

"Everything *you* want, you mean." She was angry; there was no mistaking it. "You don't give a damn about what I want. I've poured my heart and soul into this place."

"It's just a house, Birdie." He moved toward her. "And you know how long I've dreamed about this."

"What do I dream about, Jack? When is it my turn?"

"How is anybody supposed to know that you even *want* a turn, Birdie? You spend your life on the sidelines. You want a turn? Then take a chance like the rest of us. Step up to the plate. But don't rain all over me because I have the guts to go after what I want."

The color faded from her cheeks, and he knew he'd gone too far. With Birdie you could rant and rave. What you couldn't do was get too close to the truth.

She took a step back. "I'll be back. I have to think."

In silence he watched her walk out of their bedroom. He didn't bother following her. Instead, he went to the window and waited.

Sure enough, a few moments later he saw her emerge from the porch. She walked across the darkened yard to the prow of their property, then stood at the top of the stairs and stared out to sea.

Finally she came back into the house. By then he'd made a fire in the fireplace and put a frozen lasagna into the oven.

She hung up her coat and came into the living room, where Jack was waiting. For an eternity she stood there staring at him, her face streaked by dried tears. Very softly she said, "I suppose we could live in New York again—for a while."

He pulled her into his arms. "I love you, Birdie. It'll be great this time, you'll see."

"Okay. But I want to rent out this house, not sell it. This isn't a permanent move. I want that agreed upon, or it's no deal."

"Agreed."

"I'll start calling Realtors in the New York area on Monday. They should be able to find us a place by summer."

"I start work on Monday."

She pulled away from him. "We can't move by Monday."

"We can use Fox's corporate apartment until we find our own place. I'll fly to New York on Sunday. As soon as you get this place packed up, you can come and pick out your dream house."

"Let me make sure I understand this correctly." She was speaking slowly. "You have accepted a job without consulting me, accepted use of a corporate apartment I've never seen, arranged for us to move across the country, *and,* as the cherry on top of this sundae, I get to close up this house by myself."

She made it sound so bad. It hadn't seemed that way to him. Hell, they'd done it this way lots of times.

She walked toward the window.

He came up behind her, placed his hands on her shoulders, and kissed the back of her neck. "Trust me, Birdie. It'll be good for us."

"I'm sure you're right," she said at last.

"We'll be happy," he said. "You'll see."

She sighed heavily. "Of course we will."

FIVE

Jack walked up Broadway, elbowing his way through the crowd. He'd been in New York two weeks, and already he felt like a local.

It had always been one of his favorite cities. As a boy, growing up in the small, depressed logging town of Aberdeen, Washington, watching his parents work themselves into early graves, he'd had two dreams—one was to play football in the NFL, the other was to live in a city full of lights-camera-action. Now, after fifteen anonymous, wasteland years, he was back.

And it was only going to get better. The show, *Good Sports,* hadn't aired yet, but the industry talk was already hot. Fox had been running an endless series of "We've got Jumpin' Jack Flash and Warlord together again" commercials. Their faces were everywhere.

He turned onto Fiftieth Street and headed home. Funny how he already thought of an impersonal corporate apartment as home.

A doorman let him into the building. He walked through the marble lobby to the elevator. On the twenty-fourth floor he got out.

Inside the apartment, he walked past the kitchen, which was smaller than most bathrooms. In his bedroom he kicked off his shoes and sat down on the twisted pile of white sheets and blankets. He hadn't made the bed since he'd moved in. That was only one of the changes Birdie would make.

Birdie. It wouldn't be good, her reaction to these tiny rooms. She'd immediately begin a frenzied search for "the" place to call home. The thought of it exhausted him. He loved her, but lately it was easier to be apart. Here he was at last, poised to achieve everything he'd ever wanted. The city, the money, the fame. But his dream wouldn't match hers. Whatever it was that she longed for—the "turn" she whined about—she wouldn't find it in a one-bedroom apartment with a bathroom too small for a towel rack.

He'd done it her way. He'd spent two years in that godforsaken soggy rain forest. He'd done it because it was her "turn" to have the house of her dreams, but had she really thought they'd live there forever? Hell, the only place in the United States with worse year-round weather was Bering, Alaska.

When he'd lost football and kicked the drug habit, he'd tried to settle onto the responsible adult track. He'd lived in respectable houses in good school districts in towns so far from the limelight they were pitch-dark by eight o'clock at night. No more.

Now it was his turn.

IN THE last week of January, after two weeks of working like a dog, Elizabeth was finally ready to head to New York, a city that had frightened her in the best of times—and these were far from the best of times in New York. And once there, she'd have to move into an apartment she hadn't chosen and sleep beside a husband she'd forgotten how to love.

She had packed up the house and put almost everything in storage. Unfortunately, they still hadn't found anyone to rent it. There didn't seem to be a lot of people who wanted to live so far out of the way, but the Realtor was hopeful that he'd find a tenant.

She had spoken to Jack daily since he'd left. He sounded happier than he'd been in years. He adored his new job. Each time she hung up, she found herself praying, "Please, God, let me find that again, too. Let *us* find it."

She repeated that prayer many times on the trip from Portland to New York City. The flights went on and on, but they paled in comparison to the cab ride from Kennedy Airport into midtown.

When the taxi finally pulled over in front of Jack's apartment, Elizabeth's back was screaming in pain. She paid the cabdriver and hurried into the building, in desperate need of chiropractic care and an Excedrin.

Clutching the key Jack had sent her, she rode the elevator up to the twenty-fourth floor and found his apartment.

"Jack?"

There was no answer. She glanced at her watch. It was only six fifteen. He should be home in the next thirty minutes.

She set her purse down on the floor and looked around. The apartment was as elegantly impersonal as an expensive hotel room.

She had just poured herself a glass of water when the phone rang. She answered it. "Hello?"

"Birdie? Welcome to New York. Isn't the place great?"

"Oh, yeah. Great."

"I can't wait to see you." A pause crackled through the lines. "But I've got a meeting in fifteen minutes. I should be home in an hour and a half. You'll be okay there, right?"

It took a conscious effort to simply say, "Of course."

"That's my girl. I love you, Birdie. Gotta run. See you soon."

"Okay." She hung up. It was a moment before she realized that she hadn't said "I love you" in return.

With a sigh she walked over to the window. Here she was again, waiting for Jack. It seemed as if she'd passed her whole life that way, a woman set on pause.

At eight thirty her cell phone rang. She fished it out of her purse and answered. "Hello?"

"Birdie?" said a thick-as-molasses southern voice.

"Anita?" Fear sidled up to her, slipped a cold arm around her waist. "What's the matter?"

"Your daddy had a stroke. Y'all better get down here fast."

THE first thing Elizabeth did was call Jack.

"Oh, baby," he'd said softly, "I'm so sorry. I can be home in thirty minutes. Will you be okay by yourself until I get there?"

Of course she would. Her husband had never handled tragedy well. Even when he showed up, she knew she'd really be alone.

Next she called her daughters. Stephanie was loving and accommodating; she'd probably gone online during their phone conversation and ordered plane tickets. Jamie didn't say much.

She'd been hit too hard by the news. She and her grandfather were so close.

After that, Elizabeth concentrated on the details. By the time Jack got home, she'd made all the arrangements and packed his suitcase.

It took them more than two hours to get to the airport and find the gate. Once there, they sat side by side in silence.

At last the flight was called, and they boarded the plane.

"Are you okay?" Jack asked again.

Elizabeth squeezed his hand. "No."

Finally the plane landed in Nashville. She and Jack hailed a cab and headed north.

Forty-five minutes later the taxi pulled up in front of a sprawling gray hospital. Elizabeth got out and waited while Jack gathered their bags. She was close to falling apart, but she wouldn't allow herself that luxury.

She clung to Jack's hand as they walked through the electric doors and into the sterile, antiseptic-scented lobby. At the front desk she said, "We're looking for Edward Rhodes, please."

The receptionist looked up. "He's in intensive care. Sixth floor."

Jack squeezed her hand. "The elevators are right there."

She looked up at him. "Do you mind if I go alone?"

"You'll come and get me when you know something?"

"Of course."

He pulled her into his arms and kissed her hard. Then, without a backward glance, she headed toward the elevators.

On the sixth floor, she went to the ICU nurses desk. She asked for her father, then walked down the hallway toward his room.

It had glass walls on three sides. Through the glass she saw a bed amid a cluster of cranelike machines. There was a man in the bed lying perfectly still, his arms pressed in close to his body.

He didn't look like her daddy. Edward Rhodes was a man who was always in motion, a man who took up space.

She entered the room and moved toward him.

"Daddy?" Her voice cracked. She smoothed the gray-white hair away from his eyes. "Hey, Daddy, it's me, Birdie."

He was so still. There was a tube in his nose and an IV needle in his arm. She closed her eyes, wondering how to reach him.

Gradually she became aware of the smell of flowers. Gardenias.

She turned around, knowing she wasn't alone anymore.

Anita stood in the doorway. "Birdie," she said, "I'm glad you could get here so quick." She went to the bed. "Hey, Daddy," she whispered, touching his face.

"How's he doing?" Elizabeth asked.

When Anita looked up, her gray eyes floated beneath a dome of electric-blue eye shadow. "They're hopin' he'll wake up."

Elizabeth steeled herself. "But he might not?"

"The longer he's . . . out, the worse it is. They're pretty sure he's paralyzed on the left side."

"God," Elizabeth whispered. She pulled up a chair and sat beside him. Anita did the same thing, positioning herself on the opposite side of the bed. For the first few minutes they muddled through polite conversation, but after a while they gave up. They'd been there almost two hours when the door opened.

A short, stocky man in a white coat walked into the room.

"Hey, Phil," Anita said. She stood up. "He's still restin'."

The doctor looked at Elizabeth. "I'm Phillip Close," he said, extending his hand. "Edward's physician. You must be Birdie. He talks about you all the time."

Elizabeth stood up and shook his hand. She imagined her daddy boring this doctor with proud-father stories.

Phillip bent over Daddy, checked the machines, then straightened. "It's still a waiting game. I wish I could do better than that."

"Anita tells me he might be paralyzed," Elizabeth said slowly.

"Yes. And he may have suffered some brain injury. But as I said, we won't know much until he wakes up. The biggest concern now is his heart. Frankly, it's pretty weak."

"Thank you, Phillip," Elizabeth said, although it seemed ridiculous to thank someone for giving you more to worry about.

"I'll give you two some time with him," he said, then left the room.

Elizabeth stared across the bed at her stepmother. All that pancake makeup couldn't conceal Anita's pain.

"He'll make it," Elizabeth said. "He's too ornery to die."

Anita looked pathetically grateful for that small bit of comfort. "He is ornery, that's for sure."

"I . . . am . . . not . . . ornery."

Elizabeth and Anita gasped. They leaned down at the same time.

Daddy's eyes were open, but one side of his face was slack.

"We can hear you, Daddy," Elizabeth said. "We're both here."

Anita took his motionless hand, squeezing it hard. Tears bubbled along her lashes. "I knew you couldn't leave me."

He reached up and touched Anita's face. "There you are, Mother. I've been looking for you."

"I'm right here, Daddy," Anita said breathlessly, crying softly.

Elizabeth knew it was childish, but she had always felt excluded by their love. There was something special between Anita and Edward, so special that everything around them paled in comparison.

"Our Birdie is here, too. She hopped on a plane the very second she heard," Anita said, smoothing the hair away from his eyes.

Slowly he turned to look at Elizabeth. In his eyes she saw something she'd never seen before—defeat—and it scared her. "Hey, Daddy," she whispered. "You've got a nerve scaring us this way."

"Give me just a moment with my little girl, won't you, Mother?"

Anita leaned down and kissed his forehead. "I love you," she whispered fiercely, then left the room.

"Where's golden . . . boy? And my granddaughters?"

"Jack is in the waiting room. Stephie and Jamie will be here in a little while."

Edward took a few rattling breaths, then slowly lifted his hand and touched her hand. "I didn't handle things well. I surely didn't."

Elizabeth didn't know what he was talking about. Before she could ask, he went on. "Anita. Your mama. I shoulda done it differently, God knows. But your mama near killed me. . . . I swear I don't know what I should have told you."

"What are you talking about, Daddy?"

"I thought it best you didn't know, that's all. To protect you. But Anita paid the price. We all did."

"Daddy—"

"You're the best part of me, Birdie. You always were. I reckon I should have told you that more often."

"You told me all the time, Daddy."

He tried to sit up, but he quickly sank back against the pillow. "I need you to do somethin' for me, Birdie. It won't be easy for you."

"Anything, Daddy. You know that."

"You take care of Anita. You hear me?"

"Don't say that," Elizabeth said, hearing the sudden desperation in her voice. "You'll be around to take care of her."

"Don't sass me. This is important." His breathing became shallow, labored. "Promise me you'll take care of her."

"Okay." Elizabeth kissed his forehead. "I love you, Daddy."

He looked at her, but his eyes were glassy now, unfocused. As if he'd spent all his energy. "That love'll carry me through the Pearly Gates, sugar beet. It surely will. Now, ask Anita to come in here."

"No . . . please."

"It's time, Birdie. Go get your mama."

Elizabeth forced herself to move. At the door, she gave him a last smile, then left the room. "He wants you," she said to Anita.

Her stepmother made a sound that was half sigh, half sob, and hurried into the room, closing the door behind her.

Elizabeth stood close to the glass, on the outside of their love, looking in. She prayed hard. Be strong, Daddy. Be strong.

An alarm on one of the machines went off.

Anita stumbled back from the bed, screaming, "Help, help!"

Immediately nurses and doctors rushed past Elizabeth into the tiny room, pushing Anita out of the way. Elizabeth pressed against the glass, hard. *Don't you die, Daddy. Don't you dare.*

Phillip Close raced into the room, elbowed his way to her father's side. He reached for the heart paddles.

Elizabeth shut her eyes. Please, God, don't take him. Not yet.

When she opened her eyes, the doctors and nurses were standing still; the machines were cold and black. Anita was sitting by Daddy, her cries dwindled down to soundless gasps.

Slowly Elizabeth walked into the room, went up to her father's bed. She pressed a hand to Anita's frail shoulder.

"Hey, Daddy," she whispered. It was a second before she realized that she'd expected an answer. But of course, there wasn't one.

His heart—the one that had loved her so well—had given up.

THE mechanics of death ticked forward like a well-oiled clock. Everyone pitched in. An intricate ballet played out, first in the funeral parlor, then at the graveside, and now at the house.

There were pictures of Daddy everywhere. Everyone who'd come to Sweetwater after the funeral had brought a casserole and a photo. Wherever Elizabeth walked in the house, she was sure to hear her father's name spoken in a whispered voice and the remark that she, Birdie, was "holding up well."

But as hard as she tried to keep the grief away, it stalked her. When she couldn't take it anymore, she escaped to the back porch. It was the last place she should have chosen. She'd sat here so often with Daddy, listening to the cicadas and his tall tales. Now memories pressed in on her from all directions. This was where they'd come after Mama's funeral, too.

"Hold on, Birdie," she said out loud, squeezing her eyes shut. She had to get out of there. She went back into the house and disappeared into the bathroom.

She shut the door and closed the toilet lid. Then she sat down and cried at last—for all the times she had been with her father and all the times she hadn't, and for all the times she never would be.

When the tears had worn themselves out and left her dry, she got unsteadily to her feet. She splashed cool water on her face, smoothed her hair, and went back into the fray. She headed for the library, where the girls and Jack were hiding out.

Stephanie sat on the maroon sofa, the picture of decorum as usual in a plain scoop-necked long-sleeved black dress that clung to her lithe body. There were red streaks on her porcelain cheeks, and her gray eyes showed the residue of tears.

Jamie, on the other hand, had taken no great care in dressing. She sat slouched on an ottoman, her white-blond hair a tangled mass that covered half of her face. Her navy-blue dress was already wrinkled, and her pale blue eyes were swollen and red.

"I can't listen to any more stories about him," Jamie said softly, her eyes welling up.

Elizabeth understood. Everyone had loved Daddy so much, and they wanted to share their favorite story, but every word lodged in your heart like a shard of glass.

Jack rose from the leather wing chair and walked toward Elizabeth, never taking his gaze from her face. He pulled her into his arms. "Let me help you, Birdie," he said, stroking her hair.

She loved him for trying, but there was no way to help a person through something like this. Grief was the loneliest road in the world. "It helps just to have you here," she said, and it was true.

She clung to him then, taking strength from the feel of his arms around her, and for a single magic moment it felt as if they loved each other again.

SIX

JACK was back in New York, thank God.

He knew it was a weakness in him, a moral failing, but he hated death's accessories. The sobbing, the gathering—that awful, primitive ritual called a viewing. He loved his wife and his children, but two days in that grieving house had been more than he could stand.

Thankfully, Birdie had released him, saying, "Go on back to New York. There's nothing for you and the girls to do down here."

Now he was back in his office at the studio, free again.

The stack of papers and phone messages on his desk was huge. He'd forgotten how much the phone rang when you were a somebody. They'd promised him a secretary, but what he really needed was an assistant. Someone to handle the office grunt work as well as to help him formulate questions for the athlete interviews. There was a lot of research involved in looking smart off the cuff.

Jack picked up a pen and began making a list. His assistant would have to be bright, ambitious, dedicated. Someone like . . . Sally. Why hadn't he thought of it before? They had worked well together in Portland, and she was a tiger behind the scenes.

She'd do it, too. He had no doubt about that. Sally was a woman with big dreams. A chance to be a production assistant for a network show in the Big Apple would really charge her batteries.

This was business, pure and simple. That he was attracted to her didn't matter. He'd been tempted plenty of times in the past fifteen years, but he hadn't fallen out of the old marriage bed even once. Those days were behind him. And this was strictly business.

UNABLE TO SLEEP, ELIZABETH put on one of the thick terry-cloth robes Anita had placed in the guest room and went quietly downstairs. The old house creaked and moaned at her progress.

In the darkened kitchen, she made herself a cup of tea. Then she tightened the belt on the robe and went outside.

She stepped down onto the brick path that bisected the garden. This had once been her special place. So often in her youth she'd come out here, alone and searching. What she'd been looking for, of course, was her mother, and here, amid the flowers she'd tended so carefully, Elizabeth had thought she felt her mama's spirit.

She'd always tried to picture her mama in the garden, maybe trimming the roses, but all she'd ever seen of Marguerite Rhodes were black-and-white portrait shots—wedding, graduation, that sort of thing. The photographs left Elizabeth with a vague, colorless image of a pretty young woman who never laughed or spoke.

Elizabeth knelt at the edge of the rose bed. Behind her she heard the sound of a door creaking open and clicking closed, then the rhythm of footsteps on the brick path.

"Hey, Anita," she said without turning around.

"It's amazin' to think that those roses'll be bloomin' in just a few months."

"I was just thinking the same thing."

"You know," Anita said softly, "I tended those roses by hand all these years. I never let a gardener near 'em."

Elizabeth sat back on her heels and looked up at Anita. "Why?"

Anita smiled sadly. Her platinum hair was a mass of curlers; a blue flannel robe covered her from throat to foot. She looked ten years older than her actual sixty-two. "I smelled her perfume once."

Elizabeth felt a shiver. "Mama's?" she whispered.

"It was one of those days when you were in a mood, disagreeing with everything I said. So I came out here, ready to attack your mama's garden. I wanted to fight somethin' I could *see*. But when I sat out here, I smelled your mama's perfume. Shalimar. It wasn't like she spoke to me or anything weird like that. I just . . . realized I was fightin' with her baby girl, who was broken up inside. After that, whenever you made me crazy, I came out here to the garden."

Elizabeth heard the pain in Anita's voice, and for once, she understood. "No wonder you were out here so often."

"I should have done things differently, I guess. I knew you missed your mama somethin' awful."

"I started forgetting her. That was the worst part. That's why I always asked Daddy about her. But he always said, 'Keep your memories close, Birdie.' He never seemed to understand that my memories of her were like smoke. I couldn't hold on to them."

"I imagine your mama is giving him a piece of her mind about that right now."

"I don't think anyone held as much of Daddy's heart as you did, Anita." Try as she might, a slight bitterness tainted her words.

"Thank you for that." Anita turned, stared out at the fallow fields. "Why didn't you fly home with Jack and the girls?"

Elizabeth stood up, crossing her arms. "The truth is, I don't know why. I guess I just wasn't ready to go back to New York."

Anita took a step forward. Her silly pink slippers sank into the black earth. "Your daddy used to say to me, 'Mother, if that girl don't spread her wings, one day she's plumb gonna forget how to fly.' He was worried that you were missing out on your own life."

"I know." Elizabeth didn't want to be talking about this. It hurt too much. She wiped her eyes (when had she started crying anyway?) and looked at Anita. "What about you? Will you be okay?"

"I'll get by."

It wasn't really an answer, but it was all there was. "I'll call you when I get to New York, just to make sure everything is okay."

"That would be nice," Anita said.

Silence fell between them again. Elizabeth wished suddenly that things were different between her and her stepmother, that they could hold hands and comfort one another. But it was too late now to recraft a relationship whose time had come and gone.

"We've missed our chance, haven't we?" Anita asked softly.

Elizabeth nodded. She didn't know how else to respond.

"It's too bad," Anita said. "But don't you worry about me, honey. I'll be fine. You don't marry a man who is fourteen years older and expect to outlive him. I always knew I'd be alone one day."

"I'm sorry," Elizabeth said at last. "You call me if you're feeling too alone." She stepped back, needing space between them. "I better get to bed now. Six will come awfully early." She walked away, forcing herself to keep a steady pace. It was difficult.

She went inside the house, then peered out the window.

Anita was standing there shivering. Even in the fading moonlight Elizabeth could make out the glittering tear tracks on her face.

She was looking at the roses.

ELIZABETH stood in front of the bank of computers at the Nashville airport and scanned the flight information.

Her flight to New York was delayed by two hours.

Groaning, she went into one of the restaurants, found a window table, and sat down. She stared out, watching the planes take off.

She'd been working to keep the memories at bay, but now they flooded her. *You're missin' out on your own life. It's passin' you by.*

If only she could do something to change that. Maybe get on a plane and go to some strange place. But where would she go? Machu Picchu, Paris, Nepal? She didn't even have a passport. And there was only one place on earth she longed to go.

Home. Her house by the sea.

And now she was about to fly to New York, where once again she would trim her life to fit Jack's.

"I don't want to go." She whispered the words aloud.

She glanced down at her watch. And she decided.

She got up, paid for her lunch, and walked back down the busy aisle to the newsstand, where she purchased a box of stationery—the only one they had. At the top of each sheet was a drawing of Graceland and the words ELVIS WELCOMES YOU TO WILD AND WONDERFUL TENNESSEE. She went back to the restaurant and reclaimed her seat. She began to write.

Dear Jack,

I love you. It seems important to start with those words. We say them to each other all the time, and I know we mean them. I also know it's not enough anymore, is it? Not for either of us.

For twenty-four years I've been your wife. When we began, I never wanted to be anything else. Now I need to get in the game. I'm afraid if I don't do it now, I never will.

So—and here's the punch line—I'm not following you to New York. Not this time.

In all our years together there has been only one place that was mine, and I don't want to leave it.

I'm going home to Echo Beach. I need some time alone. I
need to find out who I am and who I can become.

I pray you'll understand. I love you, Jack.

E.

She didn't even reread the letter. She folded it, put it in an envelope, stamped it, and mailed it.

Then she went looking for a flight to Portland.

ELIZABETH felt rejuvenated. She had been back in Echo Beach
for two days. She'd slept late and spent the barest minimum time
on chores. She'd arranged for the furniture to be redelivered, and
she'd stocked the refrigerator. That was it. No contacting friends, no
checking on all the volunteer activities that used to munch through
so much of her time, no to-do lists. She even put off scheduling the
telephone reinstallation and kept her cell phone turned off.

Instead, she walked on the beach. It had been there for the two
years she'd lived here, yet except for that one night with the whales,
she'd never gone down there. The rickety stairs had frightened her,
as had the tides.

But it was fear that had swept Elizabeth out to sea and left her
drowning. No more. Now she tramped up and down the steps like
a local. In her walks she'd come to know every inch of Echo Beach.
She'd found "her" rock, a flat gray stone rubbed soft by the tides.
Sometimes she'd sit there for hours just staring at the ocean.

She'd begun to dream again. Although she hadn't found the
courage to try painting, she'd dug out an old sketchbook and some
charcoal. Drawing came—not easily yet, not like it once had, but it
came. After all the sagging middle years, simply picking up a piece
of charcoal felt like a triumph.

By her calculations Jack had received her letter yesterday.
That was why she hadn't reconnected the phone; she didn't want
to talk to him yet. He'd always had an ability to erode any position she'd taken until she crumpled beneath the weight of what
he wanted.

Now, sitting on her rock, she looked down at her sketch pad
and wondered what to draw this morning. Inspiration was
everywhere.

She saw a blue jay perched on a leafless branch. The deep jewel tones of its wings were a stark, beautiful contrast to the weather-grayed bark. The colors jumped out at her. It felt suddenly as if a veil had been lifted, and now she saw the world in all its vibrancy. For the first time in years, she *needed* to draw, to paint.

The first raindrop hit her forehead. It landed with a cold splat and squiggled down her cheek. She flipped up her hood, shoved all her supplies into the canvas bag at her feet, and ran for home.

By the time she'd climbed the stairs, it wasn't just raining. It was raging. Wiping her eyes, she raced across the lawn to the house. Her hands were freezing cold as she opened the door and went inside.

She grabbed a blanket and wrapped it around her, shawl-like. Then she went back out onto the porch to watch the storm. She'd never done anything like that. Always she'd been afraid of nature's furies. It was another trait she wanted to shed.

Watching the storm from the porch, instead of burrowed in the safety of her house, made her feel changed somehow. Stronger.

After a while she looked up and saw two headlights in the darkness. She stood up, pulling the blanket tightly around her.

The car stopped. The headlights snapped off, and the car door opened. Someone got out and stepped into the light. Jack.

Rain flattened his hair and dripped down the sides of his face. He tried to smile, but the smile didn't reach his eyes. "Hey, Birdie."

She wished she was surprised to see him, but she thought maybe she'd been expecting him. She said, "Come in before you drown."

He followed her into the house. Inside, rain sluiced down his pant legs and formed a puddle.

"You better get out of those wet clothes. You'll catch a cold," she said matter-of-factly. It had always been her pattern—*take care of him*. "I'll get you a robe." She turned and went upstairs.

She opened the closet door and pulled the robe off its hanger. Then she spun around and slammed into Jack.

At the contact he stumbled backward. "Sorry. I thought you knew I was behind you."

They were like a couple of fourteen-year-olds on a first date—nothing but nerves and emotions. He took the robe and went into the bathroom to change, closing the door behind him. While he was dressing, she went down to the living room and built a fire.

When she turned back around, he was there. She sat down on the sofa, looked up at him. "I guess you got my letter?"

"Yes." He said it so softly she could barely hear him.

"Then perhaps we should talk about it."

He sat down beside her. "I don't know what you want me to say. I'm sorry for taking the job without talking to you."

"Let me ask you a question. When you read my letter . . ." She looked him square in the eyes. "Tell me you weren't relieved."

The color faded from his cheeks. She knew he wanted to lie, to say, "Of course, I wasn't relieved," but instead he said, "You know how long I've dreamed of a job like this one. And now, when I finally get my shot, you leave me."

"Come on, Jack. Our whole marriage has been about your dreams. I followed you from town to town for two decades. Two decades. I've been the best wife and mother I know how to be, but now I'm empty. I need time to figure out what *my* dreams are."

He ran a hand through his hair and let out a ragged sigh. "God, Birdie. You really mean it." He sagged forward, resting his arms across his knees. Then he looked at her. "People who want time alone get divorced. Is that what you want?"

Her mouth fell open. "I didn't ask for a divorce."

"What did you think, Birdie? That we'd split up and stay married? That nothing would change?"

She made a small panicked sound. The enormity of what she'd done settled into place. When she'd asked for a separation, all she'd thought was, I need time. Just that.

Jack went upstairs. A few moments later he walked back into the living room wearing his dripping wet clothes.

She looked up at him through a blur of tears. She knew he wanted her to take it back, to be his wife again, but she couldn't do it. It took every ounce of strength she possessed to remain silent.

"I love you, Birdie." His voice broke, and for a second she saw how deeply she'd hurt him.

She wondered how long she'd carry this sad and terrible moment in her heart. "I love you, too."

"Is that supposed to *help?*" He stared at her for a minute, then walked out of the house, slamming the door behind him.

WHAT in the hell had made him say divorce?

Jack jammed on the brakes, and his rental car skidded to a stop. He hadn't been this shaken since his mother's death more than thirty years ago. If asked a week ago, he would have sworn that he and Birdie were in one of those rough patches that sometimes befall a long-term marriage. He would have said that it would pass.

He'd thought—when he read her letter—that it was her way of getting his attention. It had never occurred to him that she meant it.

Not his Birdie. How could she suddenly have found the guts to leave him? Her father's death must have really shaken her. He'd known she was unhappy, of course, but he hadn't expected this.

He almost turned the car around. The urge to go back, take her in his arms, and beg for forgiveness was so strong he felt choked by it. But what then? She was right. Here, alone in the car, he could admit it. They both deserved better.

He closed his eyes, then slowly opened them. "I loved you, Birdie," he whispered aloud. It didn't escape his notice that even when he spoke to himself, he used the past tense.

THE next day the movers showed up with the furniture. Elizabeth stumbled out of bed to greet them. As soon as they left, she went back to bed. She stayed there for three days. Then she flung the quilt aside and sat up. It was time to start this new life of hers.

She swung her feet over the edge of the bed and lumbered to a stand. If she didn't do something, she'd sink into a pit of depression.

When a woman was in this kind of trouble, there was only one thing to do. Unfortunately, the phone wouldn't be connected until sometime between noon and four o'clock.

She found a piece of paper and a pen and wrote a note to Meghann, pouring out her heart. She immediately felt better. Reaching out to someone was better than sitting here alone, wondering what she was going to do with the rest of her life.

She put on a pair of ragged sweats and green plastic gardening clogs and walked up to the mailbox to mail the letter.

By the time she got home, she was breathing hard and soaked with sweat. She definitely needed more exercise.

She was in the bedroom, peeling off her wet clothes, when something occurred to her.

The passionless women. She was one of them now.

SEVEN

With each passing day, Elizabeth felt a little more confident. Today she was determined to try painting.

She grabbed her down coat off the hook by the front door and reached for the black canvas bag that held her painting supplies. Outside, the air was crisp and cold. She crossed the porch and paused at the top of the stairs. The ocean was a smear of pastel gray and lavender. A pair of cormorants flew overhead, circling lazily.

She walked across the lawn to the top of the beach stairs and looked down at the ocean. It was high tide.

Disappointed, she sat down on the damp top step. White breakers bashed themselves against the rocky outcropping at the base of the cliff, spraying foam. Every now and again she felt a sprinkle of spindrift on her face.

"Birdie?"

Elizabeth twisted around.

Meghann was standing in the yard beside her Porsche. Her designer jeans and black cashmere sweater were streaked by rain.

"Meg!" Elizabeth stood up, grabbed her bag, and ran. When Meg pulled her into a bear hug, it was almost impossible to let go.

"Don't you dare start crying," Meghann said. "Now get me under a roof somewhere, preferably with a drink in my hand."

Elizabeth clutched Meg's hand and led her into the house, then built a fire and got out her only alcohol. A bottle of tequila.

They sat on the hearth, and they each drank two shots before another word was spoken. Finally Meghann scooted back and leaned against the sofa. "So, kiddo, how the hell are you?"

Elizabeth sighed. "It's pathetic, Meg. For years I dreamed of starting my life over, but now I'm scared to death."

"Everything you're going through is normal. It'll get better."

"Tell me you can do better than fortune-cookie scribblings. What would you tell me if I were a client?"

Meghann took a sip of tequila, then said slowly, "Well, for a woman like you, I usually—"

"Like me?"

Meghann winced. "Great mother, no real work experience."

"Oh, a woman like me. Go on." Elizabeth poured another shot.

"Anyway, usually I recommend finding a job. It's good for the self-esteem, not to mention the bank account. However, I drove through Echo Beach."

Elizabeth decided on another shot of tequila. She tossed it back. "Yeah. Maybe the fish market needs someone to wipe up salmon guts. God knows I have enough cleaning experience."

"I think you should cast your net a little farther, Birdie. No pun intended." Meghann scooted closer. "I thought about this on the drive down here. You always wanted to get your master's degree in fine arts, remember? This would be a great time to do it."

"That was a long time ago."

"Be bold, Birdie. Apply. Take the road you turned away from. Isn't that what this is all about?"

"Come on, Meg. I'm forty-five years old, and I haven't painted in twenty years. Sometimes you really don't get a second chance."

"Okay, okay. Your eye is twitching. I'll change the subject."

"Thank you."

"How about this: Move up to Seattle. You could have my second bedroom."

"I love it here, Meg. You know that."

"Here? It's another damned planet—and an uninhabited one at that. And let me tell you, that is not an ordinary rain. I'm a Seattleite; we know rain."

"Come with me." Elizabeth stood up, realizing abruptly that she was drunk. Her legs felt rubbery.

Meghann crawled to her feet. "Where are we going?"

Without answering, Elizabeth led her to the front door.

Meghann stumbled to a halt. "Outside? It's raining hard enough to put your eye out."

"A little water won't hurt you. We're going down to the beach. I go every night at this time. It's become a new ritual for me."

"That's because you have no life. For the next two days I'm here for entertainment."

Elizabeth dragged her friend forward. "Hurry up or we'll miss them. My whales are very punctual."

Meghann stopped dead. "Whales? You're kidding, right?"

Elizabeth laughed. Damn, it felt good. "Come on, Counselor. For once, you're going to follow instead of lead."

JACK arrived at the studio a little later than usual. He'd been out late last night, tossing back brewskis with Warren. He'd had reason to celebrate. *Good Sports* had premièred the week before and was an instant hit. Ratings had gone through the roof.

He went straight into a meeting, then spent the next few hours reading through and editing the script for today's show. Finally he and Warren went into the studio, where their guest—an Olympic long jumper who'd recently been diagnosed with MS—was waiting.

After the show Jack hung around the studio for a while, talking to the various staffers who'd also stayed late. An hour or so later, when the building was nearly empty, he returned to his office.

He sat down at his desk and picked up the phone, dialing a number from memory.

She answered on the third ring. "Hello?"

"Hey, Sally," he said, leaning back in his chair.

"Jack! It's great to hear from you. How're things in New York? I hear your show is popping some killer numbers."

He couldn't remember the last time someone had sounded so happy to hear from him. "Things are great. Fox thinks I'm a god."

"We all think that, Jack. It sure isn't as much fun around here without you."

"Then maybe you wouldn't mind moving to New York. I need an assistant."

It was a moment before she asked, "Are you kidding me?"

"No. This is a genuine offer, okayed by my boss. We can't pay you a lot of money, but I'm sure it's more than you're making now."

"I can be there in ten days." She laughed. "I'll live in the YWCA if I have to. Thanks, Jack. You don't know what this means to me."

"You deserve it, Sally."

After Jack hung up, he sat there a minute. He was just about to leave for home when the phone rang.

It was Warren. "Hey, Jacko. Beth has her yoga class tonight. How about dinner at Sparks? Seven thirty."

"Count me in."

Traffic was bad, and Jack didn't arrive at the restaurant until seven forty-five. The hostess, a pretty young woman in a skin-tight black dress, smiled up at him. "Welcome back to Sparks, Mr. Shore."

Jack gave her his showbiz smile. "Well, thanks. It's nice to be here. I'm meeting Warren Mitchell."

"He's already here. Follow me." She turned, and he followed her to the table, where she touched his arm, smiled sweetly up at him. "I'm here until closing. If there's *anything*"—her voice italicized the word—"you need, just let me know."

"I'll think about that, darlin'," he said, sidling into the seat. He watched her walk away.

Warren laughed. "I ordered you a Dewar's on the rocks." He raised his own glass in a salute. "It's awesome what a little TV exposure does for a guy's sex appeal, isn't it? Even old guys like us."

Jack reached for his drink. "It feels good to be a somebody again, I can tell you that."

Warren took a sip of his drink. "It couldn't have been easy going from the NFL to local sportscaster."

"It was hell."

"I wasn't there for you back then. When your knee gave out."

"There wasn't anything you could have done."

"Bull." Warren took another drink. "It scared the hell out of me, you know? One minute you were on top of the world; the next minute you were down for the count. How'd you get through it?"

Jack leaned back. That was something he hadn't thought about in years—the *how* of losing everything. After the surgeries, he'd stayed for weeks in his bedroom, holed up in the dark, pretending the pain was worse than it was, popping pills as if they were SweeTARTS.

One day Elizabeth had whipped open the curtains. "That's all the time you get, Jackson Shore. Now, I want you up and dressed in ten minutes, or I'll dump ice water on you."

True to her word, she'd dumped water on his head. And a few hours later she dared to use the prohibited words: drug addiction.

"Elizabeth got me through it," Jack said now.

"That doesn't surprise me. You got lucky with Birdie. If I'd married a girl like her instead of—"

"We broke up." It was the first time he'd said the words aloud. He was surprised by how it felt, both depressing and uplifting at the same time.

"God, you two have been married forever. Are you okay?"

The answer to that question had layers and layers. The truth was, he didn't want to look too deep. It was better to swim on the surface of that pool, to feel good about his new life. "Yeah. It had gotten pretty stale around our house."

"I know how that is. The silence'll kill you. How is she taking it?"

Warlord assumed it had been Jack's decision to separate. No one would credit Birdie with the guts to end their marriage.

"She's okay. Now, can we please talk about something else?"

"Sure, Jack," Warren said slowly. "Anything you want."

IT WAS Thursday, passionless women's night, and Elizabeth was actually looking forward to the meeting. She walked through the corridors of the community college and stepped into the classroom.

"Welcome, Elizabeth. Come on in," Sarah Taylor said when she entered the room.

Elizabeth wound through the circle of women and sat in an empty chair next to Mina.

Sarah started the meeting right away. "Who would like to begin tonight?" she asked.

To her own amazement Elizabeth raised her hand. She felt a flash of fear when everyone looked at her. "My husband and I separated."

"And how do you feel about that?" Sarah asked gently.

Once Elizabeth started talking, she found that she couldn't stop. The whole story came tumbling out. She ended up with, "I need a new life, but I don't quite know how to start. So I came here."

Mina leaned forward. "I was thinking about you this week. I was reading the college catalog, looking for classes I could take now that I can drive, and I noticed that a painting class is starting soon."

Elizabeth felt a little spark of something. "Really?"

Mina reached into her handbag and pulled out a floppy catalog. "I saved it for you." She handed it to Elizabeth.

"Thanks," she said, surprised to realize that she meant it.

After that, the discussion moved around the circle, dipping time and again into the kind of intimacy that was marked by sudden emotion—tears or laughter.

When the meeting finally broke up, Elizabeth stood around for a few minutes talking to the women. Then she drove home.

On Stormwatch Lane, she stopped, pulled her mail out of the box, and continued down the road to her house.

Once inside, she flipped through the mail. There was a big manila envelope from Meghann. She ripped it open. College catalogs fell out onto the table. N.Y.U. Columbia. S.U.N.Y. Three of the graduate programs that had accepted her all those years ago.

A Post-it note read, "You can't say you don't have time now."

ELIZABETH had avoided talking to her daughters. She called during school hours or swim practice and left cheerful messages. Dad was doing great in New York; she was working hard to get the place ready for renters. Lies that stacked up like a house of cards.

She glanced at the mantel clock. It was one forty-five.

Four forty-five in Washington, D.C. They'd be in class right now.

Coward, Elizabeth thought as she punched in the number. She was so busy devising her pert, upbeat message that it took her a moment to realize Stephanie had answered.

Elizabeth laughed nervously. "Hey, honey," she said, "it's good to hear your voice. I've been thinking about you guys a lot lately."

"Hey, Mom." Stephanie sounded tired. "Your uterine radar must be working. I'm sick."

"What's wrong?"

"Don't call nine one one or anything. I just have a stomach flu."

"Is Jamie taking care of you?"

"Oh, yeah, that's her specialty. This morning she said, 'If you think you're going to puke, aim away from my new shoes.'"

Elizabeth laughed. It was so Jamie. "I'm sure you'll be back on your feet in no time."

"I hope so. Hey, Mom, Jamie and I've been invited to go skiing in Vermont over spring break. It's the second week in March."

Thank God. Elizabeth had been worrying about how she and

Jack would handle the separation with the girls at home. It was one thing to avoid the truth by phone. It was quite another to lie to your children in person. "That sounds great."

"It's kind of expensive. Lift tickets—"

"Your dad can afford it." Elizabeth winced. She should have said, "We can afford it."

"Thanks, Mom. So how's it going with the house? How much longer will you be in Oregon?"

"I don't know. Nobody seems to want to live this far out, and we can't leave the house empty." She paused. "How're classes going?" she said to change the subject.

It worked. Stephanie told several funny Jamie stories about how her sister had gotten into and out of trouble.

Elizabeth laughed. "She gets that from my dad. He never once looked before he leaped. He said it ruined the surprise." Her voice snagged on the thought: *He's gone.*

"Are you okay, Mom?"

"Sure. It's just that sometimes I miss your granddad so much."

"I know." Stephanie was quiet for a moment. "Listen, Mom, I really feel lousy. I think I'm gonna crash. Tell Dad to call me tonight. I want to hear how his big interview with Jay went."

Jay who? "Okay," Elizabeth said. "I love you."

"Love you guys, too. Bye."

For the last few days Jack's life had been a full-speed running game. Drew Grayland's arraignment had been broadcast on *Court TV*, and the whole sordid story had come out. All across America, students and parents were protesting the lack of athlete accountability. Female students from dozens of universities had filed rape charges against football and basketball players.

And at the heart of the story stood Jack Shore.

Now he was on the edge of his seat. Literally.

Sally sat beside him. "You're going to be great," she said for at least the fifteenth time in as many minutes.

To be honest, he needed her to say it again and again. That was a big part of why he'd hired her. She was great for his ego—and of course, she was a damned fine assistant. She'd organized every nuance of this opportunity, hadn't she?

There was a knock at the door. In walked Avery Kormane, the

woman who'd shown him to the small, windowless waiting room and conducted his preinterview. "How're you doing?"

"Has anyone ever puked on *The Tonight Show*, or will I be the first?"

Avery Kormane smiled. "You'll do fine. Just focus on Jay if you get nervous. He's a nice guy. He'll catch you if you fall."

Sally had chosen Jay Leno for that very reason. When the offers started pouring in last week, Jack had gravitated toward Letterman. It was Sally who'd reminded him that Leno was a lot easier.

Avery glanced at her watch. "Follow me."

Jack did as he was told. Sally stuck to his side like glue. They walked through the industrial maze of backstage hallways until finally they came to the edge of the stage.

Jack's palms were sweating like geysers. He wished Elizabeth were here. It took only a look from her to calm him.

Applause shook the soundstage. On the wall, a red light flashed.

Avery tapped his shoulder. "You're on, Jack. Break a leg."

He stumbled around the corner. Jay Leno was coming toward him, hand outstretched. "Jumpin' Jack Flash," he said, smiling.

And Jack's nerves dissipated. He'd forgotten that: He was the Flash. "Hey, Jay." He waved at the crowd, who applauded wildly.

He followed Jay across the brightly lit stage and took his seat.

"So," Jay said, sitting behind his desk, "you've been stirring up the sports world a bit."

"I was in the right place at the right time when the story broke."

Jay grinned. "I'll bet it's good to be back in the limelight."

"It is."

"What were the non-football years like?"

"Like trading in a Ferrari for a used Volvo."

"Ouch," Jay said, and the audience laughed. "What made you do it? A lot of athletes are plenty pissed off at you."

"I'm a father," Jack said simply. "It could have been one of my daughters in that room with Drew Grayland."

The interview lasted another few minutes. Then it was over. Jay stood up, clapped Jack on the back. "You were great."

Jack waved and left the stage. He felt like he'd just led his team to a Super Bowl victory.

ON FRIDAY AFTERNOON Meghann called Elizabeth.

"Tonight's the big night," Meghann said. "The painting class you told me about. God, I wish I could be there."

Elizabeth smiled a little. "You mean you wish you were driving me to class."

"And walking you to the door."

"I did consider not going."

"Of course you did. But if you don't do it now . . ." Meg let the sentence trail off, unfinished.

"I know. And I'm going. I *am*."

"Good. Call me when you get home. Meanwhile, remember how talented you are. And keep moving. Don't slow down until you're in that classroom."

"Okay."

Elizabeth followed her best friend's advice. She got to the community college right on time. She parked and went inside.

Outside classroom 108, a sign read BEGINNING PAINTING/5:00.

Cautiously she opened the door. Inside the small classroom there were six or seven people—all women—seated in a semicircle. In front of them was a table draped in white fabric. A brown wooden bowl sat in the middle; it was piled high with bright red apples.

Elizabeth tried to move invisibly toward a vacant seat. She held her canvas bag against her chest as if it were a bulletproof vest.

Behind her the door opened, then closed softly. A male voice said, "Welcome to Beginning Painting."

He walked between the chairs in an easy, loose-hipped way. When he reached the blackboard and turned around, Elizabeth drew in a sharp breath. He was young—no more than twenty-nine or thirty—but God, he was good-looking.

"I'm Daniel Boudreaux," he said, flashing a smile. "I'm your instructor for the next six weeks." His blue-eyed gaze moved from face to face. It paused for a moment on Elizabeth, or had she imagined that? "Hopefully, this'll be the start of a love affair that will last the rest of your lives." He moved away from the blackboard and stood by the table with the fruit. "Let's talk about composition."

Elizabeth's heart was pounding hard. Soon, she thought, soon he'll say, "Okay, class, let's begin."

"Like anything, painting requires preparation. We'll start with acrylics and make a working palette. Now pin your paper up."

Elizabeth clipped a long, rough sheet of paper onto the easel in front of her chair.

"Now look at the fruit. Really look at it. Study the lines, the way light reflects on the flat surfaces and disappears in the hollows. Painting is about *seeing*. Look at the bowl. Discern the colors that combine within it. When you're ready, begin. Later on we'll start with sketches and ideas, but for now I want you to dive right in."

Elizabeth heard the sound of paintbrushes being smashed into paint, the thwop of overwet bristles hitting the paper.

She cleared her mind of everything except the fruit. Just that. Light and shadow; color, lines, and composition.

Suddenly she realized with a start that she wasn't alone. He was beside her—Daniel—and he was bending down.

"Is something wrong?" he asked.

She felt herself flush. "I'm sorry. What did you say?" She turned to look up at him so fast they almost conked heads.

He stepped back and laughed. "What's your name?"

"Elizabeth."

"Okay, Elizabeth, what's wrong? You haven't started."

"I can't see it yet."

"The apples? You could move closer."

"No . . . the painting."

"Ah. Now, that's an interesting answer. Close your eyes."

She followed his direction and immediately wished she hadn't. In the darkness he felt nearer somehow.

"Describe the fruit."

"It's in a wooden bowl, hand-carved, I think, by someone who wasn't very good. The table is covered with a white cotton cloth. The apples are McIntosh, red with strands of green and black. There's a feather at the edge of the table, maybe a blue jay's."

He was quiet for a moment. "I've set them out badly," he said at last. "How should I have done it?"

"The tablecloth should be yellow. There should be one apple. No, an orange. No bowl. Everything else is clutter."

He leaned closer. Then he touched her hand. The next thing she knew, she was holding a paintbrush.

She opened her eyes. He was looking right at her.

"Show me what you can do, Elizabeth."

Suddenly all she could see was the painting—her painting. A single plump Sunkist orange. The shadow it cast was the palest lavender. She dipped the sable tip into the yellow paint and began.

She couldn't stop. Her blood was on fire, her hands a whir of motion. When she finished, she was shaking. She looked around.

The room was empty.

She glanced up at the clock. It was eight o'clock. An hour after the end of class. "Oh, my God." She laughed, feeling great.

Daniel came up beside her. For a long moment he looked at her painting, then at her.

She felt a tightening in her stomach that reminded her of high school. And she knew what it was. Attraction.

Oh, Lord. Could he read it on her face? What if he asked her out—what would she say? "You're too young. Too handsome. I'm too old. My underwear is the size of a circus tent."

He smiled slowly. "Why are you in my class?"

"I haven't painted in a long time."

Her fingers were trembling as she removed her painting from the easel. Holding it gently, she slung her canvas bag over her shoulder and headed out.

She was at the door when he said, "You have talent, you know."

She smiled all the way home. She even laughed out loud.

ELIZABETH taped the painting to the refrigerator and stared at it. She couldn't remember the last time she'd felt this good. She poured herself a glass of wine, then grabbed the phone and called Meghann. The answering machine picked up.

"I painted, Meg. Painted! Yee-ha. And just for the record, my instructor is a doll. Call me when you get home."

Laughing, she put on a Smash Mouth CD—*Hey now, you're an All Star*. She sang along, dancing by herself in the living room. As she twirled past the fireplace, she caught sight of a photo of Jack and the girls on the mantel.

Suddenly she wished Jack were here right now. He would be proud of her. The old love, the feeling that had been such a part of her, came flooding back, reminding her that life had once been good with him. She'd almost forgotten that.

She moved on to another photograph, an old shot taken years ago. She was dressed in a plaid skirt and a Shetland sweater. Jack wore a letterman's jacket and a football star's cocky smile.

The University of Washington. The sandcastle years.

She closed her eyes, swaying to the music, remembering those days, the first time he'd kissed her.

They'd been studying together, sitting on a flat, grassy place in the Quad. It was late spring. The cherry trees were just past full bloom, and tiny pink blossoms floated randomly to the ground.

She flopped back onto the grass and rested her hands behind her head.

Jack lay down next to her on his side, with his head supported on one hand. "You're so beautiful. I guess your Harvard fiancé tells you that all the time."

"No." Her voice was barely above a whisper. A pink cherry blossom petal landed on her cheek.

He brushed it away, and at the contact, she shivered. Slowly he leaned toward her, giving her plenty of time to roll away.

She lay very still, breathing too quickly.

It wasn't much of a kiss—no more than a quick, scared brushing of lips. But inexplicably, she started to cry.

"Could you ever love a guy like me?"

"Oh, Jack," she answered, "why do you think I'm crying?"

She touched the photograph now, let her finger glide across his handsome face. No other man's kiss had ever made her cry.

For the first time in weeks she wondered if there was still a chance for them.

The phone rang.

Meghann.

Elizabeth swooped down to answer it. "Meg, my instructor's a real hunk!"

"Uh . . . Birdie?"

Elizabeth winced. "Oh, hi, Anita."

"I'm sorry to call so late. It's just . . . you said you'd call."

Elizabeth heard the quiver in her stepmother's voice. She curled up on the sofa. "I'm sorry, Anita. Things have been a little crazy here. How are you doing?"

Anita laughed. It was a fluttery, sorrowful sound. "Oh, honey, I try not to think about myself too much."

Elizabeth felt a spark of kinship with her stepmother. "That's what we women do, isn't it? We push our lives underwater and float on the surface. Then one day you realize it's someone else's pool."

"What in the Sam Hill are you talkin' about?"

"Sorry, Anita, but you've got enough on your plate. You don't need my mess piled on top."

"You just can't do it, can you, Birdie?"

"Do what?"

"Share your life with me. I thought now, with Edward gone, we might change things between us."

"I was trying to protect you," Elizabeth answered, stung. "Jack and I have separated. But the girls don't know, so don't say anything."

"Oh, my." Anita released a breath. "What happened?"

"Nothing. Everything." Elizabeth took a big swallow of wine. How could she explain her own formless dissatisfaction to a woman who'd wanted so little from her own life? "It's just a bump in the road, Anita. I'm sure we'll be fine."

Anita sighed again. "Well, I'm sorry y'all are havin' problems. That's what you want me to say, isn't it?"

Elizabeth decided to move onto easy ground. "Enough about me. How've you been? I've been thinking about you."

"This big ole house has a lot of ghosts," Anita answered. "Sometimes it's so quiet I think I'll go crazy."

"You know what's helped me? Sitting on the beach. Maybe a change of scenery would do you some good."

"You think?"

This was definitely better. The scenery was a safe topic. "There's something magical about sitting on a beach all by yourself. It's funny, I used to be scared of this beach. Now I can't be away from it too long." Her voice snagged on a suddenly exposed shoal. "I always wanted you and Daddy to see it."

"I know, honey. We thought we had time."

Time. So often it seemed to slip through your fingers like silk. But sometimes you could reach back into what was and take hold. "I took a painting class tonight," Elizabeth said softly.

"Oh, Birdie, that's wonderful. I hated it when you gave up on your talent."

"You thought I had talent? You never told me that."

"Ah, honey, I told you. Well. You take care now, y'hear?"

"You, too, Anita. And think about sitting on a beach."

"I'll do that, honey. I could use a change of scenery."

EIGHT

IF THERE was still a sun out there tethering the earth in its orbit, you'd never have known it. The sky was as heavy as granite.

On a day like this, neither stormy nor clear, there was nothing to do except build a fire, curl up on the sofa with a cup of tea, and read. So that was exactly what Elizabeth did.

The phone rang, and she answered. "Hello?"

"Mom?"

It was Jamie. "Hey, Sunshine," Elizabeth said, "it's good to hear your voice. How did the swim meet go?"

Jamie burst into tears.

"Honey, what's the matter?"

"I h-hate swimming. I'm sick of it. And I'm about thirty seconds away from flunking out."

Elizabeth sat up straighter, pulled her knees toward her chest. "What about that tutor we hired for you?"

There was a short pause. Then Jamie said, "I'm dating him. Michael. He is soooo cute. He plays the saxophone in a jazz quartet. How sexy is that?" Then she came back to the point. "Anyway, I don't need a tutor. I need time to study. That's why I want to quit swimming. Dad's making buttloads of money now—he told me that—so you guys can afford my tuition, right?"

"One point at a time, kiddo. What's really going on here? Why do you want to quit swimming?"

"Bottom line? I'm not good enough."

Elizabeth's heart ached at those softly spoken words. "Go on."

"To be honest, I might have quit a long time ago, except Dad came to every swim meet, and when I won, he acted like I'd cured cancer. But he's not on the sidelines anymore. He doesn't even call and ask how I did."

"Your dad loves you. You know he does. Neither one of us cares if you swim. We just want you to be happy."

"So you'll tell him I quit?"

Elizabeth laughed. "No way. You'll have to talk to him yourself, but I'll tell you this, honey—it's dangerous to quit something because you think you're not good enough. That can be an ugly pattern that repeats itself throughout your life. Believe me, I know."

"You want me to finish out the season?"

"I'm sure your coach would appreciate it."

"I hate it when you do that."

"Do what?"

"Pretend to agree with me and then lob some grenade of common sense."

Elizabeth smiled. It was a perfect description of motherhood. "I'll support whatever decision you make, honey. Is Stephie there?"

"Stephie who?" Jamie said bitterly.

So that was part of the problem. Stephanie was getting ready to graduate; Jamie hated to admit that she'd miss her big sister. "She's too busy for you, I take it?" Elizabeth said gently.

A pause. "Yeah." Jamie sighed. "I gotta run. Michael is picking me up in an hour. I'll have Stephie call you tomorrow. Love you."

"Love you, too. Bye."

After Elizabeth hung up, she stared down at the phone. Her first thought was, Call Jack. He needed to know what was going on with Jamie. A heads-up would make the "I want to quit swimming" conversation run a lot smoother.

She dialed his work number.

JACK was in a meeting with Sally when the phone rang. He waited for his secretary to answer, then remembered that she'd gone to lunch. He picked up the phone and said, "Jackson Shore."

"I almost hung up." Elizabeth's voice sounded forced, nervous.

"Hey, Birdie," he said after a stunned pause.

Sally glanced at the door.

"Am I catching you at a bad time?" Elizabeth asked.

Her voice sounded different, uncertain, though it didn't surprise him. In a few short weeks they'd become strangers.

Sally stood up. "I'll leave you alone for a minute," she whispered.

He nodded, mouthed, "Thanks."

"Who's that?" Birdie asked.

He felt guilty suddenly, though there was no need. "It's just my assistant. We were in a meeting." He watched Sally leave the room, then said, "So, Birdie, what's going on?"

"How's your job?"

"Honestly, I love it. I feel twenty years younger."

"I'm proud of you, Jack. I knew you'd be good at it. That was never the issue."

He smiled. Her opinion had always mattered more than anyone else's, more even than his own. He'd never owned success completely until Elizabeth kissed him and said, "You did it, baby."

"Thanks," he said. "How about you? How are you doing?"

"I'm taking a painting class."

To his amazement he felt a spark of jealousy. He'd tried for years to get her to paint again. Still, when he said, "That's great, Birdie," he meant it.

"I talked—"

"Do you—"

They spoke at once; then both laughed. Jack said, "You first."

"I just talked to Jamie. She's having a hard time. You know . . . school, swimming, Dad's death, Stephie's graduation. It's a lot for her to deal with by herself. I think you should call her."

"Okay."

"Good." Then, "I'm having a hard time lying to them. Are you?"

"Lying? What do you mean?"

"You know. Telling them I'm getting the house ready for renters. Pretty soon I think we'll have to tell them the truth."

Jack felt as if he'd been punched in the gut. As much as he loved his new life, he wasn't ready to contemplate the end of their family.

The one thing he'd always counted on, the bedrock of his life, was that Birdie loved him. Her plea for a short-term separation hadn't actually altered that belief. But now he wondered.

"There's a chance for us, isn't there?" he asked.

It took Elizabeth a moment to answer. "I hope so."

He smiled, relieved. "I hope so, too, baby."

Elizabeth said, "Don't forget about Jamie. She's fragile right now. Be gentle."

"I'm always gentle with her."

"Well, I'd better let you get back to work."

"Yeah. It was good talking to you," he said, and they were strangers again.

"Good talking to you, too."

Jack realized he was waiting for her to say "I love you," when he heard the dial tone.

ELIZABETH felt a sudden urge to call him back and say, "We can't be this far apart."

But they were distant now, emotionally as well as physically. That was what she'd wanted. It was why he'd sounded so confident and happy when he answered the phone—and so guarded and awkward when he realized who'd called.

After twenty-four years of sharing every moment of life, they'd drifted to separate coasts and picked up separate lives. Their conversations came in a kind of Morse code—hurried sentences punctuated by elongated pauses.

She tried to cull through the rubble of her emotions to find the truest one. Only a few days ago she'd seen an old photo of them and thought, There's still a chance for us. But every day took them farther away from the love that had once bound them together.

She was at a crossroads suddenly, one she hadn't even seen approaching. And yet here she was, standing at the corner of what she'd dreamed of and what she'd left behind.

If she picked up the phone and called Jack, she would turn back into who she'd been.

Someday (and yes, she knew she still held that hope close) she would feel strong enough, sure enough of herself, to call Jack and say, "I love you. Let's try again."

But not today.

THE week flew by. After years of trudging through a gray, wintry landscape of other people's choices, Elizabeth had finally emerged onto a sunny blue day of her own.

Each morning she woke with a sense of expectation that made

her smile as she went about her daily chores. Then, at noon, no matter what pressed at her to be done, she ignored everything and painted.

At first she'd tried to fix her class project. She'd added brush-strokes and dabs of color, trying to add a complexity to the image that she couldn't quite achieve. But the problem with the orange was that it wasn't *hers*. The best in art revealed something of the artist's soul, and Elizabeth's soul had never cared much for fruit.

When she trolled around for something else to paint, she saw possibilities everywhere, but only one true choice. The ocean.

She had started by stretching and priming a canvas in the way she'd been taught years ago. Then she took her easel and the can-vas and her paints and brushes out to the edge of the yard. She set up the easel and began to put her love of the sea onto canvas.

She saw the ocean in tiny increments, in slashes of hue and texture, in light and shadow. And just that, seeing it as she'd once been able to, made her feel young again.

Each day she'd added a new layer of color to her canvas, and gradually she felt it return—her own potent magic. Her painting revealed everything she loved about this view and everything she longed to be. Dangerous, rough-edged, vibrant.

Today, at last, she would take her work to class. She couldn't wait to show it to Daniel.

At three o'clock she wrapped the canvas in cheesecloth and carefully placed it in the backseat of her car. She took a shower, brushed her hair until it shone, and dressed in a black jersey tunic and straight-legged pantsuit. A chunky turquoise-and-silver neck-lace was her only accessory.

All in all, she looked good.

She got to the classroom and found it empty. When she looked at her watch, she saw that she was almost twenty minutes early.

"Idiot," she said aloud.

"Did you say something?"

And suddenly he was there, standing in the open doorway.

"I came early—" she stammered.

He smiled. "Do you have something to show me?"

"The painting," she said. "You told us to paint something that moved us. I chose the view from my house."

"Let me see."

She went to the blackboard, where an empty easel waited.

Her fingers shook as she set her canvas on the easel.

Daniel came up beside her, moving so quietly she didn't hear him. Suddenly he was just there. "It's Tamarack Cove," he said. "I used to kayak there with my grandfather. There's a tide pool—"

"By the black rocks, yes. I didn't know that was the name of my cove. I should have known, I guess, since I live there, but I don't spend a lot of time reading maps."

"You really don't know how talented you are, do you?" His voice was soft as beach sand.

The compliment made her feel about twenty years old. "You're nice to say that," she said, praying her cheeks didn't turn red.

He took a step toward her. "Come have coffee with me after class," he said.

She stepped back so fast she slammed into a desk. "I'm married." She lifted her left hand, wiggled her fingers. "I mean, we're separated right now, but that's not a divorce." She tried to shut up, but couldn't. The silence would be horrible. "I have two daughters. With my luck, they're your age."

His touch stopped her. "It's just coffee," he said.

If possible—and frankly, she doubted it—she felt *more* idiotic. "Coffee. It's a beverage, that's all. You don't care if I'm married."

"Not for coffee."

Her cheeks were on fire, she was certain of it. "I don't know what got into me. I'm sorry," she said.

"Don't be sorry. Just meet me after class. There's something I'd like to discuss with you."

She nodded. "Sure. Coffee would be great."

JACK had received one of the coveted tickets for the première of Disney's newest blockbuster movie. He'd dressed carefully in a black Armani turtleneck sweater and charcoal-gray wool slacks. He was just about to grab his coat when the phone rang. It was probably the car service. He answered quickly. "Hello?"

"Dad?"

Jamie. He'd been missing her calls all week. "Hey, baby, how're you doing?"

"You didn't return my last call."

"I know. I'm sorry. I've been so busy lately."

"Yeah, Dad. I know."

He glanced at the clock. It was six thirty-seven. The car service would be here any second. Damn. "Look, honey, I've got—" His second line beeped. "Just a minute. I have to put you on hold." He depressed the button and answered. "Hello?"

"Mr. Shore? Your car is here."

"Thanks, Billy. I'll be right down," he said to the doorman. Then he went back to Jamie. "My car is here, honey. I've got to run."

"But I need to talk to you."

"What is it?" he asked, looking around for his coat.

"I'm quitting the swim team."

He grabbed the black lambskin blazer off the kitchen table. Then it hit him. He stopped. "You're what?"

She sighed. "I'm quitting the swim team."

He glanced at the clock again. It was now six forty-three. The movie started in seventeen minutes. If he left right now, he'd be on time. "You're just having a rough time, honey. You know how much you love the sport. Back when I was playing for the—"

"Not another football anecdote, please. And I don't like swimming. I never did."

He sat down on the bed. "You're exaggerating."

"Dad, you're not listening. *I'm quitting.* At the end of this season I'm done. I would have discussed it with you last week, but you never called me back. I'm going to tell my coach tomorrow."

"Don't do that." He didn't know what to say, and he didn't have time to think about it now. "Look, honey, I have to run. Honest. I've got important business tonight. People are counting on me. I'll call you back tomorrow, and we'll talk about this. I promise."

"You do that." She paused. "And Dad?"

"Yeah?"

"Strangers aren't the only people who count on you. How come they're the only ones that matter?" Before he could respond, she hung up.

What in the hell did she mean by that?

THE newest art gallery in Echo Beach was on the corner of First and Main. A sign above the door read ECLECTICA.

Elizabeth glanced down at the piece of paper Daniel had given her. This was the place.

Just go see her, he'd said over coffee. *She's new in town and could use a little help.*

Elizabeth had wanted to decline, but when Daniel looked at her with those incredibly blue eyes, she'd automatically nodded.

Now she wished she'd been firmer. Most of the so-called art galleries in Echo Beach carried knickknacks—coasters made out of polished driftwood, dried sand dollars in brown mesh netting, that sort of thing. She stayed away from them.

Still, a promise was a promise.

She opened the door and went inside. As she entered, a bell tinkled overhead. She looked around.

To her left was a table filled with stunning wood sculptures. Most of them were women—nudes—from neck to hips. On the next table was an exhibit of black-and-white photographs. Each print captured the spirit of the coast in a strikingly original shot: a beach at low tide on a windy day; a misty, ethereal image of a lighthouse.

"Amazing," Elizabeth said softly to herself.

"It is, isn't it?"

Elizabeth spun around as a woman stepped out from behind a hanging tapestry. She was at least six feet tall and nearly as wide. Her hair was a bird's nest of brown frizz that hung to her waist.

She smiled. "I'm Large Marge. I never could figure out how a petite, retiring gal like me got saddled with a nickname like that, but there you have it."

Elizabeth offered her hand. "I'm Elizabeth Shore. Daniel Boudreaux asked me to stop by and see you."

Marge grabbed Elizabeth's hand and pumped it hard. "He told me about you. I'm glad you stopped by. I wanted to talk to you about the Stormy Weather Arts Festival."

"It's a big deal around here. I'd be happy to help you organize your gallery's event if that's what you're interested in. I know who's who."

"Organization skills I got. Local artists are scarce as hens' teeth." She studied Elizabeth. "Danny boy tells me your work might be worth exhibiting."

Elizabeth laughed. "Yeah, right."

Marge said softly, "He told me you'd be scared."

Elizabeth's smile faded. "I just started painting again after years away from it."

"Are you any good?"

"I was." It was as confident as she could be.

Marge made a clicking sound. "Danny's take is good enough for me. I'd like to show your work for the festival."

"Well . . . I suppose I could think about it."

Marge glanced at the wall clock. "I'll give you three minutes."

Elizabeth didn't need psychic abilities to hear Meghann's voice in her head: *Damn it, Birdie, don't you dare hesitate.* "How many pieces would you need?"

"Five. Is that possible?"

Elizabeth had no idea. "They won't sell, you know."

"I'm sure we've both survived worse. Come on, say you'll do it."

"I'll try."

Large Marge grinned. "Are you still here? You ought to be home painting. Now git."

IN THE past five days Jack had been in six cities. He'd interviewed Alex Rodriguez, Ken Griffey, Jr., Randy Johnson, Shawn Kemp, and Brian Bosworth.

When the interviews were finished, he spent three days in the editing room, working the narration and music into the one-hour special he'd titled *Breakable Gods*. He'd loved every minute of it.

"You did a hell of a job," the show's executive producer, Tom Jinaro, said now, leaning back in his chair.

"Thanks." Jack had been confident coming into this meeting. He knew his special was a virtuoso blend of news and entertainment.

Tom leaned forward. "I've been in this business a long time, Jack. I've seen people come and go—mostly go. But you're the real deal." He smiled. "What I'm going to tell you now can't leave this room."

"What is it?"

"One of the guys is quitting the Fox *NFL Sunday* show. I can't tell you which one. But we're looking at you to fill his slot."

The only show bigger was *Monday Night Football*.

Jack drew in a sharp breath. "Thanks." It was all he could say. Any more, and he might start laughing.

"It's not for sure, but it's close. So let me give you some advice, man to man. You had a bad-boy image in the NFL, and it doesn't seem like you've changed. I hear you practically live at Kel's pub."

Jack started to disagree, but Tom stopped him with a laugh. "Save the denials for your curiously absent wife. I don't care what you do, as long as it doesn't hurt our ratings. But opportunities can vanish in an instant. Stay away from drugs and underage women."

"Don't worry. Nothing is going to derail me this time."

"Glad to hear it. Now get going."

Jack couldn't remember when he'd felt so good. He left the office and walked home strutting. When he entered the apartment, he almost yelled, "Birdie, I'm home," but stopped himself just in time.

The apartment was as quiet as a tomb. Disappointment poked a hole in his good mood. He hadn't realized how lonely success could be if you had no one to share it with.

He made himself a drink, gulped it down, poured another.

Maybe he should go out, have a few drinks at Kel's. But he didn't feel like going out. What he felt like was talking to his wife. He wanted to show her the tape of *Breakable Gods* and watch her smile at him afterward. He needed that now.

It was funny how profoundly you could need something that for years you hadn't even noticed was missing.

He made himself another drink and put a CD into the player. The apartment swayed for a second, then righted itself.

He was a little drunk. But why should he stay sober anyway?

The doorbell rang. His heart lurched. Against all common sense, he thought, Birdie. He hurried to the door and opened it.

Sally leaned against the door frame, a bottle of Dom Perignon in one hand. "I sneaked past the doorman. I hope that's okay with you."

"Uh. Sure."

"I saw the final edit," she said, smiling. "You're a genius, Jack."

Her words were precious water that irrigated his dry heart.

He stepped back to let her inside. He smacked into the wall and stumbled sideways. "Oops. Sorry."

She grabbed his arm to steady him. With one foot she kicked the door shut. "I guess you don't need champagne."

"I'm a little drunk," he said.

She moved in close to him. He felt her small, lithe body pressing against his, and he groaned. "Sally . . ." He didn't know what to say.

Excuses staggered through his quickly shrinking brain. He had mumbled, "Wait, Sally," when she kissed him.

That was the end of even pseudo-rational thought. He gave in. It was that simple. For months—years, really—he'd been holding himself in check, keeping steady to the vows he'd made to Birdie.

But now she was living in Oregon, and she'd made it very clear that she didn't want him. Nothing had ever hurt like admitting that.

Sally gazed up at him. "Well?"

His mouth was dry. "You know I'm still married," he said, feeling that sentence was a personal triumph of self-control.

"Of course I know. I don't want your ring." Smiling slowly, she whispered, "Take me to bed."

Four little words that were his undoing.

NINE

ELIZABETH finished the day on autopilot. As she prepared some chicken for her dinner, she thought, *Exhibit. My work.*

Once the meal was in the oven, she went into the pantry and pulled out the seascape. She would finish it by tomorrow morning and then start something else.

Maybe she'd try a watercolor next. She'd be more likely to make her five-works-by-the-festival deadline if she didn't work in oil.

She thought she heard a car drive up. Then a door slam.

Maybe Meghann had cleared her schedule and headed south for a girls' weekend. Elizabeth hurried to the door and flung it open.

Anita stood there wearing a flowing white dress and pink ballet slippers. Beside her was a huge suitcase and a long, narrow cardboard box. A taxi drove away. "Hey, Birdie," she said, smiling uncertainly, "this is the beach I picked for my change of scenery."

Elizabeth didn't quite know how to react. First there was Anita's appearance. She looked like something out of a Grimm's fairy tale, nothing like the Texas gold digger that was her usual style. Gone were the bright, garish colors and peroxided hair. Now a simple white braid hung over one shoulder. There was something almost otherworldly about her, a fragility that bespoke great sadness.

And even more disconcerting was the fact that she was here, invading the solitude that had cost Elizabeth so dearly.

"I hope you don't mind me just showin' up. I was lookin' through travel magazines for a place to go, and I saw an ad for Oregon beaches. And I thought, Hell's bells, it must be a sign."

"You look . . . different," Elizabeth said clumsily.

Anita laughed. "Oh, that. All that was for Edward. This is my natural hair color."

For Daddy? Her father had wanted his wife to look like Dolly Parton? Elizabeth couldn't process that.

She didn't want to invite Anita in, but what choice did she have?

You take care of her, you hear?

"Come on in." Elizabeth grabbed the huge suitcase (how long did Anita intend to stay?) and dragged it over the threshold.

Anita stepped inside, looked around. "So this is the famous beach house. Your daddy always wanted to see it."

That sentence brought them together for a moment. "Come on, I'll show you to the guest bedroom." Elizabeth turned and walked through the house, dragging the rolling suitcase behind her. When she reached the foot of the stairs, she looked back.

Anita had stopped. "I didn't know where else to go, Birdie," she said quietly. "Is it okay? That I'm here, I mean. I won't stay long."

Elizabeth looked at her stepmother. Amazingly, she couldn't see the woman she'd fought with for most of her life. This new Anita was fragile, a lost soul. "Of course it's okay, Anita. We're family."

For better or for worse, it was true.

JACK came awake, groaning. He felt as if he'd been hit in the head with a crowbar. He opened one eye. The clock read eight oh seven.

He bolted upright and glanced to the left. The bed was empty.

He pushed the covers aside and got out of bed. Then he stumbled into the bathroom, where he saw that Sally had written a note on the mirror. In lipstick.

Great sex
xxoo
Sally

A headache kicked him in the skull, pounded.

Last night never would have happened if Birdie had moved to New York. If she hadn't left me. (Yeah, try that one on for size.)

"Never again," he said out loud. "It was a onetime thing."

Birdie didn't have to know. Ever.

By the time he'd showered, shaved, dressed, and walked to the office, he felt better. Stronger and more sure of himself. He'd made a mistake—a whopper of one, to be sure—but it would stand alone. A high-rise of stupidity in the vast prairie of the rest of his life.

He sat down at his desk and immediately started working.

Suddenly the door opened. Sally stood there dressed in a slim black suit with an emerald-green silk blouse.

She closed the door behind her. "I'm sorry I left while you were still sleeping. I needed to be at work early," she said.

"Don't mention it." Really, he thought, don't mention it.

Smiling, she strolled toward him. She placed her hands on his desk and leaned forward. He could see the lacy edge of her bra. "You'll never guess who called this morning," she said.

"Who?" He kept his gaze pinned to her face. *Nothing below the collar. Or the top button at the very lowest.*

"Your publicist. He asked me to pass along an offer . . . from *People* magazine."

"*People?*" He rose out of his chair. "What did they want?"

Sally hitched one hip onto the edge of his desk. "They want to feature you in the Fifty Most Beautiful People issue."

He didn't mean to do it, but he reached out, pulled her into his arms. He gazed down at her heart-shaped face and felt a sharp tug of desire. God help him, he wanted her again already.

ELIZABETH tossed and turned all night. At dawn she got dressed and tiptoed across the hall, then eased the door of the guest bedroom open. Anita was still sleeping.

She wrote a quick "gone to the beach" note, then went outside.

Hugging her canvas supply bag, she climbed down to the beach. The ocean was energetic today, surging forward and back.

She left the bag by her rock and kept walking, faster and faster, until it seemed completely natural to break into an easy jog. She took energy from the surf; it made her feel powerful and free. For a few glorious minutes she forgot that Anita had shown up last night dragging a suitcase big enough for a two-month stay.

Finally, breathing hard, she turned around and came back to her rock. She sat down and stared out at the sea.

"Birdie, honey? Is that you?"

She turned. Anita was standing a few feet away, wearing a long floral skirt and a heavy cable-knit white sweater.

Elizabeth reluctantly scooted sideways on the rock. "Here. There's plenty of room."

Anita sat down. "Whew! Those stairs are a killer. No wonder you've lost weight."

Elizabeth turned. "I have?"

"At least ten pounds, honey. Your clothes hang on you."

"I guess exercising was the key all along."

"I do yoga myself," Anita said.

Elizabeth hadn't known that. Come to think of it, she didn't know much about Anita's life. "What else do you do?"

"Regular things. I belong to a book group that meets once a month. I play bridge with the girls on Thursday mornings. Course your daddy took up most of my time." She stopped, fell silent. Then, softly, she said, "I don't dream about him. Every night I go to bed waitin' to see his face in my sleep, but he doesn't come."

Elizabeth knew that feeling. "I've waited my whole life to dream about Mama. It's never happened."

After another long pause Anita added, "I always knew I'd outlive him. I thought I was prepared for it. What a fool I was. You can't prepare for losin' someone you love."

Elizabeth knew there was nothing for her to say. But maybe Anita had come to Echo Beach because she needed to talk about Daddy. "How did you and Daddy meet?" she asked.

Anita gave her a grateful smile. "I was working in the beauty salon. Lordy, I still remember the first time I saw him. He looked like a Saturday-matinee hero. He had a mustache in those days, and his eyes were dark as night. I reckon I fell in love with him right then."

Elizabeth frowned. Daddy had shaved off that mustache when Mama died. He'd never worn one since. "You knew my mother," she said suddenly.

Anita started to speak—to deny it, Elizabeth was certain. But when their eyes met, Anita sighed heavily. "Not really. She was with him that day, though. Getting her hair cut."

"Tell me about her."

"I don't know much, really. I heard stories, of course. By all accounts, your mama was the most beautiful, most adventurous woman in Springdale."

"I've heard that line for years. Tell me something real. Why wouldn't Daddy ever talk about her?" She gazed at Anita. "Please."

"Before you were born, your mama ran away for a spell."

"She left Daddy?"

"In the middle of the night, from what I heard. It took him a while to find her. She was way to North Carolina by then, but he tracked her down and brought her home. After that, folks said, she was different. Sad and quiet."

"Depression." Elizabeth had never imagined such a thing. Her mama, the woman everyone said was so bold and adventurous, depressed. She didn't quite know how to process this new information.

"She loved you. But the rumor was that she never did shake that sadness. She'd stopped smilin'. That's what I heard most of all. That she'd left her smile in North Carolina."

"I begged Daddy for stories about her. He'd never say anything."

"Maybe he didn't have any stories to give you. Sometimes unhappiness can settle over a thing and bury it until there's nothin' else left."

Nothing else left. Just unhappiness. Elizabeth knew how that felt. "That's how it got between Jack and me."

"It's easy, sometimes, to forget why you fell in love." Anita stared out at the ocean. "I left your Daddy once, you know."

"No, I didn't know. Where did you go?"

"That doesn't matter. It didn't even matter then." Anita was quiet for a moment. "He overwhelmed me sometimes. And I was young when we got married. I didn't know what I wanted. So I lived his life. For a long time that was okay."

Elizabeth knew that feeling.

"But I wanted to have a child," Anita went on. "So after Edward and I got back together, we tried. I had three miscarriages. Each one took a bigger piece of me, until . . ." She shrugged. "Three was enough, I guess. I figured God knew what He was doing."

Elizabeth felt herself softening toward Anita, glimpsing a woman she'd never imagined before. It felt strangely like coming home.

Anita turned to her. "I have something for you. I brought it all the way from Tennessee. And it wasn't easy."

None of this was easy, Elizabeth thought but didn't say. Instead, she helped her stepmother to her feet. They climbed up the rickety wood steps and emerged onto the soggy grass.

When they reached the porch, Elizabeth noticed the big cardboard box leaning against the house.

Anita rushed inside and came back out holding a knife. "Open the box," she said.

Elizabeth took the knife, split the box down the seam, and opened it. Inside, she saw shiny green poles, white knotted rope.

"It's Daddy's hammock."

"Y'all used to snuggle together in that thing for hours."

"We used to watch the fireflies together," Elizabeth whispered.

"He'd want you to have it," Anita said. "It'd be perfect over there by the stairs, so you can sleep in it on sunny days and listen to the ocean . . . and remember how much he loved you."

Elizabeth looked up at Anita, her eyes stinging. She couldn't say anything, not even thank you.

Anita smiled. "You're welcome."

MARCH howled into New York on an arctic blast. In the middle of a night so cold that even Times Square was deserted, it began to snow. By morning it was snowing so hard that Jack, standing at his window, could barely see the buildings across the street.

He was just about to head into the shower when the phone rang.

"Hello, Mr. Shore. This is the Bite Me insurance agency, and we need authorization to distribute your assets, since you have Fallen Off the Face of the Planet."

He couldn't help laughing. *"Mea culpa,"* he said. It was always better to take responsibility with Jamie. Otherwise she'd chew you up and spit you out.

"Obviously *mea culpa.* That's not even a question. I suppose you've been so busy big-manning it that you didn't have time to call me back about the swim team."

"I'm sorry, baby. I meant to get back to you. Things have been crazy around here. I'm working fifteen hours a day."

"That must be why you were out when I called you last night at two o'clock in the morning. Working."

Thank God he wasn't talking to her face to face. He felt himself flush. "I took a sleeping pill last night. I've been having trouble sleeping lately—you know, without your mom."

"I didn't even know you missed her. You never mention her."

"I do . . . miss her."

"Well, Stephie and I have come up with a plan. We're gonna fly into Kennedy on Friday morning. You'll meet us at the airport. Then we'll all fly to Oregon together for the weekend."

"Huh?"

"It's Mom's birthday. You didn't forget, did you?"

Damn. "No, no. Of course not. I was going to fly out to be with her for the weekend, but then this thing at work—"

"Don't even finish that sentence. No one's gonna die if you take Friday off. You're a TV personality, Dad, not a cardiac surgeon."

What a mess. "You're right," he said dully.

"You can meet us at the airport, right? We'll buy the tickets online and put them on your Visa."

"Sure. Why not?"

"And Dad, it's a surprise. So don't tell her, okay?"

Jack closed his eyes. "Oh, it'll be a surprise, all right."

ELIZABETH and Anita stayed up late into the night, talking—two women who'd known each other all their lives and yet had never really known each other at all. To their mutual surprise they found a lot of common ground.

In the morning, after breakfast, they walked along the beach, talking some more. It was a glorious spring day, bursting with sunlight.

Later, while Anita napped, Elizabeth went to town and stocked up on groceries. It was late afternoon by the time she got home.

Anita was on the porch, staring out at the ocean. She wore a long, flowing white dress and a beautifully knit coral sweater.

Elizabeth felt a flash of inspiration. "Could I paint your picture?"

Anita pressed a pale hand to her chest. "You want to paint me?"

"I've only just started again. But if you'd be willing—"

"I could sit on that log over there by the cliff."

Elizabeth turned. Sure enough, there was a perfect log on the edge of the property. Behind it, the ocean stretched to the horizon.

She looked at Anita. "Stay here. I'll be right back." She raced into the house and got her painting supplies. She was outside again in less than five minutes.

She set up the easel, then looked around for Anita.

Her stepmother was standing by the log, her back to Elizabeth. Beyond her the twilight sky was pure magic. Pink, purple, gold, and orange lay in layers above the sparkling silver ocean.

"Don't move!" Elizabeth cried.

She let pure instinct overtake her. She'd never worked with such purpose. Mixing colors, slashing lines, trying to capture the lonely beauty of the scene in front of her.

She painted furiously, wordlessly, until the last bits of light disappeared. "That's it, Anita," she said. "No more for tonight."

Anita's body seemed to melt downward and become smaller. Suddenly Elizabeth realized how much she'd asked of the woman. "I'm sorry. Did it hurt to stand so still for so long?"

"I loved every moment of it."

"You must be starving. I know I am. Come on inside."

Anita glanced eagerly at the easel. "Can I see?"

"No." Elizabeth heard the hard edge to her voice and was instantly contrite. "Sorry. I mean not yet. Is that okay?"

Anita waved her hand in the air. "Of course, honey."

Elizabeth carried the painting into the house and put it in the walk-in pantry to dry. "Dinner'll be ready in a while," she said to Anita. "Go on upstairs. Take a hot bath."

"Darlin', you read my mind."

Elizabeth set the table and made a chicken salad, then called for Anita. When there was no answer, she went upstairs and found her stepmother sitting on the end of the bed. Her head was bowed, and she was holding a small lace-trimmed pillow.

"Anita? You okay?"

"I guess." Anita smoothed her hand across the pillow. "Your daddy always tried to get me to take up needlepoint, but I never could master it. Such a feminine thing."

The pillow was one of the few mementos Elizabeth had of her mother. She had often tried to imagine her in a rocking chair, working with that beautiful silk thread, but all she could draw up was a black-and-white image of a young woman looking into the camera.

Anita looked up. Her face was pale; there were tears in her eyes. "Your mama made this pillow," she said. "That day she came into the beauty salon? She stitched the whole time."

"I try to picture her sometimes."

Anita set the pillow down and stood up, then guided Elizabeth toward the mirror that hung above the bureau.

"When I first saw your mama, I thought she was the loveliest woman I'd ever seen." Anita pulled the hair back from Elizabeth's face. "You're the spittin' image of her."

As a girl, Elizabeth had spent hours searching through family photographs for pictures of her mother, but she'd only found a few.

She'd been looking in the wrong place, and no one had ever told her. All she'd needed to see Mama was a mirror. Now, as she looked into her own green eyes, she saw a hint of the woman she'd spent all her life missing. "Thank you, Anita," she said in a shaky voice.

"You're welcome, honey."

BLEARY-EYED and hungover, Jack padded into the bathroom and turned on the shower. Unfortunately, the hot water couldn't wash away his regret. He'd slept with Sally again last night.

He wished he could believe it wouldn't matter, but he knew better. This separation wasn't a license to screw around. If he found out that Birdie had been unfaithful, he would kill the guy.

She'd forgiven him once, but that was years ago, when they were different people. The new Birdie was a woman he couldn't predict.

He had just started shaving when the phone rang. Naked, he walked into the bedroom to answer it. "Hello?"

"Hel-lo, Dad." Jamie sighed disgustedly. "I told you he was still at home. He forgot us," she went on, clearly talking to her sister.

Damn. Today was the day they were going to Oregon. "I was just walking out the door."

"Often, people leave for the airport *before* the plane lands," Jamie said. "How long until you'll be here?"

He glanced at the clock. It was eight forty-eight. "An hour, max. Our plane doesn't leave until—"

"Eleven forty-nine."

"Right. I'll meet you at the gate by ten."

Jamie sighed. "We'll be there, Dad."

Jack hung up, took two aspirin, and rushed to get dressed. In ten minutes he was in a cab, heading for Kennedy. That gave him plenty of time to figure out what to say beyond "I'm sorry."

Maybe Stephanie would buy it, but not Jamie. She'd stare daggers at him and ignore him.

He needed Birdie. She'd always been the glue that held their family together. She'd guided him toward an easy relationship with his daughters. Without her he had no idea what to say.

"You can quit being strong, you know," Anita said as they sat in the kitchen eating an early lunch. A few presents sat on the counter.

"What do you mean?"

"A happy birthday from your stepmother doesn't quite cut it. Admit it. You miss your family."

"I'm fine." But suddenly Elizabeth was drowning in sorrow. She had buried herself in denial because she knew how much a birthday without Jack and the girls would hurt. No one had even called her today. She forced a smile. "I'm going to go paint now. I need to finish four more pieces before the festival."

Anita stood up from the table. "Do you mind if I tag along? I could knit while you paint."

"I'd appreciate the company," Elizabeth answered truthfully.

Ten minutes later she and Anita were climbing down the steps.

Elizabeth was feeling good again. The girls would call tonight. Most definitely. "The tide's out," she observed. "We can spend hours down here."

Flipping a blanket out on the sand, Anita sat down and started knitting. A pile of fuzzy white yarn settled in her lap like an angora bird's nest.

Elizabeth set up her easel, tacked the paper in place, and looked around for a subject. She settled on the ocean. It was definitely a watercolor day—no oils or acrylics.

Happy with that decision, she got started.

She worked at a furious pace for the next few hours, but it felt as if only minutes had passed when Anita suddenly said, "It's past two o'clock! We need to get back to the house. Come." She stuffed her knitting back in her bag and headed for the stairs.

Elizabeth watched her stepmother go huffing and puffing up the steps. You'd think there was a prize for the winner, she thought.

She picked up her supplies, carefully held her painting with two fingers, and climbed the stairs. She was almost at the top when she smelled smoke and heard voices. She paused, looking around.

Balloons poked through the open windows of her house and drifted upward. Suddenly the front door banged open. Marge from the art gallery, Anita, and Meghann crowded onto the porch singing "Happy Birthday." Elizabeth almost dropped her art supplies. No one had ever thrown her a surprise party before.

Meghann rushed toward her, arms outstretched. Then all three of them were there, laughing and talking at once. Elizabeth couldn't remember the last time she'd felt so special.

Marge took the still damp watercolor from her. "Oh, Birdie, this is exquisite. Is it for me?"

The compliment warmed her. "Of course."

Marge walked away, and Meghann moved closer. "Anita planned all this," she said. "It's not what I would have expected of her. You know—after all the stories."

Elizabeth flinched. "She's not who I thought she was," she said, ashamed. "I'll be right back."

She walked across the yard to where Anita was bent over a new red barbecue, busily moving oysters from a bucket onto the grill.

At Elizabeth's approach, Anita straightened. "Surprise."

"This is all your doing?" Elizabeth said. She knew how much she'd hurt her stepmother over the years, yet Anita had still organized this party. It was the kind of thing Elizabeth would do for her daughters. "Thank you," she said, knowing it wasn't enough. She grasped her stepmother's hand, held it. "I want us to start over."

Anita's eyes rounded. "Oh, my . . ."

Meghann came up beside them. "Can I interest you ladies in a margarita? Don't worry, Anita, I can make you a virgin."

Anita laughed shakily, wiped her eyes. "Honey, there ain't nothin' you can do that'll make me a virgin again, but I'll sure as tootin' take a margarita."

After that the party kicked into high gear. Marge set a portable stereo out on the porch and started playing raucous music. They barbecued oysters on the grill and cooked clams in a coffee can filled with butter, wine, and spices. A salmon, drenched in lemon and onion slices, lay on an alder plank on the grill.

Elizabeth couldn't remember when she'd had so much fun.

JACK turned onto Stormwatch Lane. "This road is still terrible." He heard the testiness in his voice and wished he'd tempered it. It wasn't enough that they were getting close to Birdie. No. The girls had to choose today to give him the near silent treatment.

They were mad at him for forgetting to meet them, and he could understand that. So he confined himself to safe topics.

"We got lucky," he said now. "It's a beautiful day."

"Totally," Jamie said. "I can't believe it's not raining."

The view was breathtaking. For the two years Jack had lived here, all he'd noticed was the rain and gray skies. But now he saw the grandeur of the coastline with its jagged cliffs and endless gray beach. Today's sunlight turned the sea into glittering silver.

No wonder Elizabeth loved it here. It was spectacularly wild. How was it that he'd never noticed the beauty before?

He rounded the last bend in the road and slowed down. There were a few cars parked in the driveway. When he got out of the car, he noticed music—some old disco song, maybe a Gloria Gaynor.

His heart was a jackhammer trying to crack through his rib cage. He should have called Birdie. Warned her.

The girls ran on ahead. Jack followed but couldn't work up much speed. When they reached the yard, the first thing he noticed were the women standing around a table. He barely had time to register that Anita and Meghann were there, when Elizabeth turned around.

The girls ran toward her, screaming.

Jack couldn't move. He knew suddenly how it felt to return from war and see the face of the woman you loved. The thought of what he'd done last night with Sally made him feel physically ill.

"Dad, get over here!" Stephanie yelled, waving her hand.

Elizabeth looked up, saw him. He walked toward her, then clumsily took her in his arms. "Happy birthday, Birdie."

"Hey, Jack," she said, "it's good to see you."

There was something about the way she said his name that wounded him. When she drew back, he had trouble letting her go.

THE party continued. At dusk Marge pulled out a paper bag full of fireworks, and they all went down to the beach to light them.

Elizabeth stood apart from the crowd, watching her daughters and friends in the flickering red-and-gold glow of the falling sparks.

Jack was off by himself; he'd stayed that way all day. Oh, he'd mingled, been friendly, but he'd kept his distance.

"That's the end of the show, kids," Marge said when the sparks from the last of the firecrackers finally faded away.

Within a few minutes they'd cleaned up the beach and gone up the stairs. Marge got into her car and drove away. Then Anita and Meghann drove off, having decided to spend the night at the Inn Between in Echo Beach.

Elizabeth watched them leave. Finally she was in her darkened yard with only her family around her.

"I'm exhausted," Stephanie said. "We're on East Coast time, don't forget." She looped an arm around her mother's shoulder. Together the four of them went into the house.

Elizabeth led the girls to the guest bedroom. Jamie plopped down on the bed. Stephanie lay down beside her.

"The party meant the world to me," Elizabeth said.

"We missed you," Jamie said simply, kicking off her shoes. She pulled off her jeans and crawled into bed.

Stephanie went down the hall. When she came back, she was wearing a baggy flannel nightgown. She kissed Elizabeth, then crawled into bed beside her sister.

Elizabeth wasn't ready to leave yet, to face Jack. "I want to hear about your new boyfriend, Jamie."

"That's it," Stephanie said. "If she's going to blab about Michael, I'm going to sleep. G'night, Mom." She rolled onto her side.

Elizabeth sat down on the floor. Jamie pushed the covers aside and slid down beside her. "How did you know Dad was the one?"

"The first kiss pretty much cinched the deal," Elizabeth said, remembering. "When your dad kissed me the first time, I cried."

"Why?"

"I guess that's what you do when you're falling and there's no way to land safely. Love is dangerous territory."

Jamie looked at her mother. "Can I tell you a secret?"

"Always."

"I don't really want to quit swimming. I just wanted Dad's attention. Not that I got it."

"He's a little crazy right now. Be patient with him. It's a big deal to have a dream come true in the middle of your life."

"I know. I just want things to be easier, I guess."

"Life isn't supposed to be easy, Jamie. Who cares if you never swim in the Olympics? What matters is knowing you tried."

"So you'd still be proud of me if I stayed on the swim team but never won a race?"

"You're fishing for compliments now."

Jamie gave Elizabeth a kiss on the cheek, then climbed up into bed. "G'night, Mom. I love you."

"I love you, too," Elizabeth said, standing up. She flicked off the light and went downstairs.

Jack had built a fire. It crackled loudly and sent spiraling, dancing gold light across the rug. He looked acutely uncomfortable.

Elizabeth sat down on the sofa, close but not too close.

For a long time neither spoke. Finally she said, "I used to remind you guys endlessly about my birthday."

"We know." He laughed, then seemed to relax, as if he'd been afraid of what she'd say.

"I always thought you'd forget. Why did I think that, Jack? Why did I assume I was so unimportant?"

He faced her. There was a sadness in his eyes that she hadn't often seen. "Because I would have forgotten. Not every year, but at some point. Not because I didn't care, but because I never had to think for myself. You always did it for me. You were my backbone; you kept me standing." He sighed. "And I took you for granted."

Elizabeth knew he wouldn't have thought that—let alone said it—a few months ago. "I guess we're both learning a few things about ourselves lately."

"I'm not the father I thought I was." He looked surprised by his own admission. "Without you, the girls and I have nothing to talk about. They think I'm an idiot."

This was a new side to Jack, vulnerable. It changed him somehow, shifted the balance of power between them. "They're nineteen and twenty, Jack. They think anyone who remembers Kennedy should be in a nursing home. I used to treat Anita the same way."

Minutes ticked past before he spoke again. "We're going to have to tell them, aren't we?"

She almost touched him then, but something held her back. Fear, maybe. If she touched him now, when her heart was swollen and tender, it might begin again, and she wasn't ready for that. This journey of hers wasn't finished yet. "Yes," she said. "We won't mention divorce, just separation."

He smiled, but it was bleak and bitter. "We can call it anything we want. Hell, call it a vacation, but they're not stupid."

She wasn't quite sure why, but the way he said it made her want to cry. "We haven't made a decision about the future, Jack. We're just taking a break. That's all. There's still a chance for us," she said fiercely.

He touched her face gently, as if she were spun from glass that he'd broken long ago. "I want to believe that."

"Me, too."

TEN

It was late Saturday afternoon when everything fell apart.

Jamie was sitting cross-legged on the floor by the fire. Her small, pointed chin was jutted out in the bulldog expression that meant trouble. "Okay, you guys, spill it," she said. "Steph and

I aren't idiots. We know something is going on between you two."

Stephanie, in the rocking chair in the corner of the room, paled visibly. "Leave me out of it," she said.

Elizabeth, who was sitting on the sofa next to Jack, didn't answer. Obviously she was leaving it up to him.

He gazed at his beloved daughters. The thought of telling them, of actually speaking the toxic words aloud, made him almost sick to his stomach. He couldn't do it. They would always remember that it was his voice that had torn their family apart.

"So?" Jamie demanded again.

He was so deer-in-the-headlights frozen that he didn't notice when Elizabeth got up and walked around the sofa.

She was behind him now. She squeezed his shoulder, and the gentleness of her touch hurt more than any punch. "I know you guys sense that something is not normal with Dad and me," she said. Her voice was surprisingly calm. "The truth is, we've separated."

Stephanie's mouth dropped open. "Oh, my *God*."

"I know this is difficult to hear," Elizabeth said quickly. "But we'll be okay. We'll always be a family, no matter what."

"Oh, this is great. We'll *always* be a family. What a crock." Jamie shot to her feet. The color had faded from her cheeks, and Jack could see that she was close to tears.

Elizabeth's hold on Jack's shoulder tightened. It occurred to him to reach up, to lay his hand on hers, but he was paralyzed by what was unfolding. He could barely breathe.

"Honey, let us explain," Elizabeth said evenly. "Your dad and I were so young when we got married."

Stephanie's head shot up. "That's your reason? Because you got married too young?" She burst into tears.

This was ripping Jack's heart out. He glanced up at Birdie. She gazed down at him. And then her beautiful face crumpled.

Jack didn't think. He got up and pulled her into his arms on the sofa. "We'll get through this," he whispered against her wet cheek.

He had never loved her more than he did right then. She'd been stronger in this than he could have been, and now he saw the cost of that strength. He looked at his daughters and knew he'd never forget this moment. *This* was the price for every bad choice he'd ever made. And of all his poor choices, none had been worse than not loving Birdie enough to fight for their marriage.

"This is hard on all of us," he said. "But we love you guys. And we love each other. For now, that's all we know. You can either help us through this or you can be angry and shut us out. But we need you now—both of us do. We need to be a family."

That took the wind out of Jamie's sail. The anger seemed to seep out of her. Without it, she crumpled to her knees.

Elizabeth slid to the floor beside her. "My girls," she whispered.

Jamie and Stephanie launched themselves at her. The three of them clung together, crying.

Jack stared down at them longingly. He wanted to join them, but he couldn't move. They'd always been a trio first, a family second.

It was Jamie who looked up at him first. "Daddy," was all she said, reaching out.

Elizabeth reached behind her, felt around for Jack's hand. When she found it, she squeezed hard.

He slid to his knees off the sofa and took them all in his arms.

Elizabeth felt as if she'd just gone two rounds with Evander Holyfield. She sat in the porch swing, gliding back and forth. A full moon hung above the ocean, its light a silver beacon across the waves. The last four hours had been the worst time of her life.

They'd all sat together, alternately weeping and shouting. Jamie had vacillated between fury and despair; Stephanie had been silent, refusing to accept that her parents might not get back together.

Now, finally, the girls had gone to sleep.

She heard the screen door open and bang shut. Jack stepped onto the porch. With a sigh he slumped down onto the swing beside her.

"I don't know how you had the guts to tell them," he said. "When they started crying . . . It was awful."

"It's my fault," she said. "I refused to go to New York. I wrote that letter. I had to be the one to tell them."

"We both know better, Birdie. This is a thing we did together."

It meant so much to her, those few and precious words. He'd shouldered part of her guilt. "I still love you," she said, turning to face him. "Until tonight I'd forgotten that."

He looked at her steadily. "For years I asked you what was wrong. You never really answered, did you?"

"You don't know what it's like to disappear, Jack. How could you? You've always been so sure of yourself."

"Are you kidding, Birdie? I went from all-star to nobody."

"That's different. I'm talking about who you are inside. Not what your job is."

"You never understood," he said. "For a man, what you do is who you are. When I lost football, I lost myself."

"You never told me that."

"How could I? I was ashamed, and I knew what it had been like for you as a player's wife."

He was right. She'd grown to hate his football years; the better he did in the sport, the farther he moved from the family.

"I'm sorry, Jack."

"Don't say that. We've wasted too many years on that."

"Not wasted," she said softly. "We did okay, Jack. We built a home, created two beautiful, loving young women." She managed a smile. "Not too bad for a couple of kids who ran off to get married in the last semester of college."

He stood up and offered her his hand. "You're something special, you know that?"

He'd never said that to her before. The simple compliment meant more to her than she'd thought possible. "You, too."

"Well. Good night, Birdie."

"Good night."

She went to her bedroom alone.

The next morning, Jack, Stephanie, and Jamie flew east.

THE make-believe spring lasted until the end of March. Then the rains returned with a vengeance. Each day, Elizabeth walked to the mailbox in her raincoat and knee-high boots. Time and again she returned empty-handed. Twice in the past weeks Stephanie had written. Short letters containing burning, unanswerable questions. Who stopped loving whom? Were you lying to us all those years? Do you want a divorce?

Jamie hadn't written at all. Nor had she returned any of the phone messages Elizabeth left on their machine.

Elizabeth had always been so close to her daughters. This new distance—and their hurt and anger—was almost unbearable.

"It would have been better to go back to Jack," she said to Anita for at least the hundredth time since the birthday party weekend. "Everyone would be happier." She stepped back from her painting, frowned, then added a streak of purple to the sunset. It was the painting she'd begun when Anita first arrived. She'd finished four of the pieces for the Stormy Weather Arts Festival, but the rain had forced her inside, so she'd turned her attention back to the portrait.

At the kitchen table, Anita sat knitting. She barely looked up. "I don't suppose everyone would be happier."

"Everyone *else*, then," Elizabeth said. "Okay. That's it. I'm done."

"Can I finally see it?" Anita asked.

Elizabeth nodded, suddenly nervous. She stepped aside and let her stepmother stand directly in front of the easel.

Anita stood there forever, saying nothing. In the painting she looked frail and ethereal yet somehow powerful. There was the barest sadness in her gray eyes, though a hint of a smile curved her lips.

"I was never this beautiful," she finally said in a throaty voice.

"Yes, you are."

"Lordy, I wish your daddy could see this. He'd put it up on the wall and make sure everyone saw it. 'Come on in,' he'd say to our guests. 'See what my little girl did.' " Anita finally turned to Elizabeth. "I guess now it'll be me sayin' that."

Elizabeth was a wreck. The Stormy Weather Arts Festival started in less than an hour, and she—fool that she was—had agreed to show her paintings to the world. She couldn't remember when she'd been this scared.

"Was I drunk?" she muttered to herself, changing her clothes for the third time. The decision of what to wear was simply too big.

She finally put on an ankle-length black knit dress and went downstairs.

Anita was already there, standing by the front door. "How are you doing?" she asked.

"Terrible. I'd rather pull out my own toenails than go to the gallery today. Maybe I won't go. What if I throw up?"

Anita came forward, grabbed her by the shoulders. "Breathe."

Elizabeth did as she was told and relaxed a little.

"We're all afraid," Anita said. "It's the going on that matters."

"Thanks," Elizabeth said, pulling her stepmother into a hug.

When she drew back, Anita said, "We'd better get going. We don't want to be late."

Echo Beach was dressed for a party. Banners and balloons were everywhere. The weather was surprisingly good—steel-gray clouds and cold breezes, but no rain.

Elizabeth stood on the sidewalk outside Eclectica. A sign filled the window. It read MEET LOCAL ARTIST ELIZABETH SHORE.

Anita said, "Good luck, honey," and shoved her into the gallery.

The members of the Women's Passion Support Group were waiting inside. At Elizabeth's entrance they burst into applause.

She stumbled to a halt. "Hey, you guys," she said, hating the tremor in her voice. "It was nice of you to come."

Everyone began talking at once. "Your work is incredible!" "Amazing! When did you start painting?" "Where did you learn?"

She couldn't answer any single question, but it didn't matter. Their enthusiasm was the balm she needed to calm her ragged nerves. She relaxed enough to be hopeful. She even allowed herself to dream of success, a wonderful review, a sellout of her work.

"Elizabeth." Marge came forward, holding a bouquet of roses. "These are for you."

"Oh, you didn't have to do that."

Marge grinned. "I didn't." She handed Elizabeth the flowers.

The card read, "We're mad, but we still love you. Good luck. Jamie and Stephanie. P.S. We're proud of you."

Proud of you. The words blurred before her eyes.

Anita moved closer. "I told them. I hope you don't mind."

"I don't mind," Elizabeth whispered. "Thank you, Anita."

Her stepmother touched her arm. "Everything's going to be fine."

By ten o'clock the streets were packed with tourists and locals. A band played oldies in the parking lot of the Windermere Realty office, and every store was crowded with shoppers.

Out-of-towners bought ice-cream cones and kites, sweatshirts and place mats. They bought wind chimes made of old spoons and watercolors of the shore. What they didn't buy was Elizabeth's work.

Marge stood at the cash register, ka-chinging up sales. As the day dragged on, the walls around Elizabeth's work cleared out.

One by one the members of the Women's Passion Support Group left. But Anita stayed; she sat on a stool in the corner, ostensibly knitting, but Elizabeth knew that her stepmother was really watching her, waiting for signs of meltdown.

The bell above the door tinkled. Elizabeth steeled herself to smile at someone else who wouldn't want her work.

Daniel stood there, filling the doorway. Sunlight gilded his blond hair. "How's it going?" he asked.

"Not good. Actually, that's an overstatement."

He walked past her, stood in front of her work. Then he turned to her. "These are beautiful. You really have a remarkable talent."

"Yeah. I know." She was an eyelash away from losing it. Before he could see how weakened she was, she rushed out of the store.

He followed her out. "How about a latte?"

"Great."

They strolled down the busy street together. At the ice-cream shop, he bought two chocolate-chip cones and two lattes. Then they went onto the promenade and sat down on a cement bench.

"You have nothing to be ashamed of," he said.

"I know." Her agreement sounded hollow, even to her own ears. "It's more of a free-form depression."

"Did you think it would be easy?"

"I thought *something* would sell."

He touched her cheek. "Does that matter so much?"

"No, but—" The tears she'd been swallowing all day burst out.

Daniel took her in his arms. He stroked her hair and let her cry. Finally she drew back, hiccuping, feeling like a fool. "I'm sorry. It's just been an awful day."

"Don't give up, Birdie. You have talent. I knew that the first time I saw you paint. I think maybe you've given up too easily before."

She realized suddenly that she was in his arms, that he was holding her tightly. Slowly she looked up.

He took her face in his hands, wiped the tears with his thumbs. "It took guts to show your work today. There's nothing worse than standing naked in public and saying, Here I am."

She stared at his mouth. All she heard was "naked."

"You should be proud of yourself, Elizabeth. Anything else

would be a crime." He leaned toward her. She saw the kiss coming and braced for it. Her heart raced.

His lips pressed against hers. He tasted of coffee. She slid her arms up around his neck and pulled him closer.

And . . . nothing. No Fourth of July, no fireworks.

When he drew back, he was frowning. "No good, huh?"

Elizabeth was surprised. "I guess I'm more married than I thought."

"Too bad." He stood up and pulled her to her feet. Then he held on to her hand and led her across the street. They cut through the crowd, threaded their way toward the gallery.

Elizabeth realized a second too late where he was taking her. She tried to stop. "Come on, Daniel. It's a death by hanging in there."

"Then put your neck in the noose; it's what artists do." He smiled down at her. "I expect big things of you, Elizabeth Shore. Now get in there where you belong."

Marge smiled at her entrance, obviously relieved to see her. "I'm glad you came back."

"I didn't want to." When she glanced at the door, she saw that Daniel was gone. "Chicken," she muttered.

"It's always difficult on the artist. I should have warned you."

"Difficult?" Elizabeth said. "Difficult is making hollandaise sauce. This is a near-death experience."

Elizabeth hung around for a while, watching tourists mill through the gallery. Finally she couldn't take it anymore. The last thing she saw as she and Anita left was the wall filled with her work.

Jack stood at his office window staring out at the beautiful spring day. This ought to be the best day of his life. Twenty-four hours ago they'd offered him the best job in broadcasting: *NFL Sunday.*

He'd been dreaming of a moment like this for years, and yet now that it was here, he felt curiously numb.

The door to his office cracked open. "There you are," Warren said. "I just heard the news about your photo shoot. *People* magazine, huh? Pretty hot stuff."

"I'll probably be the oldest guy in the issue."

Warren frowned. "That's it. There's something wrong with you. Let's go."

Jack grabbed his coat and followed Warren out of the building. By tacit consent they went straight to Kel's pub on the corner and headed for the back booth.

"Double bourbon on the rocks," Warren said when the barmaid appeared.

She looked at Jack.

"Club soda with lime."

"Now I *know* something's wrong," Warren said. "A club soda?"

"I've been drinking pretty hard lately. It blurs the lines." He paused, then said, "Fox just offered me *NFL Sunday*."

Warren sat back. "Most guys would kill for that job, Jack. Here you are, slurping club soda and practically crying. What gives?"

It wasn't Jack's way to talk about stuff like this, but the loneliness was killing him. And if there was anyone who ought to understand marital problems, it was the thrice-married Warren. "We told the girls about the separation."

"Ouch. How'd they take it?"

"Badly. They cried and screamed. Then they went back to school. I've been getting the silent treatment ever since."

"It'll pass. They'll come to accept their new family after a while. Trust me."

There it was—the source of his sleepless nights. *New family.* "What if I can't accept it, either?"

"What do you mean?"

"I miss Birdie." There, he'd said it.

"You made a bad trade, Jacko. You thought the heat of all this was real, but at the end of the day, all that matters is finding a woman who loves the real you." He looked at Jack. "You never should have let Birdie go."

"She left me."

"Birdie left you?"

"The marriage went to hell slowly. I'm not even sure when. I think it started with me, though, when I lost football. All I could think about was what I'd lost. I married so young; I never got to be the young hotshot of my imagination." He sighed. "For years I dreamed about going back in time and making a different choice. I was desperate to be *someone* again. Then this job came along, and I got it all back." He smiled bitterly. "I'm free, rich, and famous. I can do anything I want. Hell, I'm sleeping with a beautiful woman half my age, and she doesn't care that I don't love her. It's what I always dreamed of. And I hate it. I miss Birdie all the time."

"Have you told her?"

Jack looked up. "What if she doesn't love me anymore?"

Warren sipped his drink. "Then you aren't gonna have a movie ending, my friend. Sometimes a bad choice can haunt you forever."

THE drive home from the gallery seemed to take forever. Elizabeth had failed. The realization was like a canker sore; no matter how much it hurt, you couldn't leave it alone.

She felt Anita looking worriedly at her from the passenger seat, but fortunately, her stepmother kept her opinions to herself. This was not the time for one of those pumped-up pep talks.

When Elizabeth had parked the car, she turned to Anita and forced a tired smile. "Thanks for everything today. It meant a lot to me that you were there."

Anita looked stricken. "Birdie, I don't know what to say."

"Don't say anything. Please. It was bad enough to live through. I can't talk about it, too."

Anita nodded. "I'll go cook us a nice dinner."

"I'm not very hungry. I think I'll soak in a hot bath." Suddenly she felt the first hairline crack in her composure. If she wasn't careful, she'd break like old porcelain, and that wouldn't help anyone. She opened the car door, then hurried into her beloved house.

Upstairs, she ran a bath and poured a capful of almond-scented oil into the water. She let the tub fill, undressed, and lowered herself into the hot water. She leaned her head back and closed her eyes.

Images of the endless day tumbled through her mind. The worst of it was that she'd believed in herself. She'd known better, and yet still she'd stumbled into that quicksand and been caught.

She'd believed. She'd dared. She'd dreamed. And she'd failed.

Her work wasn't good enough. That much was clear.

What now?

She stayed in the bath until the water turned cold and her skin pruned. Then, wrapped in a towel, she flopped onto her bed.

She saw the phone, and she thought, Call Jack.

She wasn't sure why exactly, except that he had always been her safe place. She picked up the receiver and punched in his number. Bits of conversation flitted through her mind as it rang. She searched for the perfect first sentence.

I love you. Nice and direct.

I miss you. Certainly true.

I need you. The God's honest truth.

But the answering machine clicked on. She hung up, then dialed her daughters' number.

Another answering machine. She left a forcibly upbeat message and a thank-you for the flowers, then hung up.

There was a knock at her door. "Birdie, honey? Dinner's ready."

"I can't eat. Sorry. But thanks for cooking. I'll see you in the morning." She heard footsteps walking away . . . then coming back.

The door opened. Anita stood there clutching a flat black metal strongbox. She patted it. "This belonged to your mama. If you want to see what's inside, you'd better come downstairs." Then she turned and walked away.

Elizabeth didn't want to follow, but Anita had dangled the biggest carrot of all. Mama.

With a sigh she rolled off the bed and got dressed.

Downstairs, she took a seat on the sofa beside Anita. The metal box was on the coffee table now, waiting.

Elizabeth stared at it. She imagined a journal of precious memories. Photographs. Mementos. She turned to her stepmother.

"I brought this with me," Anita said. "I knew I'd know if the time was right to open it." She tried to smile, but the transparent falsity of it only underscored her nervousness. "Your daddy loved you. More than anything on this earth."

"I know that."

Anita reached for the box, and Elizabeth noticed that her fingers were shaking as she handed it over.

Inside, there was a rubber-banded pile of scallop-edged photographs and a long cardboard tube.

Anita withdrew the pictures first. There on the top of the heap was Mama. She was sitting on a porch swing, wearing pink pants and a blouse with small capped sleeves and a Peter Pan collar.

She was laughing. Not smiling, not posing. Laughing. She looked marvelously, wonderfully alive.

"She's beautiful," Elizabeth said.

"Yes."

The next picture was of a different woman. Someone with intense, flashing eyes and curly black hair. She looked like an Italian peasant—the opposite of her delicate, aristocratic mother.

All the remaining pictures were of the other woman. At the beach, on a white-painted porch, at a county fair.

Elizabeth frowned in disappointment.

At last she picked up the cardboard tube, uncapped it. Inside was a rolled-up canvas. She eased it out and spread it on the coffee table. It was an exquisite painting of the dark-haired woman, done in vibrant acrylics. She was reclining on a mound of red pillows, with her black hair artlessly arranged around her. Except for a pale pink shawl that was draped across her ample hips, she was nude.

There was a sadness to the work. The woman's black eyes were filled with a desperate longing. As if, perhaps, she were looking at a lover who'd already begun to leave her.

Elizabeth glanced at the signature. Marguerite Rhodes.

Time seemed to slow down. She could hear the thudding of her own heart. "Mama was an artist?"

"Yes."

There it was, after all these years, the link between them. Elizabeth looked up. "Why didn't Daddy tell me?"

"That's the only painting there is."

"So? He knew I dreamed of being a painter. He had to know what this would have meant to me."

Anita looked terribly sad. "Remember when I told you that your mother had run away from Edward? That was in 1955."

Elizabeth noticed the date on the painting: 1955.

Anita sighed heavily. "The world was different then. Not as open and accepting of . . . things as we are now."

Elizabeth looked at the painting again. This time she saw the passion in it. And she understood the secret that had been withheld from her all these years. "Mama fell in love with this woman," she said.

"Her name was Missy Esteban. And yes, she was your mother's lover."

Elizabeth leaned back in her seat. Dozens of vague childhood memories made sense suddenly. "That's why Mama was depressed," Elizabeth said aloud. Her whole life seemed to settle into place, a puzzle with all the pieces finally where they belonged. "That's why Daddy wouldn't talk about her. He was ashamed."

"To have his wife run away was one thing. He could handle that because she came back. But when he found out that she'd fallen in love out there—and with a woman—well, there was no handlin' that for Edward. So he shut it up tighter than a drum. Pretended it had never happened."

"How did you find out?"

"Your daddy got liquored up one night and spilled the beans."

"But why don't I have any memories of Mama? She didn't die until I was six."

"She loved you, Birdie, somethin' fierce, but she was broken inside. Lost. She couldn't care for you. She would hold you close one day and then ignore you for weeks at a time. Course, she was on serious medications. Back then a woman who did a thing like that was crazy. Good girls just didn't have sex with other women." Anita reached out, touched Elizabeth's hand. "Your mama found what she wanted in life, but she turned away from it. She walked away from her love and her talent. And it killed her. I know you, Birdie. You were up in your bedroom thinking of quitting, telling yourself you were a fool to think you had talent."

Elizabeth felt transparent suddenly.

"Don't you dare give up on Elizabeth Shore," Anita continued. "You've come too far and worked too hard to go back to your old life because you're scared. If you give up, you'll be making the same mistake as your mama. It might not kill you, but it'll break you, Birdie."

Elizabeth closed her eyes. She wanted to deny it, but there was no point. She managed an uneven smile. "You're something else," she said softly. "All these years I thought I had no mother. I was wrong, wasn't I? I had two. I love you, Anita."

Anita's mouth trembled. "Your daddy always told me you'd figure that out someday."

In the hotel ballroom, waiting for his turn to speak, Jack couldn't think about anything except Birdie. Every time he tried to consider his great new job offer or the upcoming *People* magazine shoot, he wanted to pick up the phone and call his wife.

That was the thing about sobriety. It cleared the mind, left everything standing in a bright, true light.

Since his conversation with Warren, that light had been particularly unflinching. He saw the whole of his life.

Every day had been a search for more. Nothing had ever been enough. Not even Birdie. He could admit that now.

Because of the man he'd been, he was alone now. A husband estranged from his wife, a father estranged from his daughters. No responsibilities beyond the ones he chose.

But freedom wasn't what he'd thought.

The affair with Sally was hot. The sex was great—physically satisfying anyway—and afterward was perfect. She got dressed and left for her own apartment. No scenes about staying over, no pretense about love. No sharing, no laughter, no warmth.

Warren had been right. Jack had made a bad trade. True warmth for false heat. The dream wasn't full. It was frighteningly empty.

"Jack?" Sally tapped his elbow.

He came stumbling out of his thoughts. The audience was clapping. A quick look at Sally told him he'd missed his introduction.

He got to his feet and threaded his way through the crowded ballroom of the hotel. He stepped up to the microphone and gave the same speech he'd given at least a dozen times in the past few months. A plea for athletic accountability and good sportsmanship.

The local chapter of the Boys and Girls Clubs of America applauded wildly when he was done. Then he spent the next hour posing for photographs, answering questions.

Sally came up beside him. "Can we talk?" she asked. Then, without waiting for an answer, she took his arm and led him out of the ballroom and down to a quiet corner table in the bar. "I'm confused." She kept her voice lowered, pausing only long enough to order a glass of white wine.

"Why are you confused?" He knew, of course.

"You've been avoiding me all week. I don't put any pressure on you, do I? I know you're married. So what's wrong?"

In the dim light she seemed impossibly young. "For the last fifteen years—until you—I was completely faithful to my wife.

But I counted and remembered every woman I'd denied myself. I was so proud of every woman I didn't sleep with. I thought, Good for you, Jacko, you're strong as steel. Every night I went home and crawled into bed with my wife and told her I loved her. I meant it, too."

"What does this have to do with me?"

The decision that had been rolling obliquely toward him was suddenly crystal clear. "I don't want to be that guy anymore. I don't want to be sleeping with a woman simply because I can."

"That's a rotten thing to say. I know we aren't head over heels in love, but I thought we were friends."

"Come on, Sally. Friends talk. Get to know each other. They don't crawl into bed together and wake up alone."

"You never wanted to wake up with me." Hurt crept into her eyes.

"I'm still in love with my wife," he said gently. "I didn't know how much until I lost her."

Sally looked at him. "Are you saying it's over between us?"

"You deserve more than I can give you." He saw how hard she was trying to appear calm, but her lips were trembling. She thought she loved him; that had never occurred to him before. How had he been so blind? He reached out, covered her hand with his. "I'm not the one, Sally. Believe me." He remembered the first time he kissed Elizabeth, how she'd cried. "When it's right, you know it."

Sally sighed. "You know what the worst thing about that confession is? It only makes you more attractive. What about my job?"

"Tom thinks you'd make a great associate producer."

"Great. I've become one of those women who sleep their way up the ladder." She downed the rest of her wine. "I'm outta here. A girl's self-esteem can only take so much honesty. Bye, Jack."

He watched her walk away, afraid of what he'd feel. In the old days it would have been regret.

It was relief.

He paid for the drinks and went outside. As he reached the street, rain hit him in the face and made him think of Oregon. Of home.

He knew where he wanted to be right now, and it wasn't in his empty apartment, surrounded by too many regrets. Once, he'd imagined that the opportunities in a man's life were endless; now he saw how easy it was to make a wrong turn and lose everything. There wasn't always time to make amends.

For the first time in years, he prayed. Please, God, don't let it be too late.

ELEVEN

ELIZABETH sat on her favorite beach rock staring out at the view that owned such a piece of her heart. She was alone out here today. There were no seals lazing on the rocks along the shoreline, no birds diving down into the water. Waves washed forward, a foamy white line that pushed her back, back.

All last night she'd tossed and turned in bed. She'd thought of so many things. Her mother and the terrible price she paid for love. Her daddy, her children, her marriage, her art.

For the first time, perhaps, she saw the big picture. She loved Jack with all her heart. Her biggest failure had been an inability to love herself as well as she'd loved her family.

Then she'd finally taken the wheel and changed her course. She'd put her needs first and left Jack and dared to dream her own dream. She'd worked hard for it, painted until her fingers cramped up and her back ached.

But at the first bump in the road, she'd crumpled, pure and simple. One little setback and she'd folded into the old Birdie. She'd considered quitting. As if the point of art could be found in supply-and-demand economics. That pissed her off.

She stood up, walked forward. The tide tried to stop her. Icy water slid inside her rubber gardening clogs, dampened the hem of her pants. But nothing could push her back anymore. She'd never quit painting again. Even if no one ever liked her work. It would be enough that she did.

She ran forward suddenly, splashed into the freezing cold surf. It wasn't until the very last moment, when the water hit her full in the face, that she realized she wasn't going to turn around.

She dove headfirst into the next wave—something she'd never had the courage to do before. She came up on the other side, where the water was calm.

Life, she realized, was like this wave. Sometimes you had to dive into trouble to come out on the other side. That was what she'd learned at her failed art show—perspective. She needed to work harder, study more. Nothing in life came easily; it was time she said okay to that.

A wave scooped her up and sent her tumbling toward the beach. She landed spread-eagled on the shore and burst out laughing.

WHEN Elizabeth came home, wet and freezing cold, the house smelled heavenly—of vanilla, cinnamon, and freshly brewed coffee.

"Breakfast smells great," she said, shivering.

Anita was at the stove. "What happened to you?"

Elizabeth grinned. "I started over. Again."

Anita smiled back. "Well, start for the stairs and change your clothes. I'm starving."

Elizabeth ran upstairs, dried off, and changed into a pair of fleece sweats. By the time she got to the kitchen, Anita had already dished up French toast and strawberries and was sitting at her place.

Half of Anita's toast was missing. "I waited for you like one pig waits for another," she said.

Elizabeth laughed and sat down. "Daddy used to say that."

"I dreamed about him last night."

"Really? What was he doing?"

"Sitting in that white wicker rocking chair on the porch, smokin' one of his cigars. I sat down at his feet, and he squeezed my neck just like he'd done a million times. 'Mother,' he said, 'it's time.' "

Elizabeth could picture it—picture him—perfectly. She took a bite of her French toast. "So what did he mean?"

"I think he was talkin' about me. It's time for me to go home," Anita answered gently. "I've been hiding here long enough."

Elizabeth set down her fork. She was surprised at how much she wanted Anita to stay. "Are you sure you're ready?"

"I left Sweetwater because I couldn't stand to be so alone. But now I have you."

"Yes," Elizabeth answered slowly, "you do."

"Will you be okay alone?"

"Yes. But I'll miss you."

"Do you love Jack?" Anita asked suddenly.

Elizabeth would have thought she'd need to think about that, but the answer came immediately. "Yes."

Anita smiled broadly. "Well, honey, let me say this. True love is a rare thing. We lean on it for years without botherin' to look at what's holdin' us up. It lasts forever, as the poets say, but life doesn't. One minute you're in bed with your husband, and the next second you're alone. You'd best think about that."

Elizabeth knew that her stepmother was right. In her months away from Jack she'd been waiting for her new life to unfold in a line that was straight and true. No hairpin turns, no sudden drop-offs.

She'd wanted certainty. But life wasn't like that.

I love you. Those were the words that mattered.

She loved Jack. Needed him, though not in the desperate, frightened way of before. She could live without him. She knew that now. Maybe when all was said and done, that was the truth she'd gone in search of.

She could make her way alone in the world, but when she stared out over the rest of her life, she wanted him beside her. Whatever else she would search for in life, he would always be at the center of it. The place she came home to.

Anita was watching her closely.

"I'll miss you," Elizabeth said again, feeling her throat tighten.

"The planes fly east, you know." Anita took a bite of French toast. "Now, about your painting. You won't give up, will you?"

Elizabeth smiled. "Because of one little old failure? No. I won't give up. That's a promise."

Years ago, when Jack's life had been falling apart the first time, he'd been called on the carpet by his network boss. He'd begged for a second chance, but it hadn't worked.

He'd been young then, still swollen by his own importance. Begging had felt unnatural; it wasn't surprising that he'd done it poorly.

Now, all these years—and losses—later, he knew better. Some things, once lost, were worth dropping to your knees for.

He sat in his rental car thinking about all the mistakes he'd made in his life. Of this extensive list of wrongs, nothing had been as bad as taking his family for granted.

He got out of the car. The Washington, D.C., weather was bitingly cold. The promise of spring felt distant today, even though the winter air was thick with tiny pink cherry blossoms.

As he walked up the concrete steps toward the building, he realized that it was the first time he'd been here. *Shameful, Jack.*

He pushed through the double glass door and stepped into the chlorine-scented humidity. The familiar scent reminded him of all the hours he'd spent sitting on bleachers cheering Jamie on.

At the front desk, a green-haired kid sat in front of a computer screen. "Are the ECAC championships here today?" Jack asked.

"They're almost over," the kid said. "Go through the men's locker room. Take the first door on your left."

"Thanks." Jack took off his suede coat and slung it over his shoulder as he walked through the busy locker room. He emerged into the hot, damp world of an indoor pool.

Along the back wall, dozens of women in Speedo bathing suits stood clustered together. Jack eased his way up the bleachers and sat down. His gaze narrowed as he studied the Georgetown team.

A sound blared. A row of swimmers dove into the pool and raced for the other side.

Suddenly the race was over. A new group of swimmers was walking toward the edge of the pool. There she was. His Jamie.

She stepped into place, stretched, then bent into position.

It was the 200 IM. Never her best event.

The horn blared, and the swimmers dove into the water.

Slowly Jack got to his feet.

Jamie was in second place at the first turn. By the second turn she'd fallen into fourth. But at the final turn she picked up speed. Her strokes were damned near perfect.

He moved down the bleachers, stepped onto the floor. "Come on, Jamie," he yelled, still moving.

She came in third, with a time of 2:33. If it wasn't her personal best, it was close. He'd never been so proud of her.

When she got out of the pool, her teammates crowded around her. Jack stood there waiting for her to notice him.

When she finally looked up, her smile faded. In that moment, across the crowded room, everything blurred and fell away. Only the two of them were left.

He was the first to move. He closed the distance between them, mentally preparing for her anger. "Hey, Jamie. Good race."

She jutted out her chin. "I came in third."

"You swam your heart out. I was proud of you."

"Why are you here? Business in town?"

"I came to watch you swim."

"It's been a long time," she said.

"Too long."

"Well. Thanks for coming." She turned and walked away.

For a minute he was so shocked he just stood there. Then he called out, "Wait!"

She stopped but didn't turn around.

He came up behind her. "Forgive me," he whispered. "I spent too much time looking at my own life."

"Forgive you?"

His voice fell to a whisper. "Remember when you had that bad start at the state meet when you were a junior in high school? I took you aside and told you you'd had your stance wrong." He stared at her back. "I should have hugged you and told you it didn't matter. What you do is nothing compared to who you are. It took me too long to figure that out. I'm sorry, Jamie. I let you down."

She turned. Her eyes were moist. "What about you and Mom?"

"I don't know."

"Do you still love her?"

"I'll always love her. Just like I'll always love you and Stephanie. We're a *family*." He said the word gently, with a newfound reverence. "I don't know what's going to happen with me and your mom, but I know this. You're my heart, Jaybird. Always."

She looked at him then, her eyes watery with tears that didn't fall. "I love you, Daddy."

He pulled her into his arms.

By the time Elizabeth returned to the house from the airport, it was almost completely dark outside. When she opened the door and went inside, she opened her mouth to call out for Anita, but Anita was on an airplane, flying east.

She took a deep breath and went up to her bedroom, where

the papers Meghann had sent her were stacked neatly beside her bed. She picked them up, stared down at the letterheads. N.Y.U, Columbia University, S.U.N.Y. All New York schools. Near Jack.

Pretty subtle, Meg.

She tucked the papers under her arm, then grabbed a yellow legal pad and a pen. Downstairs, she took a seat at the kitchen table and began filling out the forms. When she'd finished, she went to the phone and called Meghann.

"Hey, Meg," she said without preamble, "I need you to write a letter of recommendation for me. I'm applying to grad school."

Meg screamed into the phone. "Oh, Birdie! I'm so proud of you!"

Elizabeth hung up, then called Daniel, who had the same reaction. She gave him the names and addresses of the schools.

She would have to photograph her work so she'd have slides to put in a portfolio to be included with the applications. She'd also have to write her admission essay. Three hundred words on why they should let a forty-six-year-old woman into graduate school.

She poured herself a glass of wine and returned to the kitchen table. She opened the yellow pad and began to write.

Right off the bat I should tell you that I'm forty-six years old. I'm sure your school will be inundated with applications from twenty-one-year-old students with stellar talents. Honestly, I don't see how my record can compete with theirs.

Unless dreams matter. To the young, a dream is simply a goal to reach for, a prize to win. For a woman like me, who has spent half a lifetime facilitating other people's aspirations, it has a whole different meaning.

Once, years ago, I was told that I had talent. It seemed an insubstantial thing, something that had traveled in my DNA. I didn't see then—as of course I do now—that such a thing is a gift. I let it pass me by. I got married, had children, and put aside thoughts of who I'd once wanted to be.

Life goes by so quickly. One minute you're twenty and filled with fire; the next you're forty-six and tired. But if you're very lucky, a single moment can change everything.

That's what happened to me this year. I wakened. I opened my eyes and dared to look around. What I saw was a woman who'd forgotten how it felt to paint.

Now I remember. I have spent the last few months studying

again, pouring my heart and soul onto canvas and have found—miraculously—that my talent survived. Certainly it is weaker, but I am stronger. My vision is clearer.

And so I am entreating you to give me a chance, to make a place for me in your classroom next fall. I cannot guarantee that I'll become famous or exceptional. I can, however, promise that I will give everything to the pursuit of excellence.

I will not stop trying.

JACK maneuvered his rental car down Stormwatch Lane. It was full-on night now, dark as pitch, as he pulled into the carport.

The house glowed with golden light as he went to the front door and knocked. There was no answer, so he let himself in.

She was in the living room, dancing all by herself, wearing a long white T-shirt and fuzzy pink socks. She sang along with the record, *"I can see clearly now, the rain is gone."*

She turned suddenly and saw him. A bright smile lit up her face, and it was an arrow straight into his heart.

The whole of the living room stretched between them. There was so much he wanted to say. He'd practiced the words all the way across the country, but how much would she want to hear?

"You won't believe what I did tonight," she said, coming toward him, doing a little dance.

"What?" It threw him off-balance, seeing her so shiny and bright. She looked happier than he could ever remember. Maybe it was because she *liked* being away from him.

"I applied to grad school."

"Grad school?" He felt a rush of pride that immediately turned cold. "Where?"

"Oh, I thought I'd try . . . New York." She smiled up at him. "That's where my husband lives."

He could breathe again. "I'm proud of you, baby. I always knew you had talent." He paused. "They offered me the *NFL Sunday* show."

"That's great. When do you start?"

"I haven't given them an answer. I told them I needed to talk to my wife."

"You're kidding?"

He dared to reach for her. When he took her hand, she let him lead her to the sofa. He thought about all the words he'd come prepared to offer. *I love you, Birdie.* Those were the ones that mattered most of all. Somewhere along the course of two dozen years, the two of them had let that simple phrase erode into rote. Now he wanted to have it back. "I don't want to live without you anymore."

"You don't?" Her easy smile faded away. There was a new look in her eyes, something he didn't quite recognize. It frightened him a little, reminded him that she had changed.

"You're my center, Birdie. I never knew how much I loved you until you were gone."

She leaned forward and kissed him, whispering, "I missed you," against his lips. And just that easily he was home.

After the kiss he drew back. "This time it's *our* life, Birdie. I mean it. Nothing matters more than us. Nothing. That's why I didn't agree to take the job yet."

"Oh, Jack." She gently touched his face. "I've learned something about dreams. They don't come true every day. And love . . . love is stronger than I ever imagined. Take the job. We'll find a nice loft in Chelsea or TriBeCa. Somewhere I can paint."

They would make it this time, he knew it. After twenty-four years of marriage, they had finally found their way.

"Show me your work," he said.

Her face lit up. She grabbed his hand and pulled him to his feet. Hand in hand they walked through the kitchen. She darted into the pantry, then came out holding a huge painting.

She set it up against the cupboards and stood back. "You don't have to pretend you like it," she said nervously.

He was too stunned to say anything.

Her painting was a haunting stretch of coastline in winter, painted in grays and purples and blacks. In the distance a lone figure walked along the beach. It saddened him somehow, made him think about how fast life could pass a person by, how easy it was to walk past what mattered because you were busy looking into the future. "God, Birdie, it's amazing." He turned to her. "You were painting the first time we met, remember? There was a dock in your painting, and it looked lonely, too, like this beach. I remember wanting to tell you that the picture made me feel sad, but I didn't dare."

She tilted her chin up. "I can't believe you remember all that."

"I forgot it for a long time. But nothing felt right without you. My world went from color to black and white." He touched her face, felt the warmth of her skin. "You take my breath away, Birdie."

"I love you, Jack. I'll never forget that again."

This time when Jack kissed her, he was the one who cried.

THE letter came nearly six weeks later.

Dear Ms. Shore:

We are pleased to welcome you to Columbia University School of the Arts.

BETWEEN SISTERS

CHAPTER ONE

Dr. Bloom waited patiently for an answer.

Meghann Dontess leaned back in her seat and studied her fingernails. It was time for a manicure. "I try not to feel too much, Harriet. You know that. I find it impedes my enjoyment of life."

"Is that why you've seen me every week for four years? Because you enjoy your life so much?"

"I wouldn't point that out if I were you. It doesn't say much for your psychiatric skills. It's possible, you know, that I was perfectly normal when I met you and you're actually *making* me crazy."

"You're using humor as a shield again."

"You're giving me too much credit. That wasn't funny."

Harriet didn't smile. "Let's talk about the day you and Claire were separated."

Meghann shifted uncomfortably in her seat. She knew what Harriet was poking around for. "That subject is closed."

"It's interesting that you maintain a relationship with your mother while distancing yourself from your sister."

Meghann shrugged. "Mama's an actress. I'm a lawyer. We're comfortable with make-believe."

"Meaning?"

"Have you ever read one of her interviews? She tells everyone that we lived this poor, pathetic but loving existence. We pretend it's the truth."

"You were living in Bakersfield when the pathetic but loving pretense ended, right?"

Meghann remained silent.

Harriet went on. "Claire was nine years old, if I remember."

"Don't," Meghann said.

Harriet stared at her. "Don't back away. We're making progress."

"Any more progress, and I'll need an aid car. We should talk about my practice. That's why I come to you, you know. It's a pressure cooker down in family court these days. Yesterday I had a deadbeat dad drive up in a Ferrari and then swear he was flat broke. Didn't want to pay for his daughter's tuition."

"Why do you keep paying me if you don't want to discuss the root of your problems?"

"I was sixteen when all that happened. Now I'm a whopping forty-two. It's time to move on. It doesn't matter anymore."

"Then why do you still have the nightmare?"

Meghann should have seen that coming. She glanced down at her platinum-and-gold watch. "Too bad, Harriet. Time's up. I guess we'll have to solve my pesky neuroses next week." She stood up.

"Do you like your life, Meghann?" Harriet asked.

That wasn't what she'd expected. "What's not to like? I'm the best divorce attorney in the state. I live—"

"Alone."

"In a kick-ass condo above the Pike Place Public Market and drive a brand-new Porsche."

"Family?"

"My mom stayed with me for a week last year. If I'm lucky, she'll come back for another visit just in time to watch the colonization of Mars on MTV."

"And Claire?"

"My sister and I have problems, I'll admit it. But nothing major. We're just too busy to get together." When Harriet didn't speak, Meghann rushed to fill the silence. "Okay, she makes me crazy, the way she's throwing her life away. She's smart enough to do anything, but she stays tied to that loser campground they call a resort."

"With her father."

"I don't want to discuss my sister. And I *definitely* don't want to discuss her father."

Harriet tapped her pen on the table. "Okay, how about this: When was the last time you slept with the same man twice?"

"I like variety."

"The way you like younger men, right? Men who have no desire to settle down."

"I don't want a house with a picket fence in suburbia. I'm not interested in family life."

"And the loneliness, do you like that?"

"I'm not lonely," she said stubbornly. "I'm independent. Men don't like a strong woman."

"Strong men do. And strong women face their fears. They talk about the painful choices they've made in their lives."

Meghann actually flinched. "Sorry, Harriet, I need to scoot. See you next week."

She left the office.

Outside, it was a gloriously bright June day. Early in the so-called summer. Everywhere else in the country, people were swimming and barbecuing and organizing poolside picnics. Here, in good ole Seattle, people were methodically checking their calendars and muttering that it was June, damn it.

Only a few tourists were around this morning, out-of-towners recognizable by the umbrellas tucked under their arms. Meghann crossed the busy street and stepped up onto the grassy lawn of the waterfront park. In front of her the deep-blue Puget Sound stretched along the pale horizon. She wished she could take comfort from that view; often she could. But today her mind was caught in the net of another time and place.

If she closed her eyes—which she dared not do—she'd remember it all: the dialing of the telephone number, the stilted, desperate conversation with a man she didn't know, the long drive to that Podunk town up north. And worst of all, the tears she'd wiped from her little sister's flushed cheeks when she said, *I'm leaving you.*

Her fingers tightened around the railing. Dr. Bloom was wrong. Talking about Meghann's painful choice and the lonely years that had followed it wouldn't help.

Her past wasn't a collection of memories to be worked through; it was like an oversize Samsonite with a bum wheel. All Meghann could do was drag it along behind her.

CLAIRE CAVENAUGH STOOD ON the bank of the Skykomish River, her work boots almost ankle-deep in the soft brown mud. Beside her an out-of-gas Weed Eater lay on its side. She smiled, wiped a gloved hand across her sweaty brow. The amount of manual labor it took to get the resort ready for summer was unbelievable.

Resort.

That was what her dad called these sixteen acres. Sam Cavenaugh had come across this acreage almost forty years ago, back when Hayden had been nothing more than a gas-station stop on the rise up Stevens Pass. He'd bought the parcel for a song and settled into the decrepit farmhouse that came with it. He'd named his place River's Edge Resort and begun to dream of a life that didn't include hard hats and earplugs and night shifts at the paper plant in Everett.

At first he'd worked after hours and weekends. With a chain saw, a pickup truck, and a plan drawn out on a cocktail napkin, he began. He hacked out campsites and cleaned out a hundred years' worth of underbrush and built each knotty-pine riverfront cabin by hand. Now River's Edge was a thriving family business. There were eight cabins in all, each with two pretty little bedrooms and a single bathroom and a deck that overlooked the river.

In the past few years they'd added a swimming pool and a game room. Plans for a miniature-golf course and a Laundromat were in the works. It was the kind of place where the same families came back year after year to spend their precious vacation time.

Claire still remembered the first time she'd seen it. The towering trees and rushing silver river had seemed like paradise to her. Her childhood memories before coming to River's Edge were gray: ugly towns that came and went, uglier apartments in run-down buildings. Mama had married repeatedly, but Claire couldn't remember a man ever being around for longer than a carton of milk. Meghann was the one Claire remembered. The older sister who took care of everything . . . and then walked away one day, leaving Claire behind.

Now, all these years later, their lives were connected by the thinnest of strands. Once every few months she and Meg talked on the phone. Then Meg would invariably "get another call" and hang up. Her sister loved to underscore how successful she was and how Claire had sold herself short. *Living on that silly little campground, cleaning up after people* was the usual wording. Every single Christmas she offered to pay for college. As if reading *Beowulf* would improve Claire's life.

For years Claire had longed to be friends as well as sisters, but Meghann didn't want that, and they were what Meghann wanted them to be: polite strangers who shared a blood type and an ugly childhood.

Claire reached down for the Weed Eater. As she slogged across the spongy ground, she noticed a dozen things that needed to be done before opening day. Roses that needed to be trimmed, moss that needed to be scraped off the roofs, mildew that needed to be bleached off the porch railings. She made a mental note to ask George, their handyman, to scrub out the canoes this afternoon.

She tossed the Weed Eater in the back of the pickup. It hit with a clanging thunk that rattled the rusted bed.

"Hey, sweetie. You goin' to town?"

She turned and saw her father standing on the porch of the registration building. He wore a ratty pair of overalls and a flannel shirt.

He pulled a red bandanna out of his hip pocket and wiped his brow as he walked toward her. "I'm fixing that freezer. Don't you go pricing new ones."

There wasn't an appliance made that he couldn't repair. "You need anything from town?" she asked.

"Smitty has a part for me. Could you pick it up?"

"You bet. And have George start on the canoes when he gets here, okay?"

"I'll put it on the list. You here for dinner?"

"Not tonight. The princess has a Tee Ball game at Riverfront Park, remember? Five o'clock."

"Oh, yeah. I'll be there."

Claire nodded, knowing that he would. He hadn't missed a single event in his granddaughter's life. "Bye, Dad."

She wrenched the truck's door handle and yanked hard. The door screeched open. She climbed up into the seat.

Dad thumped the truck's door. "Drive safely. Watch the turn at milepost seven."

She smiled. He'd been giving her that exact bit of advice for almost two decades. "I love you, Dad."

"I love you, too. Now go get my granddaughter. If you hurry, we'll have time to watch *SpongeBob SquarePants* before the game."

CHAPTER TWO

THE west side of the office building faced the Sound. A wall of floor-to-ceiling windows framed the beautiful view.

Meghann sat alone at a long, kidney-shaped conference table. The glossy cherry-and-ebony-wood surface bespoke elegance and money. When a person sat down at this table and looked at that view, the point was clear: Whoever owned this office was damn successful.

It was true. Meghann had achieved every goal she'd set for herself. When she'd started college as a scared, lonely teenager, she'd dared to dream of a better life. Now she had it. Her practice was among the most successful and most respected in the city.

She glanced down at her watch: 4:20. Her client was late.

You would think that charging well over three hundred dollars an hour would encourage people to be on time.

"Ms. Dontess?" came a voice through the intercom.

"Yes, Rhona?"

"Your sister, Claire, is on line one."

"Put her through. And buzz me when May Monroe gets here."

Meghann pushed the button on her phone and forced a smile into her voice. "Claire, it's good to hear from you."

"The phone works both ways. So how's life in Moneyland?"

"Good. And in Hayden? Everyone still sitting around waiting for the river to flood?"

"That danger's passed for the year."

"Oh"—Meghann stared out her window—"so how's that beautiful niece of mine? Did she like the skateboard?"

"She loved it." Claire laughed. "But really, Meg, someday you'll have to ask a salesperson for help. Five-year-old girls don't generally have the coordination for skateboards."

"You did. We were living in Needles that year." Meg immediately wished she hadn't said that. It always hurt to remember their past together. For a lot of years Claire had been more of a daughter to Meghann than a sister. Certainly, Meg had been more of a mother to Claire than Mama ever had.

"Just get her a Disney movie next time. You don't need to spend so much money on her. She's happy with a Polly Pocket."

Whatever that was. An awkward silence fell between them. Meghann looked down at her watch; then they both spoke at once.

"What are you—"

"How's work going?"

"Good. And the camp?"

"Resort. We open in two weeks. The Jeffersons are having a family reunion here with about twenty people."

"A week without phone access or television reception? Why am I hearing the *Deliverance* theme music in my head?"

"Some families like to be together," Claire said in that crisp you've-hurt-me voice.

"I'm sorry. You're right. I know you love the place."

"Yeah"—Claire paused—"I'm going to Lake Chelan tomorrow."

"The yearly trip with the girlfriends," Meghann said. "What do you call yourselves? The Bluesers?"

"Yeah."

"You all going back to that same place?"

"Every summer since high school."

Meghann couldn't imagine still being friends with people she'd gone to high school with. "Well, have fun."

"Oh, we will. This year, Charlotte—"

The intercom buzzed. "Meghann? Mrs. Monroe is here."

"Damn. Sorry, Claire, I've got to run."

"Oh, right. I know how much you love to hear about my college-dropout friends."

"It's not that. I have a client who just arrived."

"Yeah, sure. Bye."

"Bye." Meghann disconnected the call just as her secretary showed May Monroe into the conference room.

"Hello, May," Meghann said, walking briskly toward her client. "Thank you, Rhona. No calls, please."

Her secretary nodded and left the room, closing the door.

May Monroe stood in front of a large oil painting, a Nechita original entitled *True Love*. Meghann had always loved the irony of that; here, in this room, true love died every day of the week.

May wore a serviceable black jersey dress and black shoes that were at least five years out of date. Her wedding ring was a plain gold band. Looking at her, you would never know that her husband drove a jet-black Mercedes and had a regular Tuesday tee time at the Broadmoor Golf Course. May probably hadn't spent money on herself in years. Not since she'd slaved at a local restaurant to put her husband through dental school.

"Please, May, sit down."

May jerked forward like a marionette who'd been moved by someone else. She sat in one of the black suede chairs.

Meghann took her usual seat at the head of the table. Spread out in front of her were several manila file folders with bright pink Post-it notes fanned along the edges of the paperwork. Meghann looked at her client. "As I told you at our last meeting, I hired a private investigator to check into your husband's financial affairs."

"It was a waste of time, right?"

"Not exactly."

May stared at her for a long moment, and then she stood up and went to the silver coffee service set out on the cherry-wood credenza. "I see," she said. "What did you find out?"

"He has more than six hundred thousand dollars in an account in the Cayman Islands, which is under his own name. Seven months ago he took almost all of the equity out of your home. Perhaps you thought you were signing refinance documents?"

May turned around. She was holding a coffee cup and saucer. The porcelain chattered in her shaking hands as she moved toward the conference table. "The rates had come down."

"What came down was the cash. Right into his hands."

"Oh, my," she whispered.

"It gets worse," Meghann went on, trying to be gentle with her words but knowing how deep a cut she'd leave behind. "He sold the practice to his partner, Theodore Blevin, for a dollar."

"Why would he do that? It's worth—"

"So you wouldn't be able to get the half you're entitled to."

At that, May's legs seemed to give out on her. She crumpled into her chair. The cup and saucer hit the table with a clatter.

Coffee burped over the porcelain rim and puddled on the wood. May immediately started dabbing the mess with her napkin. "I'm sorry."

Meghann touched her client's wrist. "Don't be." She got up, grabbed some more napkins, and blotted the spill.

"Do any of those documents say why he did this to me?"

Meghann reached into the file and pulled out a photograph. Very gently she pushed it toward May. "Her name is Ashleigh."

"Ashleigh Stoker. I guess I know why he always offered to pick Sarah up from piano lessons."

Meghann nodded. It was always worse when the wife knew the mistress, even in passing. "Washington is a no-fault state; we don't need grounds for a divorce, so his affair doesn't matter."

May looked up. She wore the vague, glassy-eyed expression of an accident victim. "It doesn't matter?" She closed her eyes. "I'm an idiot." The words were more breath than sound.

"No. You're an honest, trustworthy woman who put a selfish man through ten years of college so *he* could have a better life."

"It was supposed to be *our* better life."

"Of course it was."

Meg reached out, touched May's hand. "You trusted a man who told you he loved you. Now he's counting on you to be good ole accommodating May, the woman who puts her family first and makes life easy for Dr. Dale Monroe."

May looked confused, maybe even a little frightened. "What should we do? I don't want to hurt the children."

"He's the one who's hurt the children, May. He's stolen money from them. And from you."

"But he's a good father."

"Then he'll want to see that they're provided for, and he'll hand over half of the assets without a fight."

"And if he doesn't?"

"Then we'll make him."

"He'll be angry."

Meghann leaned forward. "You're the one who should be angry, May. This man lied to you, cheated on you, and stole from you."

"He also fathered my children," May answered. "I don't want this to get ugly. I want him . . . to know he can come home."

Oh, May. Meghann chose her words carefully. "We're simply

going to be fair, May. I don't want to hurt anyone, but you sure aren't going to be left destitute by this man. Period. He's a very very wealthy orthodontist. I won't let him hurt you anymore."

"You think a few rounds of paperwork and a pile of money in the bank will protect me from that?" She sighed. "Go ahead, Ms. Dontess, do what you need to do to protect my children's future. But let's not pretend you can make it painless, okay? It already hurts so much I can barely breathe, and it has just begun."

Across the blistered expanse of prairie grass, a row of windmills dotted the cloudless horizon. Their blades turned in a slow and steady rhythm. Sometimes, when the weather was right, you could hear the creaking thwop-thwop-thwop of each rotation. Today it was too hot to hear anything except the beating of your own heart.

Joe Wyatt stood on the poured-concrete slab that served as the warehouse's front porch, holding a now warm can of Coke—all that was left of his lunch.

He stared at the distant fields. The heat was getting to him, and it was only the second week of June. There was no way he could handle summer in the Yakima Valley. It was time to move on again.

The realization exhausted him.

He wondered how much longer he could do this, drift from town to town. Loneliness was wearing him down, whittling him away to a stringy shadow. Once—it felt long ago—he'd hoped that one of these places would feel right, that he'd come into some town, think, This is it, and rent an apartment instead of a seedy motel room. He no longer harbored such dreams. He knew better. After a week in the same room he started to feel things, remember things. If he settled in, got comfortable, he invariably dreamed about Diana.

That was okay. It hurt, of course, because seeing her face—even in his dreams—filled him with an ache that ran deep in his bones, but there was pleasure, too, a sweet remembrance of how life used to be, of the love he'd once been capable of feeling. If only the dreams stopped there, with memories of Diana sitting on the green grass of the quad in her college days or of them cuddled up in their big bed in the house on Bainbridge Island.

He was never that lucky. The sweet dreams invariably soured

and turned ugly. More often than not he woke up whispering, "I'm sorry." The only way to survive was to keep moving.

He'd learned in these vagrant years how to be invisible. If a man cut his hair and dressed well, people saw him. But if a man let himself go, if he forgot to cut his hair and wore a faded Harley-Davidson T-shirt and carried a ratty backpack, no one noticed him.

Three years ago, when he'd first run away, he'd carried an expensive suitcase. He still remembered standing in his bedroom, packing for a trip without destination or duration, wondering what a man in exile would need. He'd packed khaki slacks and merino wool sweaters and even a black Joseph Abboud suit.

By the end of his first winter alone, he'd understood that those clothes were the archaeological remains of a forgotten life. All he needed in his new life were two pairs of jeans, a few T-shirts, a sweatshirt, and a rain slicker. Everything else he'd given to charity.

He closed his eyes, and Diana came to him. "I'm tired," he said to her.

It's no good, what you're doing.

"I don't know what else to do."

Go home.

"I can't."

You break my heart, Joey.

And she was gone.

CLAIRE stood at the kitchen sink, thinking about the phone conversation she'd had with Meg yesterday.

"Mommy, can I have another Eggo?"

"How do we ask for that?" Claire said absently.

"Mommy, may I *please* have another Eggo?"

Claire turned away from the window and dried her hands on a towel. "Sure." She popped a frozen waffle into the toaster. While it was warming, she looked around the room for more dirty dishes—and saw the place through her sister's eyes.

It wasn't a bad house, certainly not by Hayden standards. Small, yes: three tiny bedrooms tucked into the peaked second floor, a single bathroom on each floor, a living room, and a kitchen with an eating space that doubled as a counter. In the six years Claire had lived here, she'd painted the once moss-green walls a creamy French vanilla and replaced the orange shag carpeting with hardwood floors. Her furniture, although mostly secondhand, was all framed in wood that she'd stripped and refinished herself.

Meg would see it differently, of course. Meg, who'd graduated from high school early and then breezed through seven years of college, who never failed to mention that she had buckets of money and had the nerve to send her niece Christmas gifts that made the others under the tree look paltry by comparison.

"My waffle's up."

"So it is." Claire took the waffle from the slot, buttered and cut it, then put the plate in front of her daughter. "Here you go."

Alison immediately stabbed a piece and popped it into her mouth, chewing in that cartoon-character way of hers.

Claire couldn't help smiling. She stared down at the miniature version of herself. Same fine blond hair, same eyes, same heart-shaped face. Alison's father had left no genetic imprint on his daughter. It was fitting. The minute he'd heard Claire was pregnant, he'd reached for his running shoes.

"You're in your jammies, Mommy. We're gonna be late if you don't hurry."

"You're right about that." Claire thought about all the things she had to do today: recaulk the showers and bathroom windows, unplug the toilet in cabin 5, and repair the canoe shed. It was early yet, not even eight o'clock, on the last day of school. Tomorrow they'd be leaving for a week of rest and fun at Lake Chelan. Claire glanced around. "Have you seen my work list, Alison?"

"On the coffee table."

Claire picked up her list from the table, shaking her head. She had absolutely no memory of leaving it there.

"I want ballet lessons, Mommy. Is that okay?"

Claire smiled. "I wanted to be a ballerina once."

"How come you're a worker bee instead?"

"Worker bee is what Grampa calls me. Really, I'm an assistant manager."

It had happened a long time ago, her choosing this life. Like most of her decisions, she'd stumbled across it without paying much attention. First she'd flunked out of Washington State University— one of the many party casualties of higher education. Without a degree or a dream Claire had found herself back in Hayden. But she loved this place, this job. She was, in that and in so many things, her father's daughter. There was something about these gorgeous sixteen acres along the river that filled her soul.

Claire never felt like a failure.

Except when she talked to her sister.

TWENTY-FOUR hours later Claire was ready to leave on vacation. She took a last pass through the house, looking for anything forgotten or left undone. She was straightening the shower curtain when she heard footsteps in the living room.

"What in the name of a frog's butt are you still doing here?"

She smiled and backed out of the minuscule bathroom.

Her father stood in the living room, dwarfing the small space. Big and broad-shouldered, he made every room seem smaller by comparison. But it was his personality that was truly oversize.

She'd first met him when she was nine years old. *Well,* he'd said as he looked down at her, *you must be my daughter, Claire. You're the prettiest girl I've ever seen. Let's go home.*

Home.

It was the word she'd waited for, dreamed of. It had taken her years—and more than a few tears—to realize that he hadn't offered the same welcome to Meghann.

"Hey, Dad. I was making sure everything was ready for you to move in."

His grin showed a row of Chiclet-white dentures. "You know damn well I ain't moving in here. I *like* my mobile home. I got my fridge and my satellite TV. That's all I need."

They'd been having this discussion ever since Claire had moved back to the property and Dad had given her use of the house. He swore up and down that the mobile home hidden in the trees was room enough for a fifty-six-year-old single man.

"Now dance on over here and give your old man a hug."

Claire did as she was told.

His big, strong arms enfolded her, made her feel safe and adored.

"I'll leave in an hour," she said. "The toilet in cabin—"

He spun her around and pushed her gently toward the door. "Get going. This place isn't going to fall apart without you."

Claire couldn't help smiling. "Okay."

"Take as long as you want. Really. You're only thirty-five. You and Alison should kick up your heels a bit. You're too responsible."

"I'm a thirty-five-year-old single mother who has never been married. That's not too responsible, and I *will* kick up my heels in Chelan. But I'll be home in a week."

He thumped her shoulder. "You've always done exactly what you wanted, but you can't blame a guy for trying. Have fun."

Claire walked out of the house and into the steely gray day. A drizzling rain fell like a beaded curtain in front of the trees.

"Come on, Mommy!" Alison's small face poked through the car's open window.

Dad hurried ahead of her and kissed his granddaughter's cheek.

Claire got into the car and started the engine. "Are we ready, Ali Kat? Do you have everything?"

Alison bounced in her seat, clinging to her stuffed orca and her Mary-Kate and Ashley lunchbox. "I'm ready!"

"We're off to see the wizard, then," Claire said, shifting into drive as she yelled a final good-bye to her father.

Claire loved Lake Chelan's Blue Skies Campground. She and her girlfriends had first vacationed there a few years after high school. There had been five of them; time and tragedy had whittled their number down to four. At first they'd been young and wild and driven to pick up local boys. Gradually, as they'd started dragging bassinets and car seats with them, the vacation had settled down a bit. Now with the kids old enough to swim and play on the playground alone, they had refound a slice of their previous freedom.

"Mom*my*, you're spacing out."

"Oh. Sorry, honey."

"*I said*, we get the honeymoon cabin this year, remember?" She bounced even harder in her seat. "Yippee! We get the big bathtub. Did you bring my skateboard, Mommy?"

"No. You're too young to ride it."

"How come Aunt Meg never comes to visit us?"

"Aunt Meg is so busy, she hardly has time to breathe."

"Eliot Zane turned blue when he didn't breathe."

"I just meant Meg is superbusy helping people."

"Oh."

Claire slid a Disney audiotape into the cassette player. The miles flew by. In no time they were speeding across the flat, arid land on the eastern side of the state.

"Is this the desert already?"

Claire nodded. Her daughter always called eastern Washington the desert. It was easy to see why. After the lush green of Hayden, this yellow-and-brown landscape seemed desolate and scorched.

"There's the water slide!" Alison said at last. She leaned forward, counting out loud. When she got to forty-seven, she yelled, "There's the lake!"

Lake Chelan filled their view to the left, a huge crystal-blue lake tucked into a golden hillside. They drove over the bridge that led into town.

Two decades ago this town had been less than three blocks long, without a national franchise to be found. But over time, word of the weather had spread west to those soggy coastal towns that so prized their plate-size rhododendrons and car-size ferns. Gradually Seattleites turned their attention eastward. It became a summer tradition—the trek across the mountains toward the flat, scorched plains. As the tourists came, so did the development. Condominium complexes sprouted along the water's edge. It had become a thriving vacation destination, with all the kiddie-required amenities— pools, water-slide parks, and Jet Ski rentals.

The road curved along the lakeshore. They passed dozens of condominium complexes. Then the shore became less inhabited again. They saw the sign: BLUE SKIES CAMPGROUND, NEXT LEFT.

"Look, Mommy, look!"

The sign showed a pair of stylized trees bracketing a tent with a canoe in front.

"This is it, Ali Kat." Claire turned left onto the gravel road.

AFTER checking in at the lodge, Claire handed Alison the key to the honeymoon cabin. "Here you go, Ali Kat. You're in charge. Show us the way."

With a yelp Ali was off, and Claire hurried along behind her. They raced across the expanse of lawn, past the boat-rental shed, and plunged into the trees. The ground here was hard-packed dirt, carpeted with a hundred years' worth of pine needles.

Finally they came to the lake. A silvery wooden dock floated on the wavy blue water, tilting from side to side in a rocking motion.

"Clara Bella!"

Claire tented a hand over her eyes and looked around.

Gina sat at the shoreline, waving. Even from here Claire could see the size of the drink in her friend's hand. Usually Gina was the conservative one, the buoy that held everyone up, but she'd finalized her divorce a few months ago, and she was adrift. Last week her ex-husband had moved in with a younger woman.

"Hurry up, Ali!" That was Gina's six-year-old daughter, Bonnie.

Alison dropped her Winnie-the-Pooh backpack and peeled off her clothes to show off her yellow bathing suit. "I'm ready."

"Don't go in past your belly button," Claire said.

"Aw, Mommy," Alison whined, then ran for the water.

Claire sat down beside Gina. "What time did you get here?"

Gina laughed. "On time, of course. That's one thing I've learned this year. Your life can fall apart, but you're still who you are. I'm the kind of woman who gets somewhere on time."

"There's nothing wrong with that."

"Rex would disagree. He always said I wasn't spontaneous enough. I thought it meant he wanted sex in the afternoon. Turns out he wanted to skydive." She shook her head, gave Claire a wry smile. "I'd be happy to shove him out of the plane now."

"I'd rig his parachute for him."

They laughed, though it wasn't funny. "How's Bonnie doing?"

"That's the saddest part of all. She barely seems to notice. Rex was never home anyway."

They were silent for a long moment. The only sound between them was the slapping of the water against the dock and the girls' high-pitched laughter. Gina turned to her. "How have you done it all these years? Been alone, I mean."

Claire hadn't thought much about her solitude since Alison's birth. Yes, she'd been alone—in the sense that she'd never been married or lived with a man—but she rarely felt lonely.

Claire looked out at Alison, who was standing up to her belly button in the water and jumping up and down. The sight made Claire's chest tighten. She knew she loved her daughter too much, but Claire had never known any other way to love. That was why she'd never been married. Men who loved their wives unconditionally were few and far between. In truth, Claire wondered if that kind of true love existed.

"You get past being lonely. And you live for your kids," she said.

"Ali shouldn't be your whole world, Claire."

"It's not like I didn't *try* to fall in love. I've dated every single guy in Hayden."

"None of them twice." Gina grinned. "And Bert Shubert is still in love with you. Miss Hauser thinks you're crazy for letting him go."

"It's sad when a fifty-three-year-old plumber with Coke-bottle glasses and a red goatee is considered an eligible bachelor just because he owns an appliance store."

Gina laughed. "Yeah. If I ever tell you I'm going out with Bert, please shoot me."

"You'll be okay, Gina," Claire said. "I promise you will."

"I don't know," Gina said quietly, and then started to cry.

Absurdly, Claire thought about the day her life had changed— when she'd learned that love had a shelf life, a use-by date that could pass suddenly and turn everything sour. *I'm leaving you,* her sister had said. Until that moment Meg had been Claire's whole world and more of a mother than Mama had ever been.

And then Claire was crying, too.

Gina sniffed. "Ten seconds in my company, and perfectly happy people start to weep."

Claire wiped her eyes. There was no point in crying about the past. "Remember the year Char fell off the dock because she was crying so hard she couldn't see?"

"Bob's midlife crisis. She thought he was having an affair."

"And it turned out he was secretly getting hair-plug treatments."

Gina embraced Claire. "Thank God for the Bluesers. I haven't needed you all this much since I was in labor."

CHAPTER THREE

LIKE sunshine, night brought out the best in Seattle. The highway— a bumper-to-bumper nightmare at morning rush hour—became, at night, a glittering red-and-gold Chinese dragon that curled along the blackened banks of Lake Union. Meghann stood at her office window. It was eight thirty. Time to head home. She'd bring the Wanamaker file with her. Get a jump on tomorrow.

Meghann was almost to the elevator when her cell phone rang. She pulled it out of her bag. "Meghann Dontess," she said.

"Meghann?" The voice was panicky. "It's May Monroe."

Meghann was instantly alert. "What's going on?"

"It's Dale. He came by tonight and said something about the papers he got today. He was crazy. What did you send him?"

"We talked about this, May. I notified Dale's lawyer that we'd be contesting the fraudulent transfer of his business and demanding an accounting of the Cayman Island accounts. I also told his attorney that we were aware of the affair with the child's piano instructor and that such behavior might threaten his suitability as a parent."

"You threatened to take away his children?"

"The kids are a shill game with guys like your husband. Pretend to want custody, and you'll get more money."

"You think you know my husband better than I do."

"I don't have to know him," Meghann answered, using the canned speech she'd perfected long ago. "Protecting you is my job. If I upset your husband in the process, that's an unfortunate necessity. He'll calm down. They always do."

"You don't know Dale," she said again.

Meghann's senses pounced on some nuance. Something wasn't right. "Are you scared of him, May?"

"Scared?" May tried to sound surprised by the question.

"Does he hit you, May?"

"Sometimes when he's drinking, I can say just the wrong thing."

Oh, yeah. It's May's fault. "Are you okay now?"

"He didn't hit me. And he never hits the children."

Meghann didn't say what came to mind. Often if a man would hit his wife, he'd get around to hitting his children.

"We need to make sure he understands that I'm not going to take his children from him. Otherwise he'll go crazy," May said. There was the barest crack in her voice.

"May, say it's three months from now. Dale's living with Dance Hall Barbie, and they come home drunk one night. I'm guessing that you've always been a buffer between your husband and kids. You probably learned how to calm him down and deflect his attention away from the children. Will Barbie know how to protect them?"

"Am I so ordinary?"

"Sadly, the situation is. The good news is, you're giving yourself—and your children—a new start. Don't weaken now."

"So what do I do?"

"Lock the doors and turn off the phone. If you don't feel safe, go to a relative's or friend's house. Tomorrow we'll get together and come up with a new game plan. I'll file some restraining orders."

"You can keep us safe?"

"You'll be fine, May. Trust me. Bullies are cowards. Once he sees how strong you can be, he'll back down."

"Okay. When can we meet?"

"How about a late lunch—say, two o'clock—at the Judicial Annex Café by the courthouse?"

"Okay."

"Good. I'll see you there." Meghann flipped the phone shut and dropped it in her purse, then pushed the elevator button. When the door opened, she stepped inside. As always, she studied her reflection in the mirrored walls. She was forty-two years old, and since it felt as if she'd been thirty a moment ago, she had to assume it would be a blink's worth of time before she was fifty.

That depressed her. She imagined herself at sixty. Alone, working from dawn to dusk, talking to her neighbor's cats, and going on singles cruises.

Outside, the night was beautiful; an amethyst sky gave everything a pink and pearlized glow. She walked briskly down the street, bypassing people without making eye contact. At her building she paused and looked up.

There was her deck. The only one in the building without potted trees and outdoor furniture. The windows behind it were black; the rest of the building was a blaze of light. Friends and families were in those lit spaces, having dinner, watching television, making love. Connecting with one another.

Meghann didn't want to go up there, put on her old U.W. sweats, eat raisin bran for dinner, and watch a rerun of *Third Watch*. Instead, she walked past her building and went into the Public Market. At this hour pretty much everything was closed up.

She turned into the Athenian, the old-fashioned tavern made

famous in *Sleepless in Seattle*. Meghann had perfected the art of scoping out a bar without being obvious. She did that now. There were five or six men at the bar. Fishermen, she'd guess, getting ready to head up to Alaska for the season.

"Hey, Meghann," yelled Freddie, the bartender. "Your usual?"

"You bet." She moved past the bar and found a place at one of the old-fashioned varnished wooden tables.

"Here ye be," Freddie said, setting a martini glass down in front of her. He shook the steel shaker, then poured her a cosmopolitan. "You want an order of oysters and fries?"

"You read my mind."

Freddie grinned. "Ain't hard to do, Counselor." He leaned down toward her. "The Eagles are coming in tonight."

"The Eagles?"

"The minor-league ball team outta Everett." He winked at her.

Meghann groaned. It was bad when bartenders started recommending whole ball teams.

She closed her eyes, reminding herself that this was the life she wanted. She'd tried marriage. It had ended exactly as she'd feared—with his betrayal and her broken heart.

When her first cosmo was gone, Meghann ordered a second.

"May I join you?"

She looked up and found herself staring into a pair of dark eyes. She could tell by the look of him—young, blond, sexy as hell—that he was used to getting what he wanted. And what he wanted tonight was her. The thought was a tonic.

"Of course." She didn't offer a half smile or bat her eyes. "I'm Meghann Dontess. My friends call me Meg."

He slid into the seat. His knees brushed hers, and at the contact he smiled. "I'm Donny MacMillan. You like baseball?"

"I like a lot of things." She flagged down Freddie, who nodded at her. A moment later he brought her another cosmopolitan. "I suppose you're a baseball player."

He grinned, and she felt the first twinge of desire. Sex with him would be great; she knew it. And it would make her forget.

THEIR first gathering at Lake Chelan had been in 1989, the year they all turned twenty-one. There had been five of them then. Best friends since grade school.

That first get-together had happened by accident. The girls had pooled their money to give Claire a weekend in the honeymoon cabin for her birthday. At the time—in March—she'd been head over heels in love. By mid-July, on the designated weekend, Claire had been out of love, alone, and more than a little depressed. Never one to waste money, she'd gone on the trip by herself, intending to sit on the porch and read.

Just before dinnertime of the first day, a battered yellow Ford Pinto had pulled into the yard. Her best friends had spilled out of the car and run across the lawn, laughing, holding two big jugs of margarita mix. They'd called their visit a love intervention, and it had worked.

Every year since then, they'd managed to come back for a week. Now, of course, it was different. Gina and Claire each had a daughter; Karen had four children, ages eleven to fourteen; and Charlotte was trying desperately to conceive.

In the past few years their parties had quieted. Instead of getting dressed up and going to Cowboy Bob's Western Roundup to slam tequila and line dance, they put the kids to bed early, drank glasses of white wine, and played hearts at the round wooden table on the porch of the lodge. They kept a running score for the week. The winner got the keys to the honeymoon cottage for the next year.

They spent their days by the lake, stretched out on red-and-white-striped beach towels. On hot days, like this one, they spent most of their time in the lake, standing neck-deep in the cool water. Talking. Always talking.

Today the weather was perfect. The sky was a bright seamless blue, and the lake was like glass. The older kids were inside, playing crazy eights and listening to Karen's son Willie's earsplitting music. Alison and Bonnie were pedaling a water bike.

Karen sat in her chair, fanning herself with a pamphlet from the water-slide park. Charlotte, completely protected from the sun by a floppy white hat and three-quarter-sleeved cover-up, was reading the latest Kelly Ripa book club choice and sipping lemonade.

Gina leaned sideways and opened the cooler, rooting noisily through it for a Diet Coke. "My marriage ends, and we're drinking Diet Coke and lemonade. When Karen's first husband left, we slammed tequila and danced the macarena at Cowboy Bob's."

"That was my second husband, Stan," Karen said. "When Aaron left, we went skinny-dipping in the lake."

"My point remains," Gina said. "My crisis is getting the *Sesame Street* treatment. You got *Animal House*."

"Cowboy Bob's," Charlotte said. "We haven't been there in years."

"Not since we started dragging around these undersized humans," Karen said. "It's hard to rock and roll with a kid on your back."

Claire pushed herself up on her elbows. The scratchy cotton of her beach towel seemed to bite into her sunburned forearms.

"Willie's fourteen this year, right?"

Karen nodded. "He's starting high school in September."

"Why couldn't he babysit for an hour or two?"

Gina sat up. "Why didn't we think of that before? He's fourteen."

Karen frowned. "With the maturity of an earthworm."

"We all babysat at his age," Charlotte said. "Hell, I was practically a nanny that summer before high school."

"He's a responsible kid, Karen. He'll be fine," Claire said.

"I don't know. Last month his fish died. Lack of food."

"They won't starve to death in two hours."

Karen looked back at the cabin. "Yeah," she said finally. "We'll leave a cell phone with him."

"And a list of numbers."

Gina smiled for the first time all day. "Ladies, the Bluesers are going to leave the building."

It took them two hours to shower, change their clothes, and make the kids' dinner. It took them another hour to convince the kids that their plan was possible.

Finally Claire took firm hold of Karen and led her outside. As they walked down the long, winding driveway, Karen paused and looked back every few feet. "Are you sure?" she said each time.

"Just keep walking." Gina leaned close to Claire and said, "She's like a car in the ice. If she stops, we'll never get her going again."

They were standing across the street from Cowboy Bob's when it hit them. Claire was the first to speak. "It's not even dark out."

"As party animals, we've lost our touch," Charlotte said.

Claire refused to be thwarted. So what if they looked like

sorority girls amid the professional drinkers that populated a place like this in the early evening? They were here to have a good time. "Come on, ladies," she said, storming forward.

Her friends fell in line behind her. Heads held high, they marched into Cowboy Bob's as if they owned the place.

Claire led the way to a round table near the empty dance floor. From here they would have an unobstructed view of the band, which was noticeably absent. A whiny western song played on the jukebox. Gina ordered a round of margaritas and onion rings.

"God it feels good to get *out*," Karen said. "I can't remember the last time I went out without having to do enough preplanning to launch an air strike."

Claire raised her glass. "To us," she said in a firm voice. "To the Bluesers. We made it through junior high and high school, through labors and surgeries, weddings and divorces. Two of us have lost our marriages, one hasn't been able to get pregnant, one of us has never been in love, and a few years ago one of us died. But we're still here. We'll *always* be here for one another. That makes us lucky women."

They clinked their glasses together.

They returned to talking about the old days, and everything made them laugh. At some point they ordered a plate of nachos. By the time the second order of food came, the band had started. The first song was a loud rendition of "Friends in Low Places."

By the time the band got around to Alan Jackson's "Here in the Real World," the place was wall-to-wall people. A group was line dancing in a thigh-slappin' way.

"Did you hear that?" Claire leaned forward and put her hands on the table. "It's 'Guitars and Cadillacs.' We *gotta* dance."

"Dance?" Gina laughed. "The last time I danced with you two, my butt hit an old man and sent him flying."

Karen shook her head. "Sorry, Charlie."

Claire stood up. "Come on, Charlotte. You want to dance?"

"I'd love to." She plopped her purse onto her chair and followed Claire to the dance floor.

The minute Claire started to move in time with the music, to swing her hips and stamp her feet and clap her hands, she remembered how much she loved this. She couldn't believe that she'd let so many quiet years accumulate.

By the time the band took a break, Claire was out of breath. A tiny headache had flared behind her left eye; she stuck a hand in her pocket and found an Excedrin.

Charlotte pushed the hair out of her eyes. "That was *great*. Come on. I'm so dehydrated, I feel like a piece of beef jerky."

Claire started to head for the table and then remembered the aspirin. She went to the bar instead and asked for a glass of tap water.

The water came, and as she swallowed the single pill, she saw a man walk onto the stage. He carried a guitar—a regular, old-fashioned guitar that didn't plug in or amp out.

He sat down easily on a rickety barstool. One black cowboy boot was planted firmly on the floor; the other rested on the stool's bottom rung. He wore a pair of faded, torn jeans and a black T-shirt. His hair was almost shoulder length and shone blond in the overhead lighting. He was looking down at his guitar, and though a black Stetson shielded most of his face, Claire could make out the strong, high bones that defined his cheeks.

"Wow." She couldn't remember the last time she'd seen a man who was so good-looking. Not in Hayden, that was for sure.

The man leaned toward the microphone. "I'm gonna fill in while the band takes a short break. I hope y'all don't mind."

Claire pushed through the crowd to the edge of the dance floor.

He strummed a few notes on the guitar and started to sing. At first his voice was too soft to be heard above the raucous din.

"Be quiet." Claire was surprised to hear the words spoken out loud; she'd meant only to *think* them. She felt ridiculously conspicuous, standing there in front of the crowd, but she couldn't move, couldn't look away.

He looked up. In the smoky darkness, with a dozen people crammed in beside her, Claire thought he was looking at her. Slowly he smiled.

Once, years ago, Claire had been running along the dock at Lake Crescent behind her sister. One minute she'd been laughing and upright; the next second she was in the freezing cold water, gasping for breath and clawing her way to the surface. That was how she felt right now.

"I'm Bobby Austin," he said softly, still looking at her. "This song is for The One. The one I've been lookin' for all my life."

His long fingers strummed the guitar strings. Then he started to sing. His voice was low and smoky, seductive as hell. Claire found herself swaying in time to the music, dancing all by herself.

When the song ended, he set down the guitar and stood up. The crowd clapped politely, then headed back to their pitchers of beer.

He walked toward Claire. She couldn't seem to move.

Directly in front of her he stopped. When he didn't say anything, she said, "I'm Claire Cavenaugh."

A smile hitched one side of his mouth. "I don't know how to say what I'm thinking without sounding like an idiot."

Claire's heart was beating so fast, she felt dizzy. "What do you mean?"

He closed the distance between them, small as it had been. Now he was so near, she could see the gold flecks in his green eyes and the tiny half-moon–shaped scar at the edge of his upper lip.

"I'm The One," he said softly.

"The one what?" She tried to smile. "The way? The light? There is no way to heaven but through you?"

"No joking. I'm the one you've been looking for."

She ought to have laughed at him, told him she hadn't heard that corny a pickup line since the year she tried shaping her eyebrows with a Lady Bic. She was long past believing in love at first sight. All of that was what she meant to say, but when she opened her mouth, she heard her heart speak. "How do you know that?"

"Because I've been lookin' for you, too."

Claire took a step backward—just far enough so that she could breathe her own air. She wanted to laugh at him. She really did.

"Come on, Claire Cavenaugh," he said softly. "Dance with me."

CHAPTER FOUR

SOME marriages ended with bitter words and ugly epithets, others with copious tears and whispered apologies; each proceeding was different. The one constant was sadness, and it was a fact, well known in family court, that no woman who'd gone through a divorce ever saw the world—or love—in quite the same way again. "Are you okay?" Meghann asked May Monroe.

Her client sat rigidly upright, her hands clasped tightly in her lap. "I'm fine," she said.

"Let's go next door and get something to eat, okay?"

In the front of the courtroom the judge stood up. She smiled at Meghann, then at George Gutterson, the opposing counsel; then she left the courtroom.

Meghann helped May to her feet. She held on to her arm to keep her steady as they headed toward the door.

"You *bitch!*" Dale Monroe surged forward. His face was a deep, purply red. A blue vein throbbed down the middle of his forehead.

"Dale," George said, reaching for his client, "don't be stupid."

Dale shook his lawyer's arm away and kept coming.

Meghann sidestepped easily, putting herself between Dale and May. "Step back, Mr. Monroe."

"That's *Dr.* Monroe, you avaricious bitch."

"Excellent word usage. You must have gone to a good liberal arts college. Now, please, step back."

"You took my children away from me," Dale said to Meghann.

"Are you suggesting *I* was the one who fraudulently transferred assets out of my wife's reach . . . or that *I* stole money and equity from my family? Maybe you're suggesting that *I* was the one who banged my daughter's piano teacher every Tuesday afternoon."

He paled and tried to make eye contact with his ex-wife.

"May, come on," he said, "I didn't do all of those things. I would have given you everything you asked for. But the kids . . . I can't see them only on weekends and two weeks in the summer."

He sounded sincere, actually. If Meghann hadn't seen the ugly truth in black and white, she might have believed him.

She spoke quickly, so May wouldn't have to. "The separation of your assets was entirely fair and equitable, Dr. Monroe. The custody issues were also fairly resolved, and when you calm down, I'm sure you'll agree. We all read the depositions that reflected your lifestyle. You were gone in the morning by six a.m.—before the children woke up—and you rarely returned home before ten p.m.— after they were in bed. You'll probably see your children more now than you did while you resided at the family home."

"Who do you think you are?" Dale whispered harshly, taking a step toward her. At his sides his fingers curled into fists.

"You going to hit me, Dale? Go ahead. Lose what little custody you have."

Meghann slipped her arm around May's waist. Together they walked out of the courtroom.

"You'll pay for this," Dale screamed to their backs.

Meghann didn't look back. Instead, she kept a steadying hand on May's waist and led her into the elevator. The moment the door closed, May burst into tears.

Meghann held May's hand, squeezing it gently. "I know it seems impossible now, but life will get better. I promise."

She led May down the courthouse steps and outside. The sky was heavy and gray with clouds. They walked down Third Street to the Judicial Annex, the favorite lunch spot for the family-court gang.

"Hey, Meg," said a few colleagues as she walked through the restaurant to a table at the back. Within moments a waitress was beside them. "Is this a champagne or a martini day?" she asked.

"Definitely champagne. Thanks."

May looked across the table at her. "We aren't really going to drink champagne, are we?"

"May, you are now a millionaire. Your children can get Ph.D.'s from Harvard if they want. And you got full custody. Hell yes, we're celebrating."

"What happened to you?"

"What do you mean?"

"My life has been hit by a Scud missile. And there you sit, drinking champagne. What's wrong with you?"

"This can be a harsh job," Meghann answered truthfully. "Sometimes the only way I can get through it is—"

A commotion broke out in the restaurant. Glass shattered. A table crashed to the floor. A woman screamed.

"Oh, no," May breathed. Her face was pale.

Meghann frowned. "What in the—" She turned in her chair.

Dale stood in the open doorway, holding a gun in his left hand. He appeared to be crying.

"Put down the gun, Dale." Meghann was surprised to hear the calmness in her voice.

"You ruined my life."

"Put the gun down. You don't want to do something stupid."

"I already did something stupid." His voice broke. "I had an affair and got greedy and forgot how much I love my wife."

May started to get to her feet. Meghann grabbed her, forced her down, and then stood up herself.

"Come on, Dale. Put the gun down. We'll get you some help."

"Where was all your help when I tried to tell my wife how sorry I was?" Tears rolled down his cheeks.

"Dale," Meghann said in a calm voice, "I know how—"

"Shut *up*. It's your fault, you bitch. You're the one who did all of this." He raised the gun, aimed, and pulled the trigger.

JOE awoke with a fever and a stinging throat. A dry, hacking cough brought him upright before he'd even fully opened his eyes. When it was over, he sat there, bleary-eyed.

A glittering layer of frost coated his sleeping bag, its presence a testament to the altitude. Though the days in this part of the state were as hot as hell, the nights were cold.

He coughed again, then climbed out of the sleeping bag. His fingers were trembling as he dug the toothbrush, soap, and toothpaste out of his pack. Squatting by the rushing rapids of Icicle Creek, he readied himself for the day.

Today was his birthday. His forty-third. In another time—another life—this would have been a day for celebration, for family. Diana had always loved a party. The year he'd turned thirty-eight, she'd rented the Space Needle and hired a Bruce Springsteen impersonator to sing the sound track of their youth. The place had been packed with friends. Everyone wanted to celebrate Joe's birthday with him.

Then.

With a sigh he pushed to his feet. A quick check of his wallet and pockets revealed that he was nearly broke again. Slinging his backpack into place, he hiked out of the national forest. By the time he reached Highway 2, his forehead was on fire. He knew he had a fever—one hundred degrees, at least.

He stared at the black river of asphalt that flowed down to the tiny town of Leavenworth. It was only a mile or so away.

By the time Joe got there, his headache was almost unbearable. At a Chevron station he spent his last two dollars on aspirin.

He was standing outside the minimart, trying to will the aspirin to take effect, when the first raindrop hit.

"Damn." Before he finished the word, the storm hit. A pounding rain that seemed to nail him in place. And suddenly he couldn't live like this anymore. He was sick and tired of being sick and tired.

Home.

He closed his eyes and thought of the small town where he'd been raised, where he'd played shortstop for the local ball team and worked at a garage after school and every summer until he went away to college. If any town would still accept him after what he'd done, it would be that one.

Moving slowly, his emotions a convoluted mixture of fear and anticipation, he went to the phone booth and stepped inside its quiet enclosure. Now the rain was only noise; it was like his heartbeat: fast, breathless. He let out a long breath, then picked up the phone, punched 0, and placed a collect call.

"Hey, little sister," he said when she answered. "How are you?"

"Oh, my *God*. I've been worried sick about you, Joey. You haven't called in—what?—eight months."

"I know. I'm sorry. How's my beautiful niece?"

"She's great."

He heard something in her voice. "What's the matter?"

"Nothing," she said. Then more softly, "I could use my big brother right about now, that's all. Has it been long enough?"

There it was, the question upon which everything rested. "I don't know. I'm tired—I know that. Have people forgotten?"

"I don't get asked so much anymore."

He didn't know if he was strong enough to stand up to his past. He hadn't been when it was his present.

"Come home, Joey. You can't hide forever. And . . . I need you."

He heard the sound of her crying; it was soft and broken, and it pulled something out of him. "Don't cry. Please."

"I'm not. I'm chopping onions for dinner." She sniffed. "Your niece is going through a spaghetti phase. She won't eat anything else." She tried to laugh.

Joe appreciated the attempt at normalcy, however forced.

"Make her some of Mom's spaghetti. That should end it."

She laughed. "Gosh, I'd forgotten. Hers was awful."

"Better than her meat loaf."

After that, a silence slipped through the lines. Softly she said, "You've got to forgive yourself, Joey."

"Some things are unforgivable."

"Then at least come home. People care about you here."

"I want to. I can't live like this anymore."

"I hope that's what this phone call means."

"I hope so, too."

IT WAS that rarest of days in downtown Seattle. Hot and humid. A haze hung over the city. If it was hot outside, it was swelter-ing in the courthouse. Meghann stared at the yellow legal pad in front of her. She hadn't written a word. Her right hand started to tremble.

"Ms. Dontess. Ahem. *Ms. Dontess.*"

The judge was speaking to her.

She blinked slowly. "I'm sorry." She got to her feet.

The judge—a thin, heronlike woman—was frowning. "Approach the bench," she said.

Meghann tried to look confident. At the bench she stopped and looked up. "Yes, Your Honor?"

The judge leaned forward to say softly, "We all know what hap-pened last week, Meghann. That bullet missed you by inches. Are you certain you're ready to be back in a courtroom?"

"Yes." Meghann's right hand was trembling.

The judge cleared her throat and nodded. "Step back."

Meghann went back to the table, slid into her seat.

Her client, a Mercer Island housewife, stared at her. "What's going on?"

Meghann shook her head. "Don't worry."

"I'll restate, Your Honor," John Heinreid said. He and Meghann had tried dozens of cases against each other. "My client would like to stay these proceedings for a time so that he and Mrs. Miller can obtain counseling. There are, after all, small children involved."

Meghann heard her client whisper, "No way."

Then Meghann planted her hands on the desk and slowly rose. Her mind went blank. She couldn't think of a single argument. When she closed her eyes, trying to concentrate, she saw the gun pointed at her, heard an echoed blast. When she opened her eyes, everyone was looking at her.

Meghann turned to her client. "It's a reasonable request, Celene. You won't look good if we fight this battle in front of the judge."

"Oh. I guess . . ." Celene frowned.

Meghann returned her attention to the bench. "We'd ask for a time limit and a follow-up court date to be set now."

"That's acceptable to us, Your Honor."

Meghann stood there as the details were worked out. Her right hand was still trembling. On autopilot, she packed up her briefcase.

"Wait. What just happened?" Celene whispered.

"We agreed to counseling. A few months or so. No more."

"Counseling? We've tried counseling—or did you forget that? It didn't work. Mr. Computer Software likes men, remember?"

Meghann had forgotten all of that. "I'm sorry, Celene."

"Sorry? *Sorry*. My children and I need to start over."

"You're right. I'll fix this. I promise I will." And she could. A phone call to John Heinreid that threatened to reveal Mr. Miller's preferred sex partners, and it'd be handled instantly. Quietly.

Celene sighed. "Look, I know what happened last week. I feel sorry for that lady—and for you. But I need to worry about myself."

"You *should* be taking care of yourself. I screwed up in here. But I'll fix it, and you won't be paying a dime for this divorce. Okay?"

Celene tried valiantly to smile. "Okay."

Meghann put a hand down on the desk to steady herself as she stood there, watching her client walk out of the courtroom. A hand pressed against her shoulder. "Meg?"

It was Julie Gorset, her partner.

"Hey, Jules. Tell me you weren't in the courtroom today."

Julie looked at her sadly. "I was. And we need to talk."

THE Pike Place Public Market was wall-to-wall people on a sunny summer's day. Now, at nighttime, it was quiet.

Meghann stood outside the Athenian's open door. She could go in there and find someone to spend time with her. But suddenly all she could think about was what would really happen. She'd meet some guy whose name wouldn't matter . . . and then be left more alone than when she'd started. A tic began in her left eye.

She reached into her handbag and pulled out her cell phone. She punched in a number, biting down on her lip as it rang. She was just about to hang up when a voice answered.

"Hello?" Then, "Meghann, I recognize your cell phone number."

"I'm going to sue whoever invented caller ID."

"It's eight thirty. Why are you calling me?" Harriet asked.

"My left eyelid is flapping like a flag on the Fourth of July. I need a prescription for a muscle relaxer."

"We talked about a delayed reaction, remember?"

"Yeah. Posttraumatic stress."

"I'll be in my office in thirty minutes."

"If you could just call in a prescription—"

"My office. Thirty minutes."

"I'll be there."

Meghann hung up the phone and put it back in her purse. It took her less than fifteen minutes to get to Harriet's office.

At precisely nine o'clock Harriet showed up. Her hair had been drawn back in a thin headband, and her face shone pink without makeup. "If you make a crack about the headband, I'll charge you double."

"Me? Be judgmental? You must be joking."

Harriet unlocked the door and pushed it open.

Meghann walked through the reception area and went into Harriet's large corner office. Harriet took her usual seat.

"Sit down, Meghann."

"Do I have to?"

"Sit."

Meghann did as she was told.

Harriet steepled her fingers and peered at Meghann over her short, clear-polished nails. "It was a week ago today, wasn't it? When your client's husband tried to shoot you."

Meghann's left foot started to tap. "Yes."

"I told you, you needed to deal with it."

"Yes, you did."

"Are you sleeping?"

"No. Every time I close my eyes, I see it all again. The gunshot whizzing past my ear . . . the way he dropped the gun afterward and sank to his knees . . . May rushing to him, holding him, telling him everything would be all right, that she'd stand behind him . . . the police taking him away in handcuffs. Today I relived it in court." She looked up. "That was lovely, by the way."

"It's not your fault. He's the one to blame."

"I know that. I also know that I handled their divorce badly. I've lost my ability to really *feel* for people." She sighed. "Today I completely screwed a client. My partner has asked me—ordered me, really—to take a vacation."

"That might not be a bad idea."

"Will I feel better in London or Rome . . . alone?"

"Why don't you call Claire? You could go stay at her resort."

"Claire and I can't talk for more than five minutes without getting into an argument."

"You could visit your mother."

"I'd rather contract the West Nile virus."

"So you're saying you have nowhere to go and no one to visit."

"All I said was where would I go?" It had been a mistake to come here. Harriet was making her feel worse. "Look, Harriet"— her voice was softer than usual, and cracked—"I'm falling apart. It's like I'm losing myself. All I want from you is a drug to take the edge off. You know me. I'll be fine in a day or two."

"The queen of denial."

"When something works for me, I stick with it."

"Only denial isn't working anymore, is it? That's why your eyelid is spasming, your hands are shaking, and you can't sleep. You can't keep running away from your own past. Someday you're going to have to settle the tab with Claire."

"This isn't about Claire, damn it."

"Sooner or later, Meg, it's always about family. The past has an irritating way of becoming the present."

"I once had a fortune cookie that said the same thing."

"You're deflecting again."

"No. I'm rejecting." Meghann got to her feet. "Does this mean you won't write me a prescription for a muscle relaxant?"

"It wouldn't help your tic."

"Fine. I'll get an eye patch."

Harriet slowly stood up. "Why won't you let me help you?"

Meghann had asked herself the same question a hundred times.

"What do you want?" Harriet asked finally.

"I don't know."

"Yes, you do. You want to stop feeling so alone."

A shudder passed through Meghann, left her chilled. "I've always been alone. I'm used to it."

"No. Not always."

Meghann's thoughts spooled back to those years, so long ago now, when she and Claire had been inseparable, the best of friends. Then Meg had known how to love.

Enough. This was getting Meg nowhere.

She grabbed her purse off the floor and headed for the door. "Send tonight's bill to my secretary. Charge whatever you want. Good-bye, Harriet." She said good-bye instead of good night because she didn't intend to come back.

She was at the door when Harriet's voice stopped her.

"Be careful. Especially now. Don't let loneliness consume you."

Meghann kept walking, right out the door and into the elevator and across the lobby.

Outside, she looked down at her watch: 9:40.

There was still plenty of time to go to the Athenian.

IN THE passenger seat of an eighteen-wheeler, Joe sat slumped against the window. The driver, a long-hauler named Erv, hit the Jake Brakes and shifted gears. The truck groaned and shuddered and began to slow down. "There's the Hayden exit."

Joe saw the familiar sign and didn't know how to feel. He hadn't been here in so long.

Home.

No. It was where he'd grown up; home was something else—or, more accurately, someone else—and she wouldn't be waiting up for him to return.

The off-ramp looped over the freeway and flattened out onto a treelined road. On the left side was a small, shingled gas station. Erv pulled up in front of the pump and came to a creaking stop.

Joe wedged the handle down and gave the door a good hard push. It creaked wearily open, and he stepped down onto the pavement of western Washington for the first time in three years.

He looked at Erv. "Thanks for the ride."

Erv nodded. "You sure you don't want to go to Seattle? It's only an hour and a half away. There ain't much here."

Joe looked down the long road. "You'd be surprised," he said softly. His sister was just down that road, waiting for him.

He slung his backpack over his shoulder and started walking. In no time he came to the small green sign that welcomed him to

HAYDEN, POPULATION 872. HOME OF LORI ADAMS, 1974 STATE SPELLING BEE CHAMPION. The town where he'd been born looked precisely as he remembered, a pretty little collection of western-themed buildings dozing peacefully beneath this warm June sun.

The buildings all had false fronts, and there were hitching posts stationed here and there along a wooden boardwalk. The stores were mostly the same—the Whitewater Diner and the Basket Case Florist Shoppe, then Mo's Fireside Tavern and the Stock 'Em Up grocery store. Every sign sparked some memory; every doorway had once welcomed him. Now . . . who knew?

He let out a long sigh and kept walking, past the four-way stop sign that introduced the start of town, past the Loose Screw Hardware Shop and the family-owned bakery.

He felt people looking at him; it beat him down, those looks that turned into frowns of recognition. Whispers followed him.

"Is that Joe Wyatt?"

"Did you see that, Myrtle? It was Joe Wyatt."

He tucked his chin close to his chest and kept moving. On Azalea Street he veered left, and then on Cascade he turned right. Here, only a few blocks from Main Street, the world was quiet again. Quaint wood-framed houses sat on impeccably trimmed lawns.

By the time he reached Rhododendron Lane, the street was almost completely deserted. He walked past Craven Farms, quiet this time of year before the fall harvest, and then turned into the driveway. Now the mailbox said TRAINOR. For years it had read WYATT.

The house was a sprawling log-built A-frame that was set amid a perfectly landscaped yard. His father had built this house by hand, log by log. One of the last things Dad had said to them was, *Take care of the house. Your mother loved it so.*

Joe felt a sudden sadness almost too sweet to bear. His sister kept the house looking exactly as it always had. Mom and Dad would be pleased. He climbed the steps, hearing the familiar creaking of the boards underfoot. After a long pause he knocked on the door.

For a moment there was no sound within, then the clattering of heavy-soled shoes and the called-out "Coming!"

The door swung open. Gina stood there, dressed in baggy black sweats and green rubber clogs, breathing hard. Her chestnut-brown hair was a bird's nest of disarray. She took one look at him, mouthed "Oh," then burst into tears. "Joey . . ."

She pulled him into her arms. For a moment he was dazed. He hadn't been touched in so long, it felt wrong somehow.

"Joey," she said again, putting her face in the crook of his neck. He felt her warm tears on his skin, and something inside of him gave way. He brought his arms around her and held on. The whole of his childhood came back to him then, drifted on the baking-bread smell of the house and the sweet citrusy scent of her shampoo.

She drew back, wiping her red-rimmed eyes. "I didn't think you'd really come back." She patted her hair and made a face. "I look like the undead. I was planting flowers in the backyard."

"You look beautiful," he said, meaning it.

"You look sick." She dragged him into the sunlit living room.

"I am. My head is pounding."

Gina hurried from the room. "Some water," she called out, "and aspirin."

He saw the photo on the mantel and walked toward it. The photograph was of five women crowded together; four of them wore matching pink dresses. They were all smiling. Gina, front and center, was in white. Diana was beside her, laughing.

"That's one of my favorite pictures," Gina said, coming up behind him.

"At the end," he said softly, "she talked about you guys. The Bluesers. She must have told me a hundred Lake Chelan stories."

Gina squeezed his shoulder. "We all miss her."

"I know."

"Did you find it out there . . . whatever you were looking for?"

He thought about that. "No," he said at last. "But now that I'm here, I want to be gone again. Everywhere I look, I'll see her."

"Tell me that wasn't true out there, too."

He sighed. His sister was right. It didn't matter where he was. Diana filled his thoughts, his dreams.

"I'm lost, Gigi. I don't know how to start over."

She touched his cheek. "You already have. You're here."

He placed his hand over hers and tried to think of something to say. Nothing came to mind, so he smiled instead. "Where's my beautiful niece? And my brother-in-law?"

"Bonnie's over at River's Edge, playing with Ali."

"And Rex? He doesn't work on Sundays."

"He left me, Joey. Divorced me."

She didn't say, "While you were gone," but she could have. His baby sister had needed him, and he hadn't been there for her. He pulled her into his arms.

She burst into tears. He stroked her hair and whispered that he was here, that he wasn't going anywhere.

For the first time in three years it was the truth.

MEGHANN couldn't get over the sight of her desk. It was clean for the first time in more than a decade. All her pending cases had been portioned out to the other attorneys. She'd promised Julie that she'd take at least three weeks of vacation, but already Meghann was having second thoughts. She hadn't taken a vacation in a decade. What in the hell would she do with all the hours that made up an ordinary day?

She retrieved her briefcase from the desk drawer and headed for the door. She allowed herself a last look at the room that was more of a home to her than her condo and quietly closed the door.

Outside, night was closing in, drawing the warmth from a surprisingly hot day. As she neared the Public Market, the crowds increased. Tourists stood in front of flower shops and outside bakery windows. She cut through Post Alley toward her building. It wasn't a route she often chose, but she didn't want to walk past the Athenian. Not now, when she felt vulnerable.

In the lobby of her building, she waved at the doorman and went up to her condo. She'd forgotten to leave the radio playing. The place was jarringly silent.

Her place was beautiful and neat, with not so much as a paper clip out of place. A pair of brocade sofas faced each other, with an elegant black coffee table in between. The west-facing walls were solid glass. The view was a blue wash of sky and Sound.

Meghann opened the black-and-gold lacquered armoire in the television room and grabbed the remote. As sound blared to life, she slumped into her favorite chair and planted her feet on the ottoman. It took less than five seconds to recognize the theme music.

It was a rerun of her mother's old television show—*Starbase IV*. Mama hurried on-screen wearing that ridiculous lime-green stretch suit with black thigh-high boots.

"Captain Wad," Mama said, "we've received an emergency message from the boys in the dehydratin' pod."

Dehydratin'.

As if a microbotanist on a Martian space station had to be from Alabama. Meg hated the fake accent. And Mama had used it ever since. Said her fans expected it of her.

Meg closed her eyes and remembered. They'd been living in Bakersfield then. . . .

Hey, girls, Mama's home.

Meghann huddled closer to Claire, holding her baby sister tightly. Mama stumbled into the trailer's living room, wearing a clinging red-sequined dress with silver fringe.

I've brought Mr. Mason home with me. You girls be nice to him now, she said in that boozy voice that meant she'd wake up mean.

Meghann knew she had to act fast. With a man in the trailer Mama wouldn't be able to think about much else, and the rent was long past due. She reached down for the wrinkled copy of *Variety* that she'd stolen from the local library. *Mama?*

Mama lit up a menthol cigarette. *What is it?*

Meghann thrust out the magazine. She'd outlined the ad in red ink. It read, "Mature actress sought for small part in science fiction television series. Open call." Then the address in Los Angeles.

Mama read the ad out loud. Her smile froze in place at the words "mature actress." After a long, tense moment she laughed and gave Mr. Mason a little shove toward the bedroom. When he went into the room and closed the door behind him, Mama knelt down and opened her arms. *Give Mama a hug.*

Meghann and Claire flew into her embrace. They waited days for a moment like this, sometimes weeks, but when Mama turned on the heat of her love, it warmed you to the bone.

Thank you, Miss Meggy. I don't know what I'd do without you. I'll surely try out for that part. Now, you two scamper off and stay out of trouble. I've got some entertaining to do.

Mama read for the role. To her—and everyone else's—amazement she nailed the audition. Instead of winning the small part she'd gone up for, she won the starring role of Tara Zyn, the space station's microbotanist.

Meghann sighed. She didn't want to think about the week Mama had gone to Los Angeles and left her daughters alone in that dirty trailer—or the changes that had come afterward. Meghann and Claire had never really been sisters since.

Beside her, the phone rang. Meghann pounced on it, eager to talk to anyone. "Hello?"

"Hey, Meggy, it's me. Your mama. How are you, darlin'?"

Meg rolled her eyes at the accent. "I'm fine, Mama. And you?"

"Couldn't be better. The Fan-ference was this weekend. Lordy, I signed s'many autographs, my fingers ache."

"Well, your fans love you."

"Thank God for small miracles. It surely is nice to talk to you, Meggy. Y'all should come down and visit me."

Mama always said that, but Meghann couldn't sit alone in this condo for three weeks. "I'm taking a vacation," she said in a rush. "Maybe I could come stay with you."

"Oh. That would be . . . fine. Maybe this Christmas—"

"Tomorrow."

"Tomorrow?" Mama laughed. "Honey, I've got a photographer from *People* magazine comin' over at three o'clock, and at my age I wake up lookin' like one o' those hairless dogs. It takes ten women all day to make me beautiful."

Meghann wanted to hang up, say forget it, but when she looked around her empty, photo-free apartment, she felt almost sick. "How about Monday, then? Maybe we could go to a spa."

"Don't you *ever* watch the E! channel? I'm leavin' for Cleveland on Monday. I'm doin' Shakespeare in some park with Pamela Anderson and Charlie Sheen. *Hamlet*."

"*You? You're* doing Shakespeare?"

"I'm gonna forget I heard that tone in your voice."

"Cut the accent, Mama. It's me. I know you were born in Detroit. Joan Jojovitch is the name on your birth certificate."

"Now you're just being rude. You always were a prickly child. It's a big break for me."

For me. Mama's favorite words. "Well, good luck. You better get a good night's sleep before the magazine shoot."

"That's the God's honest truth." Mama exhaled heavily. "Maybe y'all could come down when I'm not so busy. Claire, too."

"Sure. Bye, Mama."

Meghann hung up the phone. For the next hour she paced the apartment, trying to formulate a plan that made sense.

The phone rang. She dived for it. "Hello?"

"Hi, Meg."

"Claire? This is a nice surprise." And for once it was. "I talked to Mama today. You won't believe this. She's doing—"

"I'm getting married."

"Shakespeare in— *Married?*"

"I've never been so happy, Meg. I know it's crazy, but that's love, I guess."

"Who are you marrying?"

"Bobby Jack Austin. I met him ten days ago in Chelan. I know what you're going to say, but—"

"Ten days ago. Claire! Sometimes you sneak away for a wild weekend with men you just met. What you don't do is marry them."

"I'm in love, Meg. Please don't ruin it for me."

Meg wanted to give advice so badly, she had to curl her hands into fists. "What does he do for a living?"

"He's a singer-songwriter. He was singing in Cowboy Bob's Western Roundup when I first saw him. My heart stopped for a second. Have you ever felt that way?"

Before Meghann could answer, Claire went on. "He's a ski instructor in the winter, and he travels around in the summer, playing his music. He's two years older than I am and so good-looking, you won't believe it. Better than Brad Pitt. He's going to be a star."

Meghann let it all soak in. Her sister was marrying a thirty-seven-year-old ski bum who dreamed of being a country-and-western singer. And the best gig he could get was at Cowboy Bob's.

"Does he know what the campground is worth? Will he sign a prenuptial agreement?"

"Damn you, Meg. Can't you be happy for me?"

"I want to be," she said, and it was true. "When's the wedding?"

"Saturday, the twenty-third."

"Of *this* month?" This was crazy. "I need to meet him."

"Of course. The rehearsal dinner—"

"No way. I need to meet him *now*. I'll be at your house tomorrow night. I'll take you guys out to dinner."

"Really, Meg, you don't have to do that."

"I have to meet the man who stole my sister's heart, don't I?"

"Okay, I'll see you tomorrow." Claire paused, then said, "It'll be good to see you."

"Yeah. Bye." Meg hung up, then punched in her office number and left a message for her secretary. "I want everything we've got on prenuptial agreements delivered to my house by ten o'clock to-morrow morning." As an afterthought she added, "Thanks."

Then she headed for her computer to do some checking up on Bobby Jack Austin. *This* was what she'd do on her idiotic vacation. She'd save Claire from making the biggest mistake of her life.

CLAIRE hung up the phone. In the silence that followed, doubt crept into the room. She and Bobby *were* moving awfully fast.

"Damn you, Meg."

But even as she cursed her sister, Claire knew the doubt had been there all along, a little seed inside her, waiting to sprout and grow. She was too old to be swept away by passion.

She had a daughter to think about, after all. Alison had never known her biological father. It had been easy so far, bubble-wrapping Ali's world so that none of life's sharp edges could hurt her. Marriage would change everything.

The last thing Claire wanted to do was marry a man who had itchy feet. She had had four stepfathers before she'd turned nine. That number didn't include the men she'd been asked to call Uncle, the men who'd passed through Mama's life like shots of tequila. There and gone, leaving nothing behind but a bitter aftertaste.

Claire walked to the window. Outside, the sun was just begin-ning to set. The camp lay bathed in a rose-gold light.

Dad and Bobby strolled into view. Bobby carried a Weed Eater in one hand and a can of gasoline in the other. In the days he'd been here, he had pitched in with the work. He was good at it, though she knew he wouldn't be happy at River's Edge forever. Already he'd mentioned going on the road for a few weeks this summer. The three of them. "The Austins' road trip," was how he put it. Claire hadn't broached the idea with her father, but knew he'd be all for it.

Dad and Bobby stopped in front of cabin number 5. Dad pointed up toward the eaves, and Bobby nodded. A minute later they were both laughing. Dad put his hand on Bobby's shoulder. They moved away, toward the laundry room.

"Hey, Mommy." Claire turned around. Ali stood at the bottom of the stairs. "Grandpa's taking me to Smitty's Garage. We're gonna get the truck fixed."

As Claire watched her daughter run out the front door, she felt the pressing weight of responsibility. What if the marriage didn't work? She needed to talk to someone about this.

Not her sister, of course. A friend. She dialed Gina's number.

Gina answered on the first ring. "Hello?"

Claire slumped back into the oversize chair. "It's me. The insta-marry queen. Meghann thinks I'm being an idiot."

"Since when do we care what *she* thinks? She's an attorney, for goodness' sake. That's below invertebrates on the evolutionary chain."

Claire smiled. "I knew you'd put it in perspective. Just tell me I'm not being a selfish bitch who is going to ruin her daughter's life by marrying a stranger."

"Oh, so it's your mother we're talking about."

"I don't want to be like her." Claire's voice was suddenly soft.

"I've known you since all five of us showed up for the first day of school in the same blue shirt. You've never been selfish. And I've never seen you this happy. God has finally given you the gift of love and passion. Don't return it unopened."

"I'm scared. I should have done this when I was young."

"Of course you're scared. A smart person is afraid of marriage. If you're not ready to marry him, wait. But don't wait because your big sister made you question yourself. Follow your heart."

"What would I do without you?"

Gina laughed. "The same thing I'd do without you—drink too much and whine to strangers."

"How are you doing?"

She sighed. "Not good. Rex came by last night. The son of a bitch has lost about ten pounds and dyed his hair. Pretty soon he'll ask me to call him the Rexster again." She paused. "He wants to marry that woman."

"Ouch."

"Ouch with a blowtorch. It hurts like hell. But you haven't heard the real news: Joey's back."

"You're kidding. Where's he been?"

Gina lowered her voice. "Here and there, he says. He looks bad.

Older. He got home yesterday. He's been asleep for almost thirteen hours. I hope I never love anyone as much as he loved Diana."

"What's he going to do?"

"I don't know. I said he could stay here, but he won't. This house brings back a lot of memories. He stared at the picture of my wedding for almost an hour. Honest to God, I wanted to cry."

"Give him my love."

"You got it."

They talked for a few more minutes about ordinary, everyday things. By the time they hung up, Claire felt better.

She looked down at her left hand, at the engagement ring she wore. It was a strip of silver foil, carefully folded and twisted around her finger.

She refused to think of what her sister would say about it and remembered instead how she'd felt when Bobby put it there.

Marry me, he'd said on bended knee. His eyes had been filled with the kind of love she'd only dreamed of.

Gina was right. This love was a gift she'd been given. She wouldn't turn away from it because she was afraid. One thing motherhood had taught her—love required boldness. And fear simply came with the package.

She grabbed her sweater off the sofa and slipped it over her shoulders, then went outside. Night had almost completely fallen now; darkness enveloped the salmon-hued granite peaks.

Claire made her nightly rounds slowly, stopping to talk to several of their guests. It was completely dark by the time she reached the small row of cabins on the property's eastern edge.

Cabin 4 had a pretty little porch that faced the river. They had taken the cabin off the market this summer because of rain damage to the roof; the vacancy had given Bobby a place to stay until the wedding. *Destiny,* Dad had said when he gave Claire the key.

Now destiny sat on the edge of the porch, cross-legged, his body veiled in shadows, a guitar across his lap. He stared out at the river, plucking a slow and uncertain tune.

Claire eased into the darkness beneath a giant Douglas fir. Hidden, she watched him. The music sent shivers along her flesh.

Almost too quietly to hear, he started to sing. *"I've been walkin' all my life . . . on a road goin' nowhere. Then I turned a corner, darlin' . . . and there you were."*

Claire stepped out of the shadows. Bobby looked up and saw her. A smile crinkled the suntanned planes of his face.

He began to sing again, his gaze on her face. *"For the first time in my life . . . I believe in God Almighty . . . in the Lord my grandpa promised me . . . 'cause, honey, I see heaven in your eyes."* He strummed a few more chords, and then he thumped his hand on the guitar and grinned. "That's all I've written so far. I know it needs work." He put down the guitar and moved toward her.

With every footstep, she felt her breathing shorten, until, by the time he was standing in front of her, she couldn't draw a full breath. It was almost embarrassing to feel this much.

He took her left hand in his, looked down at the strip of foil that was supposed to be a diamond ring. "Pathetic," he whispered. "Not every woman would accept a ring like this."

"I love you, Bobby. That's all that matters."

"I'm no prize, Claire. You know that. I've made mistakes in my life. Three of 'em, to be exact."

"I'm a single mother who never married. I know about mistakes."

"I've never felt this way before," he said softly.

"What way?"

"As if my heart doesn't belong to me anymore, as if it can't beat without you. You're inside me, Claire, holding me up. You make me want to be more than I am."

"I want us to grow old together." She whispered the words.

"I want to hear our kids fight about who's touching who in the smelly backseat of a minivan."

Claire laughed. It felt so good to dream with someone.

He pulled her into his arms, danced with her to the music of the river and the crickets.

Finally Claire said, "My sister, Meghann, is coming tomorrow. She was predictably underwhelmed by our decision to get married."

Taking her hand, he led her to his porch. They sat down in the creaky oak swing and rocked gently. "I thought you said she'd boycott the wedding."

"Wishful thinking."

"Does her opinion matter?"

"It shouldn't."

"But it does."

Claire felt like a fool. "It does."

"She won't be able to change your mind about me, will she?"

"She's never been able to change my mind about anything. It's what makes her foam at the mouth."

"As long as you love me, I can take anything."

"Well, Bobby Austin . . ." She put her arms around him and leaned over for a kiss. Just before their lips touched, she whispered, "Then you can take anything. Even my sister."

CHAPTER FIVE

"It's stupid to marry a man you just met."

"Stupid is not a good word choice."

"It's inadvisable to—"

"You're her sister, not her lawyer."

Meghann had been carrying on this demented conversation with the rearview mirror for the entire drive from Seattle. How was it that she came up with closing arguments that would bring a jury to tears and she couldn't find a simple, compelling way to warn her sister of impending doom?

At the last stop before Hayden, a run-down tavern—the Roadhouse—sat huddled beneath a blinking neon sign that recommended Coors Light. Honest to God, she wanted to pull over, walk into that crowded tavern, and lose herself in the smoky darkness. It would certainly be better than saying to Claire after being separated all these years, "You're making a mistake." But she didn't slow down. Instead, she turned off the freeway and drove nine miles on a two-lane road bordered by towering evergreens.

The small green sign welcomed her to Hayden.

Meghann slowed down. It still looked like the kind of place that welcomed newcomers, where women brought homemade tuna casseroles to the families who moved in. But Meghann knew better. She'd lived here long enough to know how cruel these nice-looking people could be to a girl who ran with the wrong crowd.

Sure, a small town could comfort a person; it could also turn cold fast.

Meghann came to the one and only stoplight. When it turned green, she hit the gas and sped through town. A few miles later she came to the sign: RIVER'S EDGE RESORT. NEXT LEFT.

She turned onto the gravel road. The trees on either side were gigantic. At the first driveway she slowed again. A cute mailbox, painted to look like a killer whale, read C. CAVENAUGH.

The once wild yard had been tamed; it now looked like an English country garden. The house was Martha Stewart perfect—pale butter-yellow siding and glossy white trim, a pretty white wraparound porch decorated with hanging pots of geraniums and lobelia.

She parked and got out of the car. Lugging gifts, she walked up to the front door and knocked. No one answered.

After a long wait she walked back to the car and drove the five hundred or so yards to the campground's main office.

She walked past the swimming pool toward the long, narrow log building that served as the registration office. A bell tinkled overhead as she opened the door.

Sam Cavenaugh stood behind the desk. At her entrance he looked up. His ready smile faded slowly, then reinforced itself. "Hey, Meg. It's good to see you. It's been too damn long."

"Yeah. I'm sure you missed me." As always, Meghann felt uncomfortable around Sam, angry. She still remembered the day he told her, *Go. Just leave.* He'd thought she was a bad influence on his daughter. But what she'd really hated, the one that stayed with her was, *Just like your damn mother.*

They stared at each other. "You look good," he said at last.

"You, too." Meghann glanced down at her watch. The last thing she wanted to do was stand around not talking with Sam.

"Claire told me to watch out for you. The Ford family, over in campsite seventeen, had a little emergency with their stove, but she should be back any minute."

"Good. I'll wait for her at the house, then."

She turned and walked away, let the door slam shut behind her. She was halfway to the car when she heard his voice again.

"She's happy, you know. With this fella," he said.

Meghann turned around. "If I remember correctly, you were happy when you married Mama. I was happy when I married Eric."

Sam walked toward her. "Your mama is a piece of work, that's for sure, but I'm glad I married her."

"You must be on drugs."

"Claire," was all he said.

"Oh." Meghann felt a pinch of jealousy. There it was again—the Claire/father-daughter thing.

"Be careful with her," he said. "You're her sister."

"I know I'm her sister." Once again she walked away. She got into her car and drove to Claire's house.

This time when she knocked on the front door, she heard the patter of feet from inside. The door burst open. Alison stood there, dressed in daisy-festooned denim overalls and a pretty yellow eyelet blouse.

"You can't be Alison Katherine Cavenaugh. She's a baby."

Ali beamed at that. "I'm a big girl now."

"Yes, you are. Can you give your aunt Meg a hug?"

Alison moved forward and gave her a lukewarm hug. When she stepped back, Meg said, "I brought you a present."

"Let me guess." Claire emerged from the shadows at the end of the hallway. "A Swiss army knife."

"No. A BB gun."

"You didn't."

Meghann laughed. "The dullest-looking salesperson at Toys 'R' Us recommended this." She handed Alison a brightly wrapped box.

Ali ripped it open. "It's a Groovy Girl, Mommy. A Groovy Girl!" She flung herself at Meghann, this time hugging for real. She showed the doll to Claire, then ran upstairs.

Meghann handed Claire a bottle of wine—Far Niente 1997. "This is one of my favorites."

"Thank you."

They stared at each other. Finally Claire surged forward, pulled Meghann into a quickie hug, then let her go.

Meghann stumbled back, too surprised by the gesture to respond. "Dinner smells good, but I wanted to take you out."

"The Chuck Wagon smorgasbord isn't exactly your style."

"Oh."

"Anyway, come in. You've never been to my place."

Meghann followed Claire to the sofa and sat down beside her.

She couldn't help noticing the ridiculous engagement ring—a band of tinfoil, for God's sake. It was good she'd come up here. There was no point in putting it off. "Claire, I think—"

Then *he* walked into the room. Meghann knew instantly why her sister had fallen so hard. Bobby might be a loser as a singer, but he was a winner in the looks department. When he smiled, it was with his whole face. A man like this didn't just sweep you off your feet; he twirled you into the air so far and fast there was nowhere to go but down. He and Claire exchanged a look that radiated love.

"I'm Bobby Austin," he said, smiling.

Meghann rose and shook his hand. "Meghann Dontess."

"Claire says folks call you Meg."

"My friends do, yes."

He smiled. "I'm judging by that bite-on-a-lemon look of yours that you'd like me to stick with Miz Dontess."

"I imagine those mountain girls in Arkansas think you're charming."

"The Texas girls sure did." He put an arm around Claire. "But those days are behind me now. I've found the girl I want to grow old with." He kissed Claire lightly on the cheek; then he took the wine bottle and walked into the kitchen.

In the few moments he was gone, Meghann stood there, staring at her sister, trying to choose her words with care, but nothing seemed quite right.

Bobby returned with two glasses of wine and handed one to Meghann. "I imagine you have some questions for me," he said, sitting down.

His forthrightness threw Meghann off. Slowly she sat down in the chair opposite the sofa. They were separate entities now: Bobby and Claire versus Meghann. "Tell me about yourself."

"I love Claire."

"Something substantive."

"I'm thirty-seven years old. Graduated from Oklahoma State. Degree in music appreciation. I've . . . been married."

Meghann leaned forward, on alert. "How many times?"

He glanced at Claire. "Three."

Meghann looked at Claire. "You've got to be kidding."

He scooted forward. "I married Suellen when we were eighteen years old. She was pregnant, and where I come from—"

"You've got kids?"

"No." His voice grew soft. "Miscarriage. After that, there wasn't much reason to stay married. We lasted less than three months. I got married again at twenty-one. Unfortunately, it turned out that she wanted a different life than I did. Nice cars, nice jewelry. I got arrested when they busted her for selling cocaine out of our house. I lived with her for two years and never noticed it. I just thought she was moody as hell. Nobody believed I wasn't a part of it. Laura was the only one who counted. She was—is—a pediatrician who loves country music. We were married for ten years. It broke up about a year ago. I could tell you why, but it's none of your business. Claire knows everything, though."

A three-time loser and a felon. *Perfect.*

And now the bad sister had to break the good sister's heart.

Claire got off the sofa, moved toward her. She sat on the carved Chinese chest that served as a coffee table.

"I know you can't be happy for me, Meg."

"I want to be." It was the truth. "It's just that—"

"He wouldn't get a platinum rating. I know. And you handle divorces for a living. I know that, too. Most of all, I know that you grew up in Mama's house." She leaned forward. "I *know,* Meg."

Meghann felt the weight of those few words. Her sister had thought of all the same reasons. There wasn't anything Meghann could say that Claire didn't already know.

"It won't ever make sense, and I know it's crazy and risky and—worst of all—Mama-like. But it would mean a lot to me if you'd hug me and say you're happy for me. Even if it's a lie."

Meghann looked into her sister's pale green eyes and was reminded of their childhood. Whenever Mama had brought a new "friend" home, Claire had let herself believe that *finally* there would be a daddy in her life. Each stepfather had broken a tiny piece of Claire's heart. And yet, when the next man arrived, her sister found a way to believe again. Of course Claire believed in Bobby Austin.

There was no way she would change Claire's mind or—more important—her heart. Thus she had two choices: pretend to give her blessing or stick to her guns.

"I trust you, Claire," Meghann said at last. "If you say Bobby Austin is the man you love, that's good enough for me."

Claire released a sharp breath. "Thank you." She leaned forward and hugged Meghann, who was too surprised by it to hug her back.

Claire drew back and stood up. She went over to the sofa and sat down by Bobby, who immediately put an arm around her.

Meghann tried to think of what to say in the awkward silence that followed. "So what's the wedding plan? Justice of the peace?"

"No way." Claire laughed. "I waited thirty-five years for this. I'm having the whole enchilada. White dress. Formal church wedding. Cake. Reception with dancing. All of it."

"There's a consultant in my building," Meghann said. "I think she planned Bill Gates's wedding."

"This is Hayden, not Seattle. I'll rent the V.F.W. hall, and everyone will pitch in with potluck. It'll be great."

"Potluck? *Potluck?*" Meghann got to her feet. Apparently there was something of her mother in her after all. She wasn't going to let her sister have a Wal-Mart wedding. "I'll organize the wedding and reception," she said impulsively.

Claire's smile faded. "You?"

"I'm not a social moron. I can do this."

"But—but your job is so hectic. I couldn't ask you to take time out of your busy schedule for this."

"You didn't ask. I offered. And it so happens that I find myself . . . underutilized at work." The idea seized hold of her. Maybe it could bring them together. "This would be perfect, really. I'd *like* to do this for you, Claire."

"Oh." Claire sounded underwhelmed. "Why am I seeing *Father of the Bride* playing in my head? You never do anything in a small way, Meg."

Meghann felt awkward suddenly, vulnerable. She wasn't certain why she wanted this so badly. "I'll listen to you and do what you want. It'll be *your* wedding. I promise."

"Okay," Claire said finally. "You can help me plan my wedding."

Meghann grinned and clapped her hands. "Good. Now, what's the date again—the twenty-third? Next Saturday? That's not much time to pull this together." She headed for the kitchen, where she found a scrap of paper and began a to-do list.

"Oh, man," she heard her sister say, "I've created a monster."

By the second night in his sister's house, Joe felt as if he were suffocating. Everywhere he looked he saw glimpses of his old life. He didn't know how he was going to go forward, but he knew he couldn't stay here.

He waited until Gina left to go grocery shopping, then crammed his things—including several framed photographs of Diana that he'd taken from the house—into the old backpack and headed for the door. He left a note on the kitchen counter: "Can't stay here. Sorry. Hurts too much. I know this is a rough time for you, so I won't go far. Will call soon. Love you, J."

He walked the few miles back to town. There were a few people milling around the streets, and more than one face peered frowningly up at him, but no one approached him.

He was about to give up on finding a job here, when he came to the end of town. He stood across the street from Riverfront Park, staring at a metal Quonset hut that advertised SMITTY'S, THE BEST AUTO SHOP IN HAYDEN.

On the chain-link fence was a sign: HELP WANTED. EXPERIENCE REQUESTED, BUT WHO AM I KIDDING?

Joe crossed the street and headed toward the entrance.

A dog started barking. He noticed the BEWARE OF DOG sign. Seconds later a miniature white poodle came tearing around the corner. "Madonna, stop that damn yapping." An old man stepped out from the shadowed darkness of the Quonset hut. He wore oil-stained overalls and a Mariners baseball cap. "Don't mind the dog. What can I do ya for?"

"I saw your 'Help Wanted' sign."

"No kiddin'." The old man slapped his thigh. "That thing's been up there pret near on two years now. I—" He paused, stepped forward, frowning slowly. "Joe Wyatt?"

Joe tensed. "Hey, Smitty."

Smitty blew out a heavy breath. "I'll be damned."

"I'm back. And I need a job. But if it'd cost you customers to hire me, I understand. No hard feelings."

"You want a job *wrenching?* But you're a doctor—"

"That life is over."

Smitty stared at him a long time, then said, "You remember my son, Phil?"

"He was a lot older than me, but yeah, I remember him."

"Vietnam ruined him. Guilt, I think. He did stuff over there. . . . Anyway, I've seen a man run before. It isn't good. Of course I'll hire you, Joe. The cabin still comes with the job. You want it?"

"Yes."

Smitty nodded, then led the way through the Quonset hut and out the other end. The backyard was big and well maintained. Flowers grew in riotous clumps along the walkway. A thicket of evergreens stood clustered behind a small log cabin.

"You were a teenager the last time you lived here."

"That was a long time ago."

"Yeah." Smitty sighed. "Helga still keeps it spick-and-span clean. She'll be glad to have you back."

Joe followed Smitty to the cabin.

Inside, it was as clean as always. A red-striped woolen blanket covered an old leather sofa, and a rocking chair sat next to the river-rock fireplace. The kitchen appeared well stocked with appliances and pots and pans, and a single bedroom boasted a queen-size bed.

Joe reached out and shook Smitty's bear-claw hand. "Thank you, Smitty," he said, surprised at how deep his gratitude ran.

"There are a lot of people in this town who care about you, Joe. You seem to have forgotten that."

"That's nice to hear. Still, I'd be happier if no one knew I was here—for a while, anyway."

"It's a long road back from something like that, I guess."

"A very long road."

After Smitty left, Joe burrowed through his backpack for one of the framed photographs that he'd taken from his sister's house. He stared down at Diana's smiling face. "It's a start," he said to her.

MEGHANN woke up disoriented. She thought a radio was on in a room down the hall. Then she realized that the noise was birdsong. Birdsong, for God's sake.

Claire's house.

She sat up in bed. The beautifully decorated guest room was oddly comforting. Everywhere were handmade trinkets—proof of time spent on the little things—as well as Ali's artwork.

There was a knock at the door, then a hesitantly called out "Meg?"

She glanced at the bedside clock: 10:15. *Oh, man.* She rubbed her eyes, which felt like a sandpit from lack of sleep. As usual, she'd tossed and turned all night.

"I'm up," she said, throwing the covers back.

"Breakfast is on the table," Claire said through the closed door. "I'm going to go clean the swimming pool. We'll leave at about eleven if that's still okay."

It took Meghann a second to remember. She'd promised to go wedding-dress shopping in Hayden with the Bluesers.

"I'll be ready."

"See you then."

Meghann listened to the footsteps as Claire walked away. How long could she keep up this charade of "I'm your sister, I support your wedding"? And yet, because Meghann couldn't return to work, she found herself preparing to plan her sister's wedding. Honestly, who could possibly be worse for the job?

Meghann got out of bed and hurried down the hallway to the small second-floor bathroom. She brushed her teeth, then took a quick, very hot shower. Thirty minutes later she was ready to go, re-dressed in yesterday's clothes—a white Dolce & Gabbana blouse and a pair of low-rise Marc Jacobs jeans.

Outside, the sun shone brightly on the well-tended yard. It was late June, a glorious time of year in the Northwest. Meghann tossed her purse into her Porsche and got inside. The engine growled to life. She drove toward the resort office slowly, careful not to stir up too much dust. It was a short distance, but her high-heeled sandals couldn't handle the loose stone.

She pulled up in front of the registration building and parked. She went into the building. It was empty.

She went to the desk and found the Hayden phone book. There was one wedding consultant listing: "Royal Event Planning." In fine print it read, "Pretend you'll only get married once."

Meghann couldn't help smiling at that. She wrote down the number and put it in her purse.

She went out to her car, put the convertible top down, and waited. At eleven o'clock Claire appeared, wearing a pair of jeans and a RIVER'S EDGE RESORT T-shirt. She tossed her canvas handbag behind the seat and climbed in. "Now, this is going to town in style."

Meghann didn't know if Claire intended that remark as a put-down or not, so she kept silent.

"You sure slept late," Claire said. "I thought you usually got to the office by seven."

"I had trouble sleeping last night."

"Please don't worry about me, Meg. Please."

Meghann couldn't let her sister think the insomnia was because of the wedding. "It's not the wedding. I never sleep."

"Since when?"

"I guess it started in college. Cramming all night for exams. You know how it is."

"No, I don't."

Meghann had been trying to protect Claire, to hide the fact that the insomnia had started when their family fell apart, but college had been the wrong tack. "From what I hear, motherhood causes a few all-nighters, too."

"You know something about babies. Mama said I was colicky."

"Yeah, like Mama would know. You didn't have colic. You had ear infections. When you were sick, you wailed like a banshee. I used to carry you, screaming, down to the Laundromat. If I sat on top of the dryer, holding you, you'd eventually fall asleep. Mama always wondered what happened to all her quarters."

"No wonder I don't mind doing the laundry. Here, this is it." Claire pointed to an old Victorian house, painted Pepto-Bismol pink, with lavender trim. The white picket fence bore a hand-painted sign that read MISS ABIGAIL'S DRAWERS. COME ON IN.

Meghann looked up at the ridiculously cute house. "We could zip down to Escada or Nordstrom."

"Don't be yourself, Meg."

"Okay." She sighed. "Lead on. I'll shut my mouth."

They walked up the rickety stairs and entered the store.

"Hello!" Claire called out.

There was an immediate response—a gaggle of women's voices, then a herd of running footsteps.

A large, older woman, wearing a floral muumuu, barreled around the corner. "Claire Cavenaugh, I'm so glad to *finally* be able to show you the second floor."

"Wedding dresses are on the second floor," Claire said to Meghann. "Miss Abigail had given up on me."

Before Meghann could respond, two other women hurried into the room. One was short and wore a baggy, waistless dress and white tennis shoes. The other was tall, perhaps too thin, and dressed flawlessly in beige silk. Two of the Bluesers. Waistless dress, Meg learned, was Gina, and beige silk was Charlotte.

"Karen couldn't make it today," Gina said. "Willie had an orthodontist appointment, and Dottie sat on her glasses."

"In other words," Charlotte said, "an ordinary Karen day."

Claire fell in beside Charlotte and Abigail. They were talking about lace and beadwork and veils.

"So, Meghann," Gina said, "I'm surprised you could get away from the office. I hear you're the best divorce attorney in Seattle."

"I wouldn't miss Claire's wedding."

"I know a divorce attorney. She's good at breaking up families."

"That's what we do."

A look passed through Gina's eyes. Her voice softened. "Do you ever put them back together?"

"Not often."

Gina's face seemed to fall; it crumpled like an old paper bag, and Meghann understood. "You're going through a divorce."

Gina tried to smile. "Just finished it, actually. Tell me it'll get better."

"It will," Meg said softly. "But it may take a while. There are several support groups that might help you."

"I've got the Bluesers to cry with, but thanks. I appreciate the honesty. Now, let's go upstairs and find your sister the perfect dress."

Gina led Meg upstairs. By the time they got there, Claire was already wearing the first dress. It had huge leg-of-mutton sleeves and a skirt that looked like an upside-down teacup. Meg sat down in a white wicker chair. Gina stood behind her.

"Oh, my. That's lovely," Abigail said.

Claire stood in front of a three-paneled full-length mirror, turning this way and that.

"It's very princesslike," Charlotte said.

Claire looked at Meg. "What do you think?"

Meghann wasn't sure what was expected of her: honesty or support. She took another look at the dress and knew support was impossible. "It's hideous."

"My sister is always harsh," Claire said quietly, walking back into the dressing room.

Meghann sighed. She'd screwed up again, wielded her opinion like a blunt instrument to the back of the head. She hunkered down in her chair and clamped her mouth shut.

The remainder of the afternoon was a mind-wrecking parade of cheap dresses, one after another. Claire zipped in, got opinions, and zipped out. She didn't again ask for Meghann's opinion, and Meghann knew better than to offer it. Instead, she leaned back in her chair and rested her head against the wall.

A jab in the rib cage woke her up. She blinked, leaned forward. Charlotte, Abigail, and Claire were walking away from her into a room marked HATS AND VEILS.

Gina said to her, "I'd heard you could be a bitch, but falling asleep while your sister tries on wedding dresses is pretty rude."

"It was the only way I could keep quiet. Did she find one?"

"No."

Meghann frowned. "What do you mean I'm a bitch? Is that what Claire says?"

"No. Yes. Sometimes. You know how it is when you're drinking margaritas on a bad day. Karen calls her sister Susan the Soulless Psychopath. Claire calls you Jaws."

Meghann wanted to smile but couldn't. "Oh."

"I remember when she moved here, you know," Gina said softly. "She cried if you looked at her the wrong way. All she'd say for years was that she missed her sister. I didn't find out until after graduation what had happened to her."

"What I'd done, you mean."

"I'm not one to judge. My point is this: Claire was wounded by all of that, but whether she admits it or not, it means a lot to her that you're here."

"I told her I'd plan the wedding."

"You seem perfectly suited for it."

"Oh, yeah. I'm a real romantic." Meghann sighed.

"All you have to do is listen to Claire. When was the last time you sat down for a drink with your sister and just *talked*?"

"Let's put it this way: We wouldn't have been old enough to have wine with our meal."

"That's what I thought. Go with her now."

"But Alison—"

"Sam can take care of Ali. I'll let him know."

"Claire won't want to go with me after I nixed the dresses."

"And fell asleep. The snoring was especially poignant."

"You don't pull any punches, do you?"

"Thus the divorce. Take Claire out for dinner. Go see a movie. Do *something* sisterly. It's about time."

CLAIRE glanced sideways at her sister, who was behind the wheel. "Where are we going?" she asked for the fourth time.

"You'll see." Always the same answer.

"I need to get back to Ali," Claire said, also for the fourth time.

"We're here." Meg tucked the silver Porsche into an empty parking spot on the street. Before Claire could respond, Meghann was out of the car and standing by the meter. "Come on."

They were in downtown Seattle now. Her sister's territory. Claire fell into step beside Meghann.

"Here," Meghann said, stopping suddenly in front of a narrow white door flanked by windows on either side. A small iron-scrolled sign read BY DESIGN.

"What *is* this place?"

"You said I could plan your wedding, right?" Meg opened the door and went inside.

Claire hesitated.

"Come on." Meghann waited for her in front of an elevator.

Claire followed. A second later the elevator pinged, and the doors slid open. They went in; the doors closed.

Meghann said, "I'm sorry about this morning. I screwed up."

"Sleeping is one thing. Snoring is another."

"I know. I'm sorry."

Claire sighed. "It's the story of our lives, Meg, but we never—"

The elevator doors opened. Claire gasped.

There were mannequins everywhere, dressed in the most beautiful wedding dresses Claire had ever seen. She stepped forward. The gown in front of her was an off-the-shoulder creation. Claire peeked at the price tag. It read ESCADA $4200.

She let go of it suddenly and turned to Meghann. "Let's go."

Meg grabbed her wrist. "I want you to try on dresses *here*."

"I can't. I know you're just being you, Meg. But this . . . hurts a little. I work at a campground."

"I don't want to say this twice, Claire, so please listen and believe me. I work eighty-five hours a week, and my clients pay almost four hundred dollars an hour. Money is something I have. It would mean a lot to me to buy you this wedding gown. You don't belong in the dresses we saw this morning. I'm sorry if you think I'm a bitch and a snob, but that's how I feel."

Before Claire could answer, a woman cried out, "Meghann Dontess. In a wedding shop. Who would *ever* believe it?"

A tall, rail-thin woman in a navy-blue sheath dress strode forward. Her hair, a perfect combination of white-blond and silver, stood out from her face in a Meg Ryan–type cut.

"Hello, Risa," Meg said, extending her hand.

"And this is the great one's baby sister, yes?"

Claire heard the barest hint of an Eastern European accent, maybe even Russian, then said, "I'm Claire."

"And Meghann is letting you marry."

"She's advised against it, actually."

Risa threw back her head and laughed. "Of course she advised against it. I have heard such advice from her twice. Both times I should have listened, yes, but love will have its way." She took a step back, studying Claire from head to toe.

"You are beautiful," she said at last. "Size ten or twelve, I expect. For you I think the classics: Prada, Valentino, Armani, Wang. Come." She turned and began marching away. Her hand snaked out now and then to grab a dress.

Claire looked at Meghann. "Armani? Vera Wang?" She shook her head, unable to say, "You can't do this."

"We can always leave without buying anything," Meghann said. "Try them on. Just for fun."

A few minutes later Claire stepped into a dressing area that was bigger than her bedroom. Three floor-to-ceiling mirrors fanned out in front of her. A small wooden platform stood in the center.

"Go on. The dresses are in there." Risa gave her a gentle shove.

Claire went into the dressing room, where several gowns hung waiting. The first one was a stunning white silk Ralph Lauren with an intricate lace-and-beadwork-patterned bodice.

Claire peeled out of her wrinkled jeans and T-shirt. The gown floated over her shoulders like a cloud.

"Come on, honey. Let's see," Risa said.

Claire opened the door and stepped into the dressing area. There was a gasp at her entrance. Risa shouted, "Shoes!" and ran off.

Meg stood there, holding an armful of dresses. Her lips parted in a soft sigh.

Claire couldn't help smiling. She stepped up onto the platform and looked at herself in the mirror. No wonder Meghann had hated the gowns this morning.

Risa came back, brandishing a pair of satin pumps. "Put them on."

Claire did as she was told, then stood very still. "I think the fabric is too flimsy, don't you?" she said.

Meghann frowned. "Too flimsy? You look gorgeous."

"It hangs on every bulge. I'd have to wear undergarments made by Boeing."

"Claire, it's a size ten."

After that, Claire tried on a succession of dresses, each one more beautiful than the last. She felt like a princess, and it didn't ruin the day at all that she had to decline each one. She could tell Meghann was getting frustrated. She kept delivering armfuls of gowns.

Risa had long ago gone on to other customers.

Finally Claire came to the last dress of the day. Meghann had chosen it. An elegant white gown with a heavily beaded tank bodice and a flowing taffeta silk skirt. Claire was still fastening the back as she stepped out of the dressing room.

Meghann was completely silent.

Claire looked at her sister. "You're uncharacteristically quiet. Should I begin the Heimlich?"

"Look."

Claire lifted the heavy skirt off the ground and stepped up onto the platform. Slowly she faced the trifold mirror.

The woman who stared back at her wasn't Claire Cavenaugh. No. This woman hadn't partied her way out of a state college, she hadn't borne a child out of wedlock, and she certainly didn't manage a campground. This woman arrived in limousines and drank champagne from fluted glasses. She slept on high-thread-count sheets and always had a current passport. This was the woman she could have been if she'd gone to college in New York and done graduate work in Paris. Maybe it was the woman she could still become.

She imagined the look on Bobby's face when she walked down the aisle. Bobby, who'd knelt on one knee when he asked her to please, please be his wife. If he saw her in this dress . . .

Meghann came up behind her, stood on the platform. There they were, side by side. Mama's girls. Meghann touched Claire's bare shoulder. "Don't even try to find something wrong with this dress."

"I didn't look at the price tag, but—"

Meghann ripped the tag in half. "And you won't."

Claire looked at her sister. "You knew. You handpicked it."

Meg tried not to smile. "It's Vera Wang. Of course I knew. It means a lot to me that you've included me in your wedding."

"We're family," Claire answered after a long pause. It felt awkward, this conversation, and vaguely dangerous. "Thank you for the dress. It's what"—her voice cracked—"I always dreamed of."

Meg finally smiled. "Just because I don't believe in marriage doesn't mean I can't plan a kick-ass wedding, you know."

Risa stepped into the dressing room. "The Wang," she said softly, looking at Meg. "You said this would be her choice."

"A good guess."

"She is the picture of love, yes?" Risa went to Claire. "We'll need to take in the bust a little—just to there, don't you think?" She began pinning and pulling. "It'll be ready in time," Risa promised when she was finished, then hurried off.

"Now, how about we pick up some takeout from the Wild Ginger and eat at my place?" Meghann said.

"Alison—"

"Is having dinner at Zeke's Drive-In and joining Sam and Bobby for date night at the Big Bowl."

Claire smiled. "Bobby is going to date night at the bowling alley? And you don't believe in true love?"

In front of the Wild Ginger, Meghann double-parked, ran into the restaurant, and came out three minutes later with a paper sack. She tossed it in Claire's lap, got into the driver's seat, and drove home.

At her condo, the view was breathtaking. An amethyst almost-night sky filled every picture window. The Space Needle, decked out in summertime colors, filled one window. Everywhere else it was the midnight-blue Sound.

"Wow," Claire said.

"Yeah. It's some view," Meghann said.

Everywhere Claire looked, she saw perfection. She walked over to a small Biedermeier desk in the corner. On its shiny surface stood a single framed photograph. It was of Claire and Meghann, taken when they were kids—maybe seven and fourteen—sitting at the end of a dock with their arms looped around each other.

Surprisingly, Claire found that it hurt to see them this way. She put the photograph back and made her way to the kitchen.

"Your home is gorgeous."

"Home." Meg laughed as she handed Claire a margarita. "That's funny. I never think of it that way, but it is, of course. Thanks."

That was it. This wasn't a home. It was a really nice hotel suite—definitely four-star but cold, impersonal.

Meghann set out the plates. "Here. Let's eat out on the deck." They carried their plates and drinks outside. "We'll have to sit on the floor. The decorator chose the most uncomfortable outdoor furniture. I returned it all and haven't found the time to buy new stuff."

"How long have you lived here?"

"Seven years."

It was a beautiful night. Stars everywhere. As they ate, Claire looked at Meghann and couldn't help remembering the old days, when they'd been best friends. She wondered if that could happen again. If so, one of them would have to make the first move.

Claire took a chance. "Maybe you'd like to come stay at my house for a few nights while you're planning the wedding."

"Really?" Meghann looked up, obviously surprised.

"You're probably too busy."

"No, actually. I'm between cases right now. And I do need to spend some time in Hayden. I have a meeting there tomorrow, in fact. With the wedding consultant."

Big mistake, Claire thought. Incredible Hulk big. "It's settled, then. You'll spend a few nights at my house."

CHAPTER SIX

MEGHANN parked the car and checked her instructions again, then looked up the street. She walked two blocks, then turned right on Azalea Street. Her destination was easy to spot: a narrow Victorian house painted canary yellow with purple trim. A sign hung askew on the white picket fence out front: ROYAL EVENT PLANNING. There were glittery roses all around the pink letters.

Meghann almost kept walking. There was no way that someone who painted with glittery paint could plan a classy wedding. But it was Claire's day, and she wanted a small, casual wedding.

Meghann unlatched the picket gate and stepped into a surreal Candy Land yard. A green Astroturf walkway led her to the porch steps. At the salmon-pink door, she knocked.

The door opened. A tall man with curly bottle-blond hair and a California-dark tan stood there. "You must be Meghann Dontess. I'm Roy Royal."

She tried not to smile.

"Go ahead, have a good laugh. I'm just lucky my middle name isn't Al." He swung one hip out, planted a hand on it. "Those are some pretty sharp clothes, Ms. Dontess. We don't see much Marc Jacobs in Hayden. I can't imagine what brings you here."

"I'm Claire Cavenaugh's sister. I'm here to plan her wedding."

He screeched. "Claire! All right, girl! Well, let's get going. Only the best for Claire." He ushered her into the sitting room, toward a pink velvet settee. "Wedding at the Episcopal church, of course. Reception at the Moose Lodge, catering by the Chuck Wagon."

"That's a wedding in Hayden, huh?"

"Top drawer."

"And what does a wedding cost around here?"

"A good, solid event? Say, two thousand dollars."

Meg leaned forward. "Do you read *In Style* magazine, Roy?"

He laughed. "Are you kidding? Cover to cover."

"So you know what a celebrity wedding is like. Especially the kind they call 'simple and elegant.'"

"Simple in Hollywood just means really really expensive but no bridesmaids and an outdoor reception."

"I want the kind of wedding this town has never seen, Roy. But—and this is important—no one but you and I can know that. You have to master the phrase 'It was on sale.' Deal?"

"No kidding." He grinned and clapped. "What's your budget?"

"Money isn't something we should worry about."

He shook his head, still smiling. "Honey, that's a sentence I've *never* heard before. Okay, let's get to work."

JOE was elbow-deep in the undercarriage of an old Kubota tractor, changing the oil, when he heard a car drive up. He listened for Smitty's booming voice, but there was nothing.

"Anyone here?" someone called out. "Smitty?"

Joe rolled out from under the tractor and got to his feet. A florid, heavyset man walked into the garage. Joe recognized him. It was Reb Tribbs, an old-time logger who'd lost an arm on the job.

Joe pulled his cap down low. "What can I do for you?"

"My truck's dyin'. I just brought the damn thing to Smitty. He said he fixed it. I ain't payin' for it till it runs."

"You'll have to take that up with Smitty. But if you want to drive into the garage, I'll—"

"Do I know you?" Reb frowned and stepped closer. "Joe Wyatt." Reb made a whistling sound. "It's you, ain't it? You got some nerve comin' back here, boy. Folks around here remember what you done. Hell, I thought you were in prison."

"No." Joe stood there, listening. He deserved every word.

"You'd best get a move on. Her daddy don't need to hear that you're back in town."

"I haven't seen her dad."

"Course not. You don't have the guts."

"That's enough, Reb." It was Smitty's voice. He stood at the open garage door, holding a half-eaten sandwich in one hand and a can of Coke in the other.

"I can't believe you'd hire this piece of garbage," Reb said. "I won't bring my truck here if he's gonna work on it."

"I can lose your business and still survive," Smitty said.

Reb made a sputtering sound, then turned on his heel and marched out. As he got into his truck, he yelled out, "You'll be sorry, Zeb Smith. Trash like him don't belong in this town."

After he drove away, Smitty placed a hand on Joe's shoulder. "He's the trash, Joe. Always has been. Mean as a badger."

"You'll lose customers when word gets out that I'm here."

"Don't matter. My house is paid for. My land's paid for. I own a rental house in town that brings in five hundred a month."

"Still, your reputation is important."

Smitty squeezed his shoulder. "Last Helga and I heard about our Philly, he was living in Seattle. Under the viaduct. Heroin. Every day I hope someone offers him a helping hand."

Joe nodded. He didn't know what to say.

Then Smitty said, "I gotta make a Costco run. You think you can handle the garage for the next two hours?"

"Not if Reb is any indication."

"He isn't." Smitty tossed him the keys. "Close up anytime you want." Then he left.

Joe finished out the workday, but he couldn't forget the incident with Reb. The old man's words seemed to hang in the garage, poisoning the air. *Trash like him don't belong in this town.*

By the time he closed up shop, he felt empty again. He locked things up and was just about to turn toward his cabin when he happened to glance down the street. The neon REDHOOK sign in Mo's window caught his attention. Suddenly he wanted to sneak into that smoky darkness and drink until the ache in his chest went away.

He pulled his baseball cap low on his forehead and crossed the street. Praying that no one he knew was inside, he pushed through the scarred wooden door.

MEGHANN hadn't been to a bridal shower in more than a decade. She had no idea how to blend into this small-town crowd, and the last thing she wanted to do was stand out.

Today, after her four-hour meeting with Roy, Meghann had spent another hour in Too Many Cooks, where she bought Claire—and Bobby, although she didn't think of them as a couple, really—a Cuisinart food processor.

She'd been tired by the time she made it back to Claire's house. Pleading a headache, she'd excused herself quickly from the dinner table and ran upstairs. But now, nearly an hour later, she felt better. A quick glance at the bedside clock told her it was 6:40.

She opened her closet, deciding on a plain black dress. Armani was never wrong. She added sheer black hose and a pair of pumps, then went downstairs. The house was quiet.

"Claire?"

No answer. Then she saw the note on the kitchen table: "Dear Meg, Sorry you're feeling sick. Stay home and rest, XXOO, C."

Claire and Bobby had left without her. She glanced at her watch. It was seven o'clock. Of course they'd left. They were the guests of honor.

She dug through her purse for the pale lavender invitation. It read "Couples Shower for Claire and Bobby, 7:00." The directions were on the back.

It took her less than ten minutes to find Gina's house. Holding her gift under one arm, she climbed the porch steps and knocked on the door. *You can do this. You can fit in with her friends.*

There was a rush of footsteps; then the door opened.

Gina stood there, her face creased in laughter. Until she saw Meghann. "Oh"—she stepped back to allow entry—"I'm glad you're feeling better."

Meghann stared at Gina, who was dressed in capri pants and an oversize black T-shirt. *Great.* "I'm overdressed."

"Are you kidding? If I hadn't gained fifteen pounds since Rex left, I'd be dressed up, too. Come on. You're my date for the evening." Gina smiled. "I thought I'd been stood up."

She took Meghann by the arm and led her down a wide hallway. They finally reached the great room—a living-room/dining-room combination—that overlooked a beautifully landscaped yard. "Claire, look who made it," she said over the buzz of conversation.

Everyone stopped talking and turned toward them. The crowd was a sea of T-shirts and jeans. Except for Meghann, of course.

Claire hurried toward her, smiling. She looked gorgeous in a pair of ice-blue cotton pants and a white boat-neck cotton sweater. Her long blond hair had been pulled back from her face. "I'm so glad you could make it. When I get a headache, I can't move for hours."

Meghann felt like Jackie O at a keggar. "I shouldn't have come. I'll go."

"Please don't," her sister said. "I'm glad you're here. Really."

They stood there in an uncomfortable silence until Gina said, "I'll bet you could use a drink."

Meghann nodded. "By all means."

"Come to the kitchen with me," Gina said.

"Hurry back," Claire said. "We're going to start the games."

MEGHANN really did have a headache now.

She sat on the edge of the sofa, her knees tucked primly together. The rest of the guests sat sprawled against one another—in pairs, like on Noah's ark—in a circle on the hardwood floor. They were all talking at once, resurrecting memories and moments from a lifetime Meghann didn't know.

"Remember when Claire fell off the high dive at Island Lake Camp?"

"Or when she hid Mrs. Testern's favorite ruler?"

"Or when she called Poison Control because she caught Ali eating the diaper-pail deodorant?"

The junior and senior high school years, the girls-just-want-to-have-fun years, the Alison years. They were all a mystery to Meghann.

"Okay, everyone, it's time for the first game," Gina yelled.

She rushed into the kitchen and came out with a big white bowl. "This game is called Truth in M&M's. Everybody take as many as you want." She went around the group, handing out candy.

Meghann could tell that she wasn't the only suspicious person. No one took a handful. Meg chose two.

"For each M&M, you have to tell one thing about the bride or groom and make a prediction for the future."

A groan moved through the men.

"I'll start," Charlotte said. "I have three. Claire has a beautiful smile, and I predict Bobby will keep it on her face. She is a great cook, so I predict he'll be fat by forty. Finally, she hates to do laundry, so I predict Bobby will learn to like the stained, rumpled look."

Claire laughed the loudest of all of them.

They continued around the circle, and with each comment

Meghann felt herself edging toward uneasiness. Even the husbands here seemed to know more about Claire's everyday life than Meghann did, and she was terrified that when her turn came to make a prediction, she'd blurt out, "I predict he breaks her heart."

"Meg? Meg?" It was Gina. "Your turn."

Meghann looked down in her palm. Sweat had turned the candies into red smudges. "I have two." She tried to smile. "Claire is the best mother I know, so I predict she'll have another child."

Claire smiled at her, then leaned lovingly against Bobby. "Another one, Meg."

She nodded. "Claire loves well, but not necessarily easily, so I predict"—she barely paused—"that this is the real thing." When she looked up, Claire was frowning.

Meghann didn't know what she'd said wrong. It had seemed cheery and optimistic to her, but Claire looked ready to cry.

"I'm last," Gina said in the sudden silence. "I have only one. Claire is completely tone-deaf. So I predict that Bobby will never let her be his backup singer."

That got them all laughing and talking again.

Absurdly, Meghann felt the start of tears. She got to her feet. When no one was looking, she ducked out of the house and ran for her car. She meant to go home, wait up for Claire, and apologize for whatever wrongs she'd uttered.

Then she saw the tavern.

Meghann eased her foot off the accelerator. She knew if she went inside and had a drink—or two or three—she would feel better.

She parked her car and walked in. It was like a hundred other taverns. The bar ran the length of the room on the right side. She saw the people clustered along the bar, seated on wooden stools. Those were the hard-core drinkers.

Scattered throughout the left side of the room were round tables; most of them were full. Perfect. She walked to the closest empty space at the bar, where a tired-looking man was busily wiping up a spill. On her arrival he said, "Whaddaya want?"

She smiled. "A glass of white wine. Vouvray, if you have it."

"We have Inglenook and Gallo."

"Inglenook."

He headed down the other way and returned with a glass of wine.

She slapped her platinum credit card on the bar. "Open a tab."

The jukebox clicked, then buzzed. An old Aerosmith song came on. She headed toward the nearest table, where a man was writing on a yellow legal pad, obviously taking notes from a textbook.

She walked over to him. "May I join you?"

When he looked up, she saw that he was young. Maybe twenty-one or twenty-two. "I'm sorry, ma'am. What did you say?"

Ma'am.

"Call me Meg."

"You look familiar. Are you a friend of my mother's?"

She felt like the old lady from *Titanic*. "I thought I knew you, but I was mistaken. Sorry."

She headed toward another table. As she came within range, a woman slipped into the empty chair and kissed the man.

Meghann spun to her left and ran into a shaggy, derelict-looking guy who was on his way back from the bar. "I'm sorry," she said. "I should have signaled before I made a turn like that."

"No harm done."

He went back to his table and sat down. She saw that he was slightly unsteady on his feet.

She stood there, alone in the midst of the crowded bar. This wasn't going to be her night. She'd have to return to Claire's homey, comfortable guest room, climb into bed alone, and spend the night tossing and turning.

She looked at the derelict. His shoulders were broad; his black T-shirt stretched taut along his back. It was him . . . or loneliness.

She went to his table, stood beside him. "May I sit down?" She pulled out a chair and sat down across from him.

He looked up. Beneath the silvery fringe of hair, a pair of blue eyes stared at her. With a start she realized that he wasn't much older than she was, and he was almost handsome, in a Sam Elliott stranger-in-town kind of way.

"Whatever you're looking for," he said, "you won't find it here."

She started to flirt, to say something funny and impersonal, but before her tongue had even formed the first word, she paused. There was something about him. . . .

"Have we met?" she asked, frowning. She prided herself on her memory. Faces, she rarely forgot.

"People say that all the time. Just an ordinary face, I guess."

No, that wasn't it. She was sure she'd seen him before, but it didn't matter, really. "Are you from around here?"

"I am now."

"What do you do for a living?"

"Do I *look* like I make a living? I get by, that's all."

"That's all any of us do, really."

"Look, lady—"

"Meghann. Friends call me Meg."

"Meghann. I'm not going to take you home. Is that clear enough for you?"

That made her smile. "I don't remember asking to be taken home. You're making quite an assumption."

"Sorry. I've been alone for a while. Makes a man poor company."

Poor company. It had the ring of education to it.

She leaned closer, studying him. She liked his face. "What if I *did* want to go home with you?"

It was an eternity before he answered. "I'd say it wouldn't mean anything." His voice sounded tight. He looked scared.

She felt it suddenly—the thrill of the chase. She pressed her forefinger along the back of his hand. "What if I said that was okay?"

"I'd say that was sad."

She pulled her hand back, stung by the observation. She felt transparent suddenly, as if those blue eyes could see straight into her. "Maybe we could just get each other through this one night."

He stood up so quickly, the chair wobbled and almost fell. "I live down the street."

"I'll follow you" was all she said.

Joe felt her beside him, the warmth of her body, the way her hand brushed accidentally against his every now and then.

Stop this now, he thought. Just turn to her and say, "I made a mistake, I'm sorry." But he kept walking. Suddenly he was standing in front of his cabin. Three blocks they'd walked, and they hadn't managed a single word of conversation. He didn't know if he was thankful or not.

"This is where I live right now," he said—rather stupidly, he thought—as they were standing at the front door.

"Right now, huh?"

He opened the door and stepped aside to let her enter first.

She walked past him into the darkness.

He followed her, leaving the lights off on purpose. There were photos of Diana everywhere. He didn't want to explain why he lived this way, not to this woman in her designer dress and expensive gold-and-platinum jewelry. In fact, he didn't want to talk at all.

He went to the kitchen and grabbed some candles. There were dozens, kept on hand for winter storms when the power went out. Wordlessly he carried them into the bedroom and placed them wherever he could; then, one by one, he lit them. When he was finished, he turned and there she was, standing at the end of the bed.

He released a pent-up breath. She was beautiful. Jet-black hair, pale skin, green eyes. What was she doing here with him? He hadn't been with a woman since Diana.

She walked toward him, hips swaying slightly.

He meant to say, Go away, but instead he reached for her, pulled her against him. He was trembling.

"Are you okay?" she asked.

He didn't think, didn't speak, just swept her into his arms and carried her toward the bed.

That night, for the first time in years, Joe Wyatt made love to a woman and fell asleep holding her in his arms.

When he woke up, he was alone again.

CLAIRE flopped back onto the pillows. "You must really love me if you'll kiss me before I brush my teeth."

Bobby rolled onto his side. His handsome face was crisscrossed with sleep lines. "You still wonder, don't you?"

"No. Just prove Meg wrong. Nothing will make her crazier."

"She's trying, you know."

Claire sat up. "I can't believe you're defending her. She told me I was stupid to marry you."

He gave her that slow-growing smile that always made her go weak in the knees. "Darlin', you can't hold that against her. She's just trying to protect you."

"Control me is more like it."

"Come here," he whispered.

She leaned toward him, and they kissed.

"I'm getting to know you, Claire Cavenaugh-soon-to-be-Austin," he whispered against her lips. "You had a headache after the wedding-dress screwup and again last night after she left the party early. When Meghann hurts your feelings, you say you don't care and start chewing aspirin. I've been there, darlin'. I know what matters is that she's your sister. The only one you've got."

"No one can push my buttons like Meghann. She has a true gift for saying exactly the wrong thing."

"Yeah. My dad was like that. We never could quite make it work between us. Now he's gone, and I wish we'd tried harder."

"Okay, Sigmund Freud. I'll try talking to her. Again."

Claire went down to start the coffee. When it was ready, she poured herself a cup and went out to the back porch.

The slatted swing welcomed her. She sat there, rocking gently, staring out at the silver curve of water that defined her back property line. The sky was as blue as forget-me-nots.

The screen door screeched open and banged shut. Meghann stepped out onto the porch. She wore a fringed black peasant top and flare-legged jeans. Her hair, unbound, fell down her back in a riot of curls. She looked beautiful. "Morning."

Claire pulled a woolen blanket around her legs, hiding the ratty sweats she'd put on. "You want some pancakes?"

Meg sat down on the Adirondack chair across from the swing. "No, thanks. I'm still trying to metabolize last night's cake."

"You sure left the party early."

"It was a nice party. Gina has a great sense of humor."

"Yeah, she does."

"It must be hard on her, watching your wedding so soon after her own divorce."

Claire nodded. "She's going through a difficult time."

"It's always hard to find out you married the wrong man."

"They were married for fifteen years. Just because they got divorced doesn't mean he was the wrong man to marry."

Meg looked at her. "I would say it meant exactly that."

Claire took a sip of coffee. It occurred to her to drop the whole thing, to do what she'd always done around Meg—shut up and pretend it didn't hurt. Then she remembered her conversation with Bobby. Slowly she said, "You didn't answer my question: How come you left the shower early?"

"It wasn't that early. How were your presents?"

"They were great. Thank you for the Cuisinart, by the way. Now, why did you leave early?"

Meg closed her eyes, then slowly opened them. She looked scared. "It was the M&M game. I tried to be a good sport and play, but I barely know you, so I said something wrong. I still don't know what it was."

"You said I loved well, but not easily. I don't think it's true, that's all, and it hurt my feelings."

"It's true for me," Meg said.

Claire leaned forward. They were actually circling something that mattered. "Sometimes it's hard to love you, Meg."

"Believe me, I know." She laughed—a bitter, throaty sound.

"You judge people—me—so harshly. Your opinions are like bullwhips. Every one leaves a bloody mark."

"People, yes. But you? I don't judge you."

"I flunked out of college. I never left Hayden. I had a child out of wedlock with a man who, I discovered, was already married. Now I'm marrying a three-time loser, and I'm too stupid to protect myself with a prenuptial agreement. Stop me when it sounds familiar."

Meg frowned. "Have I hung all that on you?"

"I can't talk to you without feeling like a loser. And of course, you're rich and perfect."

"That part is true." Meg saw that her attempt at humor failed. "My therapist thinks I have control issues."

"Well, *duh*. You're a lot like Mama, you know. You both need to run the show."

"The difference is, she's psychotic. I'm neurotic. But God knows, she handed down bad luck with men." Meghann looked at her. "Have you broken the curse?" Claire's legacy from Mama was a belief that sooner or later love walked out on you. Meg had inherited something else entirely: She didn't believe in love at all.

"I have, Meg. Honestly."

Meg smiled, but there was a sadness in her eyes. "I wish I had your faith. You were lucky to have Sam."

Claire couldn't help thinking about the summer Dad had tried to be there for Meg. It had been a nightmare. Meg and Sam had had screaming fights about who loved Claire more, who knew what was best for her. It had been Claire herself who'd ended the worst of the battles. She'd cried out to Meg, *Quit yelling at my daddy*. That was the first time she'd seen her sister cry. The next day Meg had gone.

"He wanted to be there for you, too," Claire said gently.

"He wasn't my father."

They fell silent after that. Then Claire leaned toward her sister. "I'd like you to babysit Alison next week. While Bobby and I are on our honeymoon."

"I thought you weren't taking a honeymoon."

"Dad insisted. His wedding gift was a week's trip to Kauai."

"And you want *me* to babysit?"

"It would mean a lot to me. Ali needs to know you better."

Meghann looked nervous. "You'd trust me?"

"Of course."

Meg sat back. A tremulous smile curved her lips. "Okay."

Claire grinned. "No teaching her to bungee-jump."

"So skydiving lessons are out."

They were still laughing when the phone started ringing. Claire jumped up and ran inside the house to answer it. "Hello?"

"Hold for Eliana Sullivan, please."

Claire heard Meg come up behind her. She mouthed, "Mama."

"This should be good," Meg said.

"Hello?" Mama said. "Hello?"

"Hey, Mama. It's me, Claire."

Mama laughed, that throaty, sexy sound she'd cultivated over the years. "I believe I know which of my own daughters I called."

"Of course," Claire answered, although Mama confused the two of them all the time.

"Well, honey, m'houseboy said you left me a message. What's goin' on?"

Claire hated the faux southern accent. "I called to tell you I'm getting married."

"Well, I'll be damned. Who is he?"

"You'll love him, Mama. He's a nice Texas boy."

"How much money does he make?"

"That isn't important to me."

"Broke, huh? Well, I'll give you my best advice, honey. It's easier to marry the rich ones, but what the hell. Congratulations. When's the wedding?"

"Saturday, the twenty-third."

"Of June? You mean this comin' Saturday?"

"You would have had plenty of notice if you'd called me back."

"I was doing Shakespeare in the park. With Charlie Sheen, I might add. Did you see my picture in *People?*"

"I missed that. Sorry."

"Well, Saturday's difficult for me, honey. How about the first weekend in August?"

Claire rolled her eyes. "Mama, the invitations have already gone out. It's too late to change the date."

"What time on Saturday?"

"The wedding is at seven p.m. Reception to follow."

Mama sighed. "Saturday. I've been waitin' three months for my hair appointment with José. Maybe he can take me early."

Claire couldn't take any more. "I've got to run, Mama. I'll be at the Hayden Episcopal Church at seven this Saturday. I hope you can make it, but I'll certainly understand if you're too busy."

"Tell me straight up, honey. D'you think this one'll last? I'd hate to give up my hair appointment for—"

"I've got to go, Mama. Bye."

"Okay, honey. Me, too. And congratulations."

"Thanks, Mama. Bye."

Claire looked up at Meghann. "Saturday's a bad day for her. A hair appointment with José."

"We should have sent her the invite after it was over."

"I don't know why I keep expecting something different from her."

Meg shook her head. "Even a mother alligator sticks around the eggs."

"Mama would make herself an omelette." They both laughed.

CHAPTER SEVEN

FRIDAY afternoon turned gray and cold. Rain fell in tiny staccato bursts that were all but invisible to the naked eye.

Claire spent the rest of the day pretending to work. Thirty-five was too old to marry for the first time. How could she possibly be doing the right thing? But every time her worries threatened to overwhelm her, she'd turn a corner or open a door and see Bobby. "Hey, darlin'," he'd say. "I love you." Just those few and precious words, and Claire breathed easier again for an hour or so.

At around three in the afternoon her father walked her back to her house. He reached into his pocket, pulled out a small black box, and opened it. Inside was a marquise-cut yellow diamond set on a wide platinum band.

"It's your grandma Myrtle's. She wanted you to have it." Sam reached out, took her hand. "I couldn't let my baby get married with a tinfoil ring."

She tried it on. The ring fit as if it had been made for her. She pulled him into her arms. "Thanks, Dad."

After tomorrow she would be a married woman. Another man would be the center of her life. She would be Bobby's wife from now on, not Sam Cavenaugh's little girl.

When Dad drew back, there were tears in his eyes and she knew he'd been thinking the same thing.

"Always," she whispered.

He nodded in understanding. "Always."

MEGHANN wished to God she'd never agreed to let Gina host and plan the rehearsal dinner. Every moment was pure hell.

"Are you here by yourself?"

"Where's your husband?"

"You don't have children? Well, that's lucky. Sometimes I wish I could give mine away."

Meghann knew that Claire's friends were trying to include her, especially the Bluesers, but the more they tried to make her a part of the group, the more alienated she felt. She could talk about a lot of things—world politics, the situation in the Mideast, Wall Street. What she couldn't talk about were family things. Kid things.

Meghann stood at the fireplace in Gina's house. Across the room Claire stood at the kitchen bar/counter eating potato chips and laughing with Gina. As Meghann watched, Bobby came up behind Claire and whispered something in her ear. She turned into his arms. They came together like puzzle pieces, fitting perfectly.

"Okay, everyone," Gina said, coming into the room. "Now it's time for the second part of the evening."

A hush fell.

Gina smiled. "Hector is opening the bowling alley just for us! We leave in fifteen minutes."

Bowling. Rented shoes. Polyester shirts.

Meg walked across the living room and came up beside Claire, gently putting her hand on her sister's shoulder.

Claire turned. She looked so happy right then, it took Meghann's breath away. When she saw Meghann, she laughed. "Let me guess. You're not a bowler."

"Oh, I love bowling. Really. I have my own ball."

"You do, huh?"

"Unfortunately, I have a few last-minute details I need to go over for tomorrow. I have to get up early."

Claire nodded. "I understand, Meg. I really do."

"Well, bye. I'll tell Gina why I'm leaving."

Fifteen minutes later Meghann was in her car, speeding down the country road toward Hayden. Her sister's well-meaning friends had managed to underscore the emptiness of Meg's life.

She saw the sign for Mo's Fireside Tavern and slammed on the brakes. It was a bad idea to go in, she knew. There was nothing but trouble in there. And yet . . . She parked on the street and went inside.

Men sat on every barstool, at every table. There were a few women scattered throughout the crowd. She made her way through the place, boldly checking out every man.

She had toured the whole place and made her way back to the front door when she realized why she was really here. "Joe," she said softly, surprised. She honestly hadn't known that she wanted him. That wasn't good.

She left the bar and stood at her car, looking down the street at his small cabin. Light glowed from the windows. "No," she said. She shouldn't do it, but she was walking anyway, crossing the street, and entering his yard, which smelled of honeysuckle and jasmine. At the door she paused, wondering what in the hell she was doing.

Then she knocked. No one answered.

She twisted the knob and went inside. The cabin was dark. A fire crackled in the hearth. "Joe?" Cautiously she stepped forward.

No answer.

A shiver crept along her spine. She sensed that he was here, burrowed into the darkness like a wounded animal, watching her.

She started to turn for the door, when she saw the photographs—on the coffee table, the end tables, the mantel. Everywhere. Frowning, she walked from place to place looking at the pictures. They were all of the same woman, a lovely blonde with a Grace Kelly kind of elegance. Meghann picked one up.

"Do you always break into other people's homes and paw through their things?"

Meghann jumped back. Her fingers went numb for a second, and the picture crashed to the floor. She turned around, looking for him. "Joe? It's me, Meghann."

"I know it's you."

He was slumped in the corner of the room, with one leg bent and the other stretched out. Firelight illuminated his silvery hair. Sadness clung to him, made her wonder if he'd been crying.

"I shouldn't have come in. Or come here, for that matter," she said uncomfortably. "I'm sorry." She headed for the door.

"Have a drink with me."

Slowly she faced him.

"What can I get you?"

"Martini?"

"I've got Scotch. And Scotch."

She sat on the worn leather sofa. "I'll have a Scotch."

He got up, shuffled across the room. She saw now why he'd been so invisible; he had on black jeans and a black T-shirt.

She heard a splash of liquid, then a rattling of ice. As he poured her drink, she looked around the room. All those photographs of the Grace Kelly look-alike made her uncomfortable.

"Here."

She looked up. He stood in front of her. "Thank you," she said.

He took a drink straight from the bottle, then wiped his mouth with the back of his hand. "Sure." He didn't move away, just stood there, staring down at her. He was unsteady on his feet.

"You're drunk," she said, finally getting it.

"It's June twenty-second." He sat down beside her.

"Do you have something against the twenty-second?"

His gaze darted to the photographs clustered on an end table.

"Who is she, Joe?" Her voice was soft, but in the quiet room it seemed too loud, too intimate.

"My wife, Diana."

"You're married?"

"Not anymore. She . . . left me."

"On June twenty-second."

"How'jou know?"

"I know about divorces. The anniversaries can be hell." Meghann stared into his sad, sad eyes and tried not to feel anything. It was better that way, safer. But sitting here beside him, close enough to be taken into his arms, she felt . . . needy. Suddenly she wanted something from Joe, something more than sex.

He touched her face. "I can't offer you anything, Meghann."

The way he said her name, all sad and drawn out and slow, sent a shiver along her spine. She wanted to tell him that she didn't want anything from him, but she couldn't form the words. "It's okay."

"You should want more."

"So should you."

She felt fragile suddenly. "We're talking too much. Kiss me."

In the fireplace a log fell to the hearth floor with a thud. Sparks flooded into the room.

With a groan he pulled her into his arms.

CHAPTER EIGHT

THE next morning the weather in Hayden was perfect. A bright sun rode high in the cornflower-blue sky. A thin, cooling breeze rustled through the trees, making music on the deep-green maple leaves. By five o'clock Claire was showered and ready to begin dressing.

Behind her there was a knock at the door. "Come in," she said.

Meghann stood in the doorway. "I thought maybe we'd get dressed together." When Claire didn't answer instantly, Meghann said, "You probably think it's a stupid idea."

"Stop. I think it would be great."

Meghann's hair had been fashioned into a beautiful French twist.

"Your hair looks great," Claire said.

"I could do yours if you'd like."

"Really?"

"Sure. I did it all the time when you were little."

Claire crossed the room and knelt in front of the bed.

Meghann settled in behind her, began brushing her hair.

Claire closed her eyes. It felt so good.

"There. All done."

Claire climbed to her feet, then went into the bathroom and looked in the mirror. Her blond hair had been loosely drawn back from her face and twisted into an elegant roll. The hairstyle emphasized her cheekbones and made her eyes look huge. She'd never looked this pretty. Never.

"I love it," she said.

Meghann's smile was dazzling. "Really?"

Suddenly the door banged open. "Mommy!" Ali raced into the room, already wearing her beautiful ice-blue silk bridesmaid dress. "Hurry, Mommy, come look." She grabbed Claire's hand, dragged her toward the door.

Claire and Meghann followed Ali downstairs. Outside in the driveway, Dad, Bobby, and Alison stood around a candy-apple-red convertible.

Claire moved toward them, frowning. That was when she noticed the pink bow on the hood. "What in the world?"

Dad handed her a note. It read, "Dear Claire and Bobby, Best of luck on your big day. I'm still hoping to make it up there. Hugs and kisses, Mama."

Meg came up beside Claire, laid a hand on her shoulder. "Let me guess: Mama's wedding gift."

Claire sighed. "Leave it to Mama to give me a car with two seats. Am I supposed to have Ali run along behind?"

Then she laughed. What else could she do?

CLAIRE stood in the dressing room at the small Episcopal church on Front Street. The last hour had been nonstop action. The Bluesers had been in and out every few minutes, oohing and aahing over her dress, and Meghann had been busy checking details, clipboard in hand. But now the room was mercifully quiet. Claire stood in front of the mirror, unable to grasp that the woman in the glass was her. The gown fit perfectly, flowing to the floor in a cascade of white silk.

There was a knock at the door.

It was Meghann. "The church is packed. Are you ready?"

Claire swallowed hard. "I am."

Meghann took her sister's hand and led her out to the small area behind the closed church doors. Dad was already there, waiting with Ali.

"Oh, Ali Kat, you look like a princess," Claire said, kneeling down to kiss her daughter.

Alison giggled, twirled. "I love my dress, Mommy."

Behind the doors the music started. It was time.

Meghann bent down to Alison. "Are you ready, sweetie? You walk slow—like we practiced, okay?"

Ali hopped up and down. "I'm ready."

A second later the organ played "Here Comes the Bride," and Meghann opened the doors.

Claire slipped her arm through her dad's, and they slowly followed Ali down the aisle. At the end of it Bobby, dressed in a black tuxedo, waited, smiling broadly.

Dad stopped, turned to Claire. He lifted the veil and kissed her cheek, then eased away from her, and suddenly Bobby was there beside her, taking her arm, leading her up to the altar.

She looked up at him, loving him so much it scared her.

"Don't be afraid," he mouthed, squeezing her hands.

Father Tim droned on, but Claire couldn't really hear anything except the beating of her own heart. When it came time for her to say her lines, she panicked that she wouldn't remember them. But she did. When she said, "I do," it felt as if her heart were actually expanding inside her chest. In that moment, standing in front of her friends and family and staring into Bobby's eyes, she started to cry.

Father Tim smiled down at each of them, then said, "I now pronounce you husband and—"

The doors to the church banged open.

A woman stood in the doorway, arms out-flung, a cigarette in one hand. She wore a silver lamé dress that showcased her curves. Behind her, there were at least a dozen people: bodyguards, reporters, and photographers. "I can't *believe* y'all started without me."

A gasp of recognition moved through the church. Someone whispered, "It's *her.*"

Bobby frowned. Claire sighed and wiped her eyes. She should have expected this. "Bobby, you're about to meet Mama."

"I AM going to *kill* her." Meghann shot out of the pew and stepped into the aisle.

"There's my other girl." Mama threw open her arms. Again the flashbulbs erupted in spasms of blinding light.

Meghann grabbed her mother by the arm and yanked her back through the doors. The paparazzi followed, all talking at once.

Through the now closed doors Meghann could hear Father Tim's second attempt to pronounce Bobby and Claire husband and wife. A moment later applause thundered through the church.

Meghann pulled Mama into the dressing room and shut the door behind them.

"What?" Mama whined, obviously unable to frown but wanting to. Too much Botox, no doubt.

A dog barked. Mama looked down at a small travel carrier in her arms. "It's okay, honey. Meggy's makin' a mountain out of a molehill."

"You brought your *dog?*"

Mama pressed a hand to her ample breast. "You know Elvis hates to be left alone. Now, why in the *hell* did you throw me out of my own daughter's weddin'?"

Meghann felt a surge of anger. "Today was Claire's day to be a star. Can you get that, Mama? *Her* day. And you walked in right at the moment of glory and stole the show. What were you doing out here, *waiting* for the perfect moment to make your entrance?"

Mama looked away for just a second, but it was enough to confirm Meghann's suspicion. "Oh, Mama," she said, shaking her head, "that's a new low. Even for you. And who are all those people? Do you think you need bodyguards at a wedding in Hayden?"

"My fans are everywhere. They scare me sometimes."

Meghann laughed at that. "Save the acting for *People* magazine, Mama. Now, you and I are going to walk over to the reception and tell Claire how happy we are for her. You may bring one photographer, no bodyguards, and no dog. These rules are not negotiable."

They stood there, inches apart, staring at each other.

Then Mama laughed. The real thing this time, not that sexy kitten laugh she used in Hollywood, but the deep tavern sound she'd been born with.

Meghann smiled in spite of herself. How could you stay angry with a woman as shallow as Mama?

She put her arm around Meghann and pulled her close. "So are we goin' to this reception or not? I have a midnight flight home. I need to be at SeaTac by eleven."

"That means you need to leave here about eight thirty. So let's go. Claire probably thinks I killed you."

CLAIRE was the center of a laughing, talking, congratulatory crowd. She had never felt so special, so completely loved in her life. Bobby slipped an arm tightly around her waist, pulled her close. "Have I told you how beautiful you look?"

"You have."

"When you came down that aisle, you took my breath away."

They kept their arms around each other and followed the wedding guests walking to Riverfront Park. In front of them the crowd stopped; as if on cue, they parted, forming a dark aisle.

Around them the guests clapped and cheered them on. A shower of rice seemed to fall from the sky; it sprinkled their faces and crunched beneath their feet.

"Oh, my God," Claire said. She couldn't believe her eyes. A huge white tent had been set up in the park. Thousands of tiny white Christmas lights twined up the poles and across the makeshift ceilings. Claire could see the tables set up within the tent. Silvery, shimmery tablecloths draped each one. In the corner a trio of men in white tuxedos played a haunting World War II love song.

"Wow," Bobby said.

The band struck up a beautiful rendition of "Isn't It Romantic?"

"Would you like to dance, Mrs. Austin?"

Claire let him take her in his arms and lead her to the dance floor. There, with all her friends and family watching, she danced with her husband.

When the song came to an end, Claire saw her sister. She was tagging after Mama, who was clearly in her meet-and-greet mode.

"Come on, Bobby," she said, taking his hand and pulling him off the dance floor. They reached the bar, where Mama was regaling a starstruck crowd with stories of life aboard the U.S.S. *Star Seeker*.

Mama saw her coming. "Claire," she said, reaching for her with both hands, "I'm sorry I was late, darlin'. A star's life is run by others. But you were the most beautiful bride I've ever seen."

Their gazes met. In her mother's dark eyes Claire glimpsed a genuine joy, and it touched her.

"Now," Mama said quickly, "where's my new son-in-law?"

"Here I am, Miz Sullivan."

"Call me Ellie. All my family does." She moved toward him, whistling softly. "You're good-looking enough for Hollywood."

It was Mama's highest compliment.

"Thank you, ma'am."

She took his hand. "If you sing half as good as you look, you'll be on the radio in no time. Come. Tell me about your career while we dance."

"I'd be honored to dance with my new mother-in-law." Tossing Claire a quick smile, he was off.

Claire turned at last to Meghann. "Are you okay?"

"Mama brought her dog. Not to mention an entourage of bodyguards."

"She could be overcome by the hoards of her fans at any moment," Claire said in her best pseudo-southern voice.

Meghann laughed. "She has to leave at eight thirty. I believe a prayer of thanks is in order."

The band shifted into a soulful version of "As Time Goes By."

Claire stared at her sister, trying to come up with words to match her emotions. "This wedding—" she started, but her voice cracked. She swallowed hard. "You spent a fortune."

"No." Meghann shook her head. "Almost everything was on sale. They're my Christmas lights. The tent—"

Claire touched her sister's lips, shut her up. "I'm trying to say thank you."

"Oh."

"I wish . . ." She didn't even know how to word it, this sudden longing of hers.

"I know," Meghann said. "Maybe things can be different now."

"You were my best friend," Claire said. "I missed that when you . . ." *Left.* She couldn't say the harsh word, not now.

"I missed you, too."

"Mommy! Mommy! Come dance with us."

Claire twisted around and saw her dad and Alison standing a few feet away. "I believe it's customary for the bride to dance with her father," he said, smiling, holding out his calloused hand.

"And her daughter! Grandpa'll carry me." Alison was hopping up and down with excitement.

Claire gave her champagne glass to Meghann, who mouthed, "Go." She let herself be pulled onto the dance floor. As they made it to the center of the crowd, Dad bent down and scooped Alison up. The three of them clung to one another, swaying gently in time to "The Very Thought of You."

All her life Claire would look back on this night and remember how good her life was, how much she loved and was loved in return. That was what Meghann had given her.

MEGHANN gazed at the black velvet lawn of Edgar Peabody Riverfront Park. Behind her, the band was breaking down their equipment. Only a few die-hard guests were still here. Mama had left hours ago, as had Sam and Ali. Everyone else, including the bride and groom, had drifted away at around midnight. Meghann had stayed late, supervising the cleanup, but now that job was done.

She sipped her champagne and looked across the street again.

Joe was probably sleeping. She knew it was ridiculous to go to him, maybe even dangerous, but there was something in the air tonight. A heady combination of romance and magic. It smelled like roses and made a woman believe that anything was possible. For tonight, anyway.

So she hummed along with the music and walked down the gravel road. At his gate she paused. The lights were on. She debated for another minute or two, then knocked.

Moments later Joe opened the door. His hair was messed up, as if he'd been asleep; all he wore was a pair of black jeans.

He stared at her, saying nothing.

"I thought maybe we could go out," she said.

"You want us to go on a *date?* At one o'clock in the morning?"

"Sure. Why not?"

"A better question is why."

She looked up at him. When their gazes locked, she felt a flutter in her pulse. "I was in a good mood. Maybe I had too much to drink." Humiliated, she closed her eyes. "I shouldn't have come. I'm sorry." When she opened her eyes, she saw he'd moved closer.

"I'm not much for going out."

"Oh."

"But I wouldn't mind if you wanted to come in."

She felt the start of a smile. "Great."

"What I *mind*," he said, "is waking up alone. It's okay if you don't want to spend the night, but don't sneak out like a hooker."

"I'm sorry."

He smiled. It lit up his whole face, made him look ten years younger. "Okay, come on in."

She touched his arm. "That's the first time I've seen you smile."

"Yeah," he said softly, maybe sadly. "It's been a while."

MEGHANN was showered, dressed in a T-shirt and jeans, and packed. On her way out, she paused long enough to write Claire a quick note, which she left on the kitchen counter. Then she took one last look at the house that was so much a home. It was unexpectedly difficult to leave. Her condo was so cold and empty by comparison.

Finally she went to her car and drove slowly through the campground. She came to a horseshoe-shaped yard full of oversize rhododendrons. A gray mobile home squatted on cement blocks.

Meghann parked the car and got out. As always, she felt a tightening in her stomach when she thought about meeting Sam.

She walked up the gravel walkway and onto the porch. She knocked. When no one answered, she tried again.

The door swung open, hinges creaking, and there he was, filling the doorway, dressed in shabby overalls and a pale blue T-shirt that read RIVER'S EDGE. His brown hair was Albert Einstein wild.

"Meg"—he stepped back—"come on in."

She sidled past him and found herself in a surprisingly cozy living room. "Good morning, Sam. I'm here to pick up Alison."

"Are you sure you want to take her? I'd be happy to keep her."

"I'm sure you would," she answered, stung.

"I know how busy you are."

"You still think I'm a bad influence, is that it?"

He took a step toward her, stopped. "I should never have thought that. Claire's told me how good you were to her. I didn't know about kids back then, and I sure as hell didn't know about teenage girls who—"

"Please. Don't finish that sentence. Do you have a list for me? Allergies. Medications. Anything I should know?"

"She goes to bed at eight. She likes it if you read her a story. *The Little Mermaid* is her favorite."

"Great." Meg looked down the hallway. "Is she ready?"

"She's just telling the cat good-bye. She has a birthday party to go to on Saturday. If you get her here by noon, she'll make it. That way she'll be here when Claire and Bobby get home on Sunday."

Alison came racing down the hallway, carrying a black cat whose body stretched almost to the ground. "Lightning wants to come with me, Grandpa. Can I take him with me, Aunt Meg? Can I?"

Meg had no idea whether cats were allowed in her building.

Before she could answer, Sam knelt down in front of Alison and gently eased the cat from her arms. "Lightning needs to stay here, honey. You know he likes to play with his friends and hunt for mice in the woods. He's a country cat. He wouldn't like the city."

"I'm not a city girl, either," she said, puffing out her lower lip.

"No," Sam said. "You're an adventurer, though. Just like Mulan and Princess Jasmine. Do you think they'd be nervous about a trip to the big city?"

Ali shook her head.

Sam pulled her into his arms and hugged her tightly. When he finally let her go, he got slowly to his feet and looked at Meghann. "Take good care of my granddaughter."

It was not unlike what she'd said to Sam all those years ago, just before she left for good. *Take care of my sister.* The only difference was, she'd been crying. "I will."

Alison grabbed her backpack and her small suitcase. "I'm ready, Aunt Meg."

"Okay, let's go." Meg took the suitcase and headed for the door.

They were in the car and moving down the driveway when Alison suddenly screamed, "Stop!"

Meg slammed on the brakes. "What's wrong?"

Alison climbed out of her seat and ran back into the trailer. A moment later she was back, clutching a ratty pink blanket to her chest. Her eyes glistened with tears.

"I can't go 'venturing without my wubbie."

THE TELEPHONE WOKE CLAIRE UP. She sat up fast. "What time is it?" She looked around the unfamiliar hotel room for the bedside clock, found it: 5:45 a.m. "Bobby, the phone—"

She scrambled over him and picked it up. "Hello?"

"Hey, darlin'. How are you?"

Claire released a heavy breath and climbed out of bed. "I'm fine, Mama. It's five forty-five on Kauai."

"I thought y'all were the same time zone as California."

"We're halfway to Asia, Mama."

"You always did exaggerate, Claire. I *do* have a reason for callin', you know."

Claire grabbed her robe and slipped it on, then went out onto the balcony. Outside, the sky was just turning pink. The morning smelled of sweet tropical flowers and salt air. "What is it?"

"No matter what you and your bigmouthed sister remember or think you do, the truth is that I love you."

"I know, Mama."

"Now let me talk to Bobby."

"Why?"

Mama sighed dramatically. "It's about a weddin' gift for him."

"Okay, Mama. Whatever. Just a second." She went back inside. "She wants to talk to you."

Bobby got up and took the phone from Claire. "How's the sexiest mother-in-law in the world?" After a moment his smile faded. "What?" Then, "You're kidding me."

Claire placed her hand on his shoulder. "What's going on?"

He shook his head. "That's incredible, Ellie. I don't know how to thank you. . . . When?" He frowned. "You know we're here. . . . Oh, yeah. I understand. We'll call right away. And thank you. I can't tell you how much this means. . . . Yes. Good-bye."

"What did she do?" Claire asked when he hung up the phone.

Bobby's smile was so big, it creased his whole face into pleats. "She got me an audition with Kent Ames at Down Home Records. I can't *believe* it. I've been waiting ten years for a break like this."

Claire threw herself at him, holding him tightly in her arms. "You'll knock 'em dead."

He twirled her around until they were both laughing. She was still laughing when he eased her back to her feet.

"But . . ." he said, not smiling now. "The audition is Thursday. After that, Kent is leaving for a month."

"This Thursday?"

"This Thursday. In Nashville."

Claire knew that if she said no, said, "Our honeymoon won't be over by then," he'd kiss her and say, "Okay, maybe call your mama back and see if the audition can be rescheduled in a month."

Her answer was easy. "I've always wanted to see Opryland."

Bobby pulled her into his arms, gazed down at her. "I'd given up," he admitted quietly.

"Now hand me that phone," she said. "I better let Dad and Meghann know that we'll probably add a day or two onto the trip."

THE days Meghann spent hosting with Alison as her house-guest settled into a comfortable routine. By the third afternoon Meghann had let go of her obsessive need to show her niece every child-friendly venue in Seattle. Instead, they did simple things. They rented movies and made cookies and played Candy Land.

The first night, Ali came in to her room crying because she couldn't sleep. That night and each night afterward Meg slept with Ali tucked in her arms, and each morning she awoke with an un-expected sense of anticipation. She smiled easier, laughed more often. She'd forgotten how good it felt to care for someone else.

When Claire called to extend the length of her honeymoon, Meg knew she'd shocked her sister by offering—gladly—to keep Alison for a few extra days. Unfortunately, an oh-so-important birthday party back in Hayden ruined that option.

When Saturday finally came, Meghann was surprised by the depth of her emotions. All the way to Hayden she had to work to keep smiling, while Ali chattered nonstop and bounced in her seat. At Sam's house, Ali flew into her grandfather's arms and started telling him about the week. Meg kissed her niece good-bye and hurried out of the trailer. That night she hardly slept at all. She couldn't seem to stave off the loneliness.

On Monday she went back to work.

The hours stacked on top of one another, growing heavier than usual. By quitting time she was so tired, she could hardly function.

Outside, it was a balmy early summer night.

Meghann didn't want to go to the Athenian to pick up some man she didn't know. She wanted . . . Joe.

AT FOUR o'clock Joe was finished for the day. It was a good thing, because he actually had places to go and people to see.

It felt good to look forward to something, even if that something would ultimately cause him pain.

For the next hour, as Joe shaved and showered and dressed in his cleanest worn clothes, he tried to string together the sentences he would need. He tried pretty words, "Diana's death ruined something inside me"; stark words, "I screwed up"; painful words, "I couldn't stand watching her die." But none of them were the whole of it; none of them expressed the truth of his emotions.

He still hadn't figured out what he would say when he turned onto their road or, a few minutes later, when he came to their mailbox: DR. AND MRS. HENRY ROLOFF.

Joe couldn't help touching it. There had been a mailbox in Bainbridge like this one; it read DR. AND MRS. JOE WYATT.

He stared at his former in-laws' house. It looked exactly as it had on another June day, so long ago, when Joe and Di had gotten married in the backyard.

He almost turned away, but running didn't help. He'd tried that route, and it had brought him back here—to this house, to these people whom he'd once loved so keenly—to say I'm sorry.

He walked up the brick path, toward the white-pillared house. Joe didn't let himself pause or think. He reached out and rang the bell.

A few moments later the door opened. Henry Roloff stood there, pipe in hand, dressed in khaki pants and a turtleneck. "Can I—" At the sight of Joe, his smile fell. "Joey," he said, his pipe aflutter now in a trembling hand. "We'd heard you were back in town."

Joe tried to smile.

"Who is it?" Tina called out from somewhere inside the house.

"You won't believe it," Henry said.

"Henry?" she yelled again. "Who is it?"

Henry stepped back. A watery smile spilled across his face, wrinkled his cheeks. "He's home, Mother," he yelled. Then, softly, he said it again, his eyes filling with tears. "He's home."

"THIS IS THE CLUB WHERE Garth Brooks was discovered."

Claire smiled at Kent Ames, the grand pooh-bah of Down Home Records in Nashville. She and Bobby had been in Nashville for two days now. Their room at the Loews Hotel was breathtakingly beautiful. They'd splurged on romantic dinners. They'd toured Opryland and seen the Country Music Hall of Fame. Most important, Bobby had aced his auditions. All four of them.

He'd sung his songs for one executive after another until he'd finally found himself in the big corner office that overlooked the street of country-and-western dreams: Music Row.

Their lives had changed in the last twenty-four hours. Bobby was "someone." A guy who was "going places."

Now they sat at a front table in a small, unassuming nightclub, she and the executives and her husband. In less than an hour Bobby was scheduled to take the stage. It was a chance to "show his concert stuff" to the executives.

Bobby had no trouble talking to the men. They talked about people and things Claire knew nothing about—demo records and studio time and royalty rates and contract provisions.

She wanted to keep it all straight, but she couldn't seem to concentrate. The endless flight from Kauai to Oahu to Seattle to Memphis to Nashville had left its mark in a dull headache that wouldn't go away. The smoke in the club didn't help. Neither did the thudding music or the shouting conversation.

Kent Ames smiled at her. "Bobby goes on in forty-five minutes. Usually it takes years to get a spot on this stage."

Claire felt an odd tingling sensation in her right hand. It took her two tries to reach out for her margarita. When she took hold, she drank the whole thing, hoping it would ease her headache.

It didn't. Instead, it made her sick to her stomach. She slid off the barstool and stood, surprised to find she was unsteady on her feet.

"Claire?" Bobby got to his feet.

She pulled up a smile. It felt a little weak, one-sided. "I'm sorry, Bobby. My headache is worse. I think I need to lie down." She kissed his cheek, whispered, "Knock 'em dead, baby."

He put his arm around her. "I'll walk her back to the hotel."

Ryan frowned. "But your set—"

"I'll be back in time," Bobby said. Keeping a close hold, he maneuvered her out of the club and onto the loud, busy street.

"You don't have to escort me, Bobby. Really."

"Nothing matters more than you. Nothing. Those guys might as well know my priorities right off the bat."

They hurried through the lobby and rode the elevator to their floor. In their room Bobby gently put her to bed. "Go to sleep, my love," he whispered, kissing her forehead.

"Good luck, baby. I love you."

"That's exactly why I don't need luck."

Claire roused herself enough to call home. She tried to sound upbeat as she told Ali and Sam about the exciting day and reminded them that she'd be home in two days. After she hung up, she sighed heavily and closed her eyes.

WHEN Claire woke up the next morning, her headache was gone. She felt sluggish and tired, but it was easy to smile when Bobby told her how it had gone.

"I blew them away, Claire. No kidding. Kent Ames was salivating over my future. He offered us a contract. Can you believe it?"

They were curled up in their suite's window seat, both wearing the ultrasoft robes provided by the hotel. Bright morning sunlight pushed through the window. Bobby looked so handsome, he took Claire's breath away. "Of course I can believe it. I've heard you sing. How does it all work?"

"They think it'll take a month or so in Nashville. Finding material, putting a backup band together. They want me to tour through September and October. But don't worry. I told them we'd have to work out a schedule that was good for the family."

Claire loved him more at that moment than she would have imagined was possible. She grabbed his robe and pulled him close. "You will *only* have men and ugly women on your bus. I've seen movies about those tours."

He kissed her, long and slow and hard. When he drew back, she was dizzy. "What did I ever do to deserve you, Claire?"

"You loved me," she answered, reaching into his robe. "Now take me to bed and love me again."

AT SIX thirty in the morning Meghann rolled out of bed, took a shower, and dressed in a black suit with a lavender silk shell. One look in the mirror reminded her that she hadn't slept more than two hours the night before. She was at her desk by seven thirty, highlighting a deposition.

Every fifteen minutes she glanced at her phone. It was a weekday. Joe would be at work. *Call him.*

Finally, at ten o'clock, she gave up and buzzed her secretary.

"Yes, Ms. Dontess?"

"I need the number for a garage in Hayden, Washington."

"What garage?"

"I don't know the name or the address. But it's across the street from Riverfront Park. On Front Street."

"I'm going to need—"

"To be resourceful. Thanks." Meghann hung up.

Ten long minutes passed. Finally Rhona buzzed on line 1. "Here's the number. It's called Smitty's Garage."

Meghann wrote down the number and stared at it. Her heart was beating quickly. "This is ridiculous." She picked up the phone and dialed. With every ring she had to fight the urge to hang up.

"Smitty's Garage."

Meghann swallowed hard. "Is Joe there?"

"Just a sec. Joe!"

The phone clanged down, then was picked up. "Hello?"

"Joe? It's Meghann."

There was a long pause. "I thought I'd seen the last of you."

"I guess it won't be that easy." But the joke fell into silence. "I . . . uh . . . I have a deposition in Snohomish County on Friday. I thought you might like to get together for dinner."

He didn't answer.

"Forget it. I'm an idiot. I'll hang up now."

"I could pick up a couple of steaks and borrow Smitty's barbecue."

"You mean it?"

He laughed softly, and the sound of it released that achy tension in her neck. "Why not?"

"I'll be there about six. Is that okay?"

"Perfect."

"I'll bring wine and dessert."

Meghann was smiling when she hung up. Ten minutes later Rhona buzzed her again.

"Ms. Dontess, your sister is on line two. She says it's urgent."

"Thanks." Meg pushed the button. "Hey, Claire. Welcome back. Your flight must have been on time. Amazing. How was—"

"I'm at the airport. I didn't know who else to call." Claire's voice was shaky; it sounded as if she was crying.

"What's going on, Claire?"

"I don't remember the flight from Nashville. I also don't remember getting my luggage, but it's right here. I don't remember walking through the garage, but I'm sitting in my car."

"I don't understand."

"Neither do I, damn it," Claire screamed; then she started to sob. "I can't remember how to get home."

"Oh, my God." Instead of panicking, Meghann took charge. "Do you have a piece of paper?"

"Yes. Right here."

"A pen?"

"Yes." Her sobs slowed down. "I'm scared, Meg."

"Write down Eight twenty-nine Post Alley. Do you have that?"

"I'm holding it."

"Keep holding it. Now get out of your car and walk toward the terminal."

"I'm scared."

"I'll stay on the phone with you."

"Wait. I don't know which way—"

"Is there a covered walkway in front of you, with airlines listed above it?"

"Yes. It says Alaska and Horizon."

"Go that way. I'm right here, Claire. I'm not going anywhere. Take the escalator down one floor. You see it?"

"Yes."

She sounded so weak. It scared the hell out of Meghann. "Go outside. Pick up the phone that says TAXI. What's the number above the door you just came through?"

"Twelve."

"Tell the cabdriver to pick you up at door twelve, that you're going downtown."

"Hold on."

Meghann heard her talking. Then Claire said, "Okay."

"I'm right here, Claire. Everything is going to be okay."

"Who is this?"

Meghann felt an icy rush of fear. "It's Meghann."

"I don't remember calling you."

Meghann closed her eyes. It took an act of will to find her voice. "Is there a cab in front of you?"

"Yes. Why is it here?"

"It's there for you. Give him the piece of paper in your hand."

"Oh, God, Meg. How did you know I had this paper? What's wrong with me?"

"It's okay, Claire. He'll drop you off at my building. I'll be waiting for you."

THE cab pulled along the curb and stopped. Before Claire could even say thank you, the front passenger-side door opened. Meghann paid the driver, then guided Claire into the cushy interior of a Lincoln Town Car that was waiting at the curb. Meg studied her. "Are you okay now?"

Claire heard the concern in her sister's voice, and it touched her. "I'm fine now. Really. I guess I had a panic attack or something. Just take me to a quiet restaurant for a cup of coffee. I probably just need to sleep."

Meg looked at her as if she were a science experiment gone bad. "Are you kidding me? A panic attack? Believe me, Claire, I know panic attacks, and you don't forget how to get home. We're going to the hospital."

They exchanged looks then, until Claire turned away. "Bobby aced the auditions. They offered him a big fat contract."

"He won't sign it until I review it, right?"

"The standard response is 'Congratulations.' "

Meghann had the grace to blush. "Congratulations."

"I believe it belongs in *Ripley's Believe It or Not!* under the headline 'Eliana Sullivan Does Good Deed.' "

Meg pressed a hand to her breast and said, "I'm so bighearted when it comes to family," in a gooey southern drawl.

Claire started to laugh. Then she noticed that the tingling in her right hand was back. As she stared down at her hand, her fingers curled into a kind of hook. For a split second she couldn't open it. She panicked. *Please, God—*

The spasm ended.

The car pulled up in front of the hospital and let them out.

At the emergency room's reception desk, a heavyset young woman looked up at them. "Can I help you?"

"I'm here to see a doctor."

"What's the problem?"

"I have a killer headache."

Meghann leaned over the desk. "Write this down: Severe headache. Short-term memory loss."

"That's right. I forgot." Claire smiled weakly.

The receptionist shoved a clipboard across the desk. "Fill that out and give me your insurance card."

Claire retrieved the card from her wallet and handed it to the receptionist, who said, "Take a seat until we call for you."

An hour later they were still waiting. Meghann was fit to be tied. "They've got a lot of nerve calling this an *emergency* room."

Claire considered trying to calm her sister down, but the effort was too much. Her headache had gotten worse.

"Claire Austin," called out a nurse in a blue scrub suit.

"It's about time." Meghann helped Claire to her feet.

"You're a real comfort, Meg," Claire said.

"It's a gift," Meg said, guiding her toward the tiny, birdlike nurse who stood in front of the double door of the ER.

Claire clung to her sister's hand as they went through the doors. In an exam room she changed into a hospital gown, relinquished her arm for a blood pressure test and her vein for a blood test.

Again they waited. Finally someone knocked, and the door opened. In walked a teenage boy in a white coat.

"I'm Dr. Lannigan. What seems to be the problem?"

Meghann groaned.

"Hello, Doctor," Claire said. "I really don't need to be here. I have a headache, and my sister thinks a migraine is emergency-room-worthy. After a long flight I had some kind of panic attack."

"Where she forgot how to get home," Meghann added.

The doctor asked Claire to perform a few functions—lift one arm, then the other, turn her head, blink—and answer some easy questions, like what year it is, who the President is. When he finished, he asked, "Do you often get headaches?"

"When I get stressed out. More lately, though," she admitted.

"Have you made any big changes in your life recently?"

Claire laughed. "Plenty. I just got married for the first time. My husband is in Nashville, making a record."

"Ah." He smiled. "Well, Mrs. Austin, your blood work is normal, as is your blood pressure. I'm sure this is all stress. If the headaches persist, however, I'd recommend that you see a neurologist."

Claire nodded, relieved. "Thank you, Doctor."

"Oh, no," Meghann said to the doctor. "That's not good enough."

He blinked at her, stepping back.

"I watch *ER*. She needs a CAT scan or an MRI. Some damn initial test. At the very least she'll take that neurology consult now."

He frowned. "Those are costly tests. We can hardly run a CAT scan on every patient who complains of a headache, but if you'd like, I'll recommend a neurologist. You can make an appointment."

"How long have you been a doctor?"

"I'm in my first year of residency."

"Would you like to do a second year?"

"Of course. I don't see—"

"Get your supervisor in here. Now. We didn't spend three hours here so that an almost doctor could tell us that Claire is under stress. I'm under stress; you're under stress. We manage to remember our way home. Get a neurologist in here. *Now.*"

"I'll go get a consult." He clutched his clipboard and hurried out.

Claire sighed. "You're being you again. It *is* stress."

"I hope it is, too, but I'm not taking the prom king's word for it."

A few moments later the nurse was back. "Dr. Kensington has reviewed your material. She'd like you to have a CAT scan."

"She. Thank God," Meghann said.

The nurse nodded. "You can come with me," she said.

Claire clung to Meghann's hand. The walk seemed to last forever, down one corridor and another, up the elevator, until they arrived at the Center for Nuclear Medicine.

Nuclear. Claire felt Meghann's grip tighten.

"Here we are." The nurse paused outside a closed door. She turned to Meghann. "There's a chair right there. You can't come in, but I'll take good care of her, okay?"

Meghann hesitated, then nodded. "I'll be here, Claire."

Claire followed the nurse into a room that was dominated by a huge machine that looked like a white doughnut. She let herself be positioned on the narrow bed that intersected the doughnut hole. There she waited. And waited. Periodically the nurse came back, muttered something about the doctor, and disappeared again.

Finally the door opened, and a man in a white coat walked in. "Sorry to keep you waiting. I'm Dr. Cole, your radiologist. You just lie perfectly still, and we'll have you out of here in no time."

Claire forced herself to smile. She refused to think about the fact that everyone else in the room wore lead aprons, while she lay with only the thinnest sheet of cotton to protect her.

"You're done. Fine job," he said when it was finally over.

Claire was so thankful, she almost forgot the headache that had steadily increased as she lay in the machine.

In the hallway, Meghann looked angry. "What happened? They said it would take an hour."

"And it did, once they corralled a doctor."

They followed the nurse to another exam room.

"Should I get dressed?" Claire asked.

"Not yet. The doctor will be here soon."

"I'll bet," Meghann said under her breath.

THIRTY minutes later the nurse was back. "The doctor has ordered another test," she said to Meghann. "An MRI."

"An MRI?" Meg asked, feeling anxious.

"It's a clearer picture of what's going on. Very standard."

Claire's one-hour test lasted for two. Finally she was let go, and she and Meghann returned to the nuclear medicine wing, where Claire's clothes were hanging. Then they went to another waiting room. "Of course," Meg grumbled.

They were there another hour. At last a tall, tired-looking woman in a lab coat came into the waiting room. "Claire Austin?"

Claire stood up. At the suddenness of the movement she almost fell. Meg steadied her.

The woman smiled and said, "I'm Dr. Sheri Kensington, chief of neurology."

"Claire Austin. This is my sister, Meghann."

"It's nice to meet you. Come this way." Dr. Kensington led them down a short hallway and into an office that was lined with books, diplomas, and children's artwork. Behind her, a set of X-ray–like images glowed against the bright white backlighted boxes.

Claire stared at them, wondering what there was to see.

The doctor sat down at her desk and indicated that Claire and Meghann sit opposite her. "I'm sorry you had problems with Dr. Lannigan. This is a teaching hospital, and sometimes our residents are not as thorough as we would wish. Your demand for a higher level of care was a much needed wake-up call for Dr. Lannigan."

Claire nodded. "Do I have a sinus infection?"

"No, Claire. You have a mass in your brain."

"What?"

"You have a tumor. In your brain." Dr. Kensington rose slowly and went to the X-rays, pointing to a white spot. "It's about the size of a golf ball and located in the right frontal lobe, crossing the midline."

Tumor. Claire felt as if she'd just been shoved out of an airplane. She couldn't breathe; the ground was rushing up to meet her.

"I'm sorry to say this," Dr. Kensington went on, "but I've consulted with a neurosurgeon, and we believe it's inoperable. You'll want second opinions, of course. You'll need to see an oncologist also."

Meghann was on her feet. "You're saying she has a brain tumor and that you can't do anything about it?"

"We believe it's inoperable, but I didn't say we can't do anything."

"Meg, please." Claire was absurdly afraid that her sister was going to make it worse. She looked pleadingly at the doctor. "Are you saying I might die?"

"We'll need more tests, but given the size and placement of the mass, it's not a good outlook."

"Inoperable means *you* won't operate," Meg said in a growl.

Dr. Kensington looked surprised. "I don't believe anyone will. I consulted with our top neurosurgeon on this. He agrees with my diagnosis. The procedure would be too dangerous."

Meg looked disgusted. "Who *will* do this kind of operation?"

"No one in this hospital."

Meg grabbed her handbag. "Come on, Claire. We're in the wrong hospital."

Claire looked helplessly from Dr. Kensington to her sister. "Meg," she pleaded, "you don't know everything. Please . . ."

Meg went to her, knelt in front of her. "I know I don't know everything. I even know I've let you down in the past, but none of that matters now. From this second on, all that matters is your life."

Claire started to cry. She hated how fragile she felt, but there it was. Suddenly she *felt* like she was dying.

"Lean on me, Claire."

Claire gazed into her sister's eyes and remembered how Meg had once been her whole world. Slowly she nodded.

Meghann helped her to her feet; then she turned to the doctor. "You go ahead and teach Dr. Lannigan how to read a thermometer. We're going to find a doctor who can save her life."

Outside the hospital, Meghann helped Claire into the Town Car. "Are you okay?" she asked, her voice spiked and anxious.

She looked at Meg. "Do I have cancer? Is that what a tumor is?"

"We don't know what the hell you have. Certainly, those doctors don't know."

"Did you see the shadow on that X-ray, Meg? It was *huge.*"

Meghann grabbed her, shook her hard. "Listen to me. You need to be tough now. No getting by, no giving up. Tomorrow we'll start getting second opinions. First we'll go to Johns Hopkins. Then we'll try Sloan-Kettering in New York. There's got to be a surgeon who has some balls." Meghann's eyes welled up; her voice broke.

Somehow that frightened Claire even more, seeing Meg crack. "It's going to be okay," she said automatically. Comforting others was easier than thinking. "We just need to keep positive."

"Faith. Yes," Meghann said. "You hold on to the faith, and I'll start finding out everything there is to know about your condition. That way we'll have all the bases covered."

"You mean be a team?"

"Someone has to be there for you through this."

The whole of their childhood was between them suddenly, all the good times and, more important, the bad.

Claire stared at her sister. "If you start this thing with me, you have to stick around if things get tough."

Meg looked at her. "You can count on me."

Claire frowned. "I don't want to tell anyone."

"Why should we say anything until we know for sure?"

"It'll just worry Dad and make Bobby come home." She paused, swallowed hard. "I don't even want to think about telling Ali."

"We'll tell everyone I'm taking you to a spa for a week."

"Bobby will believe it. And Ali. Dad . . . I don't know. Maybe if I tell him we need time together. He's wanted us to reconcile for years. Yeah. He'd buy that."

MEETING with Diana's parents had released something in Joe. Their forgiveness, their understanding, had eased his burdens. For the first time since his wife's death, he could stand straight again. He could believe that there was a way out for him. Not medicine. He could never watch death up close again. But something . . .

And there was Meghann. To his disbelief she'd called. Asked him on a date. His first real date with a woman in more than fifteen years. Meghann, perhaps even more so than the Roloffs' forgiveness, had brought Joe back to life.

On his lunch break he got a haircut and bought new clothes. He got back to the garage by one o'clock and worked for the rest of the day.

"That's about the tenth time you've looked at that clock in the past half an hour," Smitty said at four thirty.

"I've . . . uh . . . got someplace to be," Joe said.

Smitty reached for a wrench. "No kidding."

Joe slammed the truck's hood down. "I thought maybe I'd leave a couple of minutes early."

"Wouldn't hurt my feelings none."

"A friend is coming over for dinner," Joe said.

"This friend drive a Porsche?"

"Yeah."

Smitty smiled. "Maybe you want to borrow the barbecue. Cut a few flowers from Helga's garden?"

"I didn't know how to ask."

"Hell, Joe, you just do. Open your mouth and say please. That's part of being neighbors and co-workers."

"Thank you."

"Have a nice night, Joe."

Joe left the shop and stopped by Smitty's house. He talked to Helga for a few minutes and left carrying a small hibachi. He set up the barbecue on the front porch.

Inside the house, he showered and shaved, then dressed in his new clothes and headed for the kitchen.

For the next hour he moved from one chore to the next, until the potatoes were in the oven, the flowers were on the table, and the candles were lit. He poured himself a glass of red wine and went into the living room to wait for her.

He sat down on the sofa and stretched out his legs.

From her place on the mantel Diana smiled down at him.

He felt a flash of guilt, as if he'd done something wrong. That was stupid; he wasn't being unfaithful. Still . . .

He set his glass down on the coffee table and collected the photographs, one by one, leaving a single framed picture on the end table. Just one. All the rest he took into the bedroom and carefully put away. Later he'd return a few of them to his sister's house.

When he went back into the living room and sat down, he smiled, thinking of Meghann. Anticipating the evening.

By nine thirty his smile had faded.

He sat alone on the couch, half drunk now with an empty bottle of wine beside him. The potatoes had long ago cooked down to nothing, and the candles had burned themselves out.

At midnight he went to bed alone.

CHAPTER NINE

IN THE past nine days Meghann and Claire had seen several specialists. It was amazing how fast doctors would see you if you had a brain tumor and plenty of money. Neurologists. Neurosurgeons. Neuro-oncologists. Radiologists. They went from Johns Hopkins to Sloan-Kettering to Scripps. They learned dozens of frightening new words: glioblastoma, anaplastic astrocytoma, craniotomy.

Some of the doctors were caring and compassionate; more were distant and too busy to talk for long. They each said the same thing: inoperable. It didn't matter if Claire's tumor was malignant or benign; either way it could be deadly. Most of them believed the tumor to be a glioblastoma multiforme. A kind they called the terminator. Ha-ha.

Each time they left a city, Meghann pinned her hopes on the next destination, until a neurologist at Scripps took her aside. "Look," he said, "you're using up valuable time. Radiation is your sister's best hope. Twenty-five percent of brain tumors respond positively to the treatment. If it shrinks enough, perhaps it will be operable. Take her home. Stop fighting the diagnosis and start fighting the tumor."

So they'd gone home to Seattle. The next day Meghann had taken Claire to Swedish Hospital, where they'd agreed to begin radiation treatment the next day. Once a day for four weeks.

"I'll need to stay here for the treatments," Claire said as she sat in Meghann's condo. "Hayden's too far away."

"Of course. I'll take some more time off of work."

"You don't have to do that. I can take the bus to the hospital."

"I'm not going to dignify that with an answer."

Claire looked out the window. "A friend of mine went through chemo and radiation." She stared at the sparkling city, but all she really saw was Diana wasting away. In the end, all those treatments hadn't helped at all. "I don't want Ali to see me like that. She can stay with Dad. We'll visit every weekend."

"I'll rent a car for Bobby. That way you guys can drive back and forth."

"I'm not going to tell Bobby . . . yet."

Meghann frowned. "What?"

"I am not going to call my brand-new husband and tell him I have a brain tumor. He's waited his whole life for this break. I don't want to ruin it for him."

"But if he loves you—"

"He *does* love me," Claire answered fiercely. "That's the point. And I love him. I want him to have his chance."

"It sounds to me like you're afraid he won't want to come," Meghann said. "I know you're scared, Claire. And I know Mama and I hurt you. But you have to give Bobby the chance to—"

"This isn't about the past. I'm the one who has a tumor. Me. You don't get to organize or critique my choices, okay? I love Bobby, and I am *not* going to ask him to sacrifice everything for me." Claire stood up. "We better get going. I need to tell Dad what's going on."

"What about Mama? You want to call her?"

"I'll call her if I get worse. Now let's go."

Two hours later Meg turned onto River Road, and they were there. Late afternoon sunlight drizzled down the sides of the yellow clapboard house; the garden was a riot of color. A small bicycle with training wheels lay on its side in the overgrown grass.

Claire turned to Meg. "I need to do this alone."

Meg understood. This was Claire's family, not hers. "Okay. The doctors are going to make you better."

Claire looked at Meghann. "How do I promise that? What if—"

"Promise it, Claire. We'll worry about what-if later."

Claire nodded. "You're right." Her smile was wobbly.

Meghann saw the way her sister was trembling, and she longed to reach out to her, to hold her as she had when they were kids.

Claire got out of the car and walked haltingly up the path. She turned and glanced back at Meghann. "Pick me up at six, okay?"

Meg backed out of the driveway and drove away. She didn't even know where she was going until she was there.

The cabin looked dark, unoccupied. She parked out front. Leaving her car, she walked up to the front door. She knocked.

He opened the door. "You have got to be kidding me."

That was when she remembered their date. Over a week ago. She was supposed to bring the wine and dessert. She looked past him, saw a dying bouquet of flowers on the coffee table, and hoped he hadn't bought them for their date. How long had he waited, she wondered, before he ate his dinner alone? "I'm sorry. I forgot."

"Give me one good reason not to slam the door in your face."

She looked up at him, feeling so fragile she could barely breathe. "My sister has a brain tumor."

His expression changed slowly. A look came into his eyes, a kind of harrowing understanding that made her wonder at the dark roads that had traversed his life.

He opened his arms, and she walked into his embrace. For the first time she let herself really cry.

ALISON listened carefully to Claire's explanation of a golf ball–size "owie" in her brain.

"A golf ball is little," she said at last.

Claire nodded, smiling. "Yes. Yes, it is."

"And a special gun is gonna shoot magic rays at it until it disappears? Like rubbing Aladdin's lamp?"

"Exactly like that."

"How come you hafta live with Aunt Meg?"

"It's a long drive to the hospital. I can't go back and forth every day."

Finally Ali said, "Okay." Then she got to her feet and ran upstairs. "I'll be right back, Mommy!" she yelled down.

"You haven't looked at me," Dad said when Ali was gone.

"I know."

He got up and crossed the room, then sat down beside her. She felt the comforting, familiar heat of him as he put an arm around her, pulled her close. She rested her head on his shoulder and felt a splash of tears on her face. She knew he was crying.

He sighed heavily, wiping his eyes. "Have you told Bobby?"

"Not yet."

"But you will?"

"Of course. As soon as he's finished in Nashville. I won't make him give up his big break for me."

Before Dad could say anything else, Alison bounded into the room, dragging her worn, stained baby blanket, the one she'd slept with every single night of her life. "Here, Mommy, you can have my wubbie till you get all better."

Claire took the grayed pink blanket in her hands. She held it to her face and smelled the little-girl sweetness of it. "Thanks, Ali," she said in a throaty voice.

Alison crawled up into her arms and hugged her. "It's okay, Mommy. Don't cry. I'm a big girl. I can sleep without my wubbie."

THE next morning Meghann sat in the radiation treatment waiting room at Swedish Medical Center, trying to read the newest issue of *People* magazine. It was the "Best- and Worst-Dressed" issue. Honest to God, she couldn't tell the difference. Finally she tossed the magazine on the table beside her and went up to the desk again.

"It's been more than an hour. Are you sure everything is okay with my sister?"

"I spoke with radiology five minutes ago. She's almost finished."

Meghann sighed heavily and went back to her seat. The only magazine left to read was *Field & Stream*. She ignored it.

Finally Claire came out. Meghann rose slowly. On the right side of her sister's head was a small area that had been shaved. Claire touched her bald spot, feeling it.

"They tattooed me. I feel like Damien—that kid from *The Omen*."

Meg looked at the tiny black dots on the pale, shaved skin. "I could fix your hair so you couldn't even see the . . . you know."

"Bald spot? That would be great."

They walked through the hospital and out to the parking garage.

On the drive home, Claire said, "It didn't hurt."

"Really? That's good."

"I closed my eyes and imagined the rays were sunlight. Healing me. Like that article you gave me."

Meg had given her sister a stack of literature on positive thinking and visualization. "I'm glad it helped."

Claire leaned back in her seat and looked out the window.

Meghann wished she could say something that mattered; so much was unsaid between them. With a sigh she pulled into the underground lot and parked in her space.

Still silent, they went upstairs. In the condo, Claire touched her sister briefly; her fingers were icy cold. "Thanks for coming with me today. It helped not to be alone."

Their gazes met. Again Meghann felt the weight of their distance. "I think I'll lie down," Claire said. "I didn't sleep well last night."

So they'd both been awake. "Me, either."

Claire nodded. She waited a second longer, then turned and headed for the bedroom.

Meg went to the condo's in-home office. Once, files and briefs and depositions had cluttered the glass desk. Now it was buried beneath medical books, *JAMA* articles, and clinical trials literature. Every day boxes from Barnes & Noble.com and Amazon arrived.

Meghann sat down at her desk. Her current reading material was a *JAMA* article about the potential benefits of tamoxifen to shrink tumors. She opened a yellow legal pad and began to take notes. She worked furiously, writing, writing. Hours later, when she looked up, Claire was standing in the doorway, smiling at her. "Why do I think you're planning to do the surgery yourself?"

"I already know more about your condition than that first idiot we saw."

Claire came into the room, carefully stepping over the empty Amazon boxes and the magazines that had been discarded. "I think I better read it for myself, don't you?"

"Some of it's . . . hard."

Claire reached for a standing file on the left side of the desk. She picked up a manila file with HOPE emblazoned in red ink.

"Don't," Meg said. "I've just started."

Claire opened the file. It was empty. "This goes in it," Meg said quickly, ripping several pages out of her notebook. "Tamoxifen."

"Drugs?"

"There must be people who beat brain tumors," Meghann said fiercely. "I'll find every damn one and put their stories in there."

The doorbell rang.

"Who could that be?" Meghann sidled past Claire and walked to the door. By the time she got there, the bell had rung another eight times. "Good doorman," she muttered, opening the door.

Gina, Charlotte, and Karen stood clustered together.

"Where's our girl?" Karen cried out.

Claire appeared, and the screaming began. Karen and Charlotte surged forward, enfolding Claire in their arms.

"Sam called us," Gina said when she and Meghann were alone in the hallway. "How is she?"

"Okay, I guess. The radiation went well." At Gina's frightened look Meghann added, "She didn't want to worry you guys."

"Yeah, right. She can't be alone for a thing like this."

"I'm here," Meghann answered, stung.

Gina squeezed her arm. "She'll need all of us."

Meghann nodded. Then she and Gina looked at each other.

"You call me. Whenever," Gina said quietly.

"Thanks."

After that, Gina eased past Meg and went into the living room, saying loudly, "Okay, we've got spas-in-a-bucket, gooey popcorn balls, hilarious movies, and, of course, games."

Meghann watched the four friends come together, all talking at once. She went back to her office and shut the door.

THOUGH the radiation treatments themselves lasted only a few minutes a day, they monopolized Claire's life. By the fourth day she was tired and nauseated. But the side effects weren't half as bad as the phone calls.

Every day she called home at noon. Ali always asked if the owie was all better yet; then Dad got on the phone and asked the same question in a different way.

Meghann hardly went to the office anymore. Maybe three hours a day, tops. The rest of the time she spent huddled over books and articles or glued to the Internet. She attacked the issue of a tumor the way she'd once gone after deadbeat dads.

The only time Meg seemed willing to disappear into the woodwork was at two o'clock. The designated Bobby Phone Call time.

Now Claire was alone in the living room. In the kitchen, the two-o'clock buzzer was beeping. Claire dialed Bobby's new cell phone number.

He picked up on the first ring. "Hey, baby, you're two minutes late."

Claire leaned back into the sofa's downy cushions. "Tell me about your day." She'd found that it was easier to listen than to talk. Lately her mind was a little foggy. She wondered how long it would be before he noticed that she spent their conversations listening or that her voice always broke when she said, "I love you."

"I miss you, Claire."

"I miss you, too. But it's only a few more weeks."

"Kent thinks we should have all the songs chosen by next week. Then it's into the studio. Do you think you could come down for that? I'd love to sing the songs to you."

"Maybe," she said, wondering what lie she'd come up with when the time came. She was too exhausted to think of one now. "Well, babe, I've got to run. Meg is taking me out to lunch. Then we're getting manicures."

"I thought you got a manicure yesterday."

Claire winced. "Uh, those were pedicures. I love you."

"I love you, too, Claire. Is . . . is everything okay?"

She felt the sting of tears again. "Everything's perfect."

"I MADE us a picnic lunch," Meghann said to Claire in the car the next morning after treatment.

Meghann drove onto a treelined drive. At a beautiful, gray-shingled house, she parked. "This is my partner's house. She said we were welcome to spend the afternoon here."

Meghann helped Claire out of the car and down the grassy lawn to the silvery wooden dock that cut into the blue water. "Remember Lake Winobee?" she said, guiding Claire to the end of the dock, helping her sit down without falling.

"The summer I got that pink bathing suit?"

Meghann set the picnic basket down, then sat beside her sister. They both dangled their feet over the edge.

"I stole that bikini," Meghann said. "When I got home, I was so scared I threw up. Mama didn't care; she just looked up from *Variety* and said, 'Sticky fingers will get a girl in trouble.'"

Claire turned to her sister. "I waited for you to come back, you know. Dad always said, 'Don't worry, Claire Bear. She's your sister; she'll be back.' I waited and waited. What happened?"

Meghann sighed heavily, as if she'd known this conversation couldn't be avoided anymore. "Remember when Mama went down for the *Starbase IV* audition?"

"Yes."

"She didn't come back. I was used to her being gone for a day or two, but after about five days I started to panic. There wasn't any money left. We were hungry. Then social services started sniffing around. I was scared they'd put us in the system. So I called Sam."

"I know all this, Meg."

"He said he'd take us both in."

"And he did."

"But he wasn't *my* father. I tried to fit in to Hayden; what a joke. I got in with a bad crowd and started screwing up. Every time I looked at you and Sam together, I felt left out. You were all I really had, and then I didn't have you. One night I came home drunk, and Sam told me to shape up or get out."

"So you got out. Where did you go?"

"I bummed around Seattle for a while, feeling sorry for myself. Then one day I remembered a teacher who'd taken an interest in me, Mr. Earhart. He had convinced me that education was the way out of Mama's trailer-trash life. That's why I always got straight A's. Anyway, I gave him a call—thank God he was still at the same school. He arranged for me to graduate high school early and take the SAT, which I aced. Perfect score. U.W. offered me a full scholarship. You know the rest."

"My genius sister," Claire said. For once, there was pride in her voice instead of bitterness.

"I told myself it was the best thing for you, that you didn't need your big sister anymore. But I knew how much I'd hurt you. It was easier to keep my distance, I guess. I believed you'd never forgive me. So I didn't give you the chance."

"The only thing you did wrong was stay away," Claire said.

"I'm here now."

"I know." Claire looked out to the sparkling blue water. "I couldn't have done all this without you."

"That's not true. You're the bravest person I ever met."

"I'm not so brave, believe me."

Meghann leaned back to open the picnic basket. "I've been waiting for just the right time to give you this." She withdrew a manila folder and handed it to Claire. "Here."

Claire took the folder with a sigh. It was the one labeled HOPE. Her hands trembled as she opened the file.

In it were almost a dozen personal accounts of people who had had glioblastoma multiforme tumors. Each of them had been given less than a year to live—at least seven years ago.

Claire squeezed her eyes shut, but the tears came anyway. "I needed this today."

"I thought so."

She swallowed hard, then dared to look at her sister. "I've been so afraid." It felt good, finally admitting it.

"Me, too," Meg answered quietly. Then she leaned forward and took Claire in her arms.

For the first time since childhood Claire was held by her big sister. Meghann stroked her hair, the way she'd done when Claire was young. A handful of hair fell out at Meghann's touch.

Claire drew back, saw the pile of her pretty blond hair in Meghann's hand. "I didn't want to tell you it's been falling out. Every morning I wake up on a hairy pillow."

"Maybe we should go home," Meg said finally.

"I *am* tired."

Meghann helped Claire to her feet. Slowly they made their way back to the car. Claire leaned heavily on Meg's arm.

Back in the condo, Meghann helped Claire change into her flannel pajamas and climb into bed.

"It's just hair," Claire said. "It'll grow back."

"Yeah." Meghann set the HOPE file on the nightstand and backed out of the room. At the doorway she stopped.

Her sister lay there, with her eyes closed. Tears leaked down the sides of her face, leaving tiny gray splotches on the pillow.

And Meghann knew what she had to do.

She closed the door and went to the phone. All of Claire's emergency numbers were on a notepad beside it. Including Bobby's.

IN THE PAST TWENTY-FOUR HOURS Claire had lost almost half of her hair. This morning, as she got ready for her appointment, she spent nearly thirty minutes wrapping a silk scarf around her head.

"Quit fussing," Meghann said when they arrived at the nuclear medicine waiting room. "You look fine."

Claire left for her treatment and was back in the waiting room thirty minutes later. She didn't bother putting the scarf back on.

"Let's go out for coffee," she said when Meghann stood up.

"I have to go into the office. I've got a deposition scheduled."

"Oh." Claire followed Meghann down the hospital corridor, trying to keep up. Lately she was so tired, it was hard not to shuffle like an old woman. She practically fell asleep in the car.

At the condo door, Meghann paused, key in hand, and looked at her. "I'm trying to do what's right for you. What's best."

"I know that."

"Sometimes I screw up. I tend to think I know everything."

Claire smiled. "Are you waiting for an argument?"

"Just remember that I'm trying to do the right thing."

"Okay, Meg. I'll remember. Now go to work. I don't want to miss *Judge Judy*. She reminds me of you."

"Smart-ass." Meg opened the condo door. "Bye."

Claire went into the condo, closing the door behind her. Inside, the stereo was on: Dwight Yoakam's "Pocket of a Clown."

Claire turned the corner, and there he was. Bobby.

Her hand flew to her bald spot. She ran to the bathroom, flipped open the toilet lid, and threw up.

He was behind her, holding what was left of her hair back, telling her it was okay. "I'm here now, Claire. I'm here."

She closed her eyes, holding back tears of humiliation one breath at a time. He rubbed her back.

Finally she went to the sink and brushed her teeth. When she turned to face him, she tried to smile. "Welcome to my nightmare."

He came toward her, and the love in his eyes made her want to weep. "Our nightmare, Claire."

She didn't know what to say. She was afraid that if she opened her mouth, she'd burst into tears.

"You had no right to keep this from me."

"You'd dreamed of singing for so long."

"I dreamed of being a star, yeah. I like singing, but I *love* you. I can't believe you'd hide this from me. What if . . ."

Claire caught her lip between her teeth. "I'm sorry. I was just trying to love you."

"I wonder if you even know what love is. 'I'm in the hospital every day, honey, battling for my life, but don't you worry about it, just sing your stupid songs.' What kind of man do you think I am?"

"I'm sorry, Bobby. I just . . ." She stared at him.

He pulled her toward him and held her so tightly, it made her gasp. "I love you, Claire. I *love* you," he said fiercely. "When are you going to get that through your head?"

She wrapped her arms around him, clung to him. "I guess my tumor got in the way, but I get it now, Bobby. I get it."

THE days passed slowly; each new morning found Claire a little more tired than the night before. She strove to keep a positive attitude, but her health was deteriorating rapidly.

The Bluesers came down often, separately and together, doing their best to keep her spirits up. The hardest times were weekends, when they went to Hayden; Claire tried to pretend for Ali that everything was okay.

In the evenings, though, it was just the three of them—Claire, Meg, and Bobby—in that too quiet apartment. Mostly they watched movies together. At first, when Bobby arrived, they'd tried to spend the evening talking or playing cards, but that had proved difficult. Too many dangerous subjects. None of them could mention the future without flinching, without thinking, Will there be a Christmas together? A Thanksgiving? A next summer?

Finally the radiation ended. The following morning Claire got up early. She dressed and drank her coffee out on the deck. It amazed her that so many people were already up, going about their ordinary lives on this day that would define her future.

"Today's the day," Meg said, stepping out to join her.

Behind them, the glass door opened. "Morning, ladies." Bobby came up behind Claire and kissed the back of her neck.

They stood there a minute longer, no one speaking; then they turned together and left the condo.

In no time they were at the hospital. As they entered the waiting room, Claire noticed the other patients who wore hats and scarves. When their gazes met, a sad understanding passed between them. They were members of a club you didn't want to join. Claire wished now that she hadn't bothered with the scarf. Baldness had a boldness to it that she wanted to embrace.

There was no waiting today, not on this day that would answer all the questions. She checked in and went to the MRI. Within moments she was pumped full of dye and stuck in the loud machine.

When she was finished, she returned to the waiting room and sat between Meghann and Bobby. She held their hands.

Finally they called her name.

Claire rose. Bobby steadied her. "I'm right here, babe."

The three of them began the long walk, ending finally in Dr. Sussman's office. The plaque on the door read CHIEF OF NEUROLOGY. Dr. McGrail, the chief of radiology, was also there.

"Hello, Claire. Meghann," Dr. Sussman said. "Bobby."

"Well?" Meghann demanded.

"The tumor responded to radiation. It's about twelve percent smaller," Dr. McGrail reported.

"That's great," Meg said.

The doctors exchanged a look. Dr. Sussman went to the view box, switched it on, and there they were, the gray-and-white pictures of Claire's brain. He turned to Claire. "The decrease has bought you some time. Unfortunately, the tumor is still inoperable. I'm sorry."

Sorry.

Claire sat down in the leather chair. She didn't think her legs would hold her up. "How long do I have?"

Dr. Sussman's voice was gentle. "The survival rates aren't good. Some patients live as long as a year. Perhaps a bit longer."

"And the rest?"

"Six to nine months."

Claire stared down at her brand-new wedding ring, the one Grandma Myrtle had worn for six decades.

Meghann went to Claire then, dropped to her knees in front of her. "We won't believe it. The files—"

"Don't," she said, shaking her head, thinking about Ali. She saw her baby's eyes and sunburst smile, and tears ran down her cheeks. She wiped her eyes, looked up at the doctor. "What's next?"

Meghann jerked to her feet and began pacing the room, studying the pictures and diplomas on the walls. Claire knew her sister was scared and, thus, angry.

Dr. Sussman pulled a chair around and sat down opposite Claire. "We have some options. None too good, I'm afraid, but—"

"Who is this?" Meghann's voice sounded shrill. She was holding a framed photograph she'd taken off the wall.

Dr. Sussman frowned. "That's a group of us from medical school." He turned back to Claire.

Meghann slammed the photograph on the desk so hard, the glass cracked. She pointed at someone in the picture. "Who's that guy?"

Dr. Sussman leaned forward. "Joe Wyatt."

"He's a *doctor*?"

Claire looked at her sister. "You know Joe?"

"*You* know Joe?" Meghann said sharply.

"He's a radiologist, actually." It was Dr. McGrail who answered. "One of the best in the country. At least he was. He was a legend with MRIs. He saw things—possibilities—no one else did."

Claire frowned. "Meghann, let go of it. We're long past the need for a radiologist. And believe me, Joe wouldn't be the one to ask for help. What I needed was a miracle."

Meghann said to McGrail, "What do you mean he *was* the best?"

"He quit. Disappeared, in fact."

"Why?"

"He killed his wife."

CHAPTER TEN

THE ride home seemed to last forever. No one spoke. When they got to the condo, Bobby held Claire so tightly she couldn't breathe, then stumbled back from her. "I need to take a shower," he said in a broken voice.

She let him go, knowing what he needed. She'd cried a few tears of her own in Meghann's expensive glass-block shower.

She went to the sofa, collapsed on it. She was tired and dizzy. There was a ringing in her ears and a tingling in her right hand, but she couldn't admit any of that to Meghann.

Meg sat down on the coffee table, angled toward her. "There are all kinds of clinical trials going on—"

Claire held up a hand. "Can we be real for just a minute?"

Meghann looked stricken. "What?" she demanded.

"When I was little, I used to dream about getting some rare illness that would bring you and Mama to my bedside. I imagined you crying over my death."

Meg stood up so abruptly, she banged her shin on the coffee table and swore harshly. "I . . . can't talk about you dying. I can't." She couldn't get out of the room fast enough.

"But I need you to," Claire said to the empty room. A headache started behind her eyes again. It had been lurking nearby all day. She started to lean back into the sofa, when the pain hit. She gasped at it, tried to cry out. Her head felt as if it were exploding.

She couldn't move, couldn't breathe. Alison, she thought.

Then everything went dark.

MEGHANN stood by her sister's bed, holding on to the metal bed rails. "Is the medication helping?"

Claire looked small in the hospital bed, delicate. Her attempt at a smile was heartrending. "Yeah. A grand mal seizure. Welcome to my new world. How long will I be here?"

"A few days."

"It's time to call Mama."

Meghann flinched. Her mouth trembled. "Okay."

"Tell Dad, Ali, and the Bluesers they can come to see me, too."

Meghann heard the defeat in her sister's voice. She wanted to make her sister angry enough to fight, but her voice abandoned her.

"I'm going to go to sleep," Claire said. "I'm tired."

"It's the meds."

"Is it?" Claire smiled knowingly. "Good night. And take care of Bobby tonight, okay? He's not as strong as he looks."

A few minutes later Bobby walked into the room, looking haggard. His eyes were red and swollen.

"She woke up," Meghann said. "And went back to sleep."

"Damn it." He took Claire's hand in his. "Hey, baby. I'm back. I just went for a cup of coffee." He sighed. "She's giving up."

"I know. She wants me to call everyone. Tell them to come see her. How do we tell Ali this?" Tears stung her eyes.

"I'll tell her," Claire said quietly, opening her eyes. She smiled tiredly at her husband. "Bobby," she breathed, "I love you."

Meghann couldn't stand there another second. "I've got phone calls to make. Bye." She raced from the room.

It was late now, and the hallways were quiet. She went to the bank of pay phones and dialed Mama's number.

"It's me, Mama. Meghann. Claire's sick."

"She's on her honeymoon."

"That was a month ago, Mama. Now she's in the hospital."

"This better not be one of your stunts, Meggy. Like the time you called me at work 'cause Claire had fallen out of bed, and you thought she was paralyzed."

"She has a brain tumor, Mama. The radiation treatments didn't work, and no one has the guts to operate on her."

There was a long pause. Then, "Will she be okay?"

"Yes," Meghann said, because she couldn't imagine any other response. Then, very softly, she said, "Maybe not. You should come see her. Without your entourage, Mama. Alone."

"I've got a *Starbase IV* event tomorrow at two, and a—"

"Be here tomorrow, or I call *People* magazine and tell them you didn't visit your daughter who has a brain tumor."

"I'm no good with this sort of thing."

"None of us are, Mama." Meghann hung up, then punched in

the 800 number on her calling card and dialed Sam. The phone rang, but she lost her nerve. She couldn't tell Sam this over the phone.

She slammed the receiver onto the hook and went back to her sister's room. Bobby stood by the bed, singing softly to Claire, who snored gently. It brought Meghann up short.

Bobby looked up at her. Tears glistened on his cheeks. "She hasn't opened her eyes again."

"She will. Keep singing. I'm sure she loves it."

"Yeah." His voice cracked.

Meg had never seen a man in so much pain. "I'm going to go tell Sam. If Claire wakes up—" She caught herself. "*When* Claire wakes up, tell her I'll be back soon. Do you have your keys to my place?"

"I'll sleep here tonight."

"Okay." Meghann left the room.

She practically ran for her car. Once inside, she headed north.

Ninety minutes later she reached Hayden. She slowed down through town, stopped at the light.

And there it was: the silver Quonset hut.

Joe Wyatt.

Dr. Joseph Wyatt. Of course. No wonder he'd looked familiar. His trial had been front-page news.

He's a radiologist. Probably one of the best in the country. It came rushing back to her now, the stunning news that had been lost somehow, buried beneath a thick layer of grief.

Yet when she'd come to him, sobbing about her sick sister, he'd done nothing. Nothing. And he *knew* Claire.

"Son of a bitch." She glanced sideways. The envelope containing copies of Claire's most recent MRI films was on the passenger seat.

Meghann turned the wheel hard and slammed on the brakes, parking along the curb. Then she grabbed the envelope and marched toward the cabin. She pounded on the door, screaming, until she heard footsteps coming from inside.

When he opened the door, saw her, and said "What—" she shoved him in the chest so hard, he stumbled backward.

"Hey, Joe. Invite me in." She kicked the door shut behind her.

"It's practically midnight."

"So it is, *Doctor* Wyatt."

He sank onto the sofa and looked up at her.

"You held me. You let me cry in your arms." Her voice trembled. "And you offered *nothing*. What kind of man are you?"

"The kind who knows his hero days are behind him. If you know who I am, you know what I did."

"You killed your wife." At his flinch she went on. "Your trial was a big deal in Seattle. The prosecution of the doctor who euthanized his dying wife."

"Euthanasia is a prettier word than manslaughter."

Some of the steam went out of her at the sadness in his voice. "Look, Joe, in an ordinary world I'd talk to you about what you did. But it's not an ordinary world right now. My sister is dying." She tossed the oversize manila envelope onto the coffee table in front of him. "These are her MRI films. Maybe you can help her."

"I let my license lapse. I can't practice medicine anymore. I'm sorry."

"Sorry? *Sorry?* You have the power to save people's lives, and you hide out in this dump of a cabin feeling sorry for yourself?" She stared down at him, wanting to hate him, hurt him, but she couldn't imagine how to do either one. "I *cared* about you."

"I'm sorry," he said again.

"I'll send you an invitation to the funeral." She turned on her heel and headed for the door.

"Take this with you."

She stopped, gave him one last withering look. "No, Joe. You'll have to touch them. Throw them in the trash yourself."

Then she left. She made it all the way to her car before she started to cry.

CLAIRE grew weaker. By her second day in the hospital she wanted simply to sleep.

Her friends and family had begun showing up religiously. All of them. Even Mama. The Bluesers had descended on her tiny hospital room, bringing life and laughter, flowers and fattening food. They talked and told jokes and remembered old times. Only Gina had had the guts to brave the harsh, icy landscape of Claire's fear.

"I'll always be there for Ali, you know," she said when everyone else had gone to the cafeteria.

"Thank you," was all Claire was able to say. Then, softly, "I haven't been able to tell her yet."

"How could you?"

Gina's eyes met hers, filling slowly with tears. They'd both been thinking about how a woman said good-bye to her five-year-old daughter. After a long pause Gina smiled. "So what are we going to do about your hair?"

"I thought I'd cut it off. Dye what's left of it platinum."

"Very chic. We'll all look like old housewives next to you."

"That's my dream now," Claire said, unable to help herself. "Becoming an old housewife."

Ultimately, as much as she loved to see her friends, she was glad when they went home. Late that night, in the quiet darkness, she gave in to the meds and fell asleep.

She woke with a start. Her heart was pounding too fast, skipping beats. She couldn't seem to breathe. Something was wrong.

"Claire, are you okay?" It was Bobby. He'd obviously been sleeping. Rubbing his eyes, he stood up, came to her bedside.

"Bobby," she whispered, "get into bed with me."

He looked at all the machines, the IVs, the tubes and cords. "Oh, baby . . ." He leaned down and kissed her instead.

She closed her eyes, feeling herself sinking into the pillows. "Ali," she whispered. "I need my baby—"

Pain exploded behind her right eye.

Beside her bed an alarm went off.

THERE is no pain. No ache. The tubes that connect her to the machines are gone. She wants to shout out that she is better.

She realizes suddenly that she is watching herself from above— watching the doctors work on her body. They've ripped open her gown and are ramming something on her chest.

"Clear!" one yells.

There is such relief in being above them, where there is no pain.

"Clear."

Then she thinks of her daughter, her precious baby girl, who will have to be told that Mommy has gone away.

THE doctor stepped back. "She's gone."

Meghann ran to the bed, screaming. "Don't you do it, Claire. Come back. Come back, damn it."

Someone tried to pull her away. She elbowed him hard. "I mean

it, Claire. You come back. You cannot run out on Alison this way."
She grabbed Claire's shoulders, shook her hard. "Don't you dare."

"We have a heartbeat," someone cried out.

Meghann was pushed aside. She stumbled back into the corner
of the room, watching, praying, as they stabilized her sister.

Finally the doctors left, dragging their crash cart with them.
Meg stared at Claire's chest, watching it rise and fall.

"I heard you, you know."

At Claire's voice Meg moved forward.

There was Claire, pale as parchment, smiling up at her. "I
thought, 'God, I'm dead, and she's still yelling at me.' "

JOE HAD TRIED TO THROW OUT the damn envelope at least a dozen
times. The problem was, he couldn't bring himself to touch it.

Coward.

He heard the word so clearly, he looked up. The cabin was empty.
He stared at Diana, who looked back at him from the mantel.

He didn't need to conjure up her image to know what her words
would be right now. She would be as ashamed of him as he was
of himself. She would remind him he'd once taken an oath to help
people. And not just anyone, either. This was Claire Cavenaugh, the
woman who'd sat by Diana's bedside hour after hour when she was
ill, playing dirty-word Scrabble and watching soap operas.

Now it was Claire in a bed like that, in a room that smelled of
despair. If she were here right now, Diana would have told him that
chances didn't come any plainer than this. It was one thing to run
away from nothing. It was quite another to turn your back on a set
of films with a friend's name in the corner.

He released a heavy breath and reached out, pretending not to
notice that his hands were shaking. He pulled out the films and
took them into the kitchen, where full sunlight streamed through
the window above the sink.

As he studied them, he knew why everyone had diagnosed this
tumor as inoperable. The amount of skill needed to perform the surgery was almost unheard-of. It would require a neurosurgeon with
godlike hands and an ego to match. But with a careful resection there
might be a chance. It was possible—just possible—that this one thin
shadow wasn't tumor, that it was tissue responding to the tumor.

Stu Weissman. The cowboy. Stu Weissman at U.C.L.A. might be

able to do it. Joe glanced at the clock. He knew he couldn't reach Stu on the phone until the afternoon.

There was no doubt about what he had to do next.

He took a long, hot shower, then dressed in the blue shirt he'd recently bought and the new jeans, wishing he had better clothes, accepting that he didn't. Then he retrieved the film, put it back in the envelope, and walked over to Smitty's house. Smitty was in the living room, watching TV. He looked up. "Hey, Joe."

"I know this is irregular, but could I borrow the truck? I need to drive to Seattle. I may have to stay overnight."

Smitty dug in his pocket for the keys, then tossed them.

"Thanks." Joe went to the rusty old '73 Ford pickup and got inside. The door clanged shut behind him.

He stared at the dashboard. It had been years since he'd been in the driver's seat. He started the engine and hit the gas.

Two hours later he parked in the underground lot on Madison and Broadway and walked into the lobby of his old life.

When the elevator doors pinged open, he stepped inside. Two white-coated people crowded beside him, talking about lab results. They got off on the third floor—the floor that led to the skybridge that connected this office building to Swedish Medical Center.

He couldn't help remembering when he'd walked through this building with his head held high.

On the fourteenth floor the doors opened. He stood there a half second too long, staring at the gilt-edged black letters on the glass doors across the hall: SEATTLE NUCLEAR SPECIALISTS. The business he'd started on his own. There were seven or eight doctors listed below. Joe's name wasn't there.

He walked past the row of women waiting for mammograms, then turned onto another hallway. At the far end he took a deep breath and knocked on a door.

"Come in," said a familiar voice.

Joe entered the big corner office that had once been his. Li Chinn was at his desk, reading. At Joe's entrance he glanced up. An almost comical look of surprise overtook his face. "I don't believe it."

"Hey, Li."

Li looked awkward, uncertain of how to proceed, what to say. "It's been a long time, Joe."

"Three years."

"Where did you go?"

"Does it matter? I have some film I'd like you to look at."

At Li's nod Joe went to the view box and put the film up. Li came closer, studying it. For a long moment he said nothing. Then, "You see something I do not?"

Joe pointed. "There."

Li crossed his arms, frowned. "Not many surgeons would attempt such a thing. The risks are grave."

"She's going to die without the surgery."

"She may die because of the surgery."

"You think it's worth a try?"

Li looked at him, his frown deepening. "The old Joe Wyatt never asked for other men's opinions."

"Things change," he said simply.

"Do you know a surgeon who would do it? Who *could* do it?"

"Stu Weissman at U.C.L.A."

"Ah. The cowboy. Yes, maybe."

"I can't practice. I've let my license lapse. Could you send Stu the film? I'll call him."

Li flicked off the light. "I will. You know, it's an easy thing to reinstate your license."

"Yes." Joe stood there a moment longer. Silence spread like a stain between the men. He started to leave.

"Wait." Li moved toward him. "Privately many of us would have wanted to do the same thing. Diana was in terrible pain. There was no hope. We thank God that we were not in your shoes."

Joe had no answer to that.

"You have a gift, Joe," Li said. "Losing it would be a crime. When you're ready, come back to see me. This office is in the business of saving lives, not worrying about old gossip."

"Thank you." They were small words, too small to express his gratitude. Embarrassed by the depth of his emotion, Joe mumbled thanks again and left the office.

Downstairs in the lobby, Joe found a bank of pay phones and called Stu Weissman.

"Joe Wyatt," Stu said loudly. "How are you? I thought you fell off the face of the earth. Damn shame, what you went through."

Joe didn't want to waste time with the where-have-you-been

stuff. He said, "I have a surgery I want you to do. It's risky as hell. You're the only man I know who is good enough."

"Talk to me."

Joe explained what he knew of Claire's history, told him the current diagnosis, and outlined what he'd seen on the film.

"And you think there's something I can do."

"Only you."

"Well, Joe. Your eyes are the best in the business. Send me the film. If I see what you do, I'll be on the next plane. But you make sure the patient understands the risks."

"You got it. Thanks, Stu."

Joe replaced the receiver. Now he had to speak to Claire.

He went back to the elevators, then crossed the skybridge and headed into Swedish Hospital. A few people frowned in recognition; a few whispered behind him. He ignored them and kept moving. No one had the guts to speak to him, or ask why he was back here, until he reached the ICU. There someone said, "Dr. Wyatt?"

He turned slowly. It was Trish Bey, the head ICU nurse. They'd worked together for years. She and Diana had become close friends at the end. "Hello, Trish."

She smiled. "It's good to see you back here. We missed you."

His shoulders relaxed. He almost smiled in return. "Thanks." They stood there, staring at each other for an awkward moment; then he nodded, said good-bye, and headed for Claire's room.

He knocked quietly and opened the door.

She was sitting up in bed, asleep, her head cocked to one side. He moved toward her, trying not to remember when Diana had looked like this. Pale and fragile, her hair thinning to where she looked like an antique doll that had been loved too hard and then discarded.

She blinked awake, stared at him. "Joey," she whispered, smiling tiredly, "I heard you were home. Welcome back."

He sat down beside her bed. "Hey, Claire."

"I know. I've looked better."

"You're beautiful. You always have been."

"Bless you, Joe. I'll tell Di hi for you." She closed her eyes. "I'm sorry, but I'm tired."

"Don't be in such a hurry to see my wife."

Slowly she opened her eyes. "There's no hope, Joe. You of all people know what that's like. It hurts too much to pretend. Okay?"

"I see it . . . differently."

"Are you telling me I shouldn't give up?"

"Surgery might save you. But there could be bad side effects, Claire. Paralysis. Loss of motor skills. Brain damage."

"Do you know what I was thinking just before you got here?"

"No."

"About how to tell Ali Kat that Mommy is going to die. I'd take any risk, Joe. Anything so I don't have to kiss Ali good-bye."

"I'm sending your films to a friend of mine. If he agrees with my diagnosis, he'll operate."

"Thank you, Joe," she said softly, then closed her eyes again.

He leaned down and kissed her forehead. "Bye, Claire."

He was almost to the door when she said, "Joe?"

He turned. "Yeah?"

"She shouldn't have asked it of you."

"Who?" he asked, but he knew.

"Diana. I would never ask such a thing of Bobby. I know what it would do to him."

Joe had no answer to that. It was the same thing Gina always said. He left the room and closed the door behind him. With a sigh he leaned back against the wall and closed his eyes.

"Joe?"

He opened his eyes and stumbled away from the wall. Meghann stood a few feet away, her eyes reddened and moist.

She walked toward him. "Tell me you found a way to help her."

"I've spoken to a colleague at U.C.L.A. If he agrees with me, he'll operate, but—"

Meghann launched herself at him, clung to him. "Thank you."

"It's risky as hell, Meg. She might not survive the surgery."

Meghann drew back, blinked away her tears. "We Sullivan girls would rather go down fighting. Thank you, Joe. And . . . I'm sorry for the things I said to you. I can be a real bitch."

"The warning comes a little late."

She smiled, wiped her eyes again. "You should have told me about your wife, you know."

"In one of our heart-to-heart talks?"

"Yeah, in one of those."

"It's hardly good between-the-sheets conversation. How do you make love to a woman, then tell her that you killed your wife?"

"You didn't kill her. Cancer killed her. You ended her suffering."

"And her breathing."

Meghann looked up at him steadily. "If Claire asked it of me, I'd do it. I'd be willing to go to prison for it, too."

"Pray to God you never have to find out." His voice broke.

"What do we do now?" she said. "For Claire, I mean."

"We wait to hear from Stu. And we pray he agrees with my assessment."

THE next morning Stu Weissman called Claire. She was so groggy, it took her several seconds to understand him.

"Wait a minute," she finally said, sitting up. "Are you saying you'll do the surgery?"

"Yes. But there could be a bad outlook all the way around. You could end up paralyzed or brain damaged or worse."

"Worse sooner, you mean."

He laughed at that. "Yes."

"I'll take the chance."

"Then I will, too. I'll be there tonight. I've scheduled the surgery for eight a.m. tomorrow." His voice softened. "I don't mean to be negative, Claire. But you should put your affairs in order today. If you know what I mean."

"I know what you mean. Thank you, Dr. Weissman."

ALL that day Claire said good-bye to her friends.

To Karen she joked about the gray hairs Willie was sure to cause in the upcoming years. To Charlotte she said, "Don't give up on babies; they're the mark we leave in this world. If you can't have one of your own, find one to adopt." Gina was more difficult. For almost an hour they were together, Claire dozing off now and then. "Take care of my family," she said at last.

They all pretended Claire would still be here tomorrow night, laughing and screwing up as she always had. She left her friends with that faith, and though she wanted to own it for herself, hope felt like a borrowed sweater that didn't quite fit.

The thought of the good-byes she still had left was devastating. Bobby and Sam would hold her and cry, Meg would get angry and loud, and then there was Ali. How could Claire possibly get through *that?*

CLAIRE MUST HAVE FALLEN ASLEEP again. When she woke, the sunlight outside had faded, leaving the room a soft, silvery color.

"Mommy's awake."

She saw her daughter clinging to Meghann like a little monkey, arms wrapped around her neck, feet locked around her waist.

Claire made a whimpering sound before she rallied and pulled out a tired smile. The only way to get through this moment was to pretend there would be another. For Ali she had to believe in a miracle.

"Hey there, Ali Kat." Claire opened her arms. "Come here."

Meg leaned forward and gently deposited Ali into Claire's thin arms. She hugged her daughter tightly. She was battling tears and hanging on to her smile by a thread when she whispered into her daughter's tiny shell-pink ear, "You remember how much I love you."

"I know, Mommy," Ali said, burrowing closer. She lay still as a sleeping baby, quieter than she'd lain in years. That was when Claire knew that Ali understood. Her daughter leaned close to say, "I told God I'd never ask for Cap'n Crunch again if He made you all better." Claire clung to Ali for as long as she could. "Take her home," she said when the pain became more than she could bear.

Meghann was there instantly, pulling Ali into her arms again.

But Ali wiggled out of Meg's grasp and slithered to the molded plastic chair beside the bed. She stood there on the wobbly chair, staring at Claire. "I don't want you to die, Mommy," she said.

It hurt too much even to cry. "I know that, punkin, and I love you more than all the stars in the sky. Now skedaddle on home with Grandpa and Bobby. They're going to take you to see a movie."

Meghann picked Ali up again. Claire could see that she was near tears, too. "Make Bobby go home," she said to her sister. "Tell him I said Ali needs him tonight."

Meg reached out, squeezed her hand. "We need *you*."

"I need to sleep now," was all Claire could think of to say.

HOURS later Claire came awake with a start. For a split second she didn't know where she was. Then she saw the flowers and the machines. If she squinted, she could make out the wall clock. Moonlight glinted on the domed glass face. It was four a.m.

In a few hours they'd crack her skull open.

She started to panic, then saw Meg was in the corner, sprawled in one of those uncomfortable chairs, sleeping.

"Meg," she whispered, hitting her control button; the bed tilted upward. "Meg," she said in a louder voice.

Meghann sat upright and looked around. "Is it time?"

"No. We have four more hours."

Meghann dragged the chair over to the bed. "Did you sleep?"

"Off and on." Claire glanced out the window at the moonlight. Suddenly she was so afraid, she was shaking. "Do you remember what I used to do when I had a nightmare?"

"You used to crawl into bed with me."

"Yeah. That old cot in the trailer's living room." Claire smiled. "It smelled like spilled bourbon and cigarette smoke, but when I got into bed and you hugged me, I thought nothing could hurt me." She looked up at Meghann, then very gently peeled back the blanket.

Meghann hesitated, then climbed into bed with Claire, drawing her close.

"How come we forgot all the things that mattered?" Claire asked.

"I was an idiot."

"We wasted a lot of time."

"I'm sorry," Meg said. "I should have said that a long time ago."

Claire reached for Meg's hand, held it. "I'm going to ask you something, Meg, and I can't ask this twice; saying each word is like swallowing broken glass. If the worst happens, I want you to be a part of Ali's life. She'll need a mother."

Meg squeezed Claire's hand tightly. Long seconds passed before she answered, "I'll make sure she always remembers you."

Claire nodded; she couldn't speak.

After that, they lay in the darkness, each holding the other one together until dawn lit the room and the doctors took Claire away.

MEGHANN stood at the window staring out at the jumble of beige buildings across the street. In the three hours since they'd taken Claire to surgery, Meghann had counted every window.

Someone tugged on her sleeve. Meghann looked down. There was Alison, staring up at her. "I'm thirsty."

"Okay, honey," Meg said, scooping Ali into her arms. She carried her down to the cafeteria.

"I want a Pepsi Blue. That's what you got me last time."

"It's only eleven in the morning. Juice is better for you."

"You sound like Mommy."

Meg swallowed hard. "Did you know your mommy loved Tab when she was little? But I made her drink orange juice."

Meghann paid for the juice, then carried Alison back to the waiting room. But when she leaned over to put Ali down, the girl squeezed harder.

"Oh, Ali," Meg said, holding her niece. She wanted to promise that Mommy would be better, but the words caught in her throat. She sat down, still holding Ali, and stroked her hair. Within minutes the child was asleep.

From across the room Gina looked up, then went back to her crossword puzzle. Sam, Mama, Bobby, Karen, and Charlotte were playing cards. Joe sat off in the corner reading a magazine. He hadn't looked up in hours, hadn't spoken to anyone.

Around noon the surgical nurse came out, told them all that it would be several more hours. "You should get something to eat," she said. "It won't help Claire if you all pass out."

Sam nodded, stood up. "Come on," he said to everyone. "Let's get out of here for a while. Lunch is on me."

"I'll stay here," Meghann said. "Ali needs the sleep."

When they'd gone, Meghann leaned back in her chair, rested her head against the wall. It seemed like yesterday that Meg had held Claire this way, telling her baby sister everything would be okay.

"It's been four hours, damn it. What're they all doin' in there?"

Meg looked up. Mama stood there, holding an unlit Virginia Slims cigarette. Her makeup had faded a little, been smudged off in places, and without it she looked faded, too. "I thought you went out for lunch with everyone."

"Eat *cafeteria* food? I don't think so. I'll eat an early dinner in my hotel suite."

"Have a seat, Mama."

Her mother collapsed into the plastic chair beside her. "This is the worst day of my life. And that's sayin' something."

ONE hour bled into the next until finally, around four o'clock, Dr. Weissman came into the waiting room. Meghann was the first to see him. She tightened her hold on Ali and got to her feet. Bobby stood next; then Sam and Mama; then Joe, Gina, Karen, and Charlotte. The doctor managed a tired smile.

"The surgery went well."

"Thank God," they whispered together.

"But she's a long way from out of the woods. The tumor was more invasive than we thought." He looked at Joe. "The next few hours will tell us more."

CHAPTER ELEVEN

CLAIRE woke up in recovery feeling groggy and confused. A headache pounded behind her eyes. She was about to hit her call button and ask for an Advil when it struck her: She was alive.

She tested her memory by trying to list all the towns she'd lived in as a child, but she'd only made it to Barstow when the first of the nurses came in. After that, she was poked and prodded and tested until she couldn't think.

Her family took turns sitting with her. Two of her most vivid postsurgery memories were of Bobby holding an ice pack to her head for hours at a time and of her dad feeding her ice chips when she got thirsty. Meghann had brought in Ali's newest drawing; this one was three brightly colored stick figures standing by a river. In an uncertain scrawl across the bottom it read, "I love you Momy."

By the second full post-op day Claire had become irritable. She hurt now; her body ached everywhere, and the bruises on her forehead from the iron halo had begun to throb like hell.

When it was time for her post-operative MRI, Claire visualized a clean, clear scan of her brain, saw it so clearly that by the time it was over, her temples were wet with tears.

Waiting for the results was unbearable. Meghann paced the small hospital room. Bobby squeezed Claire's hand so tightly, she lost all feeling in her fingers. Sam came in every few minutes.

Finally Claire's nurse returned. "The docs are ready for you."

Little things got Claire through the wheelchair ride—the warmth of Bobby's hand on her shoulder, the way Meghann stayed close.

When they entered the office where Claire's doctors were waiting, Dr. Weissman was the first to speak. "Good morning, Claire."

"Good morning," she answered. The men waited for Meghann

to sit down. Eventually they realized that she wasn't going to.

Dr. Weissman clicked on the view box. Claire studied the films of her brain, then looked up at the men. "I don't see any tumor."

Dr. Weissman smiled. "I think we got it all, Claire."

"Oh, my God." She'd hoped for this, prayed for it.

"Initial lab reports indicate that it was a low-grade astrocytoma."

"Not a glioblastoma multiforme? Thank God."

"Yes. That was good news. Also, it was benign."

One of the other doctors stepped forward. "You are a very lucky woman. Dr. Weissman did an incredible job. However, as you know, most brain tumors will regenerate. Twenty-eight percent—"

"Stop!" Claire didn't realize that she'd yelled out the word until she saw the startled looks on the doctors' faces. "I don't want to hear your statistics. It was benign, right?"

"Yes, but benign in the brain is a rather misleading term. All brain tumors can ultimately be fatal, benign or not."

"Yeah. Yeah," Claire said. "But it's not a cancer that's going to spread through my body, right?"

"Correct."

"So it's gone now, and it was benign. That's all I want to hear. You can talk to me about treatments from here on, but not about survival rates." She smiled at Meg. "My future is sunny."

Only Dr. Weissman was smiling. He crossed the room and bent down to her ear. "Good for you."

She looked up at him. "There are no words to thank you."

"Joe Wyatt is the man you should thank. Good luck to you."

As soon as she was back in her room, Claire broke down and cried. Bobby held her tightly, until finally she looked up at him. "I love you, Bobby. Now go get our little girl."

He hurried out.

"You were amazing in there," Meg said when they were alone.

"My new motto is Don't screw with Baldie."

"I won't." Meg grinned.

Claire reached for her sister's hand, held it. "Thanks."

Meg kissed Claire's forehead and whispered, "We're sisters." It was answer enough. "I'll go get Mama now. She'll probably bring a film crew." With a smile Meghann left the room.

"The tumor is gone," Claire practiced saying aloud to the empty room. Then she laughed.

MEGHANN FOUND EVERYONE IN the cafeteria. Bobby was already there, talking to Sam. Mama was at the food line, signing autographs. The Bluesers and Alison were sitting in the corner, talking quietly among themselves. The only one missing was Joe.

"And there I was," Mama was saying to a rapt audience, "all ready to take the stage in a dress that wouldn't zip up. I am *not*," she said, laughing, "a flat-chested woman, so y'all can imagine—"

"Mama?" Meghann said, touching her arm.

Mama spun around. When she saw Meghann, her smile faded. For a moment she looked vulnerable. "Well?" she whispered.

"Go on up, Mama. It's good news."

Mama sighed heavily. "Of *course* it is. Y'all were so dramatic." She turned back to her audience. "I hate to leave in the middle of a story, but it seems my daughter has made a miraculous recovery. I am reminded of a television movie I once did, where . . ."

Meghann walked away.

"Auntie Meg!" Alison said, jumping up, throwing herself at Meg, who scooped her up and kissed her. "My mommy is all better!"

At that a whoop went up from the Bluesers. "Come on," Gina said to her friends. "Let's go see Claire."

Bobby walked up to Meghann. "Come on, Ali Gator," he said, pulling the little girl into his arms. "Let's go kiss Mommy." He started to walk away, then paused and turned back. Very gently he kissed Meghann's cheek, whispered, "Thank you."

Meghann closed her eyes, surprised by the depth of her emotion. When she looked up again through a blur of tears, Sam was coming toward her. He reached out, touched her cheek.

"You've been Claire's rock through this nightmare," he said softly. "You have the kind of heart that saves people. And I'm sorry I didn't see that when I was younger."

"A lot of things have become clearer lately."

"Yeah." It was a moment before he said, "I'll expect you at the house this Thanksgiving. None of your lame excuses. We're family."

Meg thought of all the years she'd declined Claire's offer. Then she thought of last Thanksgiving, when she'd eaten raisin bran for dinner by herself. All that time she'd pretended that she wasn't lonely. No more pretending for her, and no more being alone when she had a family to be with. "Just try and keep me away."

Meghann went to the elevators and rode down to the lobby, then headed outside. It was a glorious sunny day. Everything about the city felt sharper, cleaner. She walked downhill, thinking about so many things—her life, her job, her family.

Maybe she'd change her career, practice a different kind of law. Or maybe she'd start a business, sort of an informational clearinghouse for people with brain tumors. The world seemed wide-open to her now, full of new possibilities.

It took her less than half an hour to walk home. She was just about to cross the street, when she saw him, standing outside the front door of her building.

Joe pulled away from the wall he'd been leaning against and crossed the street. "Gina told me where you lived."

"Stu told you about the MRI?"

"I spent the last hour with him. It looks good for Claire."

"Yeah."

He moved toward her. "I'm tired of not caring, Meg," he said softly. "And I'm tired of pretending I died when Diana did."

She looked up at him. They were close now, close enough for him to kiss her if he chose. "What chance do we have, a couple like us?"

"We have a chance. It's all any of us gets."

"We could get hurt."

"We've survived it before." He touched her face tenderly; it made her want to cry. "And maybe we could fall in love."

She gazed up into his eyes and saw a hope for the future. She saw a little of the love he was talking about, and for the first time she believed in it. If Claire could get well, anything was possible. She put her arms around him and pressed onto her toes. Just before she kissed him, she dared to whisper, "Maybe we already have."

EPILOGUE

One Year Later

THE noise was deafening. The fairgrounds were jammed with people—kids screaming from the carnival rides, parents yelling after them, carnies barking out enticements to play the games.

Alison was up ahead, dragging Joe from ride to ride. Meghann and Claire walked along behind, talking softly, carrying the collection of cheesy stuffed animals and cheap glass trinkets that Joe had won. Claire's limp was the only physical reminder of her ordeal, and it was getting less pronounced each day.

"It's time," Claire said, signaling to Joe. The four of them fell in line together, walking past the refreshment stand and turning left toward the fairgrounds' bleachers.

"There's a crowd already," Claire said. She sounded nervous.

"Of course there is," Meghann said.

"Hurry, Mommy, hurry!" Alison was bouncing up and down. At the special side door, Claire showed her backstage pass. They made their way through the staging area, past the musicians and singers who were warming up.

Bobby saw them coming and waved. Alison ran for him. He scooped her into his arms and twirled her around. "My daddy's gonna sing tonight," she said loud enough for everyone to hear.

"I sure am." Bobby looped an arm around Claire and pulled her in for a kiss. "Wish me luck."

"You don't need it."

They talked to him for a few more minutes, then left him to get ready. They climbed the bleachers and found their seats in the fourth row. Meghann helped Claire sit down; her sister was still unsteady sometimes.

"Kent Ames called last week," Claire said. "Mama ripped him a new one for canceling Bobby's contract. It seems he wants to give Bobby another chance. Said he hopes Bobby's *priorities* are straight this time." She smiled.

A man took the stage and announced, "Bob-by Jack Austin!"

The crowd applauded politely.

Alison jumped up and down, screaming, "Yay, Daddy!"

Bobby leaped up onstage with his guitar. He scanned the audience, found Claire, and blew her a kiss. "This song is for my wife, who taught me about love and courage. I love you, baby." He strummed the guitar and started to sing. His beautiful voice wrapped around the music and mesmerized the crowd. He sang about finding the woman of his dreams and falling in love with her, about standing by her side in dark times. In the final stanza his voice fell to a throaty whisper:

*"When I saw you stumble
over rocks along the way
I learned the truth of real love
and the gift of one more day."*

The applause this time was explosive. Half the women in the audience were weeping.

Meghann put an arm around her sister. "I *told* you he'd make a great husband. I liked that guy from the first moment I saw him."

Claire laughed. "Yeah, right. And what about you and Joe? You guys are practically living together. It looks to me like maybe there's a prenuptial agreement in your future."

Meghann looked at Joe, who was on his feet, clapping. Alison was in his arms. Since he'd started practicing medicine again, he said anything was possible. They'd taught each other to believe in love again. "A prenup? Me? No way. We were thinking about a small wedding. Outside—"

"Where it rains? Where bugs breed? *That* outside?"

"Maybe with hamburgers and hot dogs and—"

"Gina's potato salad."

They both said it at the same time and laughed.

"Yeah," Meghann said, leaning against her sister. "That kind of wedding."

MAGIC HOUR

ONE

It will all be over soon.

Julia Cates had lost count of the times she'd told herself that very thing, but today—finally—it would be true. In a few hours, the world would know the truth about her.

If she made it downtown, that was. Unfortunately, the Pacific Coast Highway looked more like a parking lot than a freeway. The hills behind Malibu were on fire again, and smoke hung above the rooftops and turned the normally bright coastal air into a thick brown sludge. Even the surf seemed to have slowed down, as if exhausted by the unseasonable heat.

She maneuvered through the cranky stop-and-go traffic, ignoring the drivers who cut in front of her. It was expected; the Southern California heat made everyone edgy. Finally she exited the freeway and drove to the courthouse.

Television vans were everywhere. Dozens of reporters huddled on the courthouse steps, microphones and cameras at the ready, waiting for the story to arrive. In Los Angeles, it was becoming a daily event: legal proceedings as entertainment. Julia turned a corner and drove to a side entrance, where her lawyers were waiting for her.

She got out of the car. *You're innocent,* she reminded herself. *They'll see that. The system will work.* She took a step, then another, as if she were fighting her way uphill. When she made it to the group, it took everything she had to smile, but one thing she knew:

It looked real. Every psychiatrist knew how to make a smile look genuine.

"Hello, Dr. Cates," said Frank Williams, the lead counsel on her defense team.

"Let's go," she said, wondering if she was the only one who heard the wobble in her voice. Today, of all days, she needed to be strong, to show the world that she'd done nothing wrong.

The team coiled protectively around her. They pushed through the doors and walked into the courthouse. Flashbulbs erupted in spasms of blue-white light. Cameras clicked; tape rolled. Reporters surged forward, all yelling at once.

"Dr. Cates! How do you feel about what happened?"

"Why didn't you save those children?"

"Did you know about the gun?"

Frank put an arm around Julia and pulled her along.

In the courtroom, she took her place at the defendant's table. She tried to ignore the racket behind her. Empty seats were filling up quickly; she knew it without turning around. Journalists were no doubt packed side by side, their pens ready. In the past year, they'd written an endless string of stories about her. The press had practically set up camp outside her door, reporting on her small-town roots, her stellar education, her pricey beachfront condo, her devastating breakup with Philip. What they didn't report on was her love of her job as a psychiatrist. It was, really, the only thing that mattered to her, along with the children and adolescents she'd helped.

A hush fell over the courtroom as Judge Carol Myerson took her seat at the bench. She was a stern-looking woman with artificially bright auburn hair and old-fashioned eyeglasses.

Beside Julia, Frank stood. He was an imposing man, tall and almost elegantly thin. "Your Honor," he began in a voice soft and persuasive, "the naming of Dr. Julia Cates as a defendant in this lawsuit is absurd. Although the precise limits of confidentiality in psychiatric situations are often disputed, certain precedents exist, namely *Tarasoff* v. *the Board of Regents of California.* Dr. Cates had no knowledge of her patient's violent tendencies and no information regarding specific threats. Indeed, no such specific knowledge is even alleged in the complaint. Thus, we respectfully request that she be dismissed from this lawsuit. Thank you." He sat down.

At the plaintiff's table, a lawyer stood up. "Four children are *dead*, Your Honor. They will never grow up, never leave for college, never have children of their own. Dr. Cates was Amber Zuniga's psychiatrist for three years, two hours a week, listening to her problems and prescribing medications for her growing depression. Yet we are now to *believe* that Dr. Cates didn't *know* that Amber was becoming increasingly violent and depressed. That she had no warning that her patient would buy an automatic weapon and walk into her church youth-group meeting and start shooting." The man walked out from behind the table to face Julia. "*She* is the expert, Your Honor. She should have committed Ms. Zuniga for residential treatment. We respectfully seek to keep Dr. Cates as a named defendant in this case. It is a matter of justice. The families of the slain deserve redress from the person most likely to have foreseen and prevented the murder of their children."

"It isn't true," Julia whispered as he took his seat. Amber had never even *hinted* at violence. Every teenager battling depression said they hated the kids in their school. That was light-years away from buying a gun and opening fire.

Judge Myerson read over the paperwork in front of her, then set her glasses down on the bench. The courtroom fell into silence. The children's parents, huddled in the back rows in a mournful group, were waiting to be assured that this tragedy could have been averted, that *someone* could have kept their children alive. They had sued everyone for wrongful death—the police, the drug manufacturers, the Zuniga family. They hoped that this lawsuit would be the answer, but Julia knew the grief would outlive them all.

The judge looked at the parents first. "There is no doubt that what happened at the Baptist church in Silverwood was a terrible tragedy. As a parent myself, I cannot fathom the world in which you have lived for the past months. However, the question before this court is whether Dr. Cates should remain a defendant in this case." She folded her hands on the desk. "I am persuaded that as a matter of law, Dr. Cates had no duty to warn or otherwise protect the victims in this set of circumstances. The law does not impose a duty to warn except to clearly identifiable victims, and as a matter of public policy, we must maintain the confidentiality of the psychiatrist-patient relationship unless there is a specific threat. Thus, I am dismissing Dr. Cates from the complaint without prejudice."

The gallery went crazy. Before she knew it, Julia was on her feet and enfolded in congratulatory hugs by her defense team. Behind her, she could hear the journalists running for the doors.

Julia felt a wave of relief. *Thank God.*

Then she heard the children's parents crying behind her.

"How can this be happening?" one of them said loudly. "She should have known."

Frank touched her arm. "You should be smiling. We won."

She shot a quick glance at the parents, then looked away. Were they right? *Should* she have known?

A crowd of reporters swarmed them.

"Dr. Cates! What do you have to say to the parents who hold you responsible—"

"Will other parents trust you with their children—"

Frank stepped into the fray. "My client was just released—"

"On a technicality," someone yelled.

While they were focused on Frank, Julia slipped to the back of the crowd and ran for the door. All she wanted was to be away, to get back to real life.

Julia left the courthouse. Outside, the world was brown and bleak. A thick layer of smoke darkened the sky, obliterating the sun, matching her mood.

She got into her car and drove away. Tonight she'd lay in her lonely bed listening to the surf, and she'd try again to get beyond her grief and guilt. She *had* to figure out what clue she'd missed, what sign she'd overlooked. It would hurt—remembering—but in the end, she'd be a better therapist for all this pain. And at seven o'clock in the morning, she'd get dressed and go back to work.

Helping people.

That was how she'd get through this.

GIRL crouches at the edge of the cave, watching water fall from the sky. She wants to reach for one of the empty cans around her, maybe lick the insides again, but she has done this too many times already. The food is gone. Behind her the wolves are restless, hungry. The sky grumbles and roars.

There is a strange scent in the darkness. It should send her back into the deep, black hole, but she can't quite move. Her stomach is so tight and empty it hurts.

A twig snaps. Then another.

She goes very still, willing her body to disappear against the cave wall. She becomes like her shadow, flat and motionless.

Him is coming. Already he has been gone too long, and though she is glad Him is gone, without Him, she is afraid. In a time long ago, Her would have helped some, but she is *DEAD*.

When the forest falls silent, she leans forward, poking her face into the gray light Out There. Sleepnight is coming; it will be blackness all around. What should she do?

She glances down at the pup beside her. He is on alert, too, sniffing the air. She touches his soft fur and feels the tremble in his body. He is wondering the same thing: Would Him be back? When Him left, he actually spoke to Girl.

YOUBEGOODWHILEI'MGONEORELSE.

She doesn't understand all of the words, but she knows Or Else.

Still, it is too long since he left. There is nothing to eat. She has freed herself and gone into the woods for berries and nuts, but it is the darkening season. Soon she will be too weak to find food, and there will be none anyway when the white starts falling and turns her breath into fog. Though she is afraid, terrified of the Strangers who live Out There, she is starving, and if Him comes back and sees that she has freed herself, it will be bad. She must make a move.

THE town of Rain Valley, tucked between the wilds of the Olympic National Forest and the roaring gray surf of the Pacific Ocean, was the last bastion of civilization before the start of the deep woods.

There were places not far from town that had never been touched by the sun, where shadows lay so thick and substantial that few hikers made their way into the forest. Even today, in this modern age of scientific wonders, these woods remained as they had for centuries, unexplored, untouched by man.

Less than one hundred years ago, settlers came to this beautiful spot between the rain forest and the sea and hacked down just enough trees to plant their crops. In time, they learned what the Native Americans had learned before them: This was a place that wouldn't be tamed. So they gave up farming, and salmon and timber became the local industries. For a few decades, the town prospered. But in the '90s, environmentalists discovered Rain Valley. They set out to save the birds and the fish and the eldest of the trees. The men who made their living off the land were forgotten, and the town fell into quiet disrepair.

But the people of Rain Valley were hardy souls, willing to live in a place where it rained more than two hundred days a year and the sun was treated like a wealthy uncle who only rarely came to call. They withstood gray days and dwindling ways to make a living, and remained through it all the sons and daughters of the pioneers who'd first dared to live among the towering trees.

Today, however, they were finding their spirit tested. It was October seventeenth, and autumn had recently lost its race to coming winter. Oh, the maples and alders were still dressed in party colors, but no mistake could be made: Winter was coming. For seven days, it had rained almost nonstop.

On the corner of Wheaton Way and Cates Avenue stood the police station, a squat gray-stone building with a cupola on top and a flagpole on the grassy lawn out front. Inside the austere building, the old fluorescent lighting was barely strong enough to keep the gray at bay. The people at their desks tried not to notice the constant hammering of rain on the roof.

Ellie Barton stood at the window, staring out at the street. The rain made everything appear insubstantial, a charcoal rendering of town. Catching a glimpse of herself in the water-streaked window, she saw herself as she always did, as the younger woman she'd once been—long, thick black hair, cornflower-blue eyes, and a bright, ready smile. The girl voted homecoming queen and head cheerleader. She saw herself in white, the color of brides, of hope for the future, of families waiting to be born.

"I gotta have a smoke, Ellie. You know I do. If I don't light up, I'm heading to the refrigerator."

"Don't let her do it," Cal said from his place at the dispatch desk. He sat hunched over the phone, a sheath of black hair falling across his eyes. In high school, Ellie and her friends had called him the Crow because of his black hair and sharp, bony look. "Try tough love. Nothing else has worked."

Ellie sighed. They'd had this same discussion only ten minutes before. She put her hands on her waist, resting her fingertips on her heavy gun belt. She turned to look at her best friend. "Now, Peanut, you know what I'm gonna say. This is a public building. I'm the chief of police. How can I let you break the law?"

"Exactly," Cal said. He opened his mouth to say more, but a call came in and he answered it. "Rain Valley Police."

"Oh, right," Peanut said. "And suddenly you're Miss Law and Order. What about Sven Morgenstern—he parks in front of his store every day. Right in front of the hydrant. When was the last time you hauled his car away? And Large Marge shoplifts two boxes of freezer pops and a bottle of nail polish from the drugstore every Sunday after church." They both knew she could cite a dozen more examples. This was Rain Valley, after all, not downtown Seattle. Ellie had been the chief of police for four years and a patrol officer for eight years before that. She'd never processed a crime more dangerous than breaking and entering. "Are you going to let me have a cigarette, or am I going to get a doughnut and a Red Bull?"

"They'll both kill you."

"Yeah, but they won't kill *us*," Cal said, disconnecting his call. "Hold firm, El. She's the patrol clerk. She shouldn't smoke in a city building."

"You're smoking too much," Ellie said.

"Yeah, but I'm eating less."

"Why don't you go back to the salmon jerky diet? Or the grapefruit one? Those were both healthier."

"Stop talking and answer me. I need a smoke."

"You started smoking four days ago, Peanut," Cal said. "You hardly *need* a cigarette."

Ellie shook her head. If she didn't step in, these two would bicker all day. "You should go back to your meetings," she said with a sigh. "That Weight Watchers was working."

"Six months of cabbage soup to lose ten pounds? I don't think so. Come *on*, Ellie, you know I'm ready to reach for a doughnut."

Ellie knew she'd lost the battle. She and Peanut—Penelope Nutter—had worked side by side in this office for more than a decade and been best friends since high school. Over the years, their friendship had weathered every storm, from the ruination of Ellie's two marriages to Peanut's recent decision that smoking cigarettes was the key to weight loss.

Grinning at Cal, Peanut placed her hands on the desk and pushed herself to a stand. The fifty pounds she'd gained in the past few years made her move a little slower. She walked over to the door and opened it, although they all knew there'd be no breeze to suck the smoke away on such a wet and dismal day.

Ellie went down the hall to her office in the back, dug past the signs from last month's pancake breakfast, and found a gas mask. Putting it on, she headed back down the hall. Cal burst out laughing.

Peanut tried not to smile. "Very funny."

"I may want children someday. I'm protecting my uterus."

"If I were you, I'd worry less about secondhand smoke and more about finding a date."

"She's tried everyone from Mystic to Aberdeen," Cal said. "Last month she even went out with that UPS guy. The good-looking one who keeps forgetting where he parked his truck."

It was true. Ellie couldn't help herself: She loved men. Usually—okay, always—the wrong men. Peanut called it the curse of the small-town beauty queen. But Ellie liked having fun; she liked romance. The problem was, it hadn't yet led to true love. Peanut said it was because she didn't know how to compromise, but that wasn't accurate. Ellie's marriages—both of them—had failed because she'd married good-looking men with itchy feet and wandering eyes.

Ellie lifted the gas mask and said, "Maybe Cal here can set me up with one of his geek friends from the comic book convention."

Cal looked stung by that. "We're not geeks."

Peanut laughed. "Your friends wear *Matrix* costumes in public. How you found Lisa, I'll never know."

At the mention of Cal's wife, an awkward silence stumbled into the room. The whole town knew she was a run-around. But here in the police station, they never spoke about it.

Cal went back to reading his comic book and doodling in his sketch pad. They all knew he'd be quiet for a while now.

Ellie sat down at her desk and put her feet up.

Peanut leaned back against the wall. "I saw Julia on the news."

Ellie couldn't help sighing. It had only been a matter of time before they came around to the subject of her brilliant younger sister. "She was dismissed from the lawsuit."

"Did you call her?"

"Her answering machine. I think she's avoiding me."

Peanut took a step forward. "You should try again."

"You know how jealous Julia is of me. She especially wouldn't want to talk to me now."

"You think everyone is jealous of you."

"I do not."

Peanut gave her one of those *who-do-you-think-you're-fooling?* looks that were the cornerstone of friendship. "Ellie, your baby sister looked like she was hurting. Are you going to pretend you can't talk to her because twenty years ago you were homecoming queen and she belonged to the math club?"

In truth, Ellie had seen it, too—the haunted look in Julia's eyes. "She wouldn't listen to me, Peanut. You know that. She considers me only slightly smarter than a pet rock. Maybe—"

The sound of footsteps stopped her.

Someone was *running* toward their office.

Ellie got to her feet just as Lori Forman skidded into the room, soaking wet. "You gotta come," she said to Ellie.

"Take a breath, Lori. Tell me what's happened."

"You won't believe me. Heck, I've seen it and I don't believe me. Come on. There's something on Magnolia Street."

"Yee-*ha*," Peanut said. "Hurry up, Cal. Forward the emergency calls. Something's actually happening in town."

TWO

ELLIE pulled her cruiser into an empty parking slot on the corner of Magnolia and Woodland. The rain stopped at the same time, and sunlight peered through the clouds.

Even Ellie, who'd lived here all of her life, was awed by the sudden change of weather. It was Magic Hour, the moment in time when every leaf and blade of grass seemed separate, when sunlight, burnished by the rain and softened by the coming night, gave the world an impossibly beautiful glow.

In the passenger seat, Peanut leaned forward. "I don't see nothin'."

"Me, either." This from Cal, who sat perfectly erect in the back-seat, his tall, lanky body folded into neat thirds.

Ellie studied the town square. Clouds the color of old nails moved across the sky, but Rain Valley—all five blocks of it—seemed to glow with an otherworldly light. Brick storefronts, built in the halcyon salmon-and-timber days, shone like hammered copper.

There was a crowd outside of Swain's drugstore and another across the street. "You there, Chief?" came a voice over the radio.

Ellie flicked the button and answered. "I'm here, Earl."

"Come on down to the tree in Sealth Park." There was a bunch of static, then: "Move slow. I ain't kiddin'."

"You stay here, Peanut. You, too, Cal," Ellie said as she got out of the car. Her heart was beating quickly. She moved down the street, unclasping her holster. As she neared the four-way stop, she could see people pointing toward Chief Sealth City Park.

At the corner, she paused. Earl came running at her, his boot heels sounding like gunfire on the pavement. Rain streaked his uniform.

"Shhh," she hissed.

Earl Huff's face scrunched into a ruddy fist. At sixty-four, he'd been a cop before Ellie was born, but he never failed to show her the utmost respect. "Sorry, Boss."

"What's going on? I don't see a damn thing."

"She showed up about ten minutes ago. Right after that big thunder crack. Ya'all hear it?"

"We heard it," Peanut said, her voice wheezy from moving so fast. Cal was beside her.

Ellie spun around. "I *told* you both to stay in the cruiser."

"You *meant* it?" Peanut said incredulously. "Hell, Ellie, we're not gonna miss the first real call in years."

With a sigh, Ellie turned back to Earl. "Talk to me."

"After the thunder crack, the rain stopped. Just like that. Then that amazin' sun came out. That's when old Doc Fischer heard a wolf howl. It was Mrs. Grimm who noticed the girl." He turned and pointed. "When she climbed up that there tree, we called you."

Ellie stared at the maple tree. There was a child hidden high in the autumn-colored leaves. How could anyone climb that high on rain-slicked branches?

She took a step forward to see better.

The child was little, probably no more than five or six. Even from this distance, Ellie could see how spindly and thin she was. Her long dark hair was a filthy mat, filled with leaves and debris. Tucked in her arms was a snarling puppy.

Ellie reholstered her gun and started forward. Five feet from the tree she looked up. The child appeared completely at ease on her high perch, but her eyes were wide. The poor kid was terrified.

And damn if that wasn't a *wolf* pup in her arms.

"Hey, little one," Ellie said. "What are you doing up there?"

The wolf snarled and bared its teeth.

Ellie's gaze locked on the child's. "I won't hurt you. Honestly."

There was no response; not the flinch of an eyelash.

"Let's start over. I'm Ellen Barton. Who are you?"

Again, nothing.

"I'm guessing you're running away from something. Or maybe playing some game in the woods."

It was like talking to a photograph.

"Why don't you come on down? I'll make sure you're safe."

Ellie talked for another fifteen minutes or so; then she just ran out of words. Not once had the girl responded or moved. Frankly, it didn't even appear that she was breathing.

Ellie walked back to Earl and Peanut and Cal.

"How we gonna get her down, Chief?" Earl asked, nervously smoothing his almost bald head.

Ellie had no idea. "Anyone see her climb up?"

"Mrs. Grimm. She said the kid was up to no good—maybe lookin' to steal apples out front at the market. When Doc Fischer yelled at her, the girl ran and jumped into the tree."

"Jumped?" Ellie said. "Twenty feet in the air?"

"I didn't believe it, either, Chief. They say she ran like the wind, too. Mrs. Grimm crossed herself when she was tellin' me."

Ellie felt the start of a headache. By suppertime the whole town would be saying the girl could shoot fire from her fingertips and fly from branch to branch. "We need a plan," she said.

"The volunteer fire department got Scamper outta that Doug fir on Peninsula Road."

"It's a good idea, Earl, but she's terrified. If she sees that big red ladder coming at her, she might fall."

"I'll bet she's hungry," Peanut said.

"You think everyone's hungry," Cal said.

"Earl, go to the diner and order me a nice hot meal," Ellie said. "Maybe a slice of apple pie. And clear the streets. I want everyone gone for a two-block radius."

"They won't wanna go."

"We're the *law*, Earl. Make them go home."

Earl slumped in a hangdog way and headed for the crowd at the drugstore. After a moment, they groaned loudly.

Peanut crossed her arms and made a clucking sound. "You aren't going to be Miss Popular for making them miss this."

Ellie looked at her best friend. "Them?"

Peanut's eyes rounded. "Surely you don't mean *me*, too?"

"We've got a terrified girl up there, Pea. Now you and Cal go back to the station and get me some kind of net. Make some calls. See if a kid got lost today. Cal, you tell Mel to start canvassing the town. She's not local, but maybe she's staying with someone."

An hour and a half later the shops of downtown Rain Valley had all been locked up, and the parking slots were empty. Just out of sight were two police barricades.

"I guess you're thinking it's sorta weird that a woman is the chief of police," Ellie said, sitting as still as she could on the uncomfortable iron-and-wood bench beneath the maple tree.

She glanced down at the platter at the base of the tree. Roasted chicken, orange slices, freshly baked apple pie. It smelled heavenly.

She cocked her head and looked up.

The girl stared back with an unsettling intensity. Eyes the color of a shallow Caribbean sea looked out from beneath dark lashes.

Ellie glanced across the street to the huge rhododendron in front of the hardware store. Behind it, she knew, a man from Animal Control had his rifle trained in this direction. It was loaded with a tranquilizer dart for the wolf pup.

Keep talking.

She sighed. "I didn't really set out to become a cop. I just sort of bumped into it; that's how life works for me. Now my sister, Julia, by the time she was ten years old, she wanted to be a doctor. Me, I was twenty-one the second time I got married." She smiled ruefully. "When that marriage tanked, I moved back in with my dad. That is not a high point for a girl who can legally drink, and boy, margaritas and karaoke were my life back then. Anyway, my uncle Joe, the chief of police, he made a deal with me: If I'd go to the Police Academy, he'd ignore my parking tickets. Turns out I was born for this job." She shot a glance at the girl.

No movement. Nothing.

Ellie's stomach grumbled loudly.

"Aw, hell." She reached down for the chicken and tore off a leg.

The leaves rustled. The branch creaked.

"Come on," Ellie whispered. Maybe simple was the answer. "Down. Here. Chicken. Pie. Food."

The girl dropped from the branch, landing like a cat, the pup still in her arms. Impossible. Her bones should have snapped on impact. Ellie felt her gut tighten. The girl's gaze locked on her.

Ellie didn't move, didn't even breathe.

The girl slowly released her hold on the wolf. She took a cautious step toward the chicken, sniffing like a wild animal, sniffing, sensing. The white wolf pup shadowed her every move.

Finally the girl broke eye contact and went for the food.

Ellie had never seen anything like it. The two looked more like litter mates over a kill than anything else. The girl kept tearing off chunks of chicken and stuffing them in her mouth.

Ellie reached slowly behind her and gathered up her net. In a perfect cheerleader turn, she tossed it toward the girl. It settled over the child and the wolf pup and hit the ground. When they realized they'd been caught, all hell broke loose.

The girl went crazy. She threw herself to the ground and rolled to get free, her grimy fingers clawing at the nylon net. The more she struggled to be free, the tighter she was bound.

The wolf pup snarled. When the red dart hissed into his side, he let out a surprised yelp, then staggered and fell over.

The girl howled. It was a terrible, harrowing sound.

"It's okay, honey." Ellie moved toward them. "Don't be afraid. He's not hurt. I'm going to send him to a safe place."

The girl pulled the sleeping pup into her lap and stroked him furiously, trying to waken him. At her failure, she howled again, another desperate, keening wail of pain.

As Ellie inched around behind the child, she noticed the smell. Dying black leaves and fecund, overripe earth; beneath it all was the ammonia scent of urine. She let the hypodermic slip from its place in her sleeve.

News of the girl spread through Rain Valley. Cal was working late, answering one phone call after another. By now the story being told was of a flying wolf girl with magical powers over the weather, and everyone wanted to be part of it.

Inside the hospital, the girl lay in a narrow bed, unconscious. There were several electrodes attached to her head and another pair that monitored the beating of her heart. A leather restraint anchored her left wrist to the bed rail.

Ellie stood back from the bed. Peanut was beside her. Dr. Max Cerrasin was examining the child. Every now and then he murmured under his breath; other than that, no one spoke.

Ellie had never seen him so serious. In the six years he'd lived in Rain Valley, Max had gathered quite a reputation—and it wasn't only for his doctoring skills. When he'd taken over Doc Fischer's practice, the single women had been all aflutter, waiting for him to choose one of them. Over the years, he'd dated—plenty, in fact—but no one could really lay claim to him. Lately he'd been seen going out less and less, becoming that strangest of animals in a small town: a loner.

"Well," he said at last, shoving a hand through his curly gray hair.

Ellie eased away from the wall and went to him. He wore an old, faded pair of Levi's and a black T-shirt, but it was his eyes that demanded attention. They were an electric blue, and when he looked at you, there seemed to be no one else in the room. He was the best-looking man she'd ever seen.

"What can you tell me, Max?"

"She's dehydrated, and the malnourishment is serious." He lifted the child's unbound wrist; her dirty flesh looked splotchy and gray.

Ellie flipped open her notepad. "Native American?"

"I don't think so. I'm pretty sure that under all this filth, she's Caucasian." Moving down the bed, he gently lifted her right leg at the knee. "You see those scars on her ankle?"

Ellie leaned closer. Beneath the grime, she saw it: a thick, discolored band of scar tissue. "Ligature marks."

"Almost certainly."

Peanut made a gasping sound. "The poor thing was *tied?*"

"For a long time, I'd say. The scarring is not new tissue. X-rays show a broken left forearm that healed badly, too."

"Any evidence of sexual trauma?"

"No. None." He shook his head. "I've never seen anything like this."

"What's *this*, exactly?" Ellie asked.

"Serious trauma," Max said at last.

"What can you do for her?"

"This isn't my area of expertise. If she were conscious, I could observe her, but—"

"The old day-care center is empty," Peanut said. "You could watch her through the window."

"Right. Put her there, Max. By morning Mel and Earl will find out who she is. Or when she wakes up, she'll tell us."

"If she can talk. We're in the deep end here, Ellie, and you know it. Maybe you should call in the big boys."

"Max, it's my pool. I can handle one lost girl."

JULIA stood in front of the full-length mirror in her bedroom, studying herself with a critical eye. She wore a charcoal-gray pantsuit and a pale pink silk blouse. Her blond hair was coiled back in a French twist, the way she always wore it when seeing patients. Not that she had a lot of patients left. The tragedy in Silverwood had cost her 70 percent of them.

She grabbed her briefcase and went down to her garage, where her steel-blue Toyota Prius Hybrid waited. The garage door opened, revealing the empty street outside. On this warm, brown October morning, there were no reporters out there waiting. She was no longer part of the story.

After a year of nightmares, she had her life back.

It took her more than an hour to reach her small, beautiful Beverly Hills office building. She parked in her spot and went inside.

On the second floor, she paused outside her office, looking at the sterling silver plaque on the door: DR. JULIA CATES.

She pressed the intercom button. "Hey, Gwen, it's me."

There was a buzzing sound; then the door eased open with a click.

Julia took a deep breath and opened it. The office smelled of the fresh flowers that were delivered every Monday morning. Though there were fewer patients now, she'd never cut back on the flower order. It would have been a sign of defeat.

"Hello, Doctor," said Gwen Connelly, her receptionist. "Congratulations on yesterday."

"Thanks." She smiled. "Is Melissa here yet?"

"You have no appointments this week," Gwen said gently. The compassion in her brown eyes was unnerving. "They all canceled."

"All of them? Even Marcus?"

"Did you see the *L.A. Times* today?"

"No. Why?"

Gwen pulled a newspaper out of the trash can and dropped it on the desk. The headline was DEAD WRONG. Beneath it was a photograph of Julia.

Julia reached out for the wall to steady herself.

Gwen stood up and came around the desk. She was a small, compact woman who had run this office with discipline and caring. Moving forward, she opened her arms. "You helped a lot of people. No one can take that from you."

Julia sidestepped quickly. If she were touched right now, she'd fall apart. She might never put all the pieces back together.

Gwen stopped. "It's not your fault."

"Thank you. I . . . guess I'll take a vacation." She tried to smile. It felt heavy and wooden. "I haven't gone anywhere in years."

"It'd be good for you. I'll cancel the flowers and call the building manager," Gwen said. "Let him know you'll be gone for a while."

I'll cancel the flowers.

Funny how that, of all of it, broke the skin. Julia held on to her composure by the thinnest strand as she moved Gwen toward the door and said good-bye.

Then, alone in the office, she sank to her knees on the expensive carpeting and bowed her head.

She wasn't sure how long she knelt there in the darkness, listening to the strains of her own breathing and the beat of her heart.

Finally she got awkwardly to her feet and looked around, wondering what she would do next. This practice was the very heart of her. In her pursuit of professional excellence, she'd put everything else on the back burner—friends, family, hobbies. She went to her phone and stood there, staring down at the speed-dial list.

Philip was still number seven. For five years, he'd been her best friend and her lover. Now he was another woman's husband.

With a sigh, she pushed the number two button. Her therapist, Dr. Harold Collins, answered. She'd been seeing him once a month since her residency, when it had been required of all psychiatric students. In truth, he'd been more of a friend than a doctor.

"Hey, Harry," she said. "Did you see this morning's paper?"

He sighed heavily. "Julia, I've been worried about you."

"I'm worried about myself."

"You need to start giving interviews, tell your side of the story. It's ridiculous to shoulder the blame for this thing. We all think—"

"What's the point? They'll believe what they want to, anyway. You know that."

"Sometimes fighting is the point, Julia."

"I've never been good at that, Harry." She stared out the window at the bright blue-skied day and wondered what she would do now. They talked for a while longer, but in truth, Julia wasn't listening. She'd given her career all she had; without it, she felt empty, and talking about her emptiness wouldn't help.

"I better go, Harry. Thanks for everything."

IN THESE late evening hours, the halls of the county hospital were quiet. It was Max's least favorite time; he preferred the hustle-and-bustle of daily emergencies. There were too many thoughts that waited for him in the shadowy quiet.

He made a few last notes on the girl's chart. She lay perfectly still, breathing in the deep, even way of sedated sleep. He reached down for her free hand and held it. Her fingers were thin and tiny against his palm. "Who are you, little one?"

Behind him the door opened and closed. It was Trudi High-tower, the charge nurse of the swing shift.

"How is she?" Trudi asked, coming up close to him. She was a tall, good-looking woman with kind eyes.

"Not good. Are we ready to move her?"

"All set up." She reached down, unhooked the restraint. When she lifted the heavy strap, Max touched her wrist.

"Leave it here," he said. "She's been bound enough in her life."

He bent down and scooped the sleeping child in his arms. In silence, they walked to the old day-care center. There, he tucked the girl into the hospital bed they'd moved into the room. He had to stop himself from whispering, *Sleep tight, kiddo.*

"I'll stay with her a while," he said instead.

ELLIE stared at the computer screen until the letters blurred into little black blobs on a field of white. If she read one more report of a missing child, she was going to scream.

There were thousands of them. Thousands.

Lost girls who had no way to reach out, who were counting on professionals somewhere to find and save them.

Ellie closed her eyes. There had to be more she could do, but what? She'd contacted every precinct in five counties, the Family Crisis Network and Rural Resources, as well as every state and national agency. No one knew who the kid was, and it was becoming increasingly clear that this was Rain Valley's case. Her case.

She pushed away from the desk and got to her feet. She stepped over her sleeping dogs and went to the porch, looking out across her backyard. It was almost dawn. Here, on the edge of the rain forest, the world was both utterly still and deeply alive. Wet air from the ocean left millions of dew beads on the leaves. Come dawn, those drops would fall soundlessly to the ground.

She went down the back steps, then through the pink-and-violet morning. Mist rose up from the dark grass in vapors. She was at the very edge of Fall River when she realized why she was here.

His house was on the other side, across a marshy field. As a kid, she'd hiked through that field every day and played in that yard.

For a minute, she almost started for it. She had the idea to toss stones at his window again and call out to him. Cal would understand her fears. He always had.

But those days were more than two decades old. Ellie was his boss now, not just her friend. He had his own life, his own wife and children, and even though everyone knew that Lisa wasn't good enough for him, he loved his family.

Ellie knew she was on her own. She turned and went back to her house. With a tired sigh, she sat back down and pulled up the missing-children reports. The answer had to be in here. It *had* to be.

It was her last thought before falling asleep.

She was wakened by a car horn. She came awake with a start, realizing all at once that she'd fallen asleep at her computer.

She stumbled to her feet and went to the front door.

Peanut stood in the yard, waving to her husband as he drove away.

Ellie looked down at her watch. It was 7:55 in the morning. "What in the hell are you doing here?"

"I heard you tell Max you'd meet him at eight. You're late."

WHEN they turned into the hospital parking lot, a crowd was gathered at the front door.

"Damn it," Ellie said. "They're turning this into a circus."

She parked, grabbed her notebook, and got out of the car. Peanut followed in an uncharacteristic silence. Like geese, the crowd surged into formation and flew at them. The Grimm sisters—three old ladies as identical as prongs on a fork—led the charge.

Daisy was the first to speak. "We've come for word of the child."

"Who is the poor dear?" Violet demanded.

"Can she truly fly like a bird?" Marigold asked.

"Or jump like a cat?" This came from someone in the back.

Ellie had to remind herself that these people were her constituents. More than that, they were her friends and neighbors. "We don't have any answers yet. For now, I could use your help."

"Anything." Marigold pulled a notebook out of her handbag.

Violet offered her sister a tulip pen.

"The child will need clothes and such. Maybe a stuffed animal to keep her company," Ellie said. Before she even finished, the three ex-teachers corralled the crowd and started delegating tasks.

Ellie and Peanut walked the concrete path to the hospital.

The last room on the right on the second floor had once been a day-care center for employees. In the time since the spotted owl and the protection of old-growth forests, the room had been empty.

Max stood in the hallway. At their approach, he moved to make room for them at the window, but he didn't smile.

The room beyond was small and rectangular, with red-and-yellow color-blocked walls and cubbyholes full of toys and games and books. A sink and counter took up one corner, used years ago, no doubt, for art projects and daily cleanup. Several small tables surrounded by even smaller chairs filled the center of the room. Along the left wall were a single hospital bed and several empty cribs. There were two windows in the room—the one in front of them and a second, smaller one that overlooked the rear parking lot. To their left, a locked metal door was the only entrance.

Ellie sidled close. "Talk to me, Max."

"This morning when she woke up, she went crazy. There's no other word for it: screaming, shrieking, throwing herself to the floor. When we tried to give her an injection, she bit Carol Rense hard enough to draw blood, then hid under the bed. She's been there almost an hour. Do you have an ID on her yet?"

Ellie turned. "Peanut, go to the cafeteria. Get kid food for her."

"Sure, send the fat girl for food." Peanut sighed dramatically but couldn't help smiling. She loved to be a part of things.

When she'd gone, Max said, "I don't know what to tell you, Ellie. I've never seen a case like this."

"Tell me what you do know."

"Well, I think she's probably about six years old. She's had no dental care, and there's an old knife wound on her left shoulder."

"God help us. Has she spoken?"

"No. Her vocal cords look unimpaired, but her screams are unintelligible. Her brain waves show no anomalies. She could well be deaf or mentally challenged or autistic. I'm not even sure I know what tests to run for her mental state."

"What should we do?"

He nodded toward Peanut, who was coming toward them with a tray of food. "That's a good start."

Pea had chosen a stack of pancakes, fried eggs, a waffle with strawberries and whipped cream, a glass of milk.

Max said, "I'll have an orderly crawl under the bed and get her."

"Just leave it on the table," Peanut said. "She might be odd, but she's a kid. They do things their own way."

Ellie smiled at her friend. "Any other advice?"

"No more strangers. She knows you, so you should take the food in. Talk to her in a soothing voice, but don't stay."

"Thanks." Taking the tray, Ellie went into the brightly painted room. The metal door clicked shut behind her. "Hey, it's me again. I hope you don't hold that whole net thing against me." She set the tray on one of the tables. "I thought you might be hungry."

Under the bed, the girl made a growling sound. It made the hairs on the back of Ellie's neck stand up. She backed out of the room and closed the door behind her. The lock clicked loudly into place.

In the hall, Ellie stood by Max at the window. "Will she eat it?"

"I guess we'll find out."

Several minutes later a tiny hand came out from underneath the bed. Peanut gasped. "Lookee there."

More time passed.

Finally a dark head appeared. Slowly the child crawled out from her hiding place on all fours. When she looked up at the glass and saw them standing there, her nostrils flared.

Then she dashed to the table, where she froze again and bent low over the food, sniffing it suspiciously. She threw the whipped cream to the floor, then ate the pancakes and the eggs. She grabbed the strawberries and took them to her hiding place under the bed.

"And I thought my kids had bad table manners," Peanut said. "She eats like a wild animal."

"We need a specialist. A shrink."

Peanut drew in a sharp breath. "I can't believe we didn't think of it. She'd be perfect."

Ellie looked at her. "Her clients pay two hundred an hour."

"That was *before*. She can't have many patients left."

"God knows she's qualified for this," Ellie said.

"Who are you two talking about?" Max asked.

Ellie finally looked at him. "My sister is Julia Cates."

"The shrink who—"

"Yeah. That one." She turned to Peanut. "Let's go. I'll call her from the office."

IN THE past twelve hours, Julia had begun at least a dozen projects. She'd tried organizing her closet, rearranging her furniture. She'd bought deck stain and paint stripper. It was a good time to do all of the projects she'd been putting off for . . . ten years.

The problem was her hands.

She was fine when she started a project—more than fine. She was optimistic. Unfortunately, all it took was a thought (it's time for Joe's appointment or—worse yet—Amber's) and her hands would start to shake; she'd feel herself go cold. No temperature setting was high enough to keep her warm. Late last night she'd even tried to write a book. She wanted to tell her side of the story; maybe she even needed to.

She'd sat for hours, her yellow pad in hand. By midnight, she was surrounded by balled-up yellow wads of paper. All any of them said was: *I'm sorry.*

This morning, the phone rang.

The answering machine clicked on, and she heard her own cheery message. There was a long beep.

"Hey, Jules, it's me, your big sis. It's important."

Julia picked up the phone. "Hey, El."

There was an awkward pause, but wasn't that always the way it was between them? They were four years apart in age and light-years apart in personality. "Are you okay?" Ellie finally asked.

"Fine, thanks."

"You got released from the lawsuit. That's a good thing."

"Yeah."

Another awkward pause. "Look, I need a favor."

"A favor?"

"There's a situation up here. You could really help us out."

"You don't have to try to save me, Ellie. I'm fine. I'm a big girl now. Don't worry about me. Really."

"For a shrink, you're a lousy listener. I'm telling you I need you in Rain Valley. Specifically, I need a child psychiatrist."

"You're older than I usually take."

"Very funny. Will you fly up here? And I mean right now." There was a pause, a rustling of paper. "Alaska has a flight in two hours. I can have a ticket waiting for you."

Julia frowned. "Tell me what's going on."

"There isn't time. I want you to catch the ten-fifteen flight. Will you trust me?"

Julia glanced out the floor-to-ceiling windows and tried to focus on the blue Pacific, but all she could see were the yellow balls of paper on the floor. "Why not?" she said.

She had nothing better to do.

THREE

JULIA hadn't been back to Rain Valley in years, and now she was returning on the wave of failure.

Perhaps she should have stayed in L.A. after all. There, she would have disappeared. Here, she would always be the other Cates girl *(You know, the weird one . . .)*, the tall, scarecrow-thin book-worm in the shadow of her homecoming-queen sister.

She stared out the plane's small window. Everything was gray, as if a cloud artist had painted the merest of washes over the green landscape. The four whitecapped volcanoes that stretched to Bellingham looked like the spine of some mythic, sleeping beast.

When the plane landed, she grabbed her bag from the overhead bin and merged into the line of passengers. She was almost to the exit door when one of the flight attendants recognized her.

"It's *her*," she whispered. "That doctor. The one who—"

Julia kept moving. By the end of the Jetway, she was almost running. She caught a glimpse of Ellie standing amid the crowd, dressed in her blue uniform, looking stunningly beautiful.

Ellie put her hands on her hips and stared at her. It was a

cop-assessing-the-situation look. "I haven't seen an airport sprint like that since the O.J. commercials."

"The flight attendant recognized me. She looked at me as if *I* killed those kids." She felt her cheeks heat up.

Ellie's hard look softened. "You can't let it get to you."

"It's not that easy for me. You can't understand."

"Because you think I'm only slightly smarter than an earthworm or because I have nothing in my life worth losing?"

Julia sighed. "Let's not do this, El."

"You're right. Come on."

Until Ellie backed the white Suburban out of the stall and headed for the exit, neither one of them said anything. How was it that, even after all these distant and separate years, they immediately fell into their childhood roles? One look at each other and they were adolescents again.

"Why don't you tell me why I'm here," Julia finally said.

"I'll tell you at the house. I have a lot of stuff to show you. We have a little girl who needs help. But it's . . . complicated."

"How's your friend Penelope?"

"She's good. Raising teenagers is killing her, though. The girl—Tara—keeps wanting to pierce body parts and get tattoos. It's making Pea's husband insane."

"And Penelope? How's she handling it?"

"Great. Well . . . unless you consider her weight gain. In the past year, she's gone on every diet known to man. Last week she started smoking. She says it's how the stars do it."

"That and throwing up," Julia said.

Ellie nodded. "How's Philip?"

Julia was surprised by the swift pain that came with his name. "We broke up last year. I'm too busy—I mean, I *was* too busy—for love."

Ellie laughed at that. "Too busy for love. Are you crazy?"

For the next two hours, they alternated between meaningless conversation and meaningful silences. They came to the Rain Valley exit and turned off the highway. The long, winding forest road led through towering trees.

"I was going to sell the place, move closer to town, but every time I get close to listing it, another repair needs to be done," Ellie said. "I don't need a shrink to tell me I'm afraid to leave it."

"It's just a house, El."

"I guess that's how we're different, Jules. To you, it's two bed-rooms, two baths, and a kitchen-dining-living room. To me, it's the best childhood ever." She turned onto the driveway.

"So quit threatening to sell it. Admit that it's where you want to be. Hand the memories down to your own kids."

"As you may have noticed, I don't have kids. But thanks for point-ing it out." Ellie drove into the yard and stopped hard. "We're here."

Julia realized she had said the wrong thing again. "You don't need a husband, you know. Especially not the kind *you* pick," she said. "You can have a baby on your own."

Ellie turned to look at her. "That might be how it is in the big city, but not here, and not for me. I want it all—the husband, the baby, the golden retriever." She smiled. "Actually, I've got the dogs. And I'd appreciate it if you didn't mention my husbands again."

Julia nodded. Time to change the subject again. "And how are Jake and Elwood? Still go straight for a girl's crotch?"

"They're males, aren't they?" Ellie smiled, and Julia was struck by how *beautiful* her sister still was. There wasn't a line around her eyes or her mouth. Those startling green eyes shone against the milky purity of her skin. She had strong cheekbones and full, sensuous lips. She was small and surprisingly curvy, with a smile like a halogen spotlight. No wonder everyone loved her.

Julia reached for the door, then stepped down. Everything was exactly as it should be in October. Maple trees were dropping their leaves, creating that autumn song that was as familiar to her as the rushing whisper of the nearby river. She followed Ellie across the lawn in the late afternoon light. In the glorious softness, the old house appeared to be made of hammered strips of silver. The grayed clapboards shone with a hundred secret colors. Rhododen-drons the size of house trailers dotted the yard.

Ellie opened the door and led the way inside.

Everything looked as it always had. The same slip-covered furniture—pale beige with pink cabbage roses—graced the liv-ing room. Pine antiques were everywhere—an armoire filled with Grandma Whittaker's table linens, a dining table scarred by three generations of Cateses and Whittakers. French doors flanked a river-rock fireplace; through the silvery glass panes, a ghostly rib-bon of river shone in the sunlight.

Ellie shut the door. Just as she said, "Brace yourself," two golden retrievers came thundering down the stairs. They barreled across the slick wooden floor and hit Julia like the Seahawks' front line.

"Jake! Elwood! *Down*," Ellie yelled in her best police voice.

The dogs were clearly deaf.

Julia gave them a giant shove, and they turned their lavish attention on Ellie. "Please tell me they sleep outside."

Ellie laughed. "Okay, they sleep outside." At Julia's relieved sigh, she said, "*Not!* But I'll keep them out of your room."

Ellie told the dogs to sit. On about the twelfth command, they obeyed. Ellie stepped closer to Julia.

"Jules, I really appreciate your coming. I know things have been bad for you lately, and . . . well, thanks."

If they'd been different sisters, Julia might have admitted: *I had nowhere to go, really.* Instead, she said, "No problem. Now tell me why I'm here."

JULIA sat in her mother's favorite chair and listened in growing disbelief. "She leaps from branch to branch like a cat. Come on, El. You're getting caught up in some country myth. It sounds like you've found an autistic child who simply wandered away from home and got lost."

"Max said the same thing," Ellie said. There were papers spread out across the coffee table. Photographs and fingerprint smudge sheets and missing-children reports.

"Who's Max?"

"He took over Doc Fischer's practice."

"He's probably just in over his head. You should have called the University of Washington. They'll have dozens of autism experts."

"She won't speak. Max thinks maybe she doesn't know how."

"That's not unusual for an autistic. They seem to operate in a different world. Often, these kids—"

"You didn't see her, Jules. When she looked at me, I got chills. I've never seen such . . . terror in a child."

"She looked at you?"

"Stared is more like it. I think she was trying to communicate something to me."

Autistics rarely made purposeful eye contact. "What about her physical mannerisms? Hand movements, way of walking, that sort of thing?"

"She sat in that tree for hours and never moved so much as an eyelash. When she did finally jump down, she moved with a lightning speed. And she sniffed everything in this weird, doglike way."

In spite of herself, Julia was intrigued. "She was completely soundless? Perhaps she's mute. And deaf. That would explain her getting lost. Maybe she didn't hear people calling her."

"She's not mute. She screamed and growled. Oh, yeah, and when she thought we'd killed her wolf, she howled."

"Wolf?"

"She had a wolf pup. He's out at the game farm now. Lloyd says he just sits at the gate and howls all day and all night."

Julia leaned back. "You're making this up."

"I wish I were. And are you ready for the kicker? She has a knife wound. And on her ankle—ligature-type scarring."

Julia uncrossed her arms and leaned forward. "This is a big deal."

"I know."

Julia's mind ticked through possibilities. Autism. Mental or developmental delays. Early onset schizophrenia. But there could be something darker, something infinitely more dangerous. It could be that this child had escaped from some terrible captor. Elective mutism would be a common response to that kind of trauma.

"She really touched me, Jules. I'm afraid that when the bigwig authorities get involved, they'll warehouse her in some state institution until we find her parents. There's something so broken and sad about this kid. With you, we could make a case for treating her while we search. No one could deny your credentials."

Julia said softly, "Have you been watching the news? Your state bigwigs might not be too impressed with me."

Ellie looked at her. "Since when have I cared what other people think? You're the one to save this girl."

Julia felt something inside her give way. "Thanks, El." She wished she could tell her sister what this meant to her.

Ellie nodded. "Now go unpack. I told Max we'd meet him at the hospital before four."

THIRTY MINUTES LATER JULIA WAS showered, made up, and dressed in a well-worn pair of flare-legged jeans and a pale green cashmere sweater. Ellie came downstairs dressed in her blue and black uniform. The three gold stars on her collar winked in the light. Even in the bulky outfit, she looked petite and beautiful. "You ready?"

Julia nodded and grabbed her purse. The few miles passed in surprisingly companionable conversation. Julia remarked on the changes—the new bridge, the closure of Hamburger Haven; Ellie pointed out how much had stayed the same.

Finally they turned a corner and the county hospital came into view, a modest cement building dwarfed by the bank of magnificent evergreen trees behind it. As soon as they parked, Julia was out of the car. The closer she got to the door, the more confident she felt.

She and Ellie walked side by side through the double doors. Nurses and aides wore pale salmon-hued uniforms. Their crepe soles made a squeaking sound on the linoleum-tiled floor.

At a closed door, Ellie paused. She tucked her hair behind her ears, then quickly checked her makeup in a hand mirror.

Julia frowned. "What is this, a photo shoot?"

"You'll see." Ellie knocked on the door.

A voice said: "Come in."

Ellie opened the door. They walked into a small, cramped office with a ground-level window view of a gargantuan rhododendron.

He stood in the corner of the room, wearing faded Levi's and a black cable-knit sweater. His hair was steely gray, but it was his eyes that caught Julie's attention. They were searingly blue and intense.

"You must be Dr. Cates," he said, moving toward her.

"Please, call me Julia."

His smile was literally dazzling. "Only if you'll call me Max."

She recognized instantly the kind of man he was. A player, a man who wore his sexuality like a sport coat. Los Angeles was full of men like him. She wasn't surprised at all to see that one of his ears had once been pierced. She gave him a professional smile. "I understand your patient is . . . what, autistic?"

Surprise flickered across his handsome face. He reached down for a folder that lay on his desk. "A diagnosis is your job. Juvenile minds are hardly my specialty."

"And what is your specialty?"

"Writing prescriptions, if I had to choose. I went to Catholic school." That smile again. "Thus, my penmanship is excellent."

She glanced at the diplomas on his wall. An undergraduate degree from Stanford, a medical degree from U.C.L.A. She frowned. What in the world was this guy doing *here?* Rain Valley newcomers pretty much fell into two groups: people running away from something, and people running away from everything. She couldn't help wondering which category he fell into.

She looked up suddenly and found him studying her closely. "Come with me," he said, taking her by the arm.

Julia let him lead her down the wide, white hallway. Ellie was on his other side. After a few more turns, they came to a big picture window. Max stood so close to Julia they were nearly touching. She took a step sideways to put space between them.

The room beyond the glass was an ordinary-looking playroom with a hospital bed. "Where is she?"

Max nodded. "Watch."

In silence, they waited. Finally a nurse walked past them and entered the playroom, set a tray of food on the table, then left.

Julia was about to ask a question when she saw a flash of movement under the bed. She leaned forward as the girl descended on the food like a wild animal.

Julia felt a chill move down her spine. She opened her briefcase, pulling out a notepad and pen. "What do we know about her?"

"Nothing," Ellie answered. "She just walked into town one day. Daisy Grimm thinks she came looking for food."

"From which direction?"

It was Max who answered. "From the woods."

The woods. The Olympic National Forest. Hundreds of thousands of acres of mossy darkness: Much of it was still unexplored.

"We think she was lost there for a few days," Ellie said.

"And she hasn't spoken?"

Max shook his head. "No. We don't think she understands us, either. She spends all her time under the bed. We bathed and diapered her when she was unconscious, but we haven't been able to get close enough to change the diapers."

"Tell me about those ligature marks on her ankle."

"I think—" He was interrupted by the hospital intercom system paging him to the ER, stat.

He handed her the file. "It's all in here, Julia, and it isn't pretty. If you want to get together later to discuss—"

"The charts are fine for now. Thank you, Max."

ON LEAVING the hospital, Ellie wasn't surprised to find a crowd outside. They were standing in formation, like a landing party from a distant era, with the Grimm sisters positioned at the front. As always, Daisy was in the lead. Today she wore a floral housedress beneath a heavy Cowichan sweater. Her dove-gray hair was pulled back into a tight bun.

"Chief Barton," she said, "we heard you were headed this way."

"Ned saw you turn off the highway," Violet said, nodding.

"What's the story, Chief?" yelled Mort Elzik, the reporter from the *Rain Valley Gazette*.

"Hush, Mort," Daisy said sternly, using her former principal's voice to full effect. "We've rallied the town, Chief. We have toys and books and games and clothes. That poor child will want for nothing. Shall I take them to her hospital room?"

"What happened to the wolf?" It was Mort again, trying now to push through the crowd. Suddenly everyone was talking. Daisy couldn't stop them, and Ellie didn't try.

"Who is she?" Mort asked in a loud, exasperated voice.

That shut everyone up.

"That's the sixty-four-thousand-dollar question, Mort. Peanut is back at the station doing everything she can to find out."

"I'd like to interview her."

"Wouldn't we all? I've got a psychiatrist in with her now. I'll let you know if we get any information—"

"It's Julia!" Violet yelled, clapping her hands together.

"Of course!" Marigold said. "Ned wondered who the blond woman was. You went to the airport to fetch her."

Mort started to bounce up and down. "I want to interview your sister."

"I have not confirmed that Julia Cates has been contacted in this case, *nor* that she is here." Ellie looked directly at Mort. "Is that clear? I don't want to see her name in print."

"Maybe if you promised me an exclusive—"

"Stop talking."

"But—"

"Don't break that story, Mort. Please." In a moment like this, they were still more high school newspaper geek and homecoming queen than reporter and police chief. In small towns like this, the social dynamic was like concrete; it set early and hard.

"Okay," he said, drawing the word out into a whine.

Ellie smiled. "Good."

Daisy said, "What do we do with the supplies, Chief?"

"Why don't you put everything in my carport? Be sure and get every donor's name. Thanks for all your help. That kid was lucky to stumble into our town."

"We'll take care of her," someone said.

Ellie headed across the parking lot, climbed up into her old Suburban, and drove to the station house. All the way there, she added things to her mental to-do list. Today was the day she'd find the girl's identity. It *had* to be.

Ellie parked in her spot and went into the station. Peanut handed her a cup of coffee, then reached down to her cluttered desk and pulled up a single sheet of paper from the mess.

"Here's where we are so far." Peanut put on her rhinestone-encrusted Costco reading glasses. "The Center for Lost and Missing Children is running a database search. Their first pass brought up over ten thousand potential matches."

Ellie sat down. "Ten thousand missing girls. God help us, Peanut. It would take us decades to go through all the information."

"Get this, El. There are eight hundred thousand missing-children cases a year in this country. That's almost two thousand a day."

Ellie felt overwhelmed suddenly. "Did the FBI get back to us?"

"They're waiting for proof of kidnapping or a solid identification. It could just be a lost girl from Mystic or Forks. Technically, we have no proof of a crime. And the Department of Social and Health Services is pressuring us to identify a temporary foster parent."

"Did you call the Laura Recovery Center?"

"And the attorney general. By tomorrow this girl is going to be front-page news. It won't be easy to hide Julia."

This story was going to be a hurricane of publicity, no doubt about it. And Dr. Julia Cates would be in the eye of the storm.

"No," Ellie said, frowning. "It won't."

GIRL IS COILED UP LIKE A YOUNG fern in this too-white place. The cold, hard ground makes her shiver.

She wants to close her eyes and go to sleep; the smells in here are all wrong. Her nose itches, and her throat is so dry it hurts. She longs for her river and the water that is always leaking over the steep cliff. She can hear the Sun-Haired Her, and her voice is dangerous. She is thinking of Her . . . of Him, even. Of Wolf.

Without them she feels lost. She can't live in this place where nothing green is alive and the air stinks.

She shouldn't have run away. Him always told her that she had to stay hidden because in the world, there were people who hurt little girls worse than Him did. Strangers.

SITTING on an uncomfortable plastic chair in the cheerily decorated playroom, Julia stared down at the notebook in her lap. In the last hour, she'd talked endlessly to the girl hidden beneath the bed but had received no response. Her notebook remained full of questions without answers.

In the early years of her residency, it had become clear to everyone that Julia had a true gift for dealing with traumatized children. And although she hadn't specialized in autism or mental challenges, she'd dealt with those patients. She knew, too, how profoundly deaf children acted before they learned sign language.

But none of that seemed relevant to this case. The child's brain scan showed no lesions or anomalies. The girl under the bed could be a perfectly normal child who'd been lost on a day hike and was now too terrified to speak up.

Julia put down her pen. She'd been silent for too long. Her best hope with this child lay in *connecting*. "I guess I can't write my way to understanding you, can I?" she said in gentle, soothing tones.

For the next two hours, Julia talked about nothing. The subtext on every word was *Come on out, honey, I'm a safe place.* But not once had so much as a finger appeared out from beneath the bed.

There was a knock at the door. Julia went and opened it.

Max cocked his head to the right, where two white-clad male orderlies stood. "The food and toys are here."

"Thanks."

"No response yet?"

"No, and it's impossible to diagnose her this way. I need to *study* her. That damn bed makes it impossible."

"Whatcha want us to do with this?" asked one of the orderlies.

"I'll take the stuffed animals. Store the rest of the toys for now. She's hardly ready for that kind of play. The food can go on the table." She started to say something else when it struck her.

Move the bed. How had she missed the obvious?

She shut the door, realizing a moment too late that she'd shut it in Max's face. Oops. Oh, well. She went to the nearest orderly, who was just setting down a tray of food, and said, "Take the bed out of here, please, but leave the mattress."

"Huh?"

"Just move the bed. Carefully. Put the mattress in the corner."

They placed the mattress where she'd indicated, lifted the bed off the floor, and backed out of the room, but Julia didn't notice. All she saw was her patient.

Crouched low, the girl opened her mouth to scream.

Come on, Julia thought, *let me hear you.*

But there was no sound as the child scrambled back to the wall and froze. She went perfectly still—so still she seemed to be carved of pale wood. Her only sign of life was her nostrils, which flared as if to pick up every scent.

For the first time, Julia noticed the child's beauty. Though wretchedly thin, she was still striking. She stared near Julia, but not quite at her, as if there were a dangerous animal to Julia's left. Her eyes—those amazing, blue-green eyes—missed nothing.

"You're almost looking at me," Julia said in as conversational tone as possible. "I imagine you're scared. Everything that's happened to you since yesterday has been frightening."

There was no reaction at all.

For the next twelve hours, Julia sat quietly in a chair. The child was almost completely motionless. Sometime around midnight she fell asleep, still crouched against the wall. When she finally slumped to the floor, Julia cautiously transferred her to the mattress.

At some point, Julia fell asleep, too, but by morning, when the girl finally woke, Julia was ready. Smiling easily, she began talking again. In her voice, she made sure the girl heard acceptance and caring. Hour after hour Julia talked, all through the meals, which went uneaten. By late afternoon, she was exhausted, and the girl *had* to be hungry.

Glancing at the girl sitting on the mattress, Julia grabbed a big book off the shelf and dropped it on the floor. It hit with a thwack.

The girl flinched; her eyes widened.

"So you can hear. Now can you understand me. Are you hearing words or sounds, little girl?" Cautiously, she moved toward the child, waiting for a flicker in the eyes, an acknowledgment that she was being approached. When Julia was about eight feet away, a tiny, whimpering sound leaked past the girl's lips.

Julia stopped. "That's close enough, huh? I'm scaring you. That's good, actually. You're responding normally to this strange environment." She went back and sat down.

A moment later there was a knock at the door. The girl scrambled into the corner, crouching down to appear as small as possible.

"It's just your dinner. I know you have to be hungry." Julia opened the door, thanked the nurse, then returned to the table.

As she unpacked the food, she kept up a steady stream of conversation. Macaroni and cheese, glazed doughnuts, brownies, chicken tenders with ketchup, milk, Jell-O with fruit chunks, cheese pizza, a hot dog with fries. "I didn't know what you liked so I pretty much ordered everything." Julia plucked a doughnut off the red plastic plate. "I can't remember the last time I had a glazed doughnut. Are you hungry?"

At the word *hungry*, the girl flinched. For just a moment, her gaze skittered across the room and came to rest on the table of food.

"Did you understand? Do you know what *hungry* means?"

The girl looked at her for a moment. It lasted less than a breath, but Julia felt its impact all the way to her toes.

Understanding. She'd bet her degrees on it.

Very slowly Julia walked closer to the girl than she'd been before. Once again the child snorted and whimpered.

Julia set the red plate on the floor and gave it a little push. It skidded across the linoleum. Close enough to the child that she could smell the doughnut's vanilla-y sweetness.

Julia returned to her seat. "You're hungry. That's food."

This time the girl looked right at her.

"No one will hurt you," Julia said.

The girl blinked. Minutes passed. Neither one of them looked away. Finally Julia glanced at the window by the door. Dr. Better-looking-than-God was there, watching them.

The second Julia glanced away, the girl ran for the food, snatched it up, and returned to her spot. She put most of the doughnut into her mouth and started to chew loudly.

Julia could tell when the taste kicked in. The girl's eyes widened.

"Can't beat a good doughnut, but you'd better have some protein with that." She set the hot dog down closer to the table than before.

The girl's blue-green eyes fixed on her.

"You understand, don't you? Not everything, but enough. Are you from around here?"

The girl glanced down at the hot dog.

"Neah Bay. Joyce. Sequim. Forks. Sappho. Mystic." Julia watched closely. None of the local towns prompted a response. "A lot of families go hiking in the forest, especially along Fall River."

Had the girl blinked at that? She said it again: "Fall River."

Nothing.

"Forest. Trees. Deep woods."

The girl looked up sharply.

Julia got up from her seat and moved slowly. Squatting down, she held the plate of food forward. "Were you lost in the woods, honey? Did you get separated from your mommy and daddy? I can help you. I won't hurt you. No hurt."

At that, the girl inched forward in her awkward crouch. Not once did her gaze waver or lower. She stared at Julia.

"No hurt," Julia said again as the girl neared.

The child was breathing fast; her nostrils were blowing hard. Sweat sheened her forehead. She smelled vaguely of urine because of the diapers they'd been unable to change. The hospital gown hung slack on her tiny body. Her toenails and fingernails were long and still slightly grimy.

She grabbed the hot dog, sniffed it, frowning.

"It's a hot dog," Julia said. "Your parents probably brought them on the camping trip. Where did your daddy say you were going? Maybe I could go get him."

The girl attacked her. It happened so fast that Julia couldn't respond. One second she was sitting there, talking softly, the next, she felt herself falling backward, hitting her head on the floor. The girl jumped on Julia's chest and clawed at her face, screaming unintelligible words.

Max was there in an instant, pulling the girl off Julia.

Dazed, Julia tried to sit up. She couldn't focus. When the world finally righted itself, she saw Max sedating the child.

"No!" she cried, trying to get to her feet. Her vision blurred.

Max was back at her side, steadying her. "I've got you."

Julia wrenched away from him and fell to her knees. "I can't *believe* you sedated her. Damn it. Now she'll never trust me."

"She could have hurt you," he said in a matter-of-fact voice.

"She's all of what—forty-five pounds?"

Her cheeks hurt. So did the back of her head. She couldn't believe how fast the attack had come on. The girl lay on the mattress, curled in a tight ball even in slumber, as if the whole world could hurt her. *Damn it.* "How long will she sleep?"

"Not more than a few hours."

"Next time don't sedate her without asking me, okay?" She frowned. "The question is, what did I say?"

"What do you mean?"

"You saw her. She was fine. I thought maybe she was even understanding a few words. Then *bam!* I must have said just the wrong thing." She looked back at the girl. "Poor baby."

"We should get those scratches cleaned up. God knows what kind of bacteria is under her fingernails."

Julia could hardly disagree.

As they walked down the hallway, she realized how much her head hurt. So much that she felt queasy and unsteady. "I've never seen anyone move so fast. She was like a cat."

Max guided her into an empty examining room. "Sit. I need to look at your injuries."

She sat on the table, paper rustling beneath her. Other than their breathing, it was the only sound in the room.

His touch was surprisingly gentle on her face. She winced when he dabbed the antiseptic on her wounds.

"Sorry."

"It's not your fault." He was too close. She shut her eyes.

That was when she felt his breath on her cheek.

She opened her eyes. He was right there. Her heart skipped a beat. "Thanks," she said, jerking backward. *Oh, for God's sake, Julia.* Men like Max specialized in making a girl's heart beat faster.

"You should take the rest of the day off. Have Ellie watch you. Concussions—"

"I know the risks, Max, and the symptoms. I'm sure I don't have a concussion, but I'll be careful."

"It wouldn't hurt to lie down for a while."

"That little girl is counting on me, Max. I need to go to the police station and then to the library, but I'll take it easy."

"Why do I think you don't know how to take it easy?"

She frowned. "Am I that transparent?"

"As glass. How are you getting to the station?"

"I'll call Ellie. She'll—"

"I could give you a ride."

Sliding off the table, she felt a little steadier. Then she caught a glimpse of herself in the mirror.

"Wow." She moved closer. Four angry, seeping claw marks slashed across her left cheek. "She really got me."

He handed her a tube of antibiotic ointment. "Come on. I'll take you to the station."

Instead of arguing, she fell into step beside him.

But not too close.

FOUR

"Are you sure this is how it's done?" Peanut asked for at least the tenth time in as many minutes.

"Do I *look* like Diane Sawyer?" Ellie responded sharply. Whenever she got nervous, she got snippy, and this was her first press conference. She needed to do everything right or she'd come off looking like an idiot.

"Ellie? Are you having a meltdown?"

"I'm fine."

The police station had been transformed into a makeshift press-room. They'd pushed their desks to the perimeter, dragged a podium from the rotary club storeroom, and set up ten chairs.

Cal sat at his desk, answering the phones. Peanut stood in the hallway, surveying the setup. Ellie reread the statement she'd prepared, trying to memorize her lines. She barely looked up as reporters streamed in and sat down. By six o'clock all of the chairs were filled, with photographers and videographers standing behind.

Ellie tapped the microphone. It thumped and whined. Sound ricocheted through the room. Several people covered their ears.

"Sorry." She eased back a little bit. "Thank you all for coming. As most of you know, a young girl has arrived in Rain Valley. We have no idea who she is or where she is from. Our best estimates put her age at somewhere between five and seven years. We're in the process of getting a photograph. For now, you'll find an artist's sketch on your seats. She has black hair and blue-green eyes, and she has lost a number of baby teeth. We have consulted with all available state and local agencies, as well as the Center for Missing Children, and have—as yet—been unable to identify her. We're hoping that you all run this as front-page news to get the word out. Someone must know who she is."

Mort from the *Rain Valley Gazette* stood up. "How come she doesn't just tell you her name?"

"She hasn't spoken yet," Ellie answered.

"*Can* she speak?"

"We have early indications there's no physical barrier to speech."

A man wearing a *Seattle Times* baseball hat stood up. "So she's clammed up on purpose?"

"We don't know yet. Our very best doctors are taking care of her. That's all we have for now."

"I heard she had a wolf pup with her." This from the back.

"And that she jumped from a branch that was forty feet in the air," someone else added.

The questions just kept on coming. Her personal favorite (this from Mort): "Are you sure she's human?"

From there, it was all downhill.

"You're lucky it was raining this morning. Otherwise, I'd have my motorcycle," Max said, starting his truck.

"Let me guess," she said. "Harley-Davidson."

"How'd you know?"

"The pierced ear. I'm a shrink, remember? We tend to notice the little things."

He drove out of the parking lot. "Oh. Do you like bikes?"

"The ones that go seventy miles an hour? No."

"Too fast, too free, huh?"

She stared out the window at the passing trees, wishing he would slow down. "Too many organ donors."

Several blocks passed between them in silence. Finally, Max said, "So have you formed any specific conclusions about her yet?"

She appreciated the return to professionalism. "I can tell you what I *don't* think. I don't believe she's deaf—at least, not completely. I also don't believe she's profoundly mentally challenged; however, that's a hunch. And if she is autistic, she's high functioning."

"You sound like you don't really believe that diagnosis, either."

"I need a lot more time to run tests. I can tell you this: Elective mutism is a common response to childhood trauma."

"And there's been some serious trauma in her life."

"Yes."

The weight of those words made the air between them feel heavy suddenly, and sad.

"Maybe she was kidnapped," Max said quietly.

"That's what I'm afraid of, too. This girl's physical scars could be nothing compared to her emotional trauma."

"She's lucky you're here, then."

"Actually, I'm the lucky one." The minute the words were out, Julia wished them back. She wasn't sure why she'd revealed something so personal, and to this man she hardly knew. Thankfully, he didn't respond.

He turned left onto Azalea Street and found it barricaded. "That's odd." He backed out and drove a block down Cascade, then parked. "I'll walk you in."

"That's hardly necessary."

"I don't mind."

They walked toward the police station, turned the corner, and saw the reason for the barricade.

The street was clotted with news vans. Dozens of them.

"Stop!" she said quickly, screaming the word at Max. She spun around so fast she ran into him. His arms curled around her, steadied her. If the press saw her now, with her battered face, they'd have a field day. "I need to get out of here. *Now*."

He pointed across the street. "That's the Lutheran church. Go on in. I'll send Ellie."

"Thanks." She'd only taken a step or two when he called out her name. She turned back to him, but he didn't say anything.

She rolled her eyes. "Just say what's on your mind, Max. Everyone has a damned opinion. I'm used to it."

"Do you want me to stay with you?"

Julia drew in a sharp breath and looked up at him. She was reminded suddenly of how long she'd been alone. "No . . . but thanks." Without looking at him again, she walked away.

"You decided to hold a press conference without warning me?" Julia couldn't help yelling at her sister. "Why not just tie a yellow ribbon around my throat and toss me to the wolves?"

"How was I supposed to know you'd stop by? You never came home last night, but I'm supposed to plan around your movements. Who am I? Carnac the Magnificent?"

Julia sat back in the seat and crossed her arms. In the sudden silence, rain pattered the windshield of the police cruiser.

"Maybe the media *should* know you're here. I'll tell them how much we believe—"

"You think it would be a good thing to show my face on camera? *Now?* My patient—a kid, mind you—beat me up. It hardly is a ringing endorsement of my skills."

"That's not your fault."

"*I* know that," Julia snapped. "Believe me, they won't." She had to get the girl talking. And fast. Sooner or later, Julia knew, she would be part of the story.

Ellie pulled up in front of the library. The building, an old converted taxidermy shop, sat tucked up against a stand of towering Douglas fir. Night was falling fast.

"I sent everyone home," Ellie said, reaching into her breast pocket for the key. "Just like you asked. And Jules . . . I am sorry."

"Thanks." Julia heard the wobble in her voice. It revealed more than she would have liked. She cleared her throat. "I need somewhere private to work with the child."

"As soon as we find a temporary foster parent, we can—"

"I'll do it. There should be no problem getting me approved."

"Are you sure?" Ellie asked.

"I'm sure. She'll be a full-time job for a while. Get the paperwork started from your end."

"Okay."

Headlights came up behind them, illuminating the cab. Moments later there was a knock at the window. Julia opened the car door.

Penelope stood alongside the passenger door. Behind her was a battered old pickup truck. Julia stepped out. "Benji said you could borrow his daddy's old hay truck. The keys are in it."

"Thank you, Penelope."

"Call me Peanut. Heck, we're practically related, with Ellie being my best friend and all."

Julia could have used a friend in the past year. "Thanks, Peanut."

Ellie got out of the cruiser. Her police-issue black heels crunched the gravel. She and Julia walked up the path to the library.

Ellie unlocked the door and flicked on the lights. Then she looked at Julia. "Can you really help this girl?"

Julia's anger slipped away, along with the residue of her fear. They were back on track, talking about what mattered. "Yes. Any progress on her identity?"

"No. We've input her height, weight, and eye and hair color into the system. We've also photographed her scarring. She has a very particular birthmark on her back left shoulder that the FBI advised me to keep secret. Her fingerprints don't match any recorded missing kids. We've got her DNA, so we're hoping her mother reads tomorrow's newspaper."

"What if it was her mother that tied her up and left her to die?"

"Then you'd better get the truth out of her," Ellie said quietly.

"Nothing like a little pressure."

"Jules, I believe you can do it, you know."

Julia was surprised by how much that meant to her. She nodded, then went into the brightly lit library. Behind her, she heard Ellie sigh heavily and say, "And I believe in you, too, big sis. I know you can find the kid's family." Then the door banged shut.

Julia winced. It had never occurred to her to return the sentiment. She'd always seen her sister as indestructible. Ellie had never needed approval the way she had. It was unsettling to get a glimpse of Ellie's inner nature. There was a vulnerability in there somewhere, a fragility that belied the tough-girl-meets-beauty-queen exterior. So, they had something else in common after all.

Julia walked to a row of computers. There were five of them beneath a bulletin board studded with local flyers. She pulled a legal-sized yellow tablet and a pen out of her briefcase.

The computer came on with a thump-buzz. The screen lit up. Within seconds, she was surfing the Net.

For the next few hours, she took notes on whatever childhood behavioral and mental disorders she could find, but none of them gave her that *Aha!* moment. Finally, at around eleven, she ran a search on "lost children woods."

"Feral children" came up, a phrase she hadn't seen since college. She moved the cursor and clicked.

Feral children are lost, abandoned, or otherwise forgotten children who survive in completely isolated conditions. The idea of children raised by wolves or bears is prevalent in legend, although there are few scientifically documented cases.

The most recent case, in the 1990s, had been a Ukrainian child named Oxiana Malayer, who was said to have been raised by dogs until the age of eight. She never mastered language skills. Today she lives in a home for the mentally disabled.

Julia frowned and hit the PRINT key.

It was unlikely as hell that this girl was a true wild child.

The wolf pup . . .

The way she eats . . .

But if she were . . .

This child could be the most profoundly damaged child she would ever treat, and without extensive help, the poor girl could be as lost and forgotten in the system as she'd been in the woods.

Julia picked up the page she'd printed. A little girl stared up at her from a black-and-white photograph. The child looked both frightened and strangely fixated. The caption read: "Genie. The modern equivalent of the wild child raised in a California suburb. Saved from this nightmare, she was brought into the light for a short time until, like all the wild children before her, she was forgotten by the doctors and scientists and shuffled off to her shadowy fate: life in an institution."

"I won't let anyone hurt you again," Julia vowed to the little girl asleep in the hospital. "I promise."

BY EIGHT o'clock that evening, the phones finally stopped ringing. There had been dozens of faxes and queries from reporters who hadn't come to the press conference but had somehow gotten wind of the story. And, of course, the locals had arrived in a steady stream, begging for any scrap of news about Rain Valley's unexpected guest.

"The quiet before the storm," Peanut said.

Ellie looked up from her desk to see her friend light a cigarette.

"I asked. You grunted," Peanut said before Ellie could argue.

Ellie didn't bother fighting. "What about the storm?"

"It's the quiet before. Tomorrow all hell is gonna break loose. One Flying Wolf Girl headline and every reporter in the country will want in on the story." She shook her head, exhaling smoke and coughing. "That poor kid. How will we protect her?"

"I'm working on that."

"And how will we trust whoever comes to claim her?"

"That's been bothering me from the get-go, Pea. I don't want to hand her over to the very people who hurt her, but I have damned little evidence. I'm actually hoping there's a kidnapping report. How sad is that? Then there might be blood samples and a suspect. If it's not that simple . . ." She shrugged. "Right now our job is to find Julia a place to work."

"How about the old sawmill? No one would look for her there."

"Too cold. Too indefensible. Some wily tabloid photographer would find a way in. And it's public property."

"County hospital?"

"Too many employees." Ellie frowned. "What we need is a secret location and a cone of silence."

"In Rain Valley? You must be joking. This town lives for gossip."

Of course. The answer was so obvious, she didn't know how she'd missed it. "Call Daisy Grimm. I want everybody in this town at a six a.m. meeting at the Congregational church."

"A town meeting? How dramatic. What's the agenda?"

"The Flying Wolf Girl, of course. If this town wants to gossip, we'll give them something to talk about."

For the next hour, Ellie worked on the plan, while Peanut called their friends and neighbors. By ten o'clock, they were done.

Ellie looked down at the contract she'd devised. It was perfect.

I _____ agree to keep any and all information about the wolf girl completely confidential. I swear I won't tell anyone anything that I learned at the town meeting on October 19th. Rain Valley can count on me.

_____ (signature required)

"It won't hold up in court," Peanut said, coming over to her.

"Who are you? Perry Mason?"

"I watch *Boston Legal* and *Law & Order.*"

"It doesn't need to be legally binding." Ellie rolled her eyes. "It just needs to seem like it is."

THE girl is crouched on a branch, watching him. She is so still that he wonders how his gaze found her.

Hey, he whispers, reaching out.

She drops to the leaf-carpeted floor without a sound. On all fours, she runs away.

He finds her in a cave, bound and bleeding. Afraid. He thinks he hears her say "Help," and then she is gone. There is a little boy in her place, blond-haired. He is reaching out, crying—

Max came awake with a start. For a moment, he had no idea where he was. All he saw around him were walls and moonlight.

Within minutes, he was on his motorcycle and racing down the black, empty expanse of road. He thought about that poor girl, his patient, all alone in her room.

Kids were afraid of the dark.

He hit the gas. At the hospital, he parked beside Penelope Nutter's battered red pickup. The hallways were empty and quiet, with only a few nurses on duty. Heading toward the day-care center, he noticed a light coming from the window. He peered in, expecting to see the girl curled up on the mattress, asleep. Instead, the lights were on and Julia was there, sitting on a tiny chair beside a child-size Formica table. She appeared utterly calm. Serene, even.

The girl, on the other hand, was agitated. She darted around the room, then all at once she swung to face Julia.

Julia said something. Max couldn't hear it through the glass.

The girl blew snot from her nose and shook her head, scratching her cheeks. Julia lunged, took her in her arms. The girl fought like a cat. They stumbled, fell on the mattress.

Julia held the girl immobile, ignoring the snot-flying and head-shaking; then Julia started to sing. Max could tell by the cadence of her voice, the way the sounds blended into one another.

He went to the door and quietly opened it. Just a crack.

The girl immediately looked at him and stilled, snorting.

Julia held the girl and stroked her hair and kept singing. Not once did she even glance toward the door. Slowly, the minutes ticked by. "Only Little Petunia in the Onion Patch," "Somewhere Over the Rainbow," and then "Puff the Magic Dragon."

Gradually, the girl's eyelashes fluttered shut, reopened.

Julia kept singing.

Finally the girl put her thumb in her mouth and fell asleep.

Very gently, Julia tucked her patient into bed and covered her with blankets, then went back to the table to gather her notes.

Max knew he should leave before she noticed him, but he couldn't move. "I guess this means you like watching," she said without looking at him.

He stepped into the room. "You don't miss much, do you?"

She put the last of the papers into her briefcase and then looked up. Her skin appeared ashen beneath the dim lighting; the scratches on her cheeks were dark and angry. A yellow bruise marred her forehead. But it was her eyes that got to him. "I miss plenty."

Her voice was so soft, it took him a second to really hear what she'd said.

I miss plenty. She was talking about that patient in Silverwood. He knew about that kind of guilt.

"You look like a woman who could use a cup of coffee."

"Coffee? At one o'clock in the morning? I don't think so, but thank you." She sidled past him, then herded him out of the day-care center and shut the door behind him.

"How about pie?" he said as she headed down the hallway. "Pie is good any time of the day."

She stopped, turned around. "Pie?"

He moved toward her. "I knew I could tempt you."

She laughed at that, and though it was a tired, not-quite-genuine sound, it made his smile broaden. "The pie tempted me."

He led her to the cafeteria and flipped on the lights. "Take a seat." Going back into the kitchen, he found two pieces of pie, which he covered in vanilla ice cream.

"Marionberry pie," he said, sliding into the booth seat opposite her. "A local favorite." He handed her a fork.

She stared at him, frowning slightly. "Thanks."

"You're welcome."

"So, Dr. Cerrasin," she said, "do you make a habit of luring colleagues to the cafeteria for early morning pie?"

He smiled. "Well, if by colleagues you mean doctors, I haven't taken old Doc Fischer out for pie in ages."

"How about the nurses?"

He heard a tone in her voice and looked up. "It sounds to me like you're asking about my love life."

"Love life?" She put a slight emphasis on "love." "Do you have one of those? I would be surprised."

He frowned. "You sure think you know me."

She took a bite of pie. "Let's just say I know your kind."

"No. Let's *not* say that. Whoever you're confusing me with is not sitting at this table. You just met me, Julia."

"Fair enough. Tell me about yourself, then. Are you married?"

"An interesting first question. No. Are you?"

"No. Have you ever been married?"

"Once. A long time ago."

That seemed to surprise her. "Kids?"

"No."

She looked at him sharply, as if she'd heard something in his voice. Their gazes held. Finally she smiled. "So I guess you can have pie with anyone you'd like. You've probably had pie with every woman in town."

"You give me too much credit. Married women make their own pie." He changed the course of the conversation. "How is your face feeling? That bruise is getting uglier."

"We shrinks get popped now and then. Hazard of the trade."

"You can never quite know what a person will do, can you?"

Her gaze met his. "Knowing is my job. Although by now the whole world knows I missed something important."

There was nothing he could say, so he stayed quiet.

"No platitudes, Dr. Cerrasin? No 'God doesn't give you more than you can bear' speech?"

"Call me Max. Please." He looked at her. "And sometimes God breaks your back."

It was a long moment. "How did He break you, Max?"

He slid out of the booth and stood beside her. "As much as I'd love to keep chatting, I have to be at work at seven. So . . ."

Julia put the dishes on the tray. She paused. "No more pie for me. Just so you know. Okay?"

PEOPLE took their places in the rows of oak pews in the gray predawn light. Their voices combined, rose, sounding like a Cuisinart on high, crushing ice. Ellie went to the pulpit. It took her five minutes to quiet the crowd.

"Thank you all for coming," she said finally. "I know how early it is, and I appreciate your cooperation. This is about the girl who arrived recently."

The crowd erupted, hurling questions at the podium.

"Can she really fly?"

"Where is she?"

"Where's the wolf?"

"The wolf is with Floyd at the Olympic Game Farm. He's being well cared for." Ellie took a deep breath. "Look, the point is, do we want to protect this child?"

A resounding "Yes" rose from the crowd.

"Good." She turned to Peanut. "Hand out the contracts." To the crowd, she said, "I'm going to read off your names. Please answer so I know you're here."

Ellie read off the names in alphabetical order. One by one, people responded until she came to Mort Elzik.

"He ain't here," Earl yelled.

"Okay," Ellie said. "We don't mention this meeting or the girl to Mort, or to anyone else who isn't at this meeting. Agreed?"

"Agreed," they responded in unison.

"Fair enough. As you all know by now, my sister, Julia, has come home to help. What she needs is peace and quiet, and a place to work away from the media."

The crowd went still, waiting.

"Now, here's the plan. It's a version of Hide-the-Walnut. When asked, we're going to secretly and *off-the-record* tell the press where the girl is staying. Tell them anyplace you want—except my house. That's where she'll be. They won't trespass on the police chief's land, and if they do, Jake and Elwood will give us warning."

"We're *lying* to the press?" Violet said in awe.

"We are. Until we know the girl's name. And one other thing: No one mentions Julia. No one."

"Lying," Marigold said. "This will be fun."

Daisy burst out laughing. "You can count on us, Ellie. Those reporters will be looking for the girl as far north as the Yukon. And I don't know about the rest of you, but I never *heard* of Dr. Julia Cates. I *believe* the poor child is seeing Dr. Welby."

FIVE

WHILE Ellie was parking the car, Julia ran into the hospital to the old day-care center. A few minutes later Peanut, Max, and Ellie arrived. They stood at the window, looking in. The girl lay on the floor, curled up, the mattress beside her. From this distance, she appeared to be asleep.

"She knows we're watching her," Peanut said. "Poor thing. How do we move her without terrifying her?"

"We put a sedative in her apple juice," Max said. He turned to Julia. "Can you get her to drink it?"

"I think so."

Thirty minutes later, Julia went into the day-care center. The "team" had moved away from the window. The girl didn't move a finger or bat an eyelash. She simply lay there, coiled up like a snail.

"I know you're awake," Julia said conversationally. She set down her tray on the table. On it was a plate filled with scrambled eggs and toast. A green plastic sippee cup held apple juice.

She sat down and ate a bite of toast. "Um-um. This is good, but it makes me thirsty." She pretended to take a sip. For thirty minutes, she pretended to eat and drink, talking to the child who didn't respond. Every second bothered her. They needed to move this girl *fast*, before the press came looking for her. Finally she pushed back from the table. The chair legs screeched against the linoleum floor.

All hell broke loose. The girl screamed; she jumped to her feet and started clawing at her face and blowing her nose.

"It's okay," Julia said evenly. "You're scared. You know that word? It was a loud, ugly noise, and it scared you, that's all. See how quiet everything is?" Julia moved toward the girl, who was standing in the corner thumping her forehead against the wall.

Thud. Thud. Thud.

Julia winced at each blow. Very slowly, she reached out, touched the child's rail-thin shoulder. "Shhh," she said.

The girl went totally still. Julia could feel the tension in her shoulder. "You are okay now. No hurt. No hurt." She touched the girl's other shoulder and gently turned her around.

The girl stared up at her through wary blue-green eyes. A purplish bruise was already forming on her forehead, and the scratches on her cheeks were bleeding. At this proximity, the smell of urine was almost overwhelming.

"No hurt," Julia said, expecting the girl to pull free and run.

But she stood there breathing fast, her body trembling. She was weighing the situation, cataloging her options.

"You're trying to read me," Julia said, surprised. "I'm Julia." She patted her chest. "Julia."

The girl glanced away, disinterested. Her trembling eased.

"No hurt," Julia said. "Food. Hungry?"

The girl looked at the table. "Eat," Julia said, letting go.

When there was a safe distance between them, the girl pounced on the food. She washed it all down with the apple juice.

THEIR EARLY-MORNING JOURNEY from town to the edge of the deep woods had the hazy feel of a dream. In the last stretch of valley before the big trees, no one spoke. Max was in the backseat of the police cruiser, with Julia to his right. The girl lay between them with her head in Julia's lap, her bare feet in his.

"We're here," Ellie said from the front seat as she parked.

Max scooped the sleeping child into his arms, her cheek pressed against his chest. He knew exactly how to hold her. How was it that even after all these years, it still felt as natural as breathing?

From somewhere, deep in the woods, a wolf howled.

Max stopped; Julia did the same.

Peanut said, "I am *not* feeling good about this."

"I've never heard a wolf out here," Ellie said. "It can't be *her* wolf. He's over in Sequim."

The girl moaned.

The wolf howled again, an undulating, elegiac sound.

They walked through the house, up the stairs, and into the bedroom. Max put the child on the bed and covered her with blankets. Peanut glanced nervously at the window. "She's gonna try to escape. Those are her woods."

"Here's what we need, and fast," Julia said. "Bars on the window and a dead bolt for the door. We need to cover every scrap of shiny metal with adhesive except the doorknob."

"Why?" Peanut asked.

"I think she's afraid of shiny metal," Julia answered. "And we'll need a video camera set up to observe her twenty-four/seven. We need food, too. And lots of tall houseplants. I want to turn one corner of the room into a forest."

" '*Where the Wild Things Are*,' " Peanut said.

Julia nodded, then went to the bed and sat down beside the girl.

Max followed her. Kneeling, he checked the girl's pulse and breathing. "Normal," he said, sitting back on his heels.

"If only her mind and her heart were as easy to read," Julia said.

"You'd be out of a job."

Julia surprised him by laughing.

They looked at each other. He got slowly to his feet.

"We should go get supplies from town," Ellie said.

Max nodded. "I have time to put up the bars before my shift."

"Good. Thanks," Julia said. When they were gone, she remained at her place by the bed. "You're safe here, little one. I promise." But she knew one thing for certain: This girl had no idea what it meant to be safe.

GONE is the bad smell and the white, hissing light. Girl opens her eyes slowly. There have been many changes. It is as if she has fallen in the dark water past that pool in the deep forest that Him said was the start of Out There.

This cave is different. Everything is the color of snow and of the berries she picks in summer. It is morning light. She climbs out of bed, sniffing. Wood. Flowers. Many more smells she doesn't know.

The entrance to this cave is a thick brown barrier. There is something about the shiny ball on it that is the source of its magic; she is afraid to touch it. The Strangers would come for her again with their nets and sharp points.

A breeze floats past her face. On it is the scent of her place. She looks around. There it is. The box that holds the wind.

She moves forward, holding her stomach tightly.

Carefully she puts her hand through the opening. Nothing stops her. Finally her whole arm is Out There, in her world, where the air seems to be made of raindrops.

She closes her eyes. For the first time since they trapped her, she can breathe. She lets out a long, desperate howl.

Come for me, that noise means, but she stops in the middle of it. She is so far away from her cave. There is no one to hear her.

ELLIE stood in the hallway outside the lunchroom, sipping her coffee and looking out at the melee. The station was a hive of people. She couldn't see a patch of floor or wall. It was the same way outside and down the block.

The story had broken this morning under a variety of headlines.

THE GIRL FROM NOWHERE
WHO AM I?
LOST GIRL WALKS OUT OF WOODS

The first call had come in at eight a.m. By one, the first national news van pulled in. Within two hours, the streets were jammed with reporters demanding a press conference.

"So far nothing has panned out," Peanut said, coming out of the lunchroom. "No one knows who she is."

Ellie sipped her coffee. Cal was talking into the dispatch headset at the same time he fielded questions from the crowd of reporters in front of him. Ellie smiled at him. He mouthed, *Help me.*

"Cal's losing it," Peanut said.

"I can hardly blame him. He didn't take this job to actually work."

"Who did?" Peanut said, laughing.

"That would be me. Wish me luck." Ellie waded back into the sea of clamoring, shouting reporters. She raised her hands.

"There will be no more comments by anyone in this office. We'll conduct a press conference at four o'clock."

Peanut barreled in. "You heard the chief. Everyone with a press card, *out.* Now." She herded them out, then slammed the door.

It wasn't until Ellie turned toward her desk that she saw Mort Elzick standing in the corner, wedged between two industrial-green file cabinets. Behind his thick glasses, his eyes looked huge and watery. "Y-You need to give me an exclusive, Ellie. This is my big break." He flushed. "I *know* Julia is helping on this case."

"You *think* she is. Put it in print and I'll bury you."

"Give me an exclusive. You owe it to me. Or else."

"Mention my sister and I'll get you fired."

He stepped back. "I gave you a chance. You remember that." He pushed past her and ran out of the station.

"Praise the Lord and pass the ice," Cal said. He went down to the lunchroom and came back with three beers.

"You can't drink in here, Cal," Ellie said tiredly.

"Hell," he said, "I haven't been able to read a comic book in peace all week." He handed her a Corona.

"No, thanks," Peanut said when he offered her a beer. She went into the lunchroom, then came back out holding a mug. "Cabbage soup," she said, shrugging.

Cal sat on his desk, feet swinging, and drank his beer. "Good for you, Pea. I was afraid you were going to try the heroin diet next."

Ellie heard something in Cal's voice, a rawness that confused

her. For the first time, she noticed how tired he looked. His mouth
was a thin pale line.

She couldn't help feeling sorry for him. She knew exactly what
the problem was. Cal had worked for her now for two and a half
years; before that, he'd been an at-home dad. His wife, Lisa, was
a sales rep for a New York company and was gone more than she
was home. When the kids were all in school, Cal took the dispatch
job to fill the empty hours. Mostly he read comic books and drew
action figures in his sketch pad. The past few days seemed to have
undone him. She realized how much she missed his smile. "I'll
tell you what, Cal. I'll handle the press conference. You go on
home."

"You're sure? Thanks, Ellie." Cal finally grinned; it made him
look about seventeen years old again. Cal plucked his department-
issue rain slicker off the antler hook and left the station.

Ellie looked at her desk. There was a stack of faxes two inches
tall. Each sheet of paper represented a lost child, a grieving family.
She'd gone through them carefully, highlighted the similarities. As
soon as the press conference was over, she'd call the agencies back.
No doubt she'd be on the phone all night.

Last night Julia had transformed her girlhood bedroom into a
safety zone for her and her patient. The two twin beds still graced
the left wall, but now the spaces beneath them were filled to block
hiding places. In the corner by the window, she'd gathered almost
one dozen tall potted plants and created a mini forest. A long Formica table took up the center of the room, serving as a desk and
study space. Two chairs sat tucked up beside it. Now, however, she
realized what she'd missed: a comfortable chair.

For the past six hours, the child had stood at the barred, open
window with her arm stuck outside. Somewhere around noon,
a robin had landed on the windowsill and stayed there. Now a
brightly colored butterfly landed on her outstretched hand. If
Julia hadn't written it down, she would have stopped believing
she'd seen it.

Perhaps it was the girl's stillness. She hadn't moved in hours.

As Julia watched, another bird landed on the windowsill. The
bird cocked its head and warbled a little song.

The girl imitated the sound perfectly.

The bird appeared to listen, then sang again. The girl responded.

Julia glanced at the video camera set up in the corner. The red light was on. "Are you communicating with him?" she asked, making a note of it in her records. She knew it sounded ridiculous, but the girl and the bird seemed to understand each other. At the very least, the child was an accomplished mimic.

The bird flew away. Julia reached for the books on the table that served as her makeshift desk. *The Secret Garden, Alice in Wonderland,* and *The Velveteen Rabbit.* These were only three of the many titles donated by the generous townspeople. She opened *The Secret Garden* and began to read out loud, concentrating on giving her voice a gentle, singsong cadence. There was no doubt in her mind her patient couldn't follow the story, and yet, like all preverbal children, the girl liked the sound of it.

At the end of the chapter, Julia gently closed the book. She stood slowly, stretching. Long hours sitting tucked up to a makeshift desk at the end of her girlhood bed had left her with a crick in her neck. She went into the tiny bathroom that connected to their bedroom.

"I'm just going to go to the restroom, honey. I'll be right back. Do you know what—"

The girl skidded to a stop in the doorway and shoved the door open, wincing when it banged against the wall.

"You're upset," Julia said in a soothing voice. "Upset. You're getting angry. Did you think I was leaving?"

The girl looked nervously at the door.

"We'll keep the door open, but I need to go potty. You know that word? Potty?" The girl just stood there.

"I need privacy. You should . . . aw, hell. I'm peeing," Julia said, reaching for the toilet paper.

The girl was intent now, utterly focused, completely still.

Julia stood and pulled up her pants and then flushed the toilet. At the noise, the girl screamed and threw herself backward. She started to howl.

"It's okay," Julia said. "No hurt. No hurt. I promise." She flushed the toilet again and again, then washed her hands and moved slowly to her little patient. "Would you like me to keep reading?" She knelt down. She could see the remarkable turquoise color of the child's eyes; the irises were flicked with amber. Thick black lashes lowered slowly, then opened.

"Book," Julia said, pointing at the table.

The girl walked to the table and sat down on the floor beside it.

Julia drew in a sharp breath and sat down in the nearest chair. The girl moved a little closer.

Julia returned to the story. On and on, she read about Mary and Dicken and Colin and the garden. She read until night began to press against the window. A knock sounded at the door. The dogs started barking. The girl raced to her potted-plant sanctuary and hid behind the leaves.

The door opened slowly. Behind it, the golden retrievers were crazy to get inside. "*Down*, Jake. Elwood. What's *wrong* with you two?" Ellie slipped past them and slammed the door.

"You need to get those dogs trained," Julia said.

Ellie, who had a tray of food, set it down on the table. "How's the girl doing?"

"Better, I think. She seems to like being read to."

"Has she tried to escape?"

"No. She won't go near the shiny doorknob."

Ellie's sigh was long and slow. "I wish I could say I was making progress on my end. I had seventy-six parents in my office today. All of them had lost daughters in the last few years. Their stories . . . their pictures . . . It was awful."

"How did the press conference go?"

"Long. Boring. Full of stupid questions. My personal favorite was from the *National Enquirer*. They were hoping she had wings instead of arms. Oh, and your approval came through from DSHS. You're officially her temporary foster parent."

The girl crept out from her hiding place. Nostrils flaring, she smelled the air, then streaked across the room. Running low to the ground, she disappeared into the bathroom.

Ellie whistled. "Daisy said she ran like the wind."

Julia slowly walked toward the bathroom. Ellie followed her.

The girl was on the toilet with her diapers around her ankles. "Holy cow," Ellie whispered. "Did you teach her that?"

Julia couldn't believe it herself. "She walked in on me today. The sound of the flushing scared her to death. I would have *sworn* she'd never seen a toilet before."

"You think she taught herself? By seeing you once?"

Julia didn't answer. Any noise could ruin this moment. She inched into the room and handed the girl some toilet paper. The child frowned at the wadded paper. Finally she took it and used it. When she was finished, she slithered off the toilet, pulled up her diaper, and hit the lever. At the flushing noise, she screamed and ran.

"Wow," Ellie said.

They both stared at the girl, hiding in the forest of potted plants.

"Well," Ellie said at last, "I need to get back to the office." She handed Julia a piece of paper. "These are Peanut's and Cal's home numbers. If you need to go to the library, they'll stay with the kid."

"Thanks." Julia walked her to the door and let her out.

WHILE the girl was eating, Julia slipped out of the room and went downstairs. In the carport, she found two cardboard boxes that held the town's donations. She carried one back upstairs and set it down with a thud.

The girl looked up sharply.

Julia almost laughed at the sight of her. There was as much food on her face and hospital gown as had been on her plate. Whipped cream clung to her nose, her cheeks, and her chin in a white beard.

Julia bent down and opened the box. Three items lay on top. A beautiful, lacy white dress with pink bows on it, a doll in diapers, and a brightly colored set of plastic blocks.

She stepped back. "Toys. Do you know that word? Play. Fun. Dress up."

The girl stared at her, unblinking.

Julia bent down and picked up the soft cotton dress. The girl's eyes widened. She made a low growling noise. In a movement almost too fast and silent to be believed, she got out of her chair, yanked the dress out of Julia's grasp, and returned to her potted plants.

"Well, well, well," Julia said. "I see someone likes pretty things."

The girl started to hum. Her fingers found a tiny pink satin bow and began stroking it.

"You'll need to get clean if you want to wear the pretty dress."

Julia went into the bathroom and turned on the bathwater. "When I was your age, I loved taking baths. My mom used to add lavender oil to the water. It smelled so good. Oh, look, here's a little bottle of it left in the cabinet. I'll add some for you."

When she turned around again, the girl was there, standing just inside the open door, looking in.

Julia held out a hand. "No hurt," she said. "Come."

No response.

Julia skimmed her other hand through the water. "Nice. Come on."

The girl's steps forward were small, yet she was moving. Her gaze ping-ponged between the faucet and Julia's hand.

Julia let the water stream from her fingers. "Water. Wa-ter."

The girl stared at the water with fear and fascination.

Very slowly Julia bent down to undress the girl, who offered no opposition at all. She took hold of the girl's wrist and gently urged her toward the tub. "Touch the water. Just try." She showed her how, hoping the action would be mimicked.

It took a long time, but the girl finally dipped her hand in the water. She made a sound that was half sigh and half growl.

Julia stripped down to her bra and panties, then got into the tub. "You see? This is what I want you to do." When the girl stepped closer, Julia got out. "Your turn. Go ahead."

Cautiously, the girl climbed over the edge and lowered herself into the water. The minute she was in, she made a sound, almost like a purr, and looked up at Julia. Then she slapped at the water and kicked her feet and set about exploring. She licked the tiles and touched the grout and sniffed the faucet.

Finally Julia reached for the bar of soap. "Okay. I'm going to bathe you now. Clean. Soap." Very slowly she reached out and began washing the girl's hand.

The girl watched her with the intensity of a magician's apprentice trying to learn a new trick. Slowly, as Julia kept washing her hands, the girl began to relax. She was pliable when Julia gently turned her around and began washing her hair. As Julia massaged her scalp, the child began to hum. It took Julia a moment to realize that there was a tune within the notes. "Twinkle, Twinkle, Little Star."

Julia straightened. Of all the unexpected twists today, this was the most important. "Somebody sang that to you, little one. Who was it?"

The girl kept humming, her eyes closed.

Julia rinsed the long black hair, noticing how thick and curly it was. Tendrils coiled around her fingers like vines. She saw, too, the ugly scars near her shoulder.

Julia decided to sing along with the humming. "How I wonder what you are." She finished the song, then planted a hand to her chest and said, "Julia. Ju-li-a. That's me." She grabbed the girl's hand. "Who are you?"

The only answer was that intense stare.

With a sigh, Julia stood and reached for a towel. "Come on."

To her amazement, the girl stood up and got out of the tub.

"Did you understand? Or did you stand up because I did?" Julia dried the girl off, then dressed her. "There. All done." Accidentally she bumped the bathroom door. It shut hard; the mirror on the back of it framed the child.

The girl gasped loudly. She reached out for the mirror, trying to touch the other little girl in the room.

None of this made sense. The pieces didn't fit together. The wolf. The eating habits. The song. The toilet training. Certainly she would have seen her reflection in water, at least.

"That's *you*, honey. You. You look so pretty in that dress."

Julia moved in beside her. Now they were both in the mirror. "You see? That's me. Julia. And you."

Julia saw when understanding dawned. Very slowly the girl touched her chest and mouthed a sound.

"Did you say something? Your name?"

The girl stuck out her tongue. For the next forty minutes, the child played in front of the mirror. At one point, Julia left long enough to get her notebook and digital camera. She took several photographs, then wrote "Discovery of self" and documented every moment.

Finally Julia walked out of the bathroom. "Come on. Bedtime."

The girl didn't follow. They'd finished *The Secret Garden,* so Julia reached for *Alice in Wonderland.*

" 'Alice,' " she read aloud, " 'was beginning to get very tired of sitting by her sister on the bank, and of having nothing to do.' "

She had just introduced the white rabbit when the girl came out of the bathroom in her pretty white eyelet dress with pink ribbons.

She sidled up beside Julia.

"Hello, little one. You like it when I read?"

The girl's hand thumped down hard on the book.

Julia was too startled to respond. This was the first time the girl had really tried to communicate, and she was being quite forceful about it. The girl smacked the book again and looked at Julia. Then she touched her chest.

"Alice?" Julia whispered. "Is your name Alice?"

The girl thumped the book again.

Julia closed the book. On the cover of this ancient, well-worn edition was a painting of a pretty, blond-haired Alice with a large, brightly dressed Queen of Hearts. She touched the picture of the girl. "Alice," she said; then she placed her hand on the flesh-and-blood girl beside her. "Is that you? Alice?"

The girl grunted and opened the book, smacking the page.

Julia didn't know if the reaction had been to the name or the reading, but it didn't matter. For whatever reason, the little girl had finally stepped into this world. Julia almost laughed out loud; that was how good she felt right now.

"Okay, I'll keep reading, but from now on, you're Alice. So, Alice, when you get in bed, I'll read you a story."

SIX

ELLIE was alone in the police station, going through her notes from this afternoon. She couldn't be objective anymore. All she saw when she closed her eyes were broken families. It broke her heart.

"I could hear you crying outside."

She looked up sharply, sniffing hard. "I wasn't crying. I poked myself in the eye. What are you doing here, anyway?"

Cal stood there in a black T-shirt and faded jeans, smiling gently. How was it he always showed up when she felt most alone? "You okay?"

She wiped her eyes. The smile she gave him was pure fiction; both of them knew it. "I'm out of my league, Cal. What do I do?"

"You'll do what you always do, El. Whatever it takes. Come on. I'll buy you a beer."

"What about Lisa and the girls?"

"Tara's babysitting."

"I don't need a beer, Cal. Really. Besides, I should get home. You don't need to—"

"No one watches out for you anymore, El."

"I know, but—"

"Let me."

The simple way he said it plucked at her heart. She grabbed her black leather jacket and followed him out of the station.

The streets were empty again, quiet. A full moon hung in the night sky, illuminating streets still damp from a late-night rain.

Ellie tried not to think about the case as she drove. Instead, she focused on the comforting light from Cal's headlights behind her. As she parked in her yard, "Leaving on a Jet Plane" came on the radio.

"You used to love this song," Cal said, standing by her door, looking down at her through the open window.

"Used to." Ellie got out of the car. "Now it makes me think of husband number two. Only he left on a Greyhound bus. You've got to want to get away pretty bad to ride a bus."

"He was a fool."

"I guess you're talking about every man I've ever loved. And there are a truckload of them."

"But never the right one," he said quietly, studying her.

They climbed the porch steps. Inside, Julia sat at the kitchen table, with papers strewn all around her. "Hey," she said, looking up.

"Julia?" Cal said. His face lit up in a smile.

Julia stood up slowly, staring at him. "Cal? Cal Wallace? Is that really you?"

He opened his arms. "It's me."

Julia ran for him, let him hold her. "You still give the best hugs of any man I've ever met," she said, laughing.

He pushed the hair from his eyes. "It's good to see you again, Jules. Sorry it has to be under such crappy circumstances."

Ellie opened her can of beer. She unhooked her gun belt and radio and set them on the counter. "Want one?"

"No, thanks." Julia went to the table and fished through the mess of papers. "Here, El. I have these for you."

Ellie put her beer down. "Wow. That's her?"

"It is." Julia smiled like a proud parent. "I'm calling her Alice, by the way. From Wonderland. She responded to the story."

Ellie stared at the photograph. It was of a stunningly beautiful black-haired girl in a white eyelet dress. "How'd you do this?"

Julia's smile expanded. "We had a good day. I'll tell you all about it tomorrow. Now I need to run. Will you keep an eye on her?"

"Babysit? Me? Where are you going?"

"Back to the library. I need to find out about her diet."

"Go see Max," Cal said. "He'll be able to answer your questions."

Julia laughed. "Dr. Casanova on a Friday night? I don't think so."

"Don't worry about it, Jules," Ellie said. "You're hardly his type."

Julia's smile faded. "Thanks for the tip." She reached for her purse. "And thanks for babysitting. Good to see you again, Cal."

"Are you a moron?" Cal said to Ellie the minute Julia left. "Did you see the look on your sister's face when you said she wasn't Max's type? You hurt her feelings."

"Come on, Cal. I saw a picture of her last boyfriend. Mr. World Famous Scientist did *not* look like Max."

Cal sighed. "You'll never get it."

"Get what?"

He looked at her a long time. Finally, he shook his head. "I'm outta here. See you at work tomorrow."

"Don't leave mad."

He paused at the door and turned to her. "Mad?" His voice dropped. "I'm hardly mad, Ellie. But how would you know that? The only emotions you really understand are your own."

FORTY years ago, when the Rose Theater was built, it had been on the far edge of town. Now there were small two-story homes all around it, built in the timber-rich years to house millworkers. Across the street was the library, and just down the road was the new hardware store. Sealth Park, where the girl had first shown up, was kitty-corner to it.

Max came to the movies every Friday night alone. At first there had been talk about the weirdness of his habit, and women had shown up "accidentally" to sit with him, but in time, it had settled into a routine, and there was nothing the people of Rain Valley like better than routine.

After the movie, the crowd dissipated along the sidewalk and the cars drove away, until the street was empty except for an old white Suburban and his pickup truck.

Max was halfway to his truck when a movement across the street caught his eye: A woman was leaving the library, her arms full of books. Light from a streetlamp fell down on her, made her look too alive somehow, an angel against the dark night.

Julia.

She was almost to the Suburban when he said her name.

"Hey." He came up to her. "You're working late."

She laughed. It sounded nervous. "Obsessive is a word that's often been used about me."

"How's your patient?"

"Actually, I'd like to talk about her. Later. At the hospital."

"How about right now? We could go to my house."

Julia looked confused. "Oh, I don't think—"

"This is as good a time as any." Before she could say no, he walked over to his truck and climbed in. "Follow me."

ON EITHER side of the road, a thicket of black trees stood watch, their tops pressed into the starry night sky. At the turnoff, an old forest service wooden sign pointed to Spirit Lake.

Julia hadn't been out this way in years. Even now, with all the growth that had taken place on the peninsula, this was still the boonies—a stunningly beautiful corner of rain forest she couldn't quite match to Dr. Casanova. He struck her as a big-city guy. What was he doing out here in the middle of all this green darkness?

As she turned onto the gravel road, the ever present fog off the lake gave the forest a brooding, otherworldly feel. It occurred to her that she was following a man she barely knew into the deep woods. She wasn't entirely sure why. She wasn't really ready for a consult. Unfortunately, the past year had stolen more than her reputation. Somewhere along the way, she'd lost her confidence. She needed to hear that she was on the right path.

There it was. The true reason she was here.

Up ahead, Max turned onto the driveway. The gravel lane took a hairpin turn to the left and ended abruptly in a tree-ringed meadow. Max drove into the garage. Julia parked alongside it, grabbed her briefcase, and got out of the car.

The beauty of the place stunned her. She was in the middle of a huge grassy field, ringed on three sides by enormous evergreens. On the fourth border, mist rose like steam from Spirit Lake. Close by, an owl hooted.

"The infamous spotted owl," Max said, coming up beside her.

She eased sideways. "The enemy of every logger."

"And the champion of every tree hugger. Come on."

As she got close, she saw the craftsman-style beauty of the place. Plank cedar siding, handcrafted eaves, a big wraparound porch. Even the chairs seemed to have been handmade of clean, pure fir. It was the kind of house you didn't see in Rain Valley. Expensive and hand-tooled, yet plain. It was an Aspen or Jackson Hole kind of place.

He opened the front door and let her enter first. The first thing she noticed was the spicy aroma of bayberry; somewhere, he had a scented candle burning. Sexy music floated through the speakers. A gorgeous river-rock fireplace dominated the left wall. Windows ran the length of the house, looking out to the lake. The kitchen was small but perfectly constructed; every cabinet gleamed with candlelight. A huge trestle table took up most of the dining room, with a single chair next to it. In the living room, there was an ox-blood leather sofa, a big-screen plasma TV, and a thick alpaca rug covering the wide-planked floor.

There was also a jumble of ropes and pulleys by the back door. They lay in a tangled heap beside an ice pick and a backpack.

"Rock-climbing gear," she said. "Someone is into danger, I see."

"Don't try to psychoanalyze me, Julia. Drink?" He went into the kitchen area. "I have whatever you want."

"How about a glass of white wine?"

He returned a moment later carrying two glasses. White wine for her, Scotch on the rocks for himself. She took the glass he offered and sat down at the very end of the sofa, close to the arm. "Thanks."

He smiled. "You don't have to look so terrified, Julia. I'm not going to attack you."

For a moment, she was caught by the low, soft tone of his voice and the blue of his eyes. It was a little spark, barely anything, but it made her angry. "Let me guess again, Dr. Cerrasin. If I went out to the garage, I'd find a Porsche or a Corvette. Upstairs I'd find a king-size bed with expensive silk sheets, maybe a faux fur coverlet, and a nightstand drawer full of condoms."

A frown pulled at his forehead. "Who was he?"

"Who?"

"The man who hurt you so badly."

Julia was surprised by the perceptiveness of the question. For some reason, when she looked at him now, she saw a kind of loneliness in his gaze, an understanding that made her want to answer him.

And then she would be caught.

"May we please keep ourselves on track?"

"Ah. Business." He sat down. "Tell me about the girl."

"I'm calling her Alice for now. From *Alice in Wonderland*. She responded to the story."

"Seems like a good choice."

She started slowly. "When you first examined her, did you see any evidence of what her diet had been?"

"Facts, no. Ideas, I have a few. I'd say some meat and fish and fruit. I would guess she ate no dairy and no grains at all."

Julia looked at him. "In other words, the kind of diet that would come from living off the land for a long time."

"Maybe. How long do you think she was out there?"

There was the question whose answer could both make and break her. She started with the easy stuff. "I'm sure she's not deaf, and I strongly question the idea of autistic. Strangely enough, I think she might be a completely normal child reacting to an impossibly hostile environment. I believe she understands some language, although I don't yet know if she is choosing not to speak or if she's never been taught. Either way, she's not too old to learn."

"And?" he said, sipping his drink.

Her sense of vulnerability was so strong now, she felt her cheeks warm. There was nothing to do except dive in or walk away. "Have you ever read any of the accounts of wild children?"

"You mean, like that French kid? The one Truffaut made the movie about? Come on—"

"Hear me out, Max. Please."

He leaned back and studied her. "Tell me."

She started pulling stuff out of her briefcase. Papers, books, notes. She laid them all out on the cushion between them. As Max examined each article, she outlined her thoughts. She told him about the clear signs of wildness—the apparent lack of sense of self, the hiding mechanism, the eating habits, the howling. Then she offered the oddities—the humming, birdsong mimicry, the instant toilet training.

"So you're saying she was out there, in the woods, for most of her life. And the wolf they found with her was . . . what, her brother?"

She reached for her papers. "Forget it. I should have known—"

Laughing, he grabbed her hand. "Slow down. I'm not making fun of you, but you have to admit that your theory is out there."

"Maybe she was held hostage for a while and then let go. She's definitely been around people at some point."

"If that's true, it'll take a hell of a doctor to bring her back to this world."

Julia heard the question in his voice. She wasn't surprised. What did surprise her was how much it hurt. "I am a good doctor. At least, I used to be."

He leaned closer, touched her wrist. "I believe in you, you know. If that matters."

She looked at him, even though she knew instantly that it was a mistake. Candlelight softened his face; she saw tiny flames reflected in the blue sea of his eyes. "Thanks. It does."

Later, when she was back in her car and driving home alone, she thought back on it, wondered why she'd revealed so much to him.

The only answer came buried in her own lack of confidence.

I believe in you.

The irony was that there, in that room with the soft music

playing and the stairs that undoubtedly led to a huge bed, his words were what had seduced her.

THE next morning, Ellie was parked in front of the Ancient Grounds coffee stand when her radio beeped. Static crackled through the old black speakers, followed by Cal's voice.

"Chief? You there? Out."

Chief? When was the last time he called her that? She answered, "I'm here."

"Get down here. Now, Ellie. Out."

Ellie glanced up at the woman in the coffee-stand window. "Sorry, Sally. Emergency." She hit the gas. Two blocks later she turned onto Cates Avenue and almost slammed into a news van.

There were dozens parked in the street. White satellite dishes stood out against gray sky. Reporters huddled in clusters, their black umbrellas open. She hadn't taken three steps when they pounced.

". . . comment on the report . . ."

"No one is telling us where . . ."

". . . the exact location . . ."

She pushed through the crowd and yanked the station door open. Slipping through, she slammed it shut. "Hell."

"They were camped there at eight o'clock," Cal said. "Now they're waiting for your nine-o'clock update."

"What nine-o'clock update?"

"The one I scheduled to get them the hell out of here."

Peanut came around the corner holding a newspaper. The whole top half was a photograph of the girl. Her eyes were wild and crazy-looking; her hair was a nimbus of black and studded with leaves. She looked stark-raving mad. The byline read "Mort Elzick."

Ellie felt as if she'd been punched in the gut. So this was what he'd meant by "or else" when he'd demanded the interview. "Hell."

"The good news is, he didn't mention Julia," Cal said.

Ellie skimmed the article. "Savage girl steps out of forest and into the modern world, her only companion a wolf. She leaps from branch to branch and howls at the moon."

"They're starting to think it's a hoax," Cal said quietly.

Ellie's anger turned to fear. If the media decided it was a hoax, they'd pull out of town. Without publicity, the girl's family might never be found. She reached into her canvas book bag and pulled out the photograph Julia had taken.

"Circulate this," she said to Peanut. "We're calling her Alice. Maybe a name will make her seem more real."

GIRL comes awake slowly. This place is quiet, peaceful, even though she cannot hear the river's whispering.

She is not afraid. She cannot recall ever feeling like this. Usually her first thought is: *hide*. She has spent so long trying to make herself as small as possible.

She can breathe here, too, in this strange, squared world where light comes from a magical touch and the ground does not hold onto the bad smells of Him.

She likes it here. If Wolf were with her, she would stay in this square forever, sleeping where it is soft and smells of flowers.

"Iseeyouareawakelittleone."

It is the Sun-Haired Her who has spoken. She is at the eating place, with the thin stick in her hand that leaves markings. She is smiling.

Girl likes that smile. It makes her feel safe.

From the babble of forbidden sounds, Girl hears "Come."

She moves slowly, hunched over. She knows how dangerous a moment like this can be. She should always stay afraid, but the smile makes her forget the cave. Him.

She sits where Sun Hair wants her to. Girl remembers the rules, and she knows the price of disobeying. It is a lesson Him taught her. She eats the sweet, sticky food. When she is finished, Girl waits.

Sun Hair touches her chest and says the same thing over and over. "Jool Ya." Then she touches Girl. "A lis. A lis."

Girl knows *something* is expected of her. It seems Sun Hair wants Girl to make the bad sounds, but that can't be true. Her heart is beating so fast it makes her feel sick and dizzy.

Finally Sun Hair reaches into the square hole beside her and begins putting things Girl has never seen on the table. She wants to touch them, taste and smell them. "Kraon. Colorbook." Sun Hair is talking. In all the babble of sound, Girl begins to hear, "A lis play."

Play. Girl frowns. She almost knows these sounds.

But Sun Hair keeps talking, keeps pulling things out of the secret place, making Girl want to reach out.

Then Sun Hair pulls It out.

Girl screams and falls, hits her head and screams again, then crawls on her hands and knees toward the safety of the trees.

Sun Hair is talking in a haze of noise. Girl can make out no sounds, her heart is beating so fast.

There is almost no space between them. Sun Hair holds It out. Girl screams and claws her hair, blowing her nose.

Him is here. He will hurt her now.

Noooo . . .

Julia opened the door and threw the dreamcatcher out into the hallway, then shut the door. "There," she said in a soothing voice, moving slowly. "I'm sorry, honey. Really sorry." She knelt down in front of Alice so they were almost eye to eye.

Alice was absolutely still now, her eyes wide with fear.

"You're terrified," Julia said. "You think you're in trouble, don't you?" Very slowly, Julia touched Alice's wrist. The touch was fleeting and as soft as a whisper. "It's okay, Alice. You don't have to be scared."

At the touch, Alice made a strangled, desperate sound.

"Hmmm," Julia said, making a great show of looking around the room. "What shall we do now?" After a few moments, she picked up the old, battered copy of *Alice in Wonderland*. "Where did we leave young Alice?"

She went back to the bed and sat down. With the book open on her lap, she looked up.

Between two green fronds, a tiny, earnest face peered at her.

"Come," Julia said softly. "No hurt."

Alice remained in her safe spot. Julia started to read.

It is a trick. Girl knows this. She *knows* it.

And yet . . . the sounds are so soothing.

Don't do it, she thinks. *Trick.*

Very slowly she steps from her hiding place. Her heart is hammering. She is afraid it will break through her chest and fall onto the floor. She has been bad.

Screaming is very bad. She knows this. Out There are strangers and bad people. Loud sounds attract them.

As she approaches the bed, she lowers her head, looking as weak as possible. This she learned from the wolves.

"Al is?"

She looks up. Sun Hair's eyes are as green as new leaves. There is no anger on her face.

And she is stroking Girl's hair, touching her gently.

"Is okayokaynohurt. Comeherealis."

In a single motion, Girl leaps onto the bed and curls up in the soft place next to Her. It is the safest she has felt in a long time.

JULIA sat very still, although her mind was moving at light speed.

What was the story with the dreamcatcher?

Had Alice understood *Come here?*

She turned her attention back to the book and began reading where she left off. When she finished the chapter, she glanced down at Alice. The child lay curled catlike against her.

"You have no idea what it's like to feel safe in this world, do you?" Julia's throat tightened. "This is a good place to start, with you beside me. Trust is everything."

The instant the words were out of her mouth, she remembered the last time she'd said them. She'd been in the two-thousand-dollar leather chair in her office in Southern California, listening to Amber Zuniga, who was all dressed in black and trying not to cry.

Trust is everything, Julia had said. *You can tell me what you're feeling right now.*

Julia closed her eyes. That meeting had taken place only two days before Amber's rampage. Why hadn't she—

Stop.

Those thoughts led to a dark, hopeless place, and Alice needed her. Perhaps more than anyone had ever needed her. "As I was saying—"

Alice touched her. Julia saw it but barely felt it.

"That's good, honey," she whispered. "Come into this world. It's been lonely in yours, hasn't it? Scary?"

No part of Alice moved except her hand. Very slowly she reached out and petted Julia's thigh in an awkward gentle stroking. Making a sound low in her throat, a kind of purr, she looked up at Julia. Those amazing blue-green eyes were pools of worried fear.

"No hurt," Julia said, hearing the catch in her voice. She was feeling too much right now, and that was dangerous for a psychia-trist. She stroked Alice's soft black hair. "No hurt."

It took a long time, but finally Alice stopped trembling. For the rest of the morning, Julia alternated between reading and talking. They broke for lunch, but immediately afterward Alice returned to the bed and hit the book with her palm.

By two o'clock, Alice had curled up close and fallen asleep.

Julia eased off the bed, left the room, and retrieved the dream-catcher. It had to be of critical importance.

It was a poorly made trinket. No bigger than a tea saucer and as thin as the twigs that formed its perimeter, it was hardly threaten-ing. Several cheap, shiny blue beads glittered amidst a string web.

What was its connection to Alice?

In ordinary therapy, it could take months for a child to confront fears. Perhaps years. But this case was far from ordinary. The longer Alice remained in her solitary, isolated world, the less likely it was that she would ever emerge. Julia needed to force a con-frontation between the child lost in the woods and the girl who'd returned to the world. These two halves needed to integrate into a single personality or Alice's future would be at risk.

Desperate times called for desperate measures.

SEVEN

JULIA was still trying to formulate a dreamcatcher-use plan when Ellie barged into the room. Her keys and handcuffs jangled with every step. Behind her the dogs howled and scratched at the door, barking when she shut them out.

Alice ran for the plants and hid there.

Ellie clasped her keys, stilling them. "I need to talk to you."

Julia fought the urge to roll her eyes. The interruption had come at a particularly tender time. "Fine."

Ellie said, "I'll wait for you in the kitchen," and left the bedroom.

Julia hid her notebooks. "I'll be right back, Alice."

Alice stayed in her sanctuary, but when Julia reached for the knob, the child started to whimper.

"You're upset," Julia said softly. "You're feeling afraid that I won't come back, but I will."

She went downstairs and found Ellie out on the porch. Julia sat in the rocker. A pale breeze kicked up in the yard, sent drying leaves cartwheeling across the grass. She looked at her sister. "I need to get back to her. What's up?"

Ellie looked pale, shaken even. "The reporters are leaving town. They think the whole wild-child thing is a hoax. By tomorrow, the *Gazette* may be the only paper still writing about the story."

Julia knew suddenly why her sister looked nervous.

"We need you," Ellie said softly, "to talk to the press."

"Do you know what you're asking of me?"

"What choice do we have? If the story dies, we may never know who she is. And you know what happens to abandoned kids. The state will warehouse her, ignore her."

"I can get her to talk."

"I know. But what if she doesn't know her name? We need her family to come forward."

Julia couldn't deny it. The stakes came down to her best interest versus Alice's. "I wanted to have a success that could be balanced against the failures. They won't—"

"What?"

Believe in me. "Nothing." Julia looked away. The silvery river caught her gaze, reflecting like a strand of sunlight against the green lawn. "I guess I can't be any more ruined," she said at last, shivering slightly.

"I'll be there with you all the time. Right beside you."

"Thanks. Schedule a press conference for tonight. Say, seven o'clock. I'll show them the pictures and tell them what I can and let them ask their questions."

"I'm sorry," Ellie said.

Julia tried to smile. "I've lived through it before. I guess I can live through it again. For Alice."

JULIA could hear the racket in the police station. Dozens of reporters and photographers and videographers were setting up equipment, running sound and picture checks.

She and Ellie and Cal and Peanut were crammed into the employee lunchroom like hot dogs in a plastic pack.

"You'll be fine," Ellie said for at least the tenth time in the same number of minutes. As he had each time, Cal agreed.

Earl appeared at the door. The creases in his uniform were laser sharp. "They're ready for you, Julia." He flushed, stammered. "I mean, Dr. Cates."

One by one they peeled out of the lunchroom. Julia walked down the hallway, around the corner, and into the flash of her old life.

The crowd went wild, hurling questions like hand grenades.

"Qui-*et!*" Ellie yelled, holding her hands out. "Let Julia talk."

Gradually the crowd stilled.

Julia felt their eyes on her. Everyone in the room was judging her, finding her lacking in both judgment and skill. She drew in a sharp breath and caught it. Her gaze scanned the room.

In the back row were the locals. The Grimm sisters, Barbara Kurek, Lori Forman, and several of her high school teachers. And Max. He gave her a nod and a thumbs-up.

"As all of you know, I'm Dr. Julia Cates. I've been called to Rain Valley to treat a very special patient, whom we're calling Alice. I know many of you will wish to focus on my past, but I beg you to see what matters. This child is nameless and alone in the world. We need your help in finding her family." She held up a photograph.

"Dr. Cates, what would you say to the parents of those children who died in Silverwood?"

"How do you live with the guilt—"

"Did you know Amber had purchased a gun—"

Julia kept talking until her voice gave out. By the time it was over and the reporters had all run off to meet their deadlines, she felt utterly spent. Ellie came up to her.

"Damn, Jules, that was bad," Ellie said. "I didn't know—"

"You couldn't have."

"Can I do something to help?"

"Watch Alice for me, will you? I need to be alone for a while."

Ellie nodded.

Julia walked down the steps and into the cold lavender night. At the sidewalk, she turned left for no particular reason.

"Julia."

She turned.

He stood in the shadow of the street. "I bought the motorcycle when I worked in Watts—ER. Sometimes a man needs to clear his head. Seventy-five miles an hour on a bike will do it."

She should walk away, but she couldn't do it. "I think forty miles an hour would do it. I have a smaller head."

Smiling, he handed her a helmet. She put it on and climbed onto the bike behind him, circling him with her arms.

They drove down the cool, gray streets of town. Wind beat at her sleeves and tugged at her hair when they turned onto the highway. They drove and drove, through the night, along the narrow, bumpy pavement. She clung to him.

When he turned onto his gravel driveway, she didn't care. He parked the motorcycle in the garage. Wordlessly, they went into the house.

She took a seat on the sofa while Max brought her a glass of white wine, then built a fire and turned on the stereo. The first song that came on was something soft and jazzy.

"You don't need to go to all this trouble, Max. For God's sake, don't start lighting the candles."

He sat down beside her. "And why is that?"

"I'm not going upstairs."

"I don't remember asking you to."

She couldn't help smiling at that. Leaning back in the soft cushions, she looked at him over the rim of her wineglass. A thought flitted through her mind. *Why not?* She could follow him upstairs, climb into his big bed. For a glorious while, she could forget. Women did that kind of thing all the time.

"What are you thinking about?"

She was sure he could read her mind. She felt her cheeks grow warm. "I was thinking about kissing you, actually."

"And?"

"As my sister pointed out, I'm not your kind of woman."

He drew back. "Believe me, Julia, your sister has no idea what kind of woman I want."

She heard the edge in his voice. "I've been wrong about you," she said, more to herself than to him.

"You certainly jumped to a lot of conclusions."

"Hazard of the trade. I tend to think I know people."

"So you're an expert on relationships, huh?"

She laughed ruefully. "Hardly."

"Let me guess: You're a one-man woman. A hearts-and-flowers romantic."

"Now who's jumping to conclusions?"

"Am I wrong?"

She shrugged. "I don't know how romantic I am, but I only know one way to love. All or nothing. I'm sure it sounds stupid to you."

"It doesn't sound stupid," he said in a soft voice. "You have that same passion for your work; I can tell."

"Yes," she said. "That's why today was so hard."

For a long moment, they stared at each other. Finally Max said, "When I worked in Watts, we used to get gang shootings almost every night. One bleeding, dying kid after another. I couldn't save them all."

Their gazes locked. She felt as if she were falling into the endless sky of his eyes. "On good days, I know that. Today was not a good day. This was not a good year, actually."

"Tomorrow will be better." He reached for her, pushed a thin strand of hair from her eyes.

It would have taken nothing to kiss him then, just a slight movement. "You're good at it," she said shakily, drawing back.

"What?"

"Seducing women."

"I'm not seducing you."

But you are. She put down her wineglass and stood. "Thanks for all of this, Max. You really saved me tonight."

Slowly he got to his feet and walked her to the door. Without a word, he led her to the motorcycle and drove her home.

Something is wrong.

Girl senses it the second she opens her eyes. She stands still, sniffing the air. Many things, she has learned, can be sensed if one is quiet. The coming of snow smells like apples; a hunting bear makes a sound like snoring; danger can be heard in time if one is still. This was a lesson Her could never learn. She remembers how Her used to try talking to Girl: always the noise, and the trouble that came afterward.

Now, in her safe place, hidden by the small trees, she stares through the leaves at the Sun-Haired Her, who is so silent.

Has Girl done something wrong?

Across the room, Sun Hair looks up. She looks sad, like maybe her eyes are going to start leaking again. And tired. That was how Her looked before she got dead.

"Comeherealis." Sun Hair pats the bed.

Girl knows that Sun Hair will open the magic pictures and talk and talk. Girl *loves* that. The sound of her voice, the way she lets Girl be so close. Girl shuffles forward, trying to be small. She wishes Sun Hair would have on the happy face again. At her feet, she drops to her knees. The touch on her forehead is soft. Girl looks up.

"Thisisgoingtobedifficultalis. Trustmeokay."

Girl doesn't know what to do, how to show her obedience. Another little sound escapes her.

"I'm sorry." Sun Hair reaches into a box and pulls out It.

Girl freezes, expecting Him to break into this too-light place. She scrambles backward. Finally she screams. Once she starts, she can't stop. She knows it is Bad to make so much noise and that the Strangers will come and hurt her now, but she is past the rules. She hits one of the baby trees and it falls sideways, hitting the ground.

She screams more, trying to get away from it, but the white cave wall stops her. She hits it hard, feels pain thump her head.

Sun Hair is talking to her, stringing sounds together that are as pretty as shells, but It is still there, in Sun Hair's hand.

Girl starts to scratch herself, drawing blood. Sun Hair holds her so tightly that Girl can't claw herself. "Okayokayokayokay. Nohurt. Iknowyou'rescared. It'sokayokayokay."

Girl's screaming fades. She breathes hard and fast.

Sun Hair lets go of her. Slowly the pretty woman lifts It up.

Girl's eyes widen. She feels sick inside, desperate. The air in the room darkens. Everything smells like smoke and blood.

She remembers his dark, hairy fingers twisting the strings, threading the beads. She whimpers.

"Alis. Alis. It'sokayalis. Thisisadreamcatcher."

Dreamcatcher.

She feels her tummy start to shake.

In a single motion, Sun Hair breaks the dreamcatcher, then rips the strings apart. The beads fly across the floor.

Girl gasps. This is bad. He will come now. He will hurt them.

Sun Hair reaches into the box and pulls out another one. She rips it into pieces and throws it away.

Girl watches in awe. Sun Hair ruins another and another. She holds a dreamcatcher toward Girl. "Breakit. No hurt. No hurt."

Girl understands. Sun Hair wants *her* to break His toy.

He's not here. He's Gone. Is that what Sun Hair is trying to show her?

"Comeonalis. No hurt."

Sun Hair's watery green eyes make her feel all shaky inside. Slowly, her hand trembling, she reaches out to touch It.

It will burn you. . . .

But It doesn't. It feels like nothing, just string and twig.

She rips It in half, and at the motion, she feels something new inside her, a kind of rumble that starts deep in her belly and catches in her throat. It feels so good to break His toy, to reach into the box and grab another one.

She rips them all. As she breaks and snaps, she thinks of all the ways Him hurt her, and the water streams down her face, splatters the floor. When the box is empty, she looks up. She is gulping air as if she doesn't know how to breathe.

Sun Hair takes Girl in her arms and holds her tightly.

Girl doesn't know what is happening. Her body is shaking.

"It'sokayokayokay. Nohurt. You'resafenow."

She hears that, *feels* it.

Safe.

ELLIE shut the door firmly. Behind her, the golden retrievers were going crazy, barking, scratching, whining.

"Jules? Some people are here to see you. Doctors from the state care facility and the U.W., and a woman from DSHS."

Julia should have expected it. Just the suggestion in the media that Alice was "wild" would tempt other doctors, researchers.

"I'll be right back, Alice," she said to the girl hidden in the foliage, then followed her sister downstairs.

The living room seemed full of people at first glance. On closer examination, Julia saw that there were only three men and one woman. They simply appeared to take up a lot of space.

"Dr. Cates," said the man closest to her, moving forward. He was tall and scarecrow thin, with a nose big enough to hang an umbrella on. "I'm Simon Kletch, from the state's therapeutic residential care facility, and these are my colleagues: Byron Barrett and Stanley Goldberg, from the Behavioral Sciences lab at the U.W. You know Ms. Wharton, from DSHS."

Julia said evenly, "Hello."

A silence fell. Ellie asked them all to sit. Finally Simon cleared his throat. "Rumors are that this girl in your care is a wild child, or something close to that. We'd like to see her."

"No."

He seemed surprised by that. "You know why we are here. You're making no progress with her."

"That's hardly true. In fact, we've made huge strides. She can eat and dress herself and use the toilet. I believe—"

"You're civilizing her," the behavioral scientist said sharply. "We need to study her, Dr. Cates. As she is. We men of science have sought a child like this for decades. If taught to talk, she can be a gold mine of information. Think of it. What is true human nature? Is language instinctive? What is the link between language and humanity? She can answer these questions. Even you must see that."

"Even I? What does that mean?" she asked.

"Silverwood," Dr. Kletch said.

"You've never lost a patient?" she said sharply to him.

"Of course I have. We all have. But your failure was public. I'm getting a lot of pressure to take over this girl's case."

"I'm her foster parent as well as her therapist." By sheer force of will, she didn't call Dr. Kletch a bottom-feeder. Of course he wanted to "help" Alice; she could advance his career.

"Dr. Kletch believes that the minor child belongs in a therapeutic care facility," said the woman from DSHS.

"We need to study her." This from the behavioral scientist.

"And learn from her," added Dr. Kletch.

Julia stood. "You are like all the doctors who have been associated with children like this in the past. You want to treat her like a lab rat so that you can write your papers. When you move on, she'll grow up warehoused and medicated beyond recognition. I won't let you do it. She's *my* foster child and *my* patient. The state has authorized me to care for her, and that's what I intend to do." She forced a thin smile. "But thank you for your concern."

Ellie stepped forward. "And that's the end of the meeting. Thank you all for coming." She walked through the room, herded the crowd to the door, and locked it behind them.

When it was quiet again, the dogs started to whine upstairs. Julia could hear them pacing. "Alice is upset. I should get back."

Ellie moved forward fast, touched Julia's arm. "Don't let them get to you. You're helping that little girl."

Julia looked at her sister. "I missed things with Amber. Important things. I'm afraid—"

"Don't," Ellie said. "Don't let them win. We're all afraid."

For the next two weeks, the story of the disgraced doctor and the nameless, voiceless girl was headline news. The phones at the police station were jammed with calls from doctors, psychiatrists and counselors, kooks and scientists. Everyone, it seemed, wanted to save Alice from Julia's incompetence.

Julia worked with Alice from sunup to sundown; after the child fell asleep, she went to the library and spent more hours online.

On Wednesdays and Fridays, she went to the police station, where she conducted a press conference. The reporters asked endless questions about Julia's past, about her regrets and failures and lost patients. They cared nothing for the milestones of Alice's recovery. All that mattered was that she hadn't spoken. To them, it was proof Julia could no longer be trusted to help even one troubled child.

But in time, even the rehashing of Julia's past began to lose momentum. The stories went from headline news to a paragraph or two in local-interest sections. From her podium, Julia stared out at the few reporters. The national television stations weren't here anymore. Only a few local papers were left, and their questions were asked in dull, monotone voices.

"That's all for this week," Julia said, realizing the room had gone still. "The big news is that she can dress herself. And she can take or leave television, but she can watch cooking programs all day. Maybe that will strike a chord with someone—"

"Come on, Dr. Cates," said a man at the back of the room. "No one is looking for this kid."

There was a murmur of assent from the crowd as they talked among themselves. Julia heard the papery rustle of their laughter.

"That's not true. A child doesn't simply appear and disappear in this world. Someone is missing her."

After the press conference, Peanut drove her home. Ellie came out of the house almost immediately—so quickly, in fact, that Julia suspected she'd been at the door, waiting. Julia thanked Peanut and met Ellie halfway across the yard.

"She's howling again," Ellie said miserably.

"When did she wake up?"

"Five minutes ago. She's early. How'd it go?"

"Bad," Julia said, trying to sound strong and failing.

Julia went into the house and up the stairs. With each step, the howling grew in volume.

She was already talking when she opened the door. "Now, what's all this racket about, Alice? Everything is fine. You're just scared."

Alice streaked across the room in a blur of black hair, yellow dress, and spindly arms and legs. She pressed herself against Julia so closely that there was contact from waist to calf.

She put her hand in Julia's pocket. This was how it was lately. She needed to be next to Julia always, connected.

She was sucking her thumb and looking up at Julia with a vulnerability that was both heartbreaking and terrifying.

"Come on, Alice," Julia said, pretending it was perfectly natural to have a young human barnacle attached to her hip. She got out her Denver Kit, a collection of toys helpful in gauging development.

At the table, she set out the bell, the block, and the doll. "Sit down, Alice," she said, knowing Alice would sit down when she did.

Side by side, with Alice's hand still tucked in Julia's pocket, they sat down. With the Denver Kit spread out in front of them, Julia waited for Alice to make a move.

"Come on," Julia said. "Do something. Talk to me. I need you to talk, little one. I know you can do it."

Nothing. Just the gentle in and out of the girl's breathing.

Desperation plucked at Julia's confidence.

"Please." Her voice was a whisper now, not her therapist voice at all. She thought about the passing of time and the dwindling media interest. "Please. Come on . . ."

WHEN Ellie and Peanut arrived at the station, the building was quiet. Cal was at his desk, drawing a picture of some winged creature. At their entrance, he turned the paper facedown.

As if Ellie cared to see his bizarre sketches. He'd been doing them since sixth grade. The only difference between him and every other guy she'd known was that Cal had never outgrown it.

"The DNA results are back," Cal said. "I put them on your desk."

They all looked at one another. After a long moment, Ellie sat down and opened the official-looking envelope. The pages inside had a lot of mumbo-jumbo scientist speak, but none of it mattered. At the midsection was the sentence: "No match found."

Ellie felt a wave of defeat. Hell, she'd thrown her sister to the wolves, and for what? They were no closer to an ID now than they'd been three weeks ago.

Cal and Peanut pulled chairs across the room and sat in front of the desk. "You did the best you could," Cal said gently.

"No one coulda done any better," Peanut agreed.

After that, no one spoke. A real rarity here.

Ellie pushed the papers across her desk. "Send these results out to the people who are waiting. How many requests have we gotten?"

"Thirty-three. Maybe one is the match," Peanut said.

They all knew how unlikely that was. None of the thirty-three requests had described Alice's birthmark.

Ellie rubbed her eyes. "Let's pack it in for the night. You can send out the DNA reports tomorrow, Pea."

Peanut stood up. "I'm meeting Benji at the Big Bowl. Anyone want to join me?"

"There's nothing I like better than hanging around with fat men in matching polyester shirts," said Cal. "I'm in."

Peanut glared at him. "You want me to tell Benji you called him fat?"

Cal laughed. "It'll come as no surprise to him, Pea."

"Don't get started, you two," Ellie said tiredly. "I'm going home.

You should, too, Cal. It's Friday night. The girls will miss you."
"The girls and Lisa went to Aberdeen to see her folks." He looked
at her. "You used to love bowling."

Ellie found herself remembering the summer she and Cal had
worked at the Big Bowl's lunch counter. It had been that last magical year of childhood, before all the sharp edges of adolescence
had poked through. They'd been best friends.

"That was a long time ago, Cal. I can't believe you remember it."

"I remember." There was an edge to his voice that was odd. He
walked over to the hooks by the door and grabbed his coat.

"It's karaoke night," Peanut said, smiling.

Ellie was lost, and Peanut damn well knew it. "I guess a margarita couldn't hurt." It was better than going home. The thought of
telling Julia about the DNA was more than she could bear.

LIKE a riverbank in a spring thaw, the erosion of Julia's self-
confidence was a steady, plucking movement. While she still believed that Alice understood a few words here and there, she was
making no progress in getting the girl to speak. Every day, Dr.
Kletch left a message on the machine. It was always the same.
You're not helping this child enough, Dr. Cates. Let us step in.

This afternoon, when she'd put Alice down for her nap, Julia
had knelt by the bed, stroking the girl's soft black hair, patting her
back, thinking, *How can I help you?*

She'd felt the sting of tears in her eyes; before she knew it, they
were falling freely down her cheeks.

She'd only just redone her makeup for the press conference
when a car drove up outside. She was halfway down the stairs
when she ran into Ellie, coming up.

"You okay?" Ellie asked, frowning.

"I'm fine. She's asleep."

"Well, Peanut's waiting in the car. I'll stay here today."

They drove the mile and a half to town in a heavy rain. The
drops on the windshield and roof were so loud that conversation
was impossible. While Peanut parked the car, Julia opened an umbrella and ran for the station. She was hanging up her coat and
walking to the podium when it struck her.

Every seat was empty.

No one had come.

EIGHT

ELLIE was in the living room when Julia got home. She knew how the press conference had gone by her sister's disappointed look. She saw all the new lines on Julia's face, the pallor of her skin, and the pounds she'd lost. The woman was practically a scarecrow.

"No one showed," Julia said, sitting down stiffly.

Ellie glanced up the stairs, thinking of Alice. "What do we do now?"

Julia looked down at her hands in her lap. Her sudden fragility was sad to see. "I'm making remarkable progress, but . . ."

Ellie waited. "But what?"

Julia finally looked up at her. "Maybe . . . I'm *not* good enough."

"Of *course* you're good enough." Ellie frowned. "What would you do right now if you were your old self and that girl upstairs needed your help?"

Julia shrugged. "I'd go up and try something radical. See if a little shaking up would help."

"So, do it."

"And if it's the wrong course?"

"Then you try something else. You've got to keep trying." Ellie leaned forward. "That little girl needs you to believe in yourself."

JULIA squared her shoulders and tilted her chin up, adopting a winner's stance. Combined with the fledgling hope of *Maybe I'm still okay,* it gave her the strength to open her old bedroom door.

Alice lay in her bed, curled up like a little cinnamon roll. As always, she was on top of the covers. No matter how cold the room got, she never pulled the blankets over her.

It was nearing six o'clock. Any minute, Alice would wake from her nap. Julia shut the door behind her and went to the table, where she read through her morning's notes.

Alice still spends long spans of time at the window, but only if I will stand with her. I have noticed increasing curiosity about her world. She looks under things, pulls out drawers, opens closets. Twice today she dragged me toward the door. The dogs were on the other side, whining. Alice is beginning to wonder what's beyond this room.

Julia heard a movement on the bed. The old wooden frame creaked as Alice got up. As always, the girl woke up and went straight into the bathroom. She ran nimbly, almost soundlessly, across the floor. Moments later the toilet flushed. Then Alice ran for Julia, tucking up alongside her, putting her tiny hand in Julia's pants pocket.

Julia put her notebook on a high shelf. Alice moved soundlessly beside her, never losing contact. Julia went to the chest of drawers and withdrew a pink sweater and a pair of blue overalls.

"Put these on," she said to Alice, who complied. It took her several attempts to put on the sweater—she kept confusing the neck and sleeves. When she started breathing heavily and snorting, Julia dropped to her knees.

"Here. This is where your head goes through."

Alice instantly calmed and let Julia help her, but she drew the line at shoes. She simply would not put them on.

"Come with me," Julia said, "but your feet will be cold."

Holding hands, Julia led her toward the door.

Alice halted as they drew close. A tiny, mewling sound escaped. She stared at the bright, shiny knob in horror.

"It's okay. No hurt. You're safe." Julia squeezed Alice's hand in reassurance. When the girl's trembling subsided, Julia reached for the door.

Alice tried to pull back.

Julia held fast to her hand. "It's okay. You're afraid, but no hurt." She twisted the knob and pushed the door open. The hallway was revealed, long and straight, illuminated by sconces. The dogs were there. At Alice's presence, they erupted into barking, prancing movements and started to run toward her.

Alice held out one small, pale hand and made a gurgling sound. The dogs stopped in their tracks and dropped to their haunches.

Alice looked up at Julia.

"Okay, Alice," Julia said, not sure what she was agreeing to, but she saw the question in the child's eye.

Very slowly, Alice let go of Julia's hand and moved toward the dogs. They remained perfectly still. When Alice reached them, it was as if a switch had been turned. The dogs pounced to life, licking Alice and pawing her. Alice threw herself at them, giggling when they nuzzled her throat.

Julia soaked in the new sight of Alice's smile.

Long minutes passed. Finally Alice drew back and tucked her hand in Julia's waistband. "Come on, Alice," Julia said.

Alice let herself be pulled slowly into the hallway. They paused at the stairs. Still holding the little hand, Julia took one step down.

Alice gazed at her for a long time, obviously gauging this turn of events. Finally she followed. They made their way down to the living room one step at a time. By the time they reached the sofa, it was full-on night.

Julia opened the porch door, revealing the darkness outside. The air smelled of coming winter, of dying leaves and rain-soaked grass and the last few roses on the bushes alongside the house. Alice made a quiet, gasping sound and took a step on her own, then another, until they were on the porch. The old cedar boards creaked.

She was easily led now, down the steps into the grassy yard. The sound of the river was loud; leaves floated downward. Alice let go of Julia's hand and grabbed onto her pant leg instead; then she dropped to her knees. She sat utterly still, her head bowed.

Alice lifted her face to the night sky and let out a howl that undulated on the air. It was a noise so sad and lonely that you wanted to cry, or howl along with her. It made you think of all that you'd ever loved, all that you'd lost, and all the love you'd never known.

"Go ahead, Alice," Julia said. "Let it all out."

When the howling faded, Alice sat so motionless it was as if she'd melted onto the landscape. Then, all at once, she picked up a tiny yellow dandelion from the darkness in front of her. In a single motion, she separated the root from the stem and ate the root.

"This is the world you know, isn't it?" Julia tried to get Alice to let go of her pants so the child could wander freely, but Alice wouldn't let go. "I won't leave you, but you don't know that, do you? Someone has already left you out in these woods, haven't they?"

A crow cawed; then an owl hooted. Within seconds, the forest at the edge of their property was alive with birdsong.

Alice imitated each of the calls, each of her versions flawless. The birds answered her. In the darkness, it took Julia a moment to notice what was happening. The yard was full of birds; they formed a wide circle around them.

Far away, a wolf howled. Alice answered the call.

A shiver crept down Julia's spine. Alice tugged on Julia's hand. It was the first time the girl had ever tried to lead. Julia couldn't help smiling. "That's good, little one. I'll follow."

Alice pointed at the bare rosebushes. A single bud remained. She pulled free and approached the roses with a confidence Julia had never seen before.

"Be careful, Alice," Julia said. "There are thorns."

The girl reached for a single pink bud, plucked it from the bush.

Alice petted the rose with a gentleness that surprised Julia, then slowly walked to the river, moving down the bank to the place where the grass was tamped down and dead. She dropped to her knees, howling softly. Coming up behind the girl, Julia touched her shoulder.

Alice turned around and peered up at Julia through eyes so dark and unfathomable they seemed to reflect the endless night sky.

Julia knelt in the damp grass. "Talk to me, Alice. What are you feeling right now? You don't need to be afraid. You're safe here."

THE night is full of noises. Sometimes it is so loud, Girl has trouble hearing the quiet beneath. A tightness in her chest scares her. She should feel safe on the edge of her world.

She could run away if she wanted to. But now she doesn't want to leave. This is where she wants to be. With Sun Hair.

"Talktomealis." Sun Hair is there, in front of her.

Girl is afraid and confused. What if Sun Hair doesn't want Girl to stay? Maybe she is being let go now.

Sun Hair bends down. "Canyoutalktomealis?" Sun Hair is smiling. "Ineedyoutotalkalis. Isanyofthismakingsense?"

Girl hears something. She frowns, trying to understand. *Need.*

Talk. Did Sun Hair *want* Girl to make the sounds that meant things?

No. It couldn't be. That is the Bad Thing.

Sun Hair's smile disappears. She makes a sad, lonely sound and straightens. "MaybeIwasrightandImnottheonetohelpthisgirl."

It seems now that Sun Hair is miles away from Girl and getting farther. Soon Girl won't be able to find her.

"Ineedyoutotalklittleone." Sun Hair takes a breath. "Please."

Please.

From somewhere, Girl remembers this sound. It is special, like the first bud in spring.

Sun Hair *wants* Girl to make the forbidden noises.

Girl gets slowly to her feet. She feels light-headed with fear.

Sun Hair is walking away now. Girl's fear pushes her forward. She follows, grabs Sun Hair's hand, and holds so tightly it hurts.

Sun Hair kneels. "ItsokayAlis. Imnotleavingyou."

Leaving. This is as clear as the sound of a river rising.

Girls looks at Sun Hair. It will take all her heart, everything she has inside of her to think and remember and make the forbidden noise.

"Whatisit? Areyouokay?" Sun Hair's voice is so soft.

Girl looks up into those pretty green eyes. Girl wants to be good. She licks her lips, then says quietly, "Stay."

Sun Hair makes a sound like a stone falling in deep water. "Did you say stay?"

Girl gives her the special rose. "Peas."

Sun Hair's eyes start leaking again, but this time her mouth is curled up in a way that makes Girl feel warm inside. She puts her arms around Girl and pulls Girl toward her.

It is a feeling Girl has never known before, this holding of the wholeness of her. She closes her eyes and lets her face bury into the softness of Sun Hair's neck.

"Stay," she whispers again, smiling now.

JULIA lay in her bed, staring at the ceiling. She was too wound up to sleep. Her blood seemed to be tingling just beneath her skin.

Stay.

That moment kept repeating itself, over and over. Each time she remembered it, she felt a shiver of awe at what it meant.

Until tonight, that very moment when Alice had spoken her first word, Julia hadn't even realized how lost she'd become, how far she'd fallen. Her grasp on confidence had been fragile and slippery. But now she was *back*. She was her old self.

And she'd never give up again. First thing tomorrow she would call the doctors and scientists and tell them to back off. No one would take Alice from her.

She needed to talk to someone tonight, to share her triumph. And there was only one person who would understand.

You're crazy, Julia.

She threw the covers back and got out of bed. Dressing in sweats and a T-shirt, she left the room. There was no light beneath Ellie's bedroom door. She didn't want to wake her sister. Besides, Ellie couldn't really understand the import of tonight's events.

Without letting herself think, she went out to the car.

MAX heard the car and hoped like hell it wasn't an emergency. This was his only night off, and he'd finished his second Scotch.

He heard footsteps on the porch. Then a knock on his door.

"I'm out here," he called. "On the deck."

There was a pause, a long time of quiet. He was about to call out again when he heard footsteps.

It was Julia. At the sight of him in the hot tub, she stopped dead.

She stood beneath the orangey bulb that illuminated the covered deck. He couldn't help noticing how pale she looked, how thin and drawn. Her eyes seemed too big for her fragile face.

"A hot tub, doctor? How cliché."

"I went climbing today. My back is killing me. Get in."

"I don't have a suit."

"Here. I'll turn off the light." He pressed the button, and the tub went dark. "There's wine in the fridge."

She stood there a long time. Finally she turned and left. He heard the front door open and close. A few moments later she returned, holding a wineglass and wearing a towel.

"Close your eyes," she said.

"Okay, okay," he said, laughing. "My eyes are closed."

He heard the muffled thump of the towel landing in a chair and the quiet splashing of her getting in the hot tub. He opened his eyes. She sat pressed to the tub, her arms at her sides. The white lacy bra she wore had gone transparent.

"You're staring," she said, sipping her wine.

"You're beautiful."

"I struggle to calculate how many times you've said that to women foolish enough to get into this tub."

"Actually, you're the first woman ever."

She frowned. "Really?"

"Really."

She turned slightly, looked out at the lake. The silence turned awkward. "I don't know anything about you, Max."

"What do you want to know?"

"Why are you in Rain Valley?"

He gave her the answer he gave everyone. "One too many gang shootings in L.A."

"Why do I think that's only part of the story?"

"I keep forgetting you're a shrink."

"And a good one." She smiled. "So tell me."

He shrugged. "I'd been having some . . . personal issues, so I decided to make some changes. I love the mountains."

"Sometimes you have to get away," she said quietly.

He nodded. "It was easy to leave Los Angeles. My parents are currently on leave from their teaching jobs, traveling Central America looking for some bug extinct for eons. My sister is in Thailand. Tsunami relief. My brother works for a big-time think tank in the Netherlands. Every year I get a Christmas card that says: 'My best wishes to you and yours, Dr. Kenneth Cerrasin.' "

Julia laughed.

He put down his drink. "Why are *you* here, Julia?"

"In Rain Valley? You know why."

"Here," he said, letting his voice soften.

"Alice spoke tonight. She said *stay.*"

"I knew you'd do it."

A smile overtook her face; it came all at once. The porch light bathed her skin, tangled in her hair. She moved ever so slightly toward him. Water rippled against his chest. "The thing is, I've been waiting every day for weeks for this to happen. . . ."

"And?"

"And when it happened, all I could think was that I wanted to tell you."

He couldn't have stopped himself if he'd tried—and he didn't try. He closed the tiny distance between them and kissed her. It was the kind of kiss he'd forgotten about. He whispered her name, hearing something unfamiliar in his voice.

She eased away from him.

"I'm sorry," she said, looking as shaken as he felt. "I need to go."

He reached out, took hold of her arm. "There's something between us," he said.

"Yes," she said. "That's why I'm leaving."

Without even bothering to say good-bye, she left him.

He sat there a long time, alone, staring out at nothing.

JULIA dreamed of Max all night. She was so caught in the web that when she woke, it took her a second to realize that someone was knocking on the bedroom door.

It sounded like an advancing army. It was, instead, one small, determined little girl, standing by the closed door.

Julia smiled. "I'd say someone wants to go outside again." She swung her legs out of bed and stood up.

After she dressed, Julia walked casually to their worktable, where all the books and blocks and dolls were spread out. There, she sat down and put her feet on the table. "If a girl wants to go outside, she should use her words."

Alice stamped her foot and punched the door.

"It won't work, Alice. You see, now I know you can talk." She got up and went to the window, pointing at the yard that was just beginning to turn pink with the dawn. "Outside." She said it over and over, then took the girl's hand and led her to the bathroom.

She pointed at herself in the mirror. "Ju-li-a," she said. "Can you say that? Ju-li-a."

"Her," Alice whispered.

Julia's heart did a little flip. "Ju-li-a," she said again. "Ju-lia."

She saw when Alice understood. The child made a little sound of discovery; her mouth formed an O. "Jew-lee."

Julia grinned. This was how people must feel when they scaled Everest. Giddy with triumph. "Yes. Yes. Julia." She pointed at Alice's reflection. "Now, who are you?" She touched Alice's chest, just as she'd touched her own.

Alice's frown deepened. "Girl?"

"Yes! Yes! You're a girl." She touched Alice's chest again. "Who are you? Julia. Me. And you?"

"Girl," she said again, her frown turning into a scowl.

"Do you know your name, little one?"

This time there was no answer. Alice waited a long moment, still frowning, then went to the door again and thumped with her fist.

Julia laughed. "You might not have much of a vocabulary, but you know what you want. Okay. Let's go outside."

ALICE was at the table "reading" a picture-book version of *The Velveteen Rabbit.* She hadn't moved in almost an hour.

Julia sat down beside her. Alice immediately took hold of her hand, pointed to the book, and grunted.

"Use your words, Alice."

"Read. Boo."

"Who wants me to read?"

Alice frowned heavily. "Girl?"

"Alice," Julia said gently. She had spent the better part of two weeks trying to get Alice to reveal her real name. With each passing day, however, Julia was increasingly certain that she didn't remember—or had never known—it. That devastated her. It had to mean that, in the formative years, after about eighteen months to two years, no one had called this child by name.

"Alice," she said gently. "Does Alice want Julia to read the book?"

Alice thumped the book with her palm, smiling. "Read. Girl."

"I'll tell you what. If you play with the blocks for a few minutes, I'll read to you. Okay?"

Alice made a disappointed face.

"I know." Smiling, Julia bent down and retrieved her box of big plastic blocks. She set them out on the table carefully. "Take the block that has the number one on it. One."

Alice immediately grabbed the red block and pulled it toward her.

"Good girl. Now the number four."

They kept at the counting for almost an hour. In less than two weeks, Alice had memorized all the numbers up to fifteen. But by one o'clock, she was getting cranky. It was near nap time. She smacked the book again. "Read."

"Okay, okay." Julia pulled Alice into her lap. Alice popped her thumb into her mouth and waited. Julia had only gotten through the first paragraph when there was a knock at the door.

Ellie stepped into the room. Alice made a strangled sound and ran to her hiding place in the potted plants.

Ellie sighed. "Is she *ever* going to stop being afraid of me? How do I make her understand I trapped her for her own good?"

"She can't understand that complex an idea yet."

"Thirty-nine years old and I can't make one little girl like me. No wonder I'm sterile. God saw my parenting potential."

Julia heard the heartache in her sister's voice. "I'll tell you what, Ellie. Tonight, why don't you read Alice a story. I'll go downstairs, leave you two alone."

"She'll stay in the fake forest."

"Then try again. Sooner or later, she'll give you a chance."

"Okay. I'll give it a try." She looked at Julia. "Thanks."

Julia nodded.

Ellie started to leave. At the door, she paused and turned around. "I almost forgot why I came in here. Thursday is Thanksgiving. We could order a turkey, invite people over."

"Cal's family?" Julia said.

"Of course. Is there anyone else you'd like to ask?"

"What about Max? He doesn't have any family here."

Ellie's gaze was a laser beam. "You're playing with fire, little sister, and you burn easily."

"It's just a dinner invitation."

Ellie wasn't fooled. "Yeah, right."

ELLIE basted the twenty-pound turkey with butter, placed it on the roasting pan, and put it in the oven. She looked around the kitchen. "What's next?"

"I'll get started on the potatoes." Julia headed for the porch. When she opened the door, cold air swept through, mingling with the hot air from the roaring fireplace to create a perfect mixture of warmth and crispness. On the top step, she sat down. A bag of potatoes was on the floor at her feet, along with a peeler.

Ellie poured two mimosas and followed her sister out to the porch. She handed Julia a glass and sat down.

Together they stared out at the backyard.

Alice was dressed in a pretty eyelet dress and pink tights, sitting on a wool blanket. There were birds all around her—mostly crows and robins—fighting to eat from her hand. Beside her, a bag of past-their-prime potato chips provided her with endless crumbs.

"Why don't you take her a glass of juice? She's really calm with her birds. It might be a good time to start bonding."

"She looks like a Hitchcock movie. What if the birds peck my eyes out?"

Julia laughed. "They'll fly away when you get there." She reached into her apron pocket and pulled out a red plastic measuring cup. "Give her this."

"She still gaga over the color red?"

"Yep." Julia stood. "I'll set the table. You'll be fine."

"Okay." Ellie walked down the steps across the grass. The birds flew off, and Alice jumped up, looking cornered, although the whole yard lay open behind her. Fear rounded her eyes.

"Hey," Ellie said, standing motionlessly. "No net. No shot." She held her palms out to prove it. The red cup was bright in her hand.

Alice frowned. After a minute, she pointed and grunted.

Ellie felt the magical pull of possibility unwind between them. This was the first time that Alice hadn't run from her. "Use your words, Alice." It was what Julia always said.

As the silence went on, Ellie tried another tack. She started to sing, quietly at first, but as Alice's frown faded, Ellie turned up the volume. She sang one kid-friendly song after another. When she got to "Twinkle, Twinkle, Little Star," Alice's whole demeanor changed. A curve that was almost a smile touched her lips.

"Star," Alice whispered at exactly the right time in the song.

Ellie bit back a grin by sheer force of will. When the song was over, she bent down and handed Alice the measuring cup. Alice stroked it, touched it to her cheek, then looked up expectantly.

Now what?

"Star. Peas."

Ellie did as she was asked. She was on her third go-round when

Alice cautiously moved to her. The little girl sat down in the grass.

Ellie felt as if she'd just bowled a strike in the tenth frame. She wanted to high-five someone. Instead, she kept singing.

At some point, Julia joined them. The three of them sat in the grass, beneath a graying November sky, and sang the songs of their youth while the Thanksgiving turkey browned inside the house.

MAX knew he should have left the house a half an hour ago. Instead, he'd poured himself a beer and turned on the television.

He was afraid to see Julia again.

All or nothing.

He could hear Susan's voice in his head, gently admonishing him. If she'd been here, beside him, she would have given him one of her crooked I-know-you smiles. He picked up the phone and dialed a California number. Susan answered on the first ring.

"Hey," he said.

"Hey. Happy Thanksgiving."

"To you, too."

He waited for her to say something more.

"Hard day for you, huh?" Her voice was soft, sad. He heard talking in the background. A man's voice. A child's.

"I've been invited to Thanksgiving dinner."

"That's *great.* Are you going?"

He heard the doubt in her voice. "I *am.*"

"Good."

They talked for a few minutes about little things, nothing that mattered, then came to a natural pause. Finally Susan said, "I need to get back. We've got company. Take care of yourself."

"You, too," he said.

Her voice lowered. "Let it go, Max. It's been too long."

"Maybe I will," he said softly.

In the end, as always, it was Max who hung up first.

It was time. There was no reason for him to be hiding out here, worrying, and the truth was, he *wanted* to go. It had been too long since he'd enjoyed a holiday.

When he parked at the house, he crossed the yard and slowly climbed the steps. He heard a car drive up behind him. Footsteps crunched through the gravel, accompanied by the high-pitched chatter of children's voices.

"Doc!" It was Cal's voice, calling out to him.

Before he could answer, the front door opened and Ellie stood there, staring at him. It was a cop's look: assessing.

"I'm glad you could make it," she said, stepping back to let him in. Dressed in velvet pants and a sparkly black sweater, she was every inch the legendary small-town beauty queen.

He handed her the bottles of wine he'd brought. "Thanks for inviting me." Julia was kneeling beside Alice in the living room. His heart did a little flip at the sight of her.

Ellie maneuvered him over. "Look who's here, little sis."

He stared down at Julia, wondering if she felt as out of breath right now as he did.

Slowly she stood. "Max, I'm glad you could make it."

"So," he said, "how's our wild one?"

Julia launched into a monologue, smiling often and looking at Alice with a love so obvious it made him smile, too. He felt swept along, and then he remembered: All or nothing.

He was looking at *all*.

"Max?" She frowned. "I'm putting you into a coma, aren't I?"

He touched her arm. Realizing it was a mistake, he pulled back sharply. Too late. It was like touching a light socket.

She stared up at him.

"I've been thinking about you." The words were out of his mouth before he could stop them.

"Yeah," she said. "I know what you mean."

Max had no idea what to say next. Finally he made some excuse and went to the makeshift bar set up in the kitchen.

For the next hour, he tried not to look at Julia. He laughed with Cal and Ellie and the girls and helped out in the kitchen.

At a few minutes before four o'clock, Ellie announced that dinner was ready. All the while, Julia had been kneeling beside Alice, who stood hidden behind a potted ficus tree. The child was obviously frightened, and it was literally magic when Julia finally shuttled her to the table and seated her on a booster seat between herself and Cal.

Max took the only available seat. It was next to Julia.

Ellie looked at them across a sea of food. "I'm so glad you're all here. It's been a long time since this table hosted a Thanksgiving dinner. Will everyone hold hands, please?"

Max reached right and took the hand of one of Cal's daughters. Then he reached left and touched Julia. He didn't look at her.

Ellie smiled at Cal. "Why don't you start for us?"

Cal looked thoughtful. "I'm thankful for my beautiful daughters. And to be in this house for Thanksgiving. I'm sure Lisa's missing us all. There's nothing worse than a business trip over the holidays."

His three daughters went next.

"I'm thankful for my daddy."

"My puppy."

"My pretty new boots."

Next came Ellie. "I'm thankful for my sister coming home."

Julia smiled. "And I'm thankful for little Alice here, who has shown me so much." She leaned over and kissed the girl's cheek.

All Max could think about was how warm Julia's hand felt in his, how steadied he was by her touch.

"Max?" Ellie said. They all looked at him. Waiting.

He looked at Julia. "I'm thankful to be here."

NINE

WINTER came to the rain forest like a hoard of greedy relatives, taking up every inch of space and blocking out the light. The rains became earnest in this darkening season of the year, changing from a comforting mist to a constant drizzle.

In the midst of all this dark weather, Alice blossomed. Like a fragile orchid, she bloomed within the walls of this house that each day felt more like a home. Now she strung two words together regularly—and sometimes three. She knew how to get her ideas and wants across to the two women who had become her world.

As remarkable as Alice's changes were, Julia's were perhaps even more surprising. She smiled easier and more often, and she made outrageously bad jokes. She put on a few much needed pounds.

Most important, she reclaimed her self-confidence. She was so proud of Alice's accomplishments. The two of them seemed almost to be communicating telepathically, that's how close they were. Alice still shadowed Julia everywhere, but more and more often, she would venture a little ways on her own. Sometimes she came to "Lellie," too, showing off some trinket she had found. Lately, she had begun to curl up against Ellie for story time.

It made Ellie happy. And it didn't. Sometimes Ellie watched her sister's growing bond with Alice, and it made her heart ache. They would leave this house someday, and Ellie would be alone, like before. Only it would be different now because she'd been part of a family again. Now that she'd lived in a house where a child played games and followed you around and kissed you good night, would she be okay again on her own?

"You don't look so good," Cal said to her from across the room.

"Yeah? Well, you're ugly."

Cal laughed. Taking off his headset, he walked out of their office. A few moments later he returned with two cups of coffee. "Maybe you need caffeine." He handed her the cup.

She looked up at him, wondering why she couldn't find men like him attractive—men who kept their promises and raised their children and stayed in love. "What I need is a new life."

"We're getting to that age." He pulled his chair over and put his feet on her desk. She couldn't help noticing that the white soles of his tennis shoes were covered with purple ink. His youngest daughter's name, surrounded by pink hearts and stars.

"It looks like someone wanted to decorate Daddy's shoes."

"Sarah thought my shoes were dorky. I never should have given her a set of markers."

"You're lucky to have those girls, Cal." Ellie sighed. "Both times I got married, I went off the pill and started praying."

"You're thirty-nine, not fifty-nine. The game isn't over."

"It just feels that way, huh?"

He rolled his eyes. "Oh, for God's sake, Ellie. Don't you ever get tired of telling the same story?"

He sounded angry with her. "What do you mean?"

"We're pushing forty, but you still act like you're the homecoming queen, waiting to be swept off her feet by the football captain. It's not like that. It's not about the falling in love. It's about the *landing,* the staying where you said you'd be and working to keep the love strong. You never did get that."

"That's easy for you to say, Cal. You've got a wife and kids who love you. Lisa—"

"Left me."

"What?"

"In August," he said quietly. "We tried the old being separated in the same house, but the girls were too smart for that. Just before school started, she left for good."

"And the girls?" Ellie could hardly ask the question.

"They're with me. Lisa works too much. Every now and again she remembers she's a mom and comes by. She's in love now. She wants me to sell the house and split the proceeds for the divorce."

"I can't believe you've never told me this. We work together every day. *Every* day."

"El, when was the last time you asked about my life?"

She felt stung by that remark. "I always ask how you're doing."

"And give me five seconds to answer before you launch into something more interesting. Usually about your own life." He stood up. "Forget it. You just got me on a bad day. I guess I just wanted a friend to tell me it would be okay." He headed for the door, grabbed his coat. "See you tomorrow."

She was staring at the closed door when it hit her.

I can't believe you didn't tell me.

She'd made it about her. She'd said nothing to comfort him.

I just wanted a friend to tell me it would be okay.

For years people had made little remarks about her being self-ish. Ellie had always brushed them off. Now she asked herself, *Is it true?*

Two lost marriages both gone south—she'd thought—because her husbands didn't love her enough. Was that because she wanted—needed—too much love? Did she return the amount she took? She'd loved her husbands, adored them. But not enough to follow Alvin to Alaska or to put Sammy through truck driver's school. It had always been her way or the highway.

She'd called *them* losers. Maybe it had been her all along.

When Mel came in to work the night shift, Ellie raced out to her car. She pulled up to Cal's house less than thirty minutes after he'd left the station. He opened the door. His face, usually so youthful and smiling, looked older, ruined. She wondered how long he'd looked like that, how often she hadn't noticed.

"I'm a bitch," she said miserably. "Can you forgive me?"

A tiny smile tugged at one side of his mouth. "A drama-queen apology if ever there was one."

"I'm not a drama queen."

"No. You're a bitch." His smile evened out. "It's your beauty. Women like you are used to being the center of attention."

She moved toward him. "I am a bitch, Cal. A sorry one."

He looked at her. "Thanks."

"It'll be okay, Cal," she said, hoping late really was better than never. "Lisa loves you. She'll remember that and come back."

"I thought that for a long time, El. But now I'm not sure it's what I even want."

"What *do* you want?"

"Not to be so lonely all the time." He looked at her, and in those eyes she knew so well, she saw a sadness that was new.

Ellie sighed. "Be thankful for your kids, Cal. At least you'll always have someone who loves you."

It was Friday night. After finishing his rounds, Max climbed into his truck and headed for the movie theater. But when he came to Magnolia Street, he turned left instead of right.

All the way to her house he told himself he was crazy. *All or nothing.* He'd had *all* once; it had practically killed him.

He parked, walked up to the front door, and knocked. Julia opened the door. Even in a pair of faded Levi's and a white cable-knit sweater two sizes too big she looked beautiful. "Max," she said, obviously surprised.

"You want to go to the movies?"

Idiot. He sounded like a desperate teenager.

Her answer was a smile. "Cal and Ellie are playing Scrabble, so yeah, I could go to the show. What's playing?"

"I have no idea."

She laughed. "That's my favorite."

The movie, as it turned out, was *To Have and Have Not*. They sat in the darkened theater, watching one of the great screen pairings of all time. When it was over and they walked through the lobby, Julia got the feeling they were being stared at.

"People are talking about us," she said, sidling close to him.

"Welcome to Rain Valley." He took her arm and led her out of the theater and across the street to where his truck was parked. "I'd take you out for some pie, but everything's closed."

"You do like your pie."

He grinned. "And you thought you knew nothing about me."

She turned and looked up at him. "I don't know much."

He stared down at her; she expected him to come up with some smart-ass comeback. Instead, he kissed her. When he drew back, he said quietly, "There. You know that."

All the way back to her house they talked about things that didn't matter. The movie. Salmon populations. Old-growth forests.

At her front door, she let him take her in his arms. It was amazing how comfortable she felt there. This time when he bent down to kiss her, she met him more than halfway, and when it was over and he drew back, she wanted more. For the first time with him, she was genuinely afraid. "Thanks for the movie, Max."

He kissed her again. "Good night, Julia."

By late December, the holidays were first and foremost on everyone's mind. The Rotary Club had hung the streetlamp decorations, and the Elks had decorated their Giving Tree. Local scout troops were selling wrapping paper door-to-door. Ellie had brought a Christmas tree home, and Alice had helped decorate it, carefully placing red ornaments on the tips of the branches.

Christmas Eve had dawned bright and clear, with an ice-blue sky unmarred by even the thinnest cloud. All day, as usual, Julia had been at Alice's side. They'd spent a lot of time outside in the yard.

Julia was preparing Alice for the next big step. Town.

"Town," Julia said quietly. "Remember the pictures in the books? I want us to go to town, where people live."

Alice's eyes widened. "Town?" she whispered.

"I'll be with you all the time."

She shook her head.

"I know you're scared, honey. It's a big world out there. But Julia would never hurt Alice, you know that, right?"

Alice's face pulled into a frown.

"I want to take you someplace special. Will you come with me?" Julia held out her hand.

Alice took hold, but her frown didn't soften.

"First you have to put on your boots and coat. It's cold outside."

"No."

Julia sighed. The fight over shoes never ended. "Cold outside." She reached for the boots and coat by the front door. "Come on. I'll give you a surprise if you put them on."

"No."

"No surprise? Oh, well, then."

"Stop!" Alice cried out as Julia walked away. She stuck her bare feet into the boots and put on her coat. "Smelly shoes."

Julia smiled. "You're such a good girl." Reaching down, she took hold of Alice's hand. "Will you follow me?"

Slowly, Alice nodded.

Julia led the girl out to the truck. As she opened the door, she heard the low, throaty growl Alice used to make.

"Use your words, Alice."

"Stay." Her dark eyes were huge in her tiny face.

"I won't hurt you, Alice." Julia tightened her hold on Alice's hand. "We'll go see Ellie. Come on, Alice. Please?"

Alice swallowed hard. "Okay." Very slowly, she climbed into the truck. Julia helped her into the booster seat they'd purchased last week for this very occasion. When she snapped the seat belt, Alice started to whimper. At the shutting of the door, that whimper grew into a desperate howling. Julia hurried to the driver's seat. By now, Alice was hyperventilating, trying to unhook the straps.

"It's okay, Alice. You're scared. That's okay," Julia said over and over until Alice calmed down enough to hear her. "I'm putting on my seat belt. See? I'm hooked in, too."

"Fee. Peas. Girl fee."

All at once, Julia got it. Alice's ligature marks. She should have foreseen this. "Oh, Alice," she said, feeling tears well in her eyes. She moved the car seat to the middle of the bench seat, then held the girl's hand. "Is that better?"

"Fwaid. Girl fwaid."

"I know, baby. But I won't let you go. You're safe. Okay?"

Julia started the engine.

Alice screamed and tightened her hold on Julia's hand.

"It's okay, honey," Julia said over and over. It took them ten minutes to get down the driveway. By the time they reached the highway, she had almost no feeling left in her right hand.

The lot behind the police station had three cars in it. Julia parked, then went around to open Alice's door. Before she'd even finished unstrapping her, the girl was climbing out of the truck.

Julia led Alice up the steps and opened the door.

Cal and his three daughters, Peanut and Benji with their teenage son and daughter, and Ellie were dancing to an ear-splitting rendition of "Jingle Bell Rock." Mel and his family were setting food out on the table.

Alice shrieked and started to howl.

Ellie ran for the stereo and shut it off. Silence descended. Cal was the first to move. He herded his girls toward Julia. Alice glommed onto her side, trying to disappear. The whimpering started again.

Close, but not too close, they stopped. Cal dropped down on one knee. "Hey, Alice. You remember us, I bet. I'm Cal, and these are my girls—Amanda, Emily, and Sarah."

Alice was trembling. She tightened her hold on Julia's hand.

Peanut bustled her family forward. Her husband, Benji, was a big, burly-looking man with twinkling eyes. Introductions were made quietly. Benji wished Alice a very merry Christmas, then herded his two teenagers over to the tree.

Peanut stayed behind. "I can't go over there," she said to Julia. "Eggnog." She laughed.

At the sound, Alice looked up and smiled.

Peanut showed Alice her long red fingernails. Each one sported a sparkly wreath. She leaned close to Julia, whispered, "I have a bit of gossip."

Julia laughed. "I'm hardly the one to tell."

"My sources—which are FBI good—tell that a certain doctor took a date to the movies. That's like Paris Hilton moving into a double-wide. Some things don't happen. But this one did."

"It was just a movie."

"Was it?" Peanut gave her a wink, a pat on the arm, and she left.

Alice was mesmerized by the opening of presents. She finally came out from behind Julia so she could see better. She didn't talk to anyone except Ellie, but she seemed content to watch it all. She dared to play alongside Sarah, who was a few years older. Not together, but side by side; Alice watched Sarah's every move and imitated it. By the time everyone started to leave, Alice could dress and undress Disco Barbie without help. After the party broke up, Ellie, Julia, and Alice walked downtown. Alice couldn't stop pointing at the various lights and decorations.

"What's the local lawyer's name?" Julia asked her sister.

"John MacDonald. Why?"

"I want to start adoption proceedings the day after Christmas."

"Are you sure?"

Julia pulled Alice against her. "I've never been more sure of anything in my life."

BY NOON on Christmas Day, Max had been to visit his patients and the few children on the ward; he'd also dropped off a donation at the Catholic church and called every member of his family. Now he stood in his living room, staring out at the gray-washed lake. It was raining so hard, even the trees looked colorless.

He should have put up a Christmas tree. Maybe that would have helped his mood, although he couldn't imagine why it would. He hadn't bought a tree in seven years.

He went to the sofa and sat down. Memories crowded in on him. He saw his mother studying bugs through a magnifying glass. And Susan, knitting a pale blue blanket. . . .

He got to his feet. He couldn't just sit here remembering other Christmases. He needed to do something. Go somewhere.

See Julia.

That was all it took—the thought of her, and he was in motion.

He got dressed, jumped into his truck, and drove to her house.

Julia was laughing as she answered the door. When she saw him, her smile faded. "I thought you were going to L.A. for Christmas."

"I stayed," he said softly. "If you're busy—"

"Of course not. Come in. Would you like a drink? We have some hot buttered rum that's pretty good."

"That would be great."

She led him into the living room, then headed for the kitchen. Her gap-toothed little shadow matched her step for step. They looked almost conjoined.

A gorgeous, beautifully decorated Christmas tree dominated the corner of the living room. A rush of memories hit him. *Come on, Dan-the-man, let's put up the star for Mommy.*

He turned his back on the tree and sat on the hearth, fire warming his back. A coil of sleeping dogs lay at his feet.

"Well, well, well."

At the sound of Ellie's voice, he looked up. She stood behind the sofa with her hands on her hips. "It's nice to see you again, Max."

"You, too, El."

She came around the sofa and sat down beside him. "You know what I hear? I hear you took my sister to the movies."

"That come across the police scanner?"

Ellie leaned toward him. "Hurt her and I'll cut your nuts off." She eased back. "And you like your nuts."

"I do indeed."

"Good. Then we understand each other."

Julia and Alice returned.

Ellie immediately stood. "I'm going to Cal's. You two be good." She picked up a box of packages and left the house.

Julia handed Max a cup.

They sat down side by side on the sofa. Neither said anything. Alice knelt at Julia's feet. She grunted at Julia and smacked the book.

"Use your words, Alice," Julia said calmly.

"Read. Girl."

"Not now. I'm talking to Dr. Max."

"Now." Alice hit the book again. "Peas?"

Julia smiled and touched her head. "In a little while, okay?"

Alice's whole body slumped in disappointment. She started turning the pages. Julia turned to him then.

"You're amazing," he said softly.

She was close enough to kiss him right now, and he wanted her to. He moved away from her slightly, as if distance could provide protection.

"Why didn't you go home for Christmas?" she asked.

"You."

Her gaze searched his, as if looking deep for answers. She gave him a sad, knowing smile, and he wondered what it was she thought she knew.

ELLIE walked down the driveway and turned onto the path into the woods. Although the rain had stopped, drops still fell from leaves and branches. She followed the beaten grass past the old pond that she and Cal used as their childhood fishing hole.

There's a snake in the water, Cal—get out!

That's just an ol' twig. You need glasses.

You're the one who needs glasses—

She remembered their laughter . . . the way they'd sit on that muddy bank for hours, talking about nothing.

She followed the path back around the bend, and there was the house. For a second, she expected it to look as it once had: a slant-sided shack with shutters askew on cracked windows, a battalion of snarling pit bulls chained in the yard.

She blinked, and the memory moved on. She was staring at the house Cal had built in the years before marrying Lisa. He'd worked for a construction company back then. After a forty-five-hour work week, he'd piled on the extra hours, literally building the place around his drunken, useless father, adding rooms on as money came in. The end result was a quaint shingled cabin set on a patch of velvet green grass, surrounded by two-hundred-year-old evergreens.

As always, the porch was studded with white lights; the railings were festooned with boughs. Ellie knocked on the door. When no one answered, she tried again.

Finally she heard a thunder of footsteps.

The door wrenched open, and Cal's daughters stood there, smiling brightly. Amanda, the eleven-year-old, looked impossibly grown-up in her low-rise jeans and studded silver belt and pink T-shirt; nine-year-old Emily was dressed in a green velvet dress that was at least a size too big; and eight-year-old Sarah hadn't changed out of her Princess Fiona pajamas.

At the sight of Ellie, all three smiles faded.

"It's just Aunt Ellie," Amanda said.

The trio mumbled, "Merry Christmas." Then Emily called out for her dad.

"Gee, thanks," Ellie said, watching them walk away.

Cal came down the stairs. He was moving slowly, as if maybe he'd just woken up. His black hair was a tangled mess. He wore a pair of Levi's so old that both knees were gone, and his Metallica T-shirt had seen better days.

"Ellie," he said, trying to smile.

"You look like hell," she said when the girls were gone.

"And I was going to say how *beautiful* you are."

Ellie followed him to the living room. Cal flopped down on the sofa, put his feet on the coffee table. His sigh was loud enough to set a tiny ornament jingling on the huge decorated tree.

Ellie sat down beside him. It confused her to see Cal this way. If he could become fragile, nothing was safe. "What happened?"

"Lisa didn't come for Christmas morning. She didn't send presents. I told the girls she'd call, but I'm starting to wonder."

Ellie frowned. "Is she okay?"

"She's fine. I called her parents. She's out with her new guy."

"That doesn't sound like Lisa."

Cal looked at her. "Yes, it does."

Ellie heard the wealth of pain behind those few words. She knew it was all Cal would ever tell her about his failed marriage. "I'm sorry."

"How was your Christmas?" he finally said.

"Great. We made Dad's stew. Alice never could get the whole Santa-down-the-chimney concept. She wouldn't unwrap her presents, either. She just carried the boxes around."

"By next year, she'll be a champ. Gift holidays, they learn fast. I remember the first time I took Amanda trick-or-treating."

"It was to my house."

"Yeah. She couldn't figure out why she was dressed up like a pumpkin, but once you gave her the candy, she didn't care."

"She wore my mom's green felt hat, remember?"

Cal looked at her again. "I thought you'd forgotten all that."

"How could I forget? We've been best friends for decades."

He sighed, looked over at the tree.

It was best, probably, to change the subject. "Julia wants to adopt Alice. She thinks the kid needs permanence."

"Good idea. How do you do it?"

"We start with a motion to terminate parental rights. If no one comes forward, Julia's in the clear."

"So we go from hoping they show up to hoping they don't."

"Right." Ellie paused, looked at him. They fell silent again.

Ellie got up and went into the kitchen. She poured two tequila straight shots and set them on a tray, alongside a shaker of salt. In the living room, she set the tray down on the coffee table, pushing his feet aside.

"What the—straight shots? On Christmas Day?"

"Sometimes a mood changes on its own." Ellie shrugged. "Sometimes it needs a shove." She plopped down beside him. "Bottoms up."

"What's the salt for?"

"Decoration." She clanked her glass against his and drank up. "Here's to a better year coming up."

"Amen to that." Cal downed the drink and seemed to *study* her, looking for something hidden. "You've been in love a lot. How do you keep believing in it? How do you tell someone you love them?"

"*Saying* it is easy, Cal. *Meaning* it is practically impossible." This whole conversation was depressing her. "Enough sadness. This is a holiday." She went over to the stereo. There, she put a CD in the player and turned the volume on high enough to bring the girls out of the family room.

"What's going on?" Amanda asked. The girls stood close together. All of them had sad eyes on this most magical of days.

"First off, you have presents to open," Ellie said. That made them smile a little. "Then I'm taking you bowling."

Amanda made a very grown-up face. "We don't bowl. Mom says it's for trailer trash."

"You don't know about secret bowling? After hours, with music blaring and all the junk food you can eat?"

"Mom would never agree to this," Amanda said.

"I'll have you know," Ellie said, "that your dad and I used to work at the Big Bowl. And that's why you're the only kids in Rain Valley who get to know about secret bowling. Now go get dressed."

In a flurry of laughter, the girls ran up the stairs.

Cal looked at Ellie. "We haven't snuck into the Big Bowl in twenty-five years."

"I'll call Wayne and let him know. He still keeps the keys in the gnome's hat. We can leave fifty bucks in the register."

"Thanks, El."

She smiled. "Just remember this the next time I get divorced. Tequila and bowling."

"Is that the magic potion?"

"No." Her smile faded. "But sometimes it's all there is."

TEN

It was nearing the end of January, that month when the skies were steely and tempers were lost as easily as car keys. Inside the Cates house, the only light came from artificial bulbs, and the pattern of rain sounded like a quickened heartbeat that wouldn't calm down.

It made Ellie uneasy. The woman from the Department of Social and Health Services sat stiffly erect on the sofa. Julia sat beside her, looking composed in winter white.

Helen Wharton looked across the room to where Alice played by herself. After cowering behind the potted ficus tree for almost an hour, she'd finally emerged, only to begin eating the flower arrangement. "Your home study was approved for temporary foster care, and you've repeatedly reminded us, the child is flourishing. My concern, actually, is for you, Dr. Cates. May I be frank?"

"I'd love to hear what you have to say," Julia said.

"Obviously, she's a profoundly damaged child. I doubt she'll ever be normal. All too often, we find that parents go into adoption of special-needs children with high hopes, only to realize they've taken on too much. The state has wonderful facilities for kids like her."

"There are no kids like her," Julia said. "She's been uniquely harmed, I think, and there's no way to judge her future. As you know, I'm more than qualified to treat her as a patient, and I'm entirely ready to love her as a parent."

Helen's smile came late and seemed as thin as nonfat milk. "She's lucky that you found her." She shot a glance at Alice, who was now standing at the window "talking" to a squirrel. The social worker stood up and offered Julia her hand. "I'll certainly recommend placement with you from a home-study perspective."

"Thank you."

After the social worker left, Julia's smile finally slipped.

Alice ran to her, jumped into her arms. "Scared," she whispered.

"I know, honey." Julia held her tightly, stroked her hair. "You don't like people who wear glasses. And she had an awful lot of shiny jewelry, didn't she? Still, you should have smiled at her."

"Smelly lady."

Ellie laughed. "I have to agree with the kid on that one." She headed for the coatrack by the front door and grabbed her jacket.

Julia moved toward her. "We announce once a week for three weeks in all area newspapers, huh?"

"They have sixty days from the first publication. After that, you're home free."

They. Alice's biological family.

Though they didn't speak of it, Julia and Ellie both knew that a parent could show up any time, even years from now, and lay a truer claim to the child's heart than Julia had.

"Well, it's off to work for me," Ellie said. "Bye, Alice."

Alice hugged Ellie. "Bye, Lellie."

Ellie left the house and went out to her cruiser. With a quick honk—Alice loved that noise—she was off.

Ellie drove to the station. She pulled into her parking slot and went in the back door. She was in the lunchroom, checking out what was in the fridge, when Peanut bustled into the room.

"Ellie!" she said. "There's a guy out front. And he won't talk to anyone but you."

Ellie peered down the hallway. From here, all she could see was a man—with his back to her—sitting in the chair opposite her desk. He was dressed all in black. "Who is it?"

"He wouldn't give his name. Won't take off his sunglasses, either." She snorted. "Must be from California."

Ellie adjusted the gold stars on her collar and walked into the main room of the station house. "Hello. I'm Chief Barton," she said, rounding her desk. "I understand—"

He turned to her. All she saw were chiseled cheekbones, full lips, and a mass of wavy black hair. He took off his sunglasses and revealed a pair of electric-blue eyes.

"I've come a long way to see you," he said in a worn, gravelly voice. "I'm George Azelle." He reached into his pocket and pulled out a folded piece of paper, which he set on her desk.

The name registered.

"I see you remember me." He leaned forward, pushing the paper closer to her. "I'm here about her."

"Her?"

He unfolded the paper he'd pushed forward. It was a picture of Alice. "I'm her father."

"ALICE, how many times are we going to have this same discussion?" Julia couldn't help laughing at her own comment. She and Alice did many things together these days. None of them could accurately be characterized as a discussion. "Put your shoes on."

"No."

Julia went to the window and pointed outside. "It's raining."

Alice collapsed to a sit on the floor. "No."

"We're going to the diner. Remember the diner? We were there last week. Yummy pie. Put your shoes on."

"No. Smelly shoes."

Julia threw up her hands in dramatic despair. "All right. You stay here with Jake and Elwood. I'll bring you home some pie." With slow, exaggerated movements, she put on her coat.

"Girl go?"

Julia didn't let herself smile as she turned around. Alice stood there, her little face scrunched in a scowl, her overalls splattered with paint from their last art project. Julia knelt down.

"Some places make little girls wear shoes."

"Girl no like."

"I know, honey. How 'bout this: No shoes in the car. Okay?"

Alice frowned in thought. "No socks."

"Okay."

Alice dutifully got her shoes out of the box by the front door and stepped onto the porch. The drizzling rain turned to tiny flakes of snow. "Look, Jewlee! Prittee."

It was snowing, and Alice was barefooted. *Perfect.*

Julia grabbed Alice's coat and scooped the girl into her arms.

She was halfway to the truck when she heard the phone ring.

"That's probably Aunt Ellie, telling us to watch the snow." She strapped Alice into the car seat.

"Icky. Tight. Bad," Alice said. "Smelly."

"It does not smell, and it keeps you safe."

That shut Alice up. Julia put a CD in the player and drove away.

Alice listened to the *Pete's Dragon* soundtrack until Julia pulled into a spot in front of the Rain Drop Diner and parked.

Julia leaned sideways and put Alice's clammy feet into her boots. She came around to Alice's side and helped her out of the seat.

Alice moved slowly toward the restaurant, staring down at her feet.

"Don't be afraid, Alice. I'm right here. I won't let go."

Julia opened the diner's door. A bell tinkled overhead. At the sound, Alice shrieked and threw herself at Julia.

She bent down to hug the girl, held her tightly.

The Grimm sisters were at the cash register. Rosie Chicowski was behind them, tucking a pencil in her pink, beehived hair. To the left, an old logger sat alone in a booth.

Everyone was staring at Julia and Alice.

They should have come an hour ago, between the breakfast and lunch crowds. That was what they'd done last week, and they'd had the place to themselves. Slowly Julia stood back up.

The Grimm sisters advanced, three abreast. They stared at Julia, then at Alice. Alice snorted nervously, tugged on Julia's hand.

Violet reached into her purse and pulled out a bright purple plastic coin purse. "Here you go. My granddaughter loves these."

Alice touched it reverently, took it in her small hand, and stroked her cheek with it. She blinked up at Violet. "Ank 'ou."

The three old women gasped and looked at Julia. All of them smiled at once. "You saved her," Daisy said in a stiff voice, obviously bothered by the emotion behind the words. Her sisters bobbed their heads in unison.

Julia smiled. For the first time in her life, she felt admired in this town. Accepted. "Thank you. I couldn't have done it without all of you. The town really protected us."

"You're one of us," Daisy said simply.

The trio turned and left the diner. Julia led Alice to a booth in the corner. They had ordered grilled cheese sandwiches, fries, and milk shakes from Rosie when Alice glanced up and said, "Max."

He didn't see them until he'd picked up his lunch order and turned for the door. "Hey," he said.

Julia's heart did a little flip. "No date for lunch, Doctor?"

"Not yet."

"Then perhaps you should join us."

He looked down at Alice. "May I sit next to you?"

Alice scooted sideways to make room for him.

Rosie swooped in, grinning from ear to ear. "I *knew* it was true about you two." She set out a place setting in front of Max.

"Alice is my patient," he said evenly.

Rosie winked one false-lashed eye. "Course she is."

When she was gone, Max said, "Before I finish my sandwich, everyone in town will know about this."

A few minutes later Rosie showed up with their lunches. Julia was about to tell Alice to eat one french fry at a time when she realized that Max was staring at her.

She met his gaze and saw fear in his blue eyes. He was afraid of her, of *them*. It was a fear she understood. Passion was a dangerous thing, and love even more so. But Alice had taught Julia a thing or two about love . . . and courage.

"What?" he said, unsmiling.

Julia felt something new, a kind of opening wonder. She wasn't afraid anymore. "Come here," she said softly.

Frowning, he leaned toward her.

She kissed him. For a heartbeat of time, he resisted. Then he gave in.

Alice giggled. "Kisses."

When Max drew back, he was pale. Julia laughed. "Might as well give the gossips something to talk about."

After that, they went back to their lunches as if it hadn't happened. Later, at the door, Julia said, "I'm taking Alice to the game farm in Sequim. Would you like to join us?"

He paused to look at his watch. "I'll follow you."

Julia bustled Alice back into the truck. By the time they reached the West End Game Farm, it was snowing in earnest.

Julia pulled up to the small wooden house.

"You need to put on your boots and your coat," Julia said.

"No."

"Stay in the truck, then." Julia joined Max, who stood by his car.

"What are we waiting for?" he asked.

"You'll see."

Alice climbed out, dressed for the weather except that her boots were on the wrong feet.

Just then Floyd came out of the house wearing a huge arctic parka. "Hello, Dr. Cates. Dr. Cerrasin." He bent down. "And you must be Alice. I know a friend of yours."

Alice hid behind Julia. "Follow me," Floyd said.

They hadn't taken three steps when the howling started.

Alice ran toward the sound. It floated on the icy air, sad and soulful. Alice answered in her own howl. They came together at the chain-link fence, the little girl and the wolf that was now almost half its full-grown size.

Floyd went to the gate. Alice was beside him in an instant. When the combination lock clicked, he eased the door open. Alice slipped into the pen. She and the wolf rolled around like littermates in the snow. Every time he licked her cheek, Alice giggled.

Floyd stood watching them play. "This is the first time he's stopped howling since I got him."

"She missed him, too," Julia said.

They fell silent, watching the girl and wolf roll around in the snow. She was about to ask him a question when she heard a siren. The sound was far off at first; then it drew close.

Flashing lights cut through the hazy snowfall as Ellie's police cruiser drove into the yard and parked. The lights remained on, flashing in staccato bursts of color. Ellie walked toward them in the surreal light. "He's come for her," she said without preamble.

"Who?" Julia asked, but when Ellie glanced at Alice, Julia knew. "Alice's father."

MAX carried Alice into the house. He tried not to think about how natural this felt, carrying a child.

He tried to set her down on the sofa so he could build a fire. But she wouldn't uncoil her arms from around his neck, and all the while, as he carried her around the house and built the fire, she was howling in a quiet way that broke his heart.

Finally he sat down on the couch and drew her onto his lap.

Her eyes were tightly shut. The sound she made was the physical embodiment of loss. Too much feeling and too few words.

Max tightened his hold on Alice. "It's okay, little one. Let it out." At the sound of his voice, she drew in a sharp breath. It made him realize it was the first time he'd spoken since the game farm. "Julia had to go with Ellie. They'll be back soon."

She blinked up at him. "No Jewlee leave Girl?"

"No. She'll be back."

"Wolf?" Her mouth trembled. The question was so big and complex, yet she asked it all with that one word.

"The wolf is okay, too."

She shook her head. "No. Trap. Bad."

"He needs to be free," Max said.

"Like birds."

"You know about trapped, don't you?" He stared down into her small, heart-shaped face. As much as he wanted to look away, he couldn't. She made him remember too many moments that had passed. The surprising thing was, they were *good* memories.

"Read Girl?" She pointed to a book on the coffee table. It was already open to a page.

He picked it up. She immediately resettled herself beside him. He looped one arm around her and began to read.

" 'Real isn't how you are made,' said the skin horse. 'It's a thing that happens to you. When a child loves you for a long, long time, not just to play with, but REALLY loves you, then you become Real.' "

Max's voice broke on that.

Read to me, Daddy.

He felt Alice's hand on his cheek, comforting him. Only then did he realize that he was crying.

"THE DNA is conclusive?" Julia asked. In the quiet of the truck, her voice sounded louder than she would have liked. Because of the snow and the falling night, it felt as if they were cocooned in some strange spaceship.

"The lab report indicated certainty," Ellie said. "Her DNA was tested against his and her mother's. It's a match. And he knew about the birthmark. I have a call in to the FBI."

"What's her real name?"

"Brittany."

"Brittany." Julia tested out the name, trying to make a match in her mind. "Why did it take him so long to get here?"

"There's a problem." Ellie pulled into her parking slot. In the weird mixture of light and darkness, her face seemed older and full of shadows. "Do you know who George Azelle is?"

It took Julia a moment to remember. "Oh, yeah. The guy who murdered his wife and baby daughter? Sure. He—"

"He's her father."

"No." She shook her head. There must be some mistake. The Azelle case had been a big trial. The millionaire murderer, they'd called him, referring to the dot-com empire he'd built. A circus of media attention had followed every confusing aspect of the process. The only certainty in the whole proceeding had been his guilt. "But he was *convicted*. He went to prison. How—"

"I'm not the one with the answers. He is."

Julia stepped into the freezing night. Losing Alice to a loving family was something she would have made herself deal with. "Not to a murderer," she muttered more than once on the walk up the stairs.

Inside the station, it was quiet. Cal was at his desk, and Peanut stood beside him. Both looked at Julia through worried eyes.

"He's in my office," Ellie said.

Ellie went first. Julia took a deep breath and followed her.

She might not have recognized George Azelle on the street, but she remembered him now. Tall, dark, and deadly—that was how the press had characterized him. He stood well over six feet, with broad shoulders and narrow hips. Black hair hung almost to his shoulders. His handsome face was the kind that darkened easily into anger. The kind that launched a woman's dreams, although he looked worn.

"You're the doctor," he said. "I want to thank you for everything you've done for my little girl. How is she?"

Julia moved forward. "And you're the murderer," she said. "A murder-one conviction, if I remember correctly."

His smile faded. He reached into his back pocket, tossed an envelope on Ellie's desk. "The Court of Appeals reversed the trial court's denial of a motion to dismiss. The Supreme Court agreed. I was released last week."

"On a technicality."

"If you consider innocence a technicality."

Julia tried desperately not to *feel* all this, but panic was stalking her. "She can't survive without me."

"Look, Doc, I've been locked up for *years*. I have a big house and enough money to hire the best care for her. I need to show the world she's alive, so I want her. *Now*."

"If you think I'm going to just hand Alice over, you're crazy."

"Who the hell is Alice?"

"That's what we named her. For all I know, you were behind the whole thing. You wouldn't be the first man to sacrifice a child to get rid of a wife."

She saw a flash of something in his eyes. He closed the distance between them. "I know who you are, too, Doc. I'm not the only one here with a shady past, am I? Do you really want a public fight?"

"You don't scare me."

His breath was warm and soft against her temple. "Tell Brit I'm on my way. We both know you can't stop me. See you in court."

As SOON as he was gone, Julia sank onto a cold, hard chair. Her whole body was trembling.

"Do you want to talk about it?" Ellie said.

"Talking won't help. I need information on his case."

"He gave me this." Ellie pushed a stack of papers across the desk.

Julia took them. The letters shimmied on the white pages.

"Jules—"

"Give me a minute," Julia said. "Please."

The documents represented the bare bones of the procedural history. The original motion to dismiss the case, the denial of that motion, the Appellate Court's reversal and the State Supreme Court's dismissal. The one that mattered most to Julia was the original certification for determination of probable cause, which outlined the facts of the state's case.

On April 13, 2002, at approximately 9:30 in the morning, George Azelle placed a call to the King County Police Department to report that his wife, Zoë Azelle, and his two-and-a-half-year-old daughter, Brittany, had been missing for more than twenty-four hours. The Seattle Police Department sent officers to the Azelle residence at 16402 Lakeside Drive on Mercer Island. A countywide, then statewide search ensued.

Investigations revealed that Mrs. Azelle was having an affair at the time of her disappearance and had requested a divorce. Azelle was also engaged in an affair with his personal assistant. Police learned the following facts:

In November 2001, police responded to a domestic disturbance call at the Azelle home. Officers observed bruising on Mrs. Azelle and arrested Mr. Azelle. This complaint was dismissed when Mrs. Azelle refused to testify.

On the evening of April 11, 2002, neighbor Stanley Seaman stated to his wife that the Azelles were "at it again." Seaman noted the time of the fight as 11:15 p.m. At almost noon on Sunday, April 12, 2002, Seaman witnessed Azelle loading a large trunk and a "sacklike" canvas bag onto his seaplane.

Azelle asserts that he took off from Lake Washington in his seaplane, on or about one o'clock on April 12. According to family witness testimony, he arrived at his sister's home on Shaw Island two hours later. The ordinary flight time would be slightly less than an hour. Azelle returned to his residence at 7:00 that evening.

A local flower delivery man, Mark Ulio, arrived at the Azelle home at 4:45 on Sunday with flowers ordered by Azelle, via phone, at one o'clock. No one answered at the house. Ulio reported seeing a Caucasian male in his mid-thirties wearing a yellow rain slicker and a Batman baseball cap getting into a white van that was parked across the street from the Azelle residence.

On Monday morning, Azelle told several witnesses that Zoë Azelle had "run off again." At 9:30 a.m., when Brittany did not show up at day care and Zoë missed a meeting with her therapist, Azelle reported them missing.

Upon identifying Azelle as a suspect, police arrived with a search warrant. On a rug in the living room, they found traces of blood confirmed as Brittany's. Hair samples determined to be Zoë's indicated a struggle. Based on the information obtained, Azelle was placed under arrest.

Julia sighed and set the papers back on the desk.

"He's a scum," she said. "An adulterer and almost certainly a wife beater. But according to the courts, he's not a murderer. He can't be retried for it, either. Double jeopardy." She looked at Ellie. "He's also her father. Washington courts—"

"What do we do to protect her?"

"Hire a detective, Ellie. Somewhere, sometime, this son of a bitch hit someone or sold drugs or drove drunk. Find it. We don't have to prove he's a murderer, just an unfit parent."

IT WAS just past five o'clock when they got home, but it felt like the middle of the night. An inch of snow frosted the lawn, the roof, the porch railing. Ellie parked close to the house.

"I'm not going to tell her," Julia said, staring straight ahead.

Ellie sighed. "How will you *ever* tell her? She hates it when you leave to make breakfast."

Julia couldn't imagine it. *No leave Girl, Jewlee.*

She opened the car door, walked up the steps, and opened the front door. Alice was curled up in Max's lap.

"Jewlee!" She slid out of his arms and ran.

Julia picked the little girl up. "Hey, little one."

Alice buried her face in Julia's neck.

Ellie came up behind Julia. "Hey girlie-girl."

"Hi, Lellie," Alice said in a muffled, happy voice.

Max was standing now. "Julia?" he said.

It almost undid her. "He wants her back."

He moved slowly toward her. "I'll wait up for you," he said.

"But—"

"It doesn't matter when. Come over when you can. You'll need me."

She couldn't deny that; she was in desperate need of comfort.

"I'll wait up for you," he said again. This time he didn't wait for a response. He said good-bye to each of them and left.

Silence swept in behind him.

"Max bye-bye," Alice said. "No Jewlee leave?"

Julia swallowed hard. She clung fiercely to Alice. "I won't leave you, Alice," she said, praying it would be true.

THE night smelled of wet wood and new snow. By the time Julia reached the porch steps of Max's house, he was there, on the deck, waiting for her.

She climbed the steps. He started to say something, but she

didn't want to hear his questions. She couldn't carry any more weight. She touched a finger to his lips.

He stared down at her, and for a moment—just that—she saw the man behind the smile, the man who knew a thing or two about loss. She closed the final distance between them and put her arms around him. He swept her into his arms and carried her up the stairs. She clung to him, her face buried in the crook of his neck. Seconds later they were in his room.

She drew back just enough to look at him. In the pale light from a single lamp, she saw now what she'd refused to admit before, even to herself: She'd been lost from the moment she saw him, certainly from their first kiss. She hadn't merely stepped into love; she'd tumbled headlong, like her beloved Alice, down the rabbit hole to a place where nothing made sense. It didn't matter now whether he loved her back. What mattered was the love itself, this feeling of connecting with another heart. She could see, too, that he was worried. They'd come to a place that neither had quite expected, and there was no way to know how it would end. In the past—hell, yesterday—that would have frightened her. She'd learned a lot today.

"Yesterday I was worried about a lot of things. Today I know what matters."

"Alice."

"Yes," she said softly. "And you."

ELLIE woke at dawn, edgy and nervous. The first thing she did was pull out the Azelle file. In the last twenty-four hours, she'd personally spoken to every police officer who'd worked the case. And the best private detective in King County.

Every person she spoke to said the same thing.

He was guilty. And the state hadn't proved it.

Ellie paced the living room. The dogs followed, running into her every time she turned. It was on *her* shoulders to prove that Azelle was a bad guy, but so far all she could find was innuendo and accusation.

He was an adulterer; that was a fact. The only one she'd been able to nail down. No one had uncovered previous bad acts. No drug charges, not even a Drunk and Disorderly. With a curse, she grabbed her files and left the house.

She drove straight to the Rain Drop. As usual, it was full of loggers and fishermen and millworkers having breakfast before work. Rosie Chicowski was behind the hostess desk, smoking a cigarette.

"Hey, Ellie, you're in early," she said.

"I need some caffeine."

Rosie laughed. "You got it. How about one of Barb's marionberry muffins to go with it?"

"Only one, though. Shoot me if I try to order another."

"Flesh wound or kill ya?"

"Kill me." Laughing, Ellie headed back for a nonsmoking booth. It was a moment before she saw him, sprawled across the burgundy vinyl, an empty coffee cup in front of him. He saw her and nodded.

Ellie walked over to him. "Mr. Azelle," she said.

"Hello, Chief Barton." He did not look pleased to see her.

"Can I join you? I have some questions to ask you."

He sighed. "Of course you do."

She sidled into the booth. As she was marshaling her thoughts into a question, he said, "Three years."

"Three years what?"

"I was in prison for a crime I didn't commit. Hell, I thought Zoë had left me for one of her lovers and taken our kid." His intensity was unnerving. "Imagine how it would feel to be convicted of something horrific and put in a cage to rot. So I had affairs. So I lied to my wife. So I sent her flowers after a knock-down, drag-out fight. It doesn't make me a killer."

"The jury—"

"The *jury*," he said with contempt. "They couldn't see past my life. Every newspaper and TV station called me guilty within five minutes. No one even looked for Zoë and Brit. An eyewitness saw a strange van on *my* street the day my family went missing—and no one cared. The police didn't even bother to search for a white guy in a yellow slicker and Batman baseball cap who drove a grayish Chevy van. For the last month, I've been waiting every day for the DNA analysis that would give my daughter back to me. I had to get a court order to compare her DNA to the blood found at the scene. And when I get it, I race up here . . . only to find that your sister is going to fight me for custody." He leaned across the table. "How is she? Does she still suck her thumb? Does she—"

Ellie stood up quickly, needing distance between them suddenly. "Alice *needs* Julia. Can you understand that?"

"There is no Alice," he said. "Tell your sister I'm coming, Chief Barton. I won't lose my daughter twice."

THE next forty-eight hours unfolded in a kind of faded slow motion. Julia spent every hour working. During the day, she was with Alice, teaching her new words, taking her outside to make snow angels in the backyard. If Alice wondered why she kept kissing her cheek or holding her hand, she showed no sign of it.

During the nighttime hours, Julia and Ellie and Peanut and Cal and the private detective pored through police reports and archived videotape. After a long shift at the hospital, Max showed up to help. By Monday, they knew every fact of George Azelle's life.

And none of it would help them.

"Read Girl?"

Julia glanced at the clock. "No reading now," she said softly. "Cal is bringing Sarah over to play with you. Do you remember Sarah?"

Alice frowned. "Jewlee stay?"

"Not right now, honey. I'll be back, though."

The front door opened. Ellie, Cal, and Sarah walked in. Ellie touched Julia's arm. "You ready?"

Julia forced a smile and reached for her briefcase. She followed Ellie out to the cruiser. In a silence broken only by the thump-thump of the windshield wipers, they drove to the county courthouse.

Family Court was on the main floor, at the very end of a hallway. Julia paused, straightening her navy suit; then she opened the door and went inside. Her high heels clicked on the marble floor. Ellie matched her step for step in her gold-starred uniform. They passed Max and Peanut, seated together in the back row of the gallery.

George Azelle was already seated in the front of the courtroom, with an attorney beside him. He rose and moved toward them. He wore a charcoal-gray suit and a crisp white shirt. His hair had been tamed into a smooth ponytail. "Dr. Cates. Chief Barton."

"Mr. Azelle," Ellie said.

Behind them, Julia's attorney, John MacDonald, bustled in and herded Julia and Ellie to their desk.

The judge entered the courtroom. From her seat, she stared down at all of them. "I've read your motion, Mr. Azelle. As you know, Dr. Cates has been temporary foster parent for your daughter for nearly four months and has recently begun adoption proceedings."

"That was before, Your Honor, when the child's identity was unknown," his attorney said.

"The question for this court is placement of the minor child. Obviously, public policy favors the reunification of biological families, but these are far from ordinary family circumstances."

"Mr. Azelle has a history of domestic violence, Your Honor," John said.

"Objection!" Azelle's attorney was on his feet.

"Sit down, Counsel. He's never been formally charged with that." The judge looked at Julia. "The white elephant in this courtroom is you, Dr. Cates. You're hardly the average foster parent seeking permanent custody. You're one of the preeminent child psychiatrists in this country."

"I'm not here in that capacity, Your Honor."

"I'm aware of that, Doctor. It would represent a conflict of interest. You're here because you won't withdraw your petition for adoption."

"In any other instance, Your Honor, I would have withdrawn if a family member had come forward. But I've read the records in this case, and I'm deeply concerned for the child's safety. The mother's body has never been found, and there's no finding of not guilty on the record. As you can see from my report, this is an extremely traumatized child. I'm making progress because she trusts me. To remove her from my care would cause irreparable harm."

"Your Honor," Azelle's attorney said. "She's a psychiatrist. My client can afford to replace her. The truth is, my client has already suffered a tremendous loss of time with his daughter."

The judge looked at them all. "I'm going to take this under advisement. I'll appoint a guardian *ad litem* to assess the child's special needs. Until I reach a decision, the child will remain with Dr. Cates. Mr. Azelle is to be granted supervised visitation." She hit the bench with her gavel. "Next case."

It took Julia a moment to process what had just happened. She still had custody of Alice—for now, at least. She eased away from the desk and started to leave the courtroom.

Then someone grabbed her arm. The grip was a little too tight. George Azelle pulled her aside. "I need to see her."

She had no choice but to agree. "Tomorrow. We're at sixteen seventeen River Road. Be there at one." She pulled free of his arm, and he backed away, sighing.

"So just tell me: How's my daughter? What does *developmentally delayed* mean?"

"She's been through hell, but she's coming through. She's a tough, loving little girl who needs a lot of therapy and stability." Julia reached into her briefcase and withdrew a videocassette tape. "This compilation of our sessions will answer some of your questions."

He took it cautiously. "Where has she been?" he asked.

"Somewhere in the woods, we think." Julia wouldn't let herself be fooled by the concern in his voice. "But I suspect you know that."

Julia walked to Max, who was waiting for her at the back door.

ELEVEN

WHEN Girl wakes up, she goes to the *window* and stands there, staring out at the *yard*. She loves these new words, especially when she adds *my* in front of it. This word means something is hers.

Down below, on top of the *snow,* is a pink rose. Maybe she should bring it inside. Jewlee needs to smile more.

Lately, Jewlee's eyes water all the time. This is a Bad Thing. Girl knows this. In the deep forest, Her's eyes watered more and more . . . and then one day she was DEAD.

She hears the door to the bedroom open and close.

"You've been standing at that window a long time, Alice. What do you see?"

She turns to Jewlee. "Bad?" she wonders. "No window stand?"

Jewlee smiles, and just like that, Girl feels happy. "You can stand there all day if you like." She goes to the bed she sleeps in and sits down, putting her legs out on top of the covers.

"Book time?" Girl hopes, reaching for the story from last night. Grabbing it, she rushes over to the bed. "Teeth first?"

"And pajamas."

Girl nods. She can do it all. Then she is on the bed beside Jewlee, tucked in close.

Jewlee pulls her sideways, settles Girl on her lap. Very softly, Jewlee says: "Brittany."

The word hits Girl hard. It is what Him used to say when he was mean and drunk. What does Jewlee mean? Girl feels the panic growing inside her. She scratches her cheek and shakes her head.

Jewlee holds Girl's hands and says it again. This time Girl hears the question Jewlee is asking. "Are you Brittany?"

Are you Brittany? Brittany.

She looks at Jewlee, who is so sad now it makes Girl's heart hurt.

How can Girl tell her how happy she is here, how this is her whole world now and nothing else feels right?

"Are you Brittany?"

She leans toward Jewlee, gives her a kiss. "Me Alice."

JULIA stood by the freezing cold river, watching sunlight creep over the inky dark treetops. She heard footsteps behind her.

"Hey," Ellie said, coming up beside her. "You're up early." She handed Julia a cup of coffee.

"Couldn't sleep." She took the mug, wrapped her fingers around the warm porcelain. In silence, they stared across the silvered field to the forest beyond. Cal's house was a twinkling of golden lights.

"He's going to get custody, Jules."

"I know." Julia stared down at the river.

"We need to *prove* him guilty." She paused. "Or innocent."

"The state spent millions, and they couldn't prove it."

"We have Alice. Maybe she could lead us back to where she was kept, or held. We might find evidence."

"My God, Ellie, can you imagine what that could do to her? She could snap. Go back into herself again. How could I live with that?"

"How traumatized is she going to be when George takes her away? Will she ever understand that you didn't abandon her?"

Julia closed her eyes. This was precisely the image that stalked her.

"I've thought it through from every angle. I was up all night. This is my *job*, Jules. I have to follow the facts. If we want to know the truth, this is our only hope."

"I don't think I could survive if Alice . . . cracked again."

"You've got to trust my instincts on this. We need to *know*." Ellie put her arm around Julia and pulled her close. "Come on, let's go make our girl breakfast."

MAX was getting out of the shower when he heard the doorbell ring. He toweled off, put on an old pair of Levi's, and went downstairs. "I'm coming."

He opened the door.

Julia stood there. "Ellie wants to take Alice into the woods. To see if"—her voice wavered—"if she can find . . ."

He pulled her into his arms and held her until she stopped trembling. Then he led her into the living room.

"What do I do?" Julia finally said.

He wiped the tears from her cheeks. "You already know the answer to that. It's why you've been crying."

"She could regress. Or worse."

"And what will she do if Azelle gets custody? This is the time to be her mother, not her doctor."

She looked up. "How is it you always know what to say to me?"

He tried to glance away, couldn't. Very slowly he pulled away from her and went upstairs. On the bureau, he found the framed photograph of the little boy in a baseball uniform, smiling for the camera. His two front teeth were missing. He took the picture down and handed it to her.

"That's Danny."

Frowning, she studied the small, shining face.

"He was my son."

She drew in a sharp breath. "Was?"

"That's the last picture we have of him. A week later a drunk driver hit us on the way home from a game."

Her eyes filled with tears. The sight of it should have broken him, but instead it strengthened him. It was the first time he'd said Danny's name out loud in years, and it felt good.

"I would do anything"—he stared down at her, not caring that his voice was breaking or that his eyes were watering—*"anything* to have one more day with him."

Julia looked at the picture a long time. "I love you, Max."

He took her in his arms and held her tightly. "And I love you." He kissed her. "You told me once I could have all or nothing. I chose all," he said.

She tried to smile. "It took you long enough."

"Alice, honey, are you listening to me?"

"Read Alice."

"We're not going to read right now. Remember what we talked about this morning and again at lunchtime?" Julia tried to keep her voice even. "A man is coming to see Alice."

"No. Play Jewlee."

Julia stood up. "Well, I'm going downstairs. You can stay up here by yourself if you'd like."

"No leave." Alice got up from her chair and raced to Julia's side, tucking a hand into her skirt pocket.

Julia's heart swelled painfully. "Come on," she said quietly.

Down the stairs they went. Ellie was standing by the fire, looking tired and scared. "Hey," she said, looking up at their entrance.

"Hi, Lellie." Alice pulled Julia toward her. "Read Alice?"

Ellie smiled. "The kid's like a bloodhound on the scent." She ruffled Alice's black hair. "Later."

Julia dropped to her knees. "When the man comes, don't be scared, Alice. I'm right here. So is Ellie. You're safe here."

Alice frowned.

The doorbell rang.

Upstairs, the dogs—who were barricaded in Ellie's bedroom—went crazy, jumping and barking. Julia slowly rose.

Ellie opened the door. George Azelle stood there, holding a huge teddy bear. "Hi, Chief Barton," he said, trying to look past her.

No one knew quite what to do or say. George stepped past Ellie and came into the living room. He wore Levi's and an expensive white shirt. Looking at them now, in the same room—the man with the dark, curly hair and the chiseled face, and the little girl who was his carbon copy—there was no mistaking the link between them.

He stepped forward, let the teddy bear slide down his hip. He held it negligently by one arm. "Brittany." He said the name softly. There was no mistaking the wonder in his voice.

Alice slid behind Julia.

"It's okay, Alice." Julia tried to ease away, but Alice wouldn't let her go. "She's got a strong will."

"She gets her stubbornness from me," George said.

For the next hour, they were like some terrible tableau in a French film. George tried talking about nothing, making no sudden moves, even reading aloud. At some point, Alice streaked to the potted plant and crouched there, watching him through the green, waxy leaves.

"She has no idea who I am," he finally said. Tossing the book aside, he got up, began to pace the room. "Won't she talk at all? How will she tell people what happened to her?"

"Is that what matters most to you?" Julia asked.

"Damn you," he said, but the words held no sting; they were, in fact, kind of desperate sounding. He moved toward the potted plant cautiously, as if approaching a wild and dangerous animal.

A low growling came from the leaves.

George squatted down, silent and frowning. He reached out to touch Alice. She threw herself backward so hard she could have been hurt. He pulled back. "Sorry. I didn't mean to scare you."

Alice stared up at him through an opening in the leaves.

George took a deep breath, let it out slowly. Julia heard his resignation. It was over. At least for the day. *Thank God.*

He surprised her by starting to sing "Twinkle, Twinkle, Little Star." His voice was beautiful and true.

Alice stilled as the song went on. Cautiously, she started humming along with him.

"You know me, don't you, Brittany?"

At that, the name Brittany, Alice spun away and ran upstairs.

The bedroom door slammed shut.

George got to his feet. Shoving his hands into his pockets, he looked at Julia. "I used to sing that song to her when she was a baby."

Julia was going to say something when she heard a car drive up. "Who's here, El?"

Ellie went to the front door, opened it. *"Damn!"* She slammed the door shut and turned around. "It's KIRO TV and CNN."

Julia looked at George. "You called the *press?*"

He shrugged. "You spend three years in prison, Doctor, and then judge me. I'm as much a victim here as Brittany is."

"Tell it to someone who'll believe it." She tried to rein in her anger. "You've seen her. Becoming the object of media attention could destroy her. Don't do that to Alice."

"Brittany." His gaze softened. She thought she saw true concern in his eyes. "And you've left me no other choice."

The doorbell rang.

"Do you really want to prove your innocence?" Julia said, hearing the desperate edge in her voice. As she said it, she thought, *God help me. God help her.* Then she looked at her sister, who nodded in understanding. "Brittany lived in the forest a long time. Whoever took her might have left evidence."

George went very still. "You think Brittany could lead us there?"

"Maybe," Ellie answered, moving toward him.

"Is it . . . safe? For Brittany, I mean?"

"Julia won't let her see the actual site—if we find it, that is."

The room felt full of words unspoken, fear denied. A guilty man would say no. . . .

"Okay," he said. "But we go tomorrow. No dragging it out."

The doorbell rang again. There was pounding on the door.

"Come with me," Ellie said to Julia. The two of them walked to the door, opened it. There were several reporters on the front steps, including Mort from the *Gazette*. They were already talking when the door opened.

"We're here to interview George Azelle!"

"Can you confirm that the wolf girl is his missing daughter?"

"Dr. Cates, have you cured the wild child? Is she speaking now?"

Julia stared out at the faces in front of her, feeling distant from them, disconnected. Only a few months ago she would have given anything to be asked the last question, to be able to answer it in the affirmative. Then, the reformation of her reputation meant everything to her, but now her world was infinitely different. In the end, after all the times she'd dreamed of her triumphant return, it was surprisingly easy to smile coolly and say: "No comment."

ELLIE, CAL, EARL, JULIA, AND ALICE were in the park. They needed to set out before dawn. There could be no media witnesses to this trek. George stood apart, talking to his lawyer.

"Can she do it?" Cal asked, voicing everyone's concern.

Ellie had no answer. "I don't even know what to hope for." She reached out for Cal, held his hand. The warmth and familiarity of his touch made her breathe easier. She had put together an evidence-gathering kit and invited Cal to be their official photographer. If they actually found the site, everything had to be done exactly right.

It was dark out here. Cold. Julia knelt in front of Alice.

"Scared." Alice gave a halfhearted growl.

"I know, honey. I'm scared, too. So is Aunt Ellie. But we need to see where you were before. Remember what we talked about? Your place in the woods?"

"Dark," Alice whispered, her voice trembling. "No leave Alice?"

"No," Julia said. "I'll hold your hand all the time."

Behind them a car drove up. It was the final member of their party.

Ellie walked over to the sidewalk where Floyd now stood, alongside a game-farm truck. Beside him, on a leash, was the wolf, muzzled. Ellie took the leash.

"Wolf!" Alice cried out, running for them.

The wolf jumped at Alice, knocked her down.

"Are you going to bring him back?" Floyd asked, watching the pair play on the icy grass.

"I don't think so. He belongs in the wild."

Julia went to the girl. "We need to go now, Alice."

Alice pointed to the muzzle and the leash. "Bad. Trap. Smelly."

Last night they'd decided to use the wolf to help Alice find her way back to her old life. It had seemed less dangerous in the abstract.

"I've got to keep the muzzle on." Ellie bent down and unhooked the leash. The wolf immediately nuzzled up against Alice.

"Cave, Wolf," the girl whispered, and off they went, the two of them, toward the woods.

By the time the sun crested the trees, they were so far from town that the only noises were their footsteps crunching through the underbrush and the rushing of the river. No one spoke. In ragged formation, with Julia and Alice and the wolf in the lead, they moved deeper and deeper into the woods.

The trees grew denser here, and taller, their heavy boughs blocking out the light. And still they went on, toward the heart of this old-growth forest, where the ground was always damp, where club mosses hung from leafless branches like ghostly sleeves. A pale gray mist swallowed them all from the knees down.

Around noon they stopped in a tiny clearing for lunch. They sat in a rough circle, clustered at the base of a cedar tree so big that they could all hold hands and not make a complete circle around its trunk.

"Where are we?" George asked, stretching out one leg.

Cal unfolded his map. "Best guess? Well past the Hall of Mosses in the park. Not far from Wonderland Falls, I think."

They walked for another few hours, but it was slow going. Curtains of hanging moss blocked their way. Beneath a quartet of giant trees, they made camp for the night, pitching their Day-Glo orange pup tents around the fire.

All the while, as they set up camp and cooked their supper from cans, no one said much of anything. By nightfall, the sounds of the forest were overwhelming. Only Alice and her wolf seemed at ease in all this green murkiness.

Long after everyone else had gone to bed, Ellie and Julia stayed up, sitting by the river's edge on a moss-furred nurse log. At their feet, the water rushed by, almost invisible in the darkness. Overhead, the Milky Way appeared in patches between the trees and clouds.

"How's Alice doing?" Ellie asked.

"Sleeping peacefully. She's completely at ease out here."

"Is she leading us somewhere or just walking?"

"I don't know. I hope we're doing the right thing."

Ellie slipped an arm around her baby sister and drew her close. "Have you seen how George looks at her?" Ellie said quietly.

"Yes. Every time she ignores him or turns away, he winces."

Behind them a twig snapped. George stood there, his hands jammed into his pockets. "I couldn't sleep," he said. He stared out at the forest. "I'm afraid of what we'll find."

"We're all afraid," Ellie said, tightening her hold on Julia.

ELLIE WOKE AT DAWN AND STARTED the fire. By first light, they were on their way again, fighting through deeper, denser undergrowth, pushing through spiderwebs as taut as fishing wire. It was just past noon when Alice stopped suddenly.

Looking impossibly afraid, she pointed upriver. "No Alice go."

Julia picked her up, held her tightly. "You're a very brave little girl." To Ellie, she said, "Be careful."

Julia carried Alice to the base of a behemoth cedar tree and sat down on moss. The wolf padded to their side and laid down.

Cal, Earl, George, and his lawyer came up beside Ellie, one by one. No one said a word as she led them into the green-and-black shadows that lay ahead.

They followed the river around a bend and over a hill and found themselves in a man-made clearing. Empty tin cans were everywhere, their sides furred by moss and mold. There were hundreds of them—years' worth. Old magazines and other garbage lay in a heap beside a cave. Tucked in a grove of red cedar trees was a small lean-to with no door.

The dark cave yawned at them. Ferns grew at its open mouth. In front, a nylon rope attached by a metal loop lay coiled around it.

Ellie knelt. At the end of the ragged rope was a leather cuff that had been chewed off—just big enough to encircle a child's ankle. Black blood stained the leather. Alice's small bare feet had worn a circular groove in the dirt. How long had she been out here, going round and round this stake?

Cal bent down beside her, touched her. Slowly she pushed to her feet. "Gloves on, everyone."

Walking through the crime scene, they found a pile of women's clothes, a single red patent leather high heel, a blood-spattered knife, a box of half-finished dreamcatchers, and a baby blanket so ratty they couldn't be certain what color it had been. Appliquéd daisies hung askew from the trim.

"Catalog everything, Earl," Ellie said.

Behind the lean-to was a bigger ankle strap; it, too, was caked with dried blood. Someone else had been staked out here. An adult.

"She couldn't even *see* her daughter," Ellie whispered.

Cal touched her again. "Keep moving."

She nodded, studying everything from the pile of junk by an old moss-furred stump to the dirty, stained mattress. There were animal signs everywhere; the scavengers had come in.

Back in the trees, Ellie found an old trunk, rusted almost shut. Inside she found piles of old Spokane newspaper clippings—most about prostitutes who'd disappeared from the city streets. There were also several guns and a blood-encrusted arm sling.

Down at the bottom, beneath dirty silverware, was a yellow plastic raincoat and a ratty Batman baseball cap.

Behind her, George let out an anguished cry. "He *saw* it. That flower delivery guy saw the kidnapper parked in front of my house."

Ellie didn't turn around. She couldn't see George right now. But she heard him drop to his knees in the muddy dirt.

"If they'd listened, they could have found them. Oh, my *God.*"

When he started to cry, Ellie closed her eyes. She'd done her job, found the truth.

But it wasn't the truth she'd wanted to find.

ALICE's heart is pounding in her chest. She knows she should RUN! But she can't leave Jewlee.

Still, she hears the voices here. The leaves and the trees and the river. And though there is fear in her chest, there is something else, something that makes her get to her feet.

Wolf brushes up against her, loving her. Not far, his pack is waiting for his return. This Alice knows. Below the rustling sounds and rushing water, she can hear their padding footsteps.

She bends down and frees Wolf from the smelly trap on his face. He looks up at her in perfect understanding.

She feels sad to lose him again, but a wolf needs his family. He howls and licks her face.

"Bye," she whispers.

Then he is gone.

Alice looks back up at Jewlee. She knows what she wants to tell Jewlee, but she doesn't have the words. She takes Jewlee's hand, leads her over trees Him cut down, and pushes through a patch of stinging nettles.

There it is.

A mound in the earth, covered with stones.

"Mommy," Alice says, pointing to the rocks. It is a word she thought she'd forgotten.

"Oh, baby. . . ." Jewlee pulls Alice into her arms and holds her tightly, rocking her back and forth.

Alice draws back to look at her. "Love Jewlee," she says.

Jewlee kisses Alice, just the way the mommy used to. "I love you, too."

Alice smiles. She is safe now.

TWELVE

By THREE o'clock the next day, all major network and cable news channels were interrupting scheduled broadcasts to report on the discovery of Zoë Azelle's body in the deep woods of Washington. Crime lab analysis had confirmed her identity, as well as that of the man who'd been there. His name was Terrance Spec, and he'd been convicted of first-degree rape twice. He'd also been a suspect in all those Spokane prostitute disappearances. He'd been killed in September—a hit-and-run accident on Highway 101.

Every newspaper and radio station and television show proclaimed George Azelle's innocence. The jury system had failed, they said.

George Azelle had answered questions all afternoon in the police station. The revelation that the wolf girl was his daughter had only fueled the fire. The headline LIVING PROOF had been inked across millions of newspapers.

ELLIE knocked at the closed door of the judge's chambers.
"Come in."

She opened the door to a large, austere room. Books lined the walls. Julia stood beside a huge potted plant. Both attorneys were seated in front of the judge's desk. George stood alone on the left.

Ellie went to Julia, stood beside her.

"She needs more time with me," Julia was saying. "She . . . trusts me. I can"—her voice slipped, caught on desperation—"save her."

"Will she always be a special-needs child?" the judge asked.

"I don't know," Julia answered. "She's extremely bright, but for many years, she'll need constant care and treatment."

"There must be special schools for kids like her," George said.

"There are," his attorney answered. "And other doctors who could treat her. Your Honor, Mr. Azelle is a victim here. We can't compound his tragedy by taking his daughter away again."

"No," the judge said. "And I'm sure Dr. Cates knows that."

Julia turned to George. "I sympathize with you, honestly I do—I was up all night thinking about what you've suffered— but the truth is, your daughter is what matters now. If she were taken away from me, she'd retreat back into silence and self-mutilation."

"Dr. Cates." His voice was gentle but firm. "I love my daughter. All those days behind bars, I dreamed of finding her."

"You love the *idea* of a daughter. I've read everything there is to know about you, George. You were never home for dinner or on weekends. You don't even know your daughter."

"That's not my fault," he said. "And she'll never love me as long as you're around."

Julia drew in a sharp breath. Everyone in the room knew there was nothing she could say to that. It was true.

IN A small town like Rain Valley, the only thing more prevalent than gossip was opinions. Everyone had one and couldn't wait to share it. Max figured that the meeting in the courthouse had barely finished when people started talking about it.

He called Julia every ten minutes; there was never an answer. His own phone remained silent. Finally he couldn't stand it anymore. She might think heartache had to be borne alone; she was wrong. He'd made that mistake for too long.

He got in his car and drove to her house. With every turn, he pictured her trying not to cry. But one memory of Alice laughing . . . or eating the flowers . . . and the tears would fall.

He knew. She might try to forget it, to outrun it, as he'd done. If so, years might pass before she'd realize that those memories needed to be held on to. They were all you had left.

From the outside of her house, everything looked normal. He went to the front door, knocking softly.

Ellie answered. "Hey, Max," she said.

"How is she?"

"Not good."

Ellie stepped back. "She's up in my room. First door on the left. Alice is asleep, so be quiet. I'm going to the station."

"Thanks."

He went upstairs. At the bedroom door, he drew in a deep breath, then opened it.

The room was full of shadows. All the lights were off.

Julia lay in the big king-size canopy bed, her eyes closed, her hands folded on her stomach. "Hey," he said.

She opened her eyes and looked up. Her face was red and swollen, as were her eyes. Tears had scrubbed the color from her cheeks. "You know about Alice," she said quietly.

He climbed into the big bed and took her in his arms. Saying nothing, he held her and let her cry, let her tell him her memories one by one. It was something he should have done long ago—formed all his memories into solid, durable things that would last.

She paused in her story and looked at him, her eyes shimmering with tears. "I should stop rattling on about her," she said.

He kissed her gently, giving her all of himself in that one kiss. "Keep talking," he said. "I'm not going anywhere."

It was late when Ellie finally left the station and headed home. As she climbed the porch steps to the front door, she felt as if she were carrying a heavy weight on her back. This was as bad as she'd ever felt in her life.

Julia was out on the porch, in the freezing cold, wrapped in their father's old woolen hunting coat.

Ellie grabbed one of the old quilts from the trunk on the porch and sat, wrapping it around her. "Where's Max?"

"He had an emergency at the hospital. He wanted to stay, but I sort of needed to be alone. Alice is asleep."

Ellie started to rise. "Should I—"

"No. Please. Stay." At that, Julia smiled sadly. "I sound like Alice. Brittany, I mean."

"She'll never really be Brittany to us. What will you do?"

"Without her?" Julia stared out at their backyard. In the darkness, they couldn't see much past the river. "I've been thinking a lot about that. Unfortunately, I don't have an answer." She fell suddenly silent. "Sorry. Sometimes . . ." She stood up. "I need to be with her now," she said in a small, breaking voice, and then she was gone.

Ellie felt the start of tears. She tossed the blanket aside and got up. What good would it do to sit here by herself and cry?

She walked down into the damp grass toward the river. Across the black field, she saw the twinkling yellow lights of Cal's house. Cal, the one constant man in her life, the one man on the planet who saw her as she was and loved her anyway. She needed a friend like that now.

She was at his door in no time. She knocked.

No one answered. Frowning, she opened the door and poked her head in. "Hello?"

Again there was no answer, but she saw a light down the hall. She followed it to the closed study door and knocked. "Hello?"

"Ellie?"

She pushed the door open. Cal was there alone, sitting behind a drafting table with papers spread out all around him. "Where are the girls?"

"Peanut took them to dinner so I could work."

"Work? Really? What are you doing?"

She crossed the room toward him, noticing the smudges on his hands. On the page in front of him was a faded, working sketch of a boy and girl holding hands, running. Overhead, a giant pterodactyl-type bird blotted out the sun with its enormous wingspan.

He pushed the sketch aside; beneath it was a full-color drawing of the same two kids huddled around a pale, glowing ball. A caption read: "How can we hide if they can see our every move?"

Ellie was stunned by the quality of his artwork, the vibrant colors and strong lines. The characters looked somehow both stylized and real. There was no mistaking the fear in their eyes.

"You're a talented artist," she said—rather dumbly, she thought, but it was so *surprising*. All those days while she'd been sitting at her desk, doing paperwork or talking to Peanut, Cal had been creating Art. She'd blithely assumed it was the same doodling he'd been doing since Mr. Chee's chemistry class. How could she have been with him every day and not known this? "Now I know why you said I was selfish, Cal. I'm sorry."

He smiled slowly. "It's a graphic novel about a pair of best friends. He's a good kid from the wrong side of the tracks with a mean drunk for a dad. She hides him in her barn. Their friendship, it turns out, is the last true innocence, and it falls to them to destroy the wizard's ball before the darkness falls. I just started submitting it to publishers."

"It's about us," she said. At the realization, it felt as if a doorway somewhere opened. "Why didn't you show me before?"

He tucked a strand of hair behind his ear and stood up to face her. "You stopped seeing me a long time ago, El. You saw the gangly screwed-up kid I used to be, and the quiet always-there-for-you guy I became. But you haven't really looked at me."

"I see you, Cal."

"Good. Because I've waited a long time to tell you something."

"What?"

He took her by the shoulders. And he kissed her. He backed her up against the wall and kept kissing her until her breathing was ragged and her heart was beating so fast she thought she'd faint. It was a kiss that held back nothing and promised everything.

When he drew back, he wasn't smiling. "You get it now?"

"Oh, my God."

"Everyone in town knows how I feel about you." He kissed her again, then drew back. "I was beginning to think you were stupid."

She didn't know how a nearly forty-year-old twice-divorced woman could feel like a teenage girl again, but that was exactly how she felt. All giddy and breathless. It all fit now. *Cal.*

Behind them the door opened. Peanut stood holding a pair of huge pizza boxes, three little faces hovering beside her.

Peanut said, "Go put on your jammies. Daddy will be up in a minute." When they were gone, she set the pizza boxes on the chair beside her. Her gaze moved from Cal to Ellie and back to Cal.

A smile finally tugged at the corners of her mouth. "You kiss her?"

Ellie had the thought: Peanut knew? And then Cal was pulling her toward him and she forgot about everything else. In those eyes she'd known forever, she saw love, the kind that began between two kids and lasted a lifetime. He squeezed her hand. "I did."

Peanut laughed. "It's about damn time."

JULIA KNEW SHE WAS HOLDING Alice too tightly, but she couldn't seem to let go. For the last hour, no matter what she did, she was thinking, Not yet. But time kept slipping past.

"Read Alice." The child thumped her finger on the page.

Julia should say quietly that it was time to talk of other things, of families that had been split up and fathers who came back, but she couldn't do it. Instead, she let herself keep reading, as if this were any rainy day. "'Weeks passed, and the little rabbit grew very old and shabby, but the boy loved him just as much. He loved him so hard that he loved all his whiskers off, and the pink lining to his ears turned grey, and his brown spots faded. He even began to lose his shape, and he scarcely looked like a rabbit anymore except to the boy.'" Julia watched the words blur and dance on the page.

"Want Alice real."

She touched Alice's velvety cheek. "You're real, Alice. And so many people love you."

"Love." Alice whispered softly with a kind of reverence.

Julia closed the book, then pulled Alice onto her lap so they were looking at each other. *Be strong,* she thought.

She stared into Alice's worried eyes. "There's a man. George. He's your father. He wants to love you."

"Alice loves Jewlee."

"I'm trying to tell you about your father. You have to be ready for this. He'll be here soon. You *have* to understand."

"Be Mommy?"

Julia glanced over at the suitcase she'd packed last night. She tightened her hold on Alice. Outside, she heard a car drive up.

"Mommy?" Alice said again. This time it was her little girl's voice that sounded wobbly and afraid.

"Oh, Alice," she whispered, touching her soft pink cheek. "I wish I could be that for you."

ELLIE saw the clot of news vans parked on the old highway. A police barricade had been set up across her driveway. Peanut stood in front, arms crossed, a whistle in her mouth.

Ellie hit the lights and siren; the sound cleared the street instantly. Reporters parted in groups to either side of the road. She rolled down her window to talk to Peanut.

"They're a roadside hazard. Get Earl and Mel out here to disperse the crowd. This day is bad enough without the media."

A bright red Ferrari pulled up behind the cruiser. Ellie looked in her rearview mirror. George smiled at her, but it was faded, less than real. There was a sad, haunted look in his eyes.

The Ferrari followed her down the driveway. She parked and killed the engine, then got out of the car.

George walked over to her. He looked at the house. "I told your sister I'd pick up Brittany at three."

With a sigh, she led him across the yard. They were almost to the steps when a gray Mercedes pulled up behind them and parked.

"Who's that?" she asked George.

"Dr. Correll. He's going to work with Brit."

The man got out of his car. Tall, thin, almost elegantly effete, he nodded at George; then he shook Ellie's hand. "I'm Tad Correll."

"Nice to meet you." Ellie noticed the hypodermic needle sticking out of his breast pocket. "What's that for? You a heroin addict?"

"It's a sedative. The girl might be upset by the transition."

"You think?"

The three of them headed for the house. Ellie opened the door. Julia sat on the sofa with Alice tucked in her arms. At the foot of the sofa was a small red suitcase.

Julia looked up at them. Her beautiful face glistened with tear tracks; her eyes were puffy and bloodshot. Max stood behind her, his hands resting on her shoulders.

"Mr. Azelle, Dr. Correll." Julia got to her feet. "Your reputation precedes you, Doctor."

"As does yours," Dr. Correll said. "I watched the tapes. Your work with her has been phenomenal. You should publish it."

"Jewlee?" Alice said, her voice spiking up in fear.

"It's time for you to go now," Julia said in a voice so quiet they all moved a little closer to hear.

Alice shook her head. "No go. Alice stay."

"But your daddy wants to love you, too, honey." She touched Alice's tiny face. "You remember your mommy? She would have wanted this for you."

"Jewlee Mommy." There was no mistaking the fear in Alice's voice now. She tried to hug Julia more tightly.

Julia worked to uncoil the girl's spindly arms. "I wanted to be . . . but I'm not. No Jewlee Mommy. You have to go with your father."

Alice went crazy. Kicking and screaming and growling and howling. She scratched Julia's face and her own.

"Oh, honey, don't," Julia said, trying to calm the child, but she was crying too hard to be heard.

Dr. Correll swooped in and gave Alice a shot.

The child howled at that. A huge, desperate wail. Julia held on to her as the sedative took effect.

"I'm sorry," Julia said to her.

Alice's eyes blinked heavily. "Love. Jewlee."

"And I love Alice."

Alice started to cry with no sound, no shuddering, just a moisture dripping down her cheeks. Then she looked up at Julia and whimpered three words before she fell asleep. "Real girl hurts."

Dr. Correll said, "We should hurry."

Julia nodded stiffly and carried Alice out to the Ferrari. She turned to George. "Where's her booster seat?"

"She's not a baby," he said.

"I'll get it," Ellie said. Somehow that did it to her—yanking Alice's seat out of the truck made her cry. She tried to hide her face as she fit the seat into the Ferrari.

Very slowly, Julia bent down and put the sleeping child into the car. She kissed her cheek and shut the door gently, then handed George a thick manila envelope.

"This is everything you need to know. Her naptimes, bedtimes, allergies. She loves Jell-O now—but only if it has pineapple in it—and vanilla pudding. She tries to play with pasta, so unless you want a real mess, I'd keep it away from her. And pictures of bunnies—"

"Stop." George's voice was harsh, throaty. He took the envelope in shaking hands. "Thank you. For everything. Thank you."

"If you have problems, call. I can be there in no time—"

"I promise."

"I want to throw myself in front of your car."

"I know."

She wiped her eyes, said, "Take care of my—*our*—girl."

"I will," George said.

Ellie went to her sister, put an arm around her. Julia felt too frail suddenly. Max came up, too; they bookended her.

George got into his car and drove away. Dr. Correll followed. For a few moments, their tires crunched on the driveway. Then there was no trace of them left.

Alice was gone.

SOMETIME later—Julia had no idea when—she sent Max downstairs and Ellie back to work. They'd both been smothering her all day, trying to offer a comfort that didn't exist.

She stared out the bedroom window at the empty yard.

Birds. Come spring, those birds would look for Alice. . . .

Behind her, the dogs chuffed softly to one another; they'd spent almost an hour looking for their girl. Now they were laying beside her bed. Every now and then, howls would fill the air.

Julia glanced down at her watch and thought about how long they'd been gone. A few hours, and already it felt like a lifetime.

It was five thirty. They would be nearing the city now. The majestic green of Alice's beloved forest would have given way to the gray of concrete. She would feel as alien there as any space traveler. Without Julia, her fear would be too big to handle.

"Please, God," Julia whispered aloud, praying for the first time in years, "don't let my girl hurt herself."

She turned away from the window and saw the potted plants. The hiding place. She walked over to stroke their glossy green leaves.

It was almost six now. They were probably on the floating bridge, nearing Mercer Island. The air would smell of smog and cars and the tamed blue sound.

Downstairs, the house was quiet except for the rattle of Max's cooking. She went to the kitchen. He was chopping vegetables.

"The phone keeps ringing," she said.

"It's Ellie," he said. "She wants to make sure you're okay."

He put an arm around her, and she leaned against him. He didn't ask how she was or tell her it would be okay. He simply put his hand around the back of her neck, anchoring her. Without that touch, she might have drifted away on this sea of emptiness.

"I wonder how she's doing."

"Don't," he said softly. "All you can do is wait."

"For what?"

"Someday when you think about her howling or trying to play with spiders, you'll laugh instead of cry."

Behind them the doorbell rang.

"Did you lock Ellie out?" Julia asked, wiping her eyes and trying to smile. "I shouldn't have sent her to work, anyway. I thought being with Cal would help."

She let go of him and went to the door, opening it.

Alice stood there, looking impossibly small and frightened. She was twisting her hands together, the way she did when she was confused, and she had her shoes on the wrong feet. Seeping, bloody scratches lined her cheeks.

George stood behind her, his face pale and seamed with worry. "She thinks you let her go because she was bad."

It hit Julia like a blow to the heart. She dropped to her knees, looked Alice in the eyes. "Oh, honey. You're a *good* girl. The best."

Alice started to cry. Her whole body shook.

"Use your words, Alice."

The girl shook her head, howled in a keening, desperate wail.

Julia touched her. "Use your words, baby. *Please.*"

George climbed the creaking porch steps. "I tried to buy her dinner in Olympia. She went . . . crazy. Howling. Growling. She scratched her face. Dr. Correll couldn't calm her down."

"It's not your fault," Julia said softly.

"All those years in prison . . . I dreamed she was still alive. . . . I thought she'd run into my arms and tell me how much she missed me. I never thought she wouldn't know me."

"She needs time to remember."

"No. She's not my little girl anymore. She's Alice now."

Julia's breath caught. Max came up beside her, touched her shoulder. She laid her hand on his, then said to George, "What do you mean?"

George stared down at his daughter. He looked older suddenly. "I'm not who she needs," he said. "She's too much for me to handle. Loving her and parenting her are two different things. She belongs here. With you."

Julia reached for Max's hand, clinging to it. "Are you sure?"

"Tell her . . . someday . . . that I loved her the only way I knew how . . . by letting her go. Tell her I'll be waiting for her. All she has to do is call."

"You'll always be her father, George."

He backed up, went down a step, then another. "They'll say I abandoned her," he said softly.

Julia gazed down at him. "Your daughter will know the truth, George. I swear to you. She'll always know you love her."

"I can't even kiss her good-bye."

"Someday you'll be able to kiss her, George. I promise you."

"Keep her close." He turned and walked away.

Julia knelt in front of Alice. Alice stood there, her little arms bolted to her sides, her hands curled into fists. Her mouth was trembling, and tears washed her eyes, magnifying her fear.

Julia's tears started again. There was no way to stop them, even though she was smiling now, too.

Alice watched George drive away, then turned to Julia. "Alice home?"

Julia nodded. "Alice is home."

Alice whispered, "Jewlee Mommy!" and threw herself into Julia's waiting arms. "Love Jewlee Mommy. Alice stay."

"Yes," Julia said, laughing and crying. "Alice stay."

EPILOGUE

As ALWAYS, September was the best month of the year. Long, hot, sunny days melted into cold, crisp nights. All over town, scattered randomly throughout the towering evergreens, maple and alder trees were dressed in their red-and-gold autumn finery.

At the corner of Olympic and Rainview, Julia stopped walking.

Alice immediately followed suit, tucking in close, putting her hand in Julia's pocket. It was the first time in weeks she'd done it. "Now, Alice," Julia said. "We've talked all about this."

Alice blinked up at her. Though she'd gained weight in the past nine months and grown at least an inch, she still had a tiny, heart-shaped face that sometimes seemed too small to hold those wide,

expressive eyes. Today, wearing a pink corduroy skirt with matching cotton tights and a white sweater, she looked like any other girl
on the first day of school. "Alice not scared."

Julia led Alice to a nearby park bench and sat down beneath a
huge maple tree. The leaves overhead were the color of ripe lemons.
She pulled Alice onto her lap. "I think you *are* scared."

Alice popped a thumb into her mouth, then slowly withdrew
it. She was trying so hard to be a big girl. Her pink backpack—a
recent present from George—fell to the ground beside her. "They'll
call Alice wolf girl," she said quietly.

Julia wanted to say, *No, they won't,* but she and Alice had come
too far together to tell each other pretty lies. "They might. Mostly
because they wish they knew a wolf."

"Maybe go school next year."

"You're ready now." Julia eased Alice off her lap. They stood up,
holding hands. "Okay?"

A car pulled up on the street beside them. All four doors opened
at once, and girls spilled out, giggling. The older girls ran off
ahead.

Ellie, in uniform, looking deeply tired and profoundly beautiful,
took Sarah's hand in hers and walked toward Julia.

"Of course you're on time," Ellie said. "You have one kid to
get ready. Getting these three organized is like herding ants.
And forget about Cal. His deadline's made him deaf." But as she
said it, she laughed. "Or maybe it's me, always telling him to
listen up."

Sarah, dressed in blue jeans and a pink T-shirt, carrying a
Shark Tales backpack, looked at Alice. "You ready for school?"

"Scared," Alice said. When she looked up at Julia, she added,
"I'm scared."

"I was scared on the first day of kindergarten, too. But it was
fun," Sarah said. "We had cake."

"Really?"

"You wanna walk with me?" Sarah asked.

Alice looked up at Julia, who nodded encouragingly. "Okay."

Alice mouthed: *Stay close.* Julia nodded, smiling.

The two girls began walking together. Ellie fell into step beside
Julia. "Who'd have thought, huh? You and me walking our daughters to school together."

"It's a new family tradition. How's the bathroom coming?"

"Cal ordered a Jacuzzi tub. Big enough for two." Ellie sounded like a woman head over heels in love. After two expensive weddings, complete with all the trimmings, she'd finally gotten lucky in a tiny chapel on the Vegas strip.

They crossed the street and climbed the steps to Rain Valley Elementary. All around them women were holding on to their children's hands. It was hard to let Alice go out in the world, but Julia had to do it.

As they moved down the hallway, a bell rang. Kids and parents scattered, disappeared into classrooms.

Alice looked nervously at Julia. "Mommy?"

"I'll sit right out front all day waiting for you. If you get nervous, all you have to do is look out the window, okay?"

" 'Kay." She didn't sound okay.

"You want me to walk you in?"

Alice looked at Sarah, who was motioning for her to hurry, then back at Julia. "No." *I'm a big girl,* she mouthed.

Following Sarah, Alice walked down the last bit of hallway to room 114. She gave Julia one last worried wave, then opened the door and went in. The door shut behind her.

Julia let out her breath in a sigh. Ellie looped an arm around her, drawing her close. "She's going to be fine."

Arm in arm, they walked out of the school and across the street. There, they sat down on the park bench and stared out at the town that had shaped their lives. The maple tree that had first welcomed Alice was a blaze of bright yellow leaves.

"What are you going to do now that she's in school?" Ellie asked.

Lately the question had arisen in Julia's mind, too. She'd had to ask herself who she was now, what she wanted. The answers had surprised her. For more than half of her life she'd been driven by her career, yet she'd lost it in a heartbeat. If you were lucky enough to have a loving family, you had to hold on to them with infinite care. She turned to her sister. "Max asked me to marry him."

Ellie shrieked and pulled Julia into her arms.

"I thought I'd open an office here, too. Work part-time. There are kids who need me."

Ellie drew back, wiping her eyes. "Mom and Dad would be so proud of you, Jules."

That made Julia smile. "Yeah." She closed her eyes for just a moment, a breath, and remembered all of it—the woman she'd been less than a year ago, afraid of her own spirit and the danger of sharp emotions . . . the little girl named Alice she'd taken into her heart . . . and the man who'd dared to push past his own darkness, toward the light they'd found deep in this old-growth forest. For years to come, she knew that the people of Rain Valley would talk about this special time, when a child unlike any other had walked out of the woods and into their lives and changed them all, and how it had begun in late October, when the trees were dressed in tangerine leaves and danced in the chilly, rain-scented breeze, and the sun was a brilliant shade of gold that illuminated everything.

Magic hour.

For the rest of her life, she'd remember it as the time she finally came home.

"I was born in September 1960 in Southern California," Kristin Hannah says, "and grew up at the beach, making sand castles and playing in the surf. When I was eight years old, my father drove us to Western Washington, where we called home."

After graduating college, Hannah worked for a while in a trendy advertising agency, until she decided to go to law school. Hannah was in her third year of study when her mother was diagnosed with breast cancer. The prognosis was not good. For the next several weeks, Hannah spent her days at law school and her evenings by her mother's bedside in a Seattle hospital. "As any of you know who have been through this sort of thing," recalls Hannah, "there are many things you don't want to talk about. We spent a lot of time looking for happy thoughts. It just so happened that what my mom wanted to discuss were her beloved romance novels." At one point, they tried to write a book together, a historical romance set in Scotland. The first chapter, which

was written in purple ink, "was pretty bad," Hannah says. Sadly, Hannah's mother did not win her fight against cancer, and they did not finish the book, "though my mother was sure I had a writing career ahead of me. And when she eventually turned out to be right—well, I know she sees it all, and reads everything I write, even though she's not here."

A few years passed, and Hannah was busy with other things, including marriage and a job practicing entertainment law, when she became pregnant with her son. After going through premature labor, she had to spend five months in bed. "Here I was, the classic law-school joke: practice for a year and get pregnant. I felt like a failure." By the time she'd read every book in the house and started asking her husband for cereal boxes to read, "I knew I was a goner. That's when my darling husband reminded me of the book I'd started with my mom. I pulled out the boxes of research material, dusted them off, and began writing. By the time my son was born, I'd finished a first draft and found an obsession."

The finished product, a historical romance, was "awful," says Hannah. But the seed had been planted, and Hannah continued pounding out stories. Many rejections later, she finally hit pay dirt when her novel *A Handful of Heaven* was published in 1991.

The author soon turned to full-time writing—"as full time as a woman who is also raising a child can." Her first books were historical romances, until she made a major crossover into contemporary women's fiction. "The crossover felt entirely natural. I'd come to the end of what I had to say in historical romance. I realized that I had something to say about modern women, about the choices and sacrifices we make every day. I still write about men and women falling in love—that's such a big part of life—but I also write about mothers and daughters, fathers and sons, brothers and sisters. In short, family life and love is what I focus on these days, and I love every minute of it."

Despite her success as a novelist, Hannah remained fond of the law and drew on her experiences in creating the take-no-prisoners divorce attorney Meghann in *Between Sisters*. "Law is a fabulous career for a woman, and surprisingly creative. Law is an intellectual game. The single best job in the world is probably Supreme Court Justice."

For *Magic Hour*, Hannah says that she had been drawn to the idea of a feral child for a long time. "There's something magical and mystical about the possibility of someone living completely apart from society, deep in the woods. Coincidentally, I read about two young boys who walked out of the woods of British Columbia. They claimed never to have seen a building or a store or a road or another human being. It turned out that their story was a hoax— they were runaways from Southern California—but my writer's imagination had been engaged. What if a child had been raised in the woods, apart from everyone and everything? What would happen if she came out of the darkness and into the light, literally? And I was off and running."

Hannah and her husband live on a small, rural island in Puget Sound. She sets many of her novels in the Pacific Northwest, and loves the dramatic landscapes of the northwestern United States. "When I look out my front door, I see a beautiful flower-encircled pond and thousands of hundred-year-old cedar trees." She often thinks of the settings of her books as "the town everyone wishes they'd grown up in," she says. "The kind of place where everybody knows your name and cares about what happens to you."

Hannah is the author of twenty novels and the winner of the Golden Heart, the Maggie, and the 1996 National Reader's Choice awards. Book club members should check out her website, KristinHannah.com, for discussion guides to many of her books.